THE
MAGICIANS'
DAUGHTER

TOR BOOKS BY S. C. BUTLER

Reiffen's Choice
Queen Ferris
The Magicians' Daughter

THE MAGICIANS' DAUGHTER

Book Three
of the
Stoneways Trilogy

S. C. BUTLER

A TOM DOHERTY ASSOCIATES BOOK
NEW YORK

This is a work of fiction. All of the characters, organizations, and events portrayed in this novel are either products of the author's imagination or are used fictitiously.

THE MAGICIANS' DAUGHTER: BOOK THREE OF THE STONEWAYS TRILOGY

Copyright © 2009 by S. C. Butler

Map by Ellisa Mitchell

A Tor Book
Published by Tom Doherty Associates, LLC
175 Fifth Avenue
New York, NY 10010

www.tor-forge.com

Tor® is a registered trademark of Tom Doherty Associates, LLC.

Library of Congress Cataloging-in-Publication Data

Butler, S. C. (Sam C.)
The magicians' daughter / S.C. Butler.—1st ed.
p. cm.—(Stoneways trilogy ; bk. 3)
"A Tom Doherty Associates book."
ISBN-13: 978-0-7653-1479-6
ISBN-10: 0-7653-1479-7
1. Magic—Fiction.   I. Title.
PS3602.U884M34 2009
813'.6—dc22

2009001657

First Edition: May 2009

Printed in the United States of America

0   9   8   7   6   5   4   3   2   1

This book is dedicated to everyone who ever taught me to read or write, but most especially to Charles Hamilton, Steve Marx, and Peter Taylor. They read some dreadful stuff, once upon a time.

Acknowledgments

My deepest thanks to everyone involved for their support while I stumbled my way through these three books. First and foremost are my agent, Alex Hoyt, and my editor, Patrick LoBrutto. Even when I thought I was right, they gently taught me better. Their confidence kept me going, as did the support of all the other great folks at Tor, most especially Paul Stevens, Stacy Hague-Hill, Irene Gallo, and Patrick Nielsen Hayden (not to mention Daniel Dos Santos's fantastic covers).

I'd also like to thank all the readers who helped me figure out what worked and what didn't, Susan Jett and Walter Maroney most of all. And all the great OWWies who helped me transform my purple prose to a slightly more delicate shade: Andrew Ahn, Aaron Brown, Ian Morrison, Ian Tregillis, and Sandra Ulbrich. And the fabulous Sooper-Sekrit SFs—you guys know who you are. If I didn't know you'd hex me for sure, I'd blow your cover: Jodi, Rae, Holly, Brad, Vern, Jo, Heather. Special thanks, too, to the Binghamton Scoobies, Patricia Bray, Jennifer Dunne, and Joshua Palmatier—and to Melinda Snodgrass—for their friendship and help in navigating the world of professional authors and cons.

Finally, I want to thank my family for putting up with me the last few years, especially the permanent absentmindedness that took over as I wrote myself ever more deeply into Ferris's, Reiffen's, and Avender's world. Hopefully they'll accept the finished books as some slight recompense. And, girls, if I ever write another trilogy, I promise you'll get a book apiece.

Contents

SPIT

HUBLEY

A maid that's fair must not despair
That love will never find her.
And hearts not cold will gain great gold
As long as they stay kinder.
But seasons change and some men range
Till other passions find them.
And fairest heart won't even start
To bring them back or bind them.

–MINDRELL THE BARD

1

Babies First

s it brushed the river, the dawn breeze grabbed Reiffen's cloak. Around him the blankets of the dead and dying fluttered. Those still alive coughed wetly, low and thick from bloody lungs.

He refused to look at them. Any of them. If even a single blanket fell aside from one of those wretched faces, he might have to notice what he'd done. Already flies hovered, their hum thick and throbbing as a hive's. A sweet stink clung to the air, though there hadn't been enough time yet for the dead to start rotting.

Knowing the smell would seek the low ground by the river, he climbed the bank in search of cleaner air. The rows of the dead stretched into the fog around him; after a few steps he no longer had any idea where he was. His feet kicked up cinders from the burnt earth until the air was as thick with charred dirt as it was with flies. The morning fog turned black.

A spotted glow rose from the ground. The dead had opened their eyes.

They didn't reach for him: Reiffen's nightmare wasn't that simple. Reliving their last moments, his victims crouched on their knees and vomited at his feet. Blood and rheum spilled across his boots, soaking the earth like rain. His stomach churned. Other corpses appeared, sissit as well as men, crawling out of the fog to press against their fellows. Perhaps Reiffen could have forced his way through the hunched, crooked crowd, but, whether from pity or revulsion, he couldn't bring himself to touch them. The dead, too, kept their careful distance, crouching on hands and knees. Broken jaws retched rotting teeth; cracked lips oozed black blood. Spittle foamed at their chins.

He decided to flee, but found he couldn't. Though his boots had barely sunk halfway into the mud, the ground gripped them with frozen strength. His alarm increased as he struggled, but every attempt to get free only drove him deeper.

A young woman stumbled out of the mist, her dress tattered. "Help me," she cried.

Was it Ferris? Reiffen's fear gripped his throat. But the woman was too thin, her hair too wild. Her eyes were blue instead of brown. The fog swallowed her like a leaping nokken as she ran away, her dress streaming behind her.

The Black Wizard followed, towering higher than the trees. Only the Wizard didn't charge angrily after the woman as Reiffen expected, but started toward Reiffen instead. Corpses of men and sissit burst in gouts of pus and pale skin at the giant's every step. But his color lightened as he came closer, his robes turning from black to gray as the quickening wind flicked away the ash. Not Ossdonc, after all, but Fornoch. The one among the Three whom Reiffen hadn't been able to slay.

Gobbets of earth splashed around him as Reiffen scrabbled to pull himself free. He coughed at the taste of it, as foul as someone else's bile, and choked as he tried to breathe. The mud gulped him down, waist and chest and shoulders, till his eyes were at the level of the Wizard's enormous ankle. Clean toes showed at the edge of a spotless sandal. Fingers reached down for Reiffen's face.

"Take my hand," said the Wizard. "Your time has not yet come."

To be saved again by Fornoch was more than Reiffen could

bear. And it felt so good to give up, to let his whole body relax and accept the sinking. To forget about all the things he was supposed to do, all the things his mother and everyone else expected from him. To leave the magic behind. He let his chin dip into the cold sludge. Mud and blood seeped between his lips. Soft paste swallowed his eyes.

The Gray Wizard's thick fingernails gouged Reiffen's scalp as he grabbed him by the hair.

"There is no escape," he warned, his words hammering down like pellets of lead. Reiffen was drawn out of the earth with a loud pop. "Not for you."

The Wizard paused. Reiffen's fear sprouted like a licking flame.

"Nor for your daughter, either."

He woke with his heart pounding. Throwing off the blankets, he scrambled out of bed onto the cold dirt floor. Sandy, thinking it was time to play, pattered over to sniff his master's knees.

"Are you all right?" Ferris sat up in the bed, her voice cutting the darkness.

"I'm fine," Reiffen said.

"You don't look fine. Was it the dream about Rimwich again?"

"Yes."

"There's still some milk left from yesterday. I'll heat it for you."

"I said I was fine."

"Oh, please."

Though he could only see the outline of her face in the fireglow, he caught Ferris's irritation easily enough. Which reassured him greatly. Some things never changed.

"If you think you can have a nightmare that bad without talking to me about it," she said, "then I'm going home to Valing right now."

"You can't cast the traveling spell on your own."

"I'm sure you're gentleman enough to take me, if I ask." She patted the empty spot on the bed. "It'll be easier for both of us if you come back and let me make you feel better."

Checking to make sure the owl he had set to stand watch in the woods outside had noticed nothing unusual, Reiffen allowed his wife to pull him back into the comfort of the covers. Already the late-summer nights in the northern forest were as cold as a Valing fall.

"Not you, Sandy." Ferris pushed the yellow dog back to the floor as it tried to scramble up beside them.

Wrapped in his wife's arms, Reiffen told her about his dream. Except for the part at the end, when Fornoch had mentioned a child.

"I wish I'd never done any of it," he said.

Soft breath caressed his ear. "It was war. Ossdonc and his army would have killed us all if you hadn't stopped them."

"I know. But there's no honor in killing men, or sissit, in their sleep."

"As far as I'm concerned, there's no honor in killing anyone, ever. Sometimes it's just something you have to do. The Wizards wouldn't have thought twice about it."

"I didn't learn magic in order to be a Wizard."

"And you aren't. A magician, maybe, but not a Wizard. Believe me, no one thinks less of you for what you did. Redburr told me he thought you'd done it very cleverly."

"Redburr isn't human. He doesn't understand."

"That doesn't mean he isn't right."

"It doesn't mean he understands, either. You have no idea what that night was like. No one does. All those people, with no idea what was happening to them. I killed them all so easily. Sometimes I wish there was a way I could go back and undo everything. Too bad the traveling spell won't work for time as well as place."

"I know you'd make everything better if you could, dear heart." Ferris kissed his cheek softly. "It's one of the reasons I love you, and why you shouldn't feel so guilty. But the main thing is no one's going to bother Banking and Wayland again any time soon. The Keeadini are back across the Westing, scared to death you're going to put the plague on them the way you did the Wizards' army. And there was talk in Malmoret before I left that Cuspor has already pledged never to attack another Banking ship."

"Lovely." Bitterness edged Reiffen's voice. "The world's at peace because everyone's afraid I'll kill them. Meanwhile Fornoch, who's the real danger, is still out there somewhere dreaming up who knows what wickedness. For all we know, he's found another child to teach everything he taught me."

"Then maybe we should get to work." Ferris threw the blanket off her shoulders and sat up. Her long hair danced free in the firelight, frosting her skin. "The quicker you teach me magic, the quicker there will be two of us to stand against them."

Laughing at the way she waved her hands while pretending to cast spells, Reiffen pulled her down beside him. He liked the way she never flinched at the touch of his thimbles. As he didn't flinch at hers.

"Be careful," he said, "or I'll think you're too eager. Magic is a sacred trust, not to be granted lightly."

"Fiddle." Ferris slapped her husband's chest playfully. "I'd never have dragged you back to Valing for Father to marry us if I thought you weren't going to teach me magic. After the way you held off Usseis all by yourself, I'm sure the two of us will defeat Fornoch easily."

"In an open fight, yes. But fighting Fornoch in the open isn't what worries me. That's exactly the sort of thing he'll most avoid. More likely he'll try to set us against each another."

"As if that could ever happen."

Later, after Ferris had finally driven the nightmare from his mind, she rested on her side while Reiffen snuggled behind her, his arm around her waist. Her belly felt warm and smooth beneath his fingers, except for the empty spot where the thimble covered the end of his pinky.

"Where shall we live, dear heart?" he asked.

"Is there any question?" she murmured. "Valing, of course."

"I don't think that would work at all."

She rolled around to face him. "You know perfectly well everyone's forgiven you, now they know Skimmer and Rollby are safe. And Icer's forgotten his burns completely."

"Only because he's moved in with Old Mortin on the lower dock. The two of them are starting to make Redburr look like an abstainer."

"That's right." Ferris poked Reiffen gently on the nose with the tip of her finger. "You do have that to answer for, dearest."

"Yes, and I'd like to keep nokken drunkenness the vilest thing I can be blamed for in Valing. Which might not be the case if we bring magic there. Our power is not always going to attract the best sort of people."

"We've already discussed that. We're going to choose our apprentices only from people who want to do good. Even if we make mistakes, we'll weed out the bad ones."

"I'd still rather establish ourselves somewhere where we hurt as few people as possible. Grangore, perhaps, where we'll be close to the Dwarves. And there's another thing."

Sitting up, Reiffen retrieved a small pouch from the pile of clothes at the foot of the bed. Sandy's head poked up hopefully as a shadow before the fire.

"We have to discuss this as well." He poured a small, glowing stone out of the bag and into his hand. Not nearly as bright as a Dwarf lamp, the gem pulsed like Ferris's moonstone necklace. But the throbs of blue color that came from Reiffen's stone were as regular as heartbeats, where the moonstones flickered wild as frightened birds. Each steady flash from Reiffen's stone faded slowly, the light retreating. But even at its brightest the glow was only enough to cast a dark blue shadow on his hand.

"I've been meaning to give you this for several days," he said.

"What is it?"

"Can't you guess?"

The stone's throbbing quickened as Ferris reached for it. The color brightened, too. She drew her hand back, afraid she'd done something wrong, and the pace of the throbbing ebbed. Reiffen grinned, the same way he had when they were children and he'd just proven his cleverness by swiping cake from Hern's kitchen.

"Is it something of Uhle's?" she asked.

"Fashioning this is far beyond Uhle's power. Or any other Dwarf's."

His wife's eyes narrowed as she realized what he was offering her, and sparked in time with the flashing jewel. "Is it . . . a Living Stone?"

He nodded. This time Ferris accepted the gem when he offered it. It glowed brighter than ever in her palm, its beating quick as her heart. Unlike the sharp facets of a Dwarf lamp, the Living Stone was like Durk, smooth as a river-rounded pebble. Its color was darker than a Dwarf lamp as well, perhaps because it put out less light.

"Did you make it?" she asked.

"No." Reiffen shook his head. "Fornoch made it."

Ferris handed the stone straight back to him. "I don't want it then."

"He made it for you. I asked him to."

"And you trust him?"

"He made my stone. And Giserre's. It saved her life once, as mine saved me when Usseis broke my neck. They have never done anything but what Fornoch said they would."

"Giserre told me her monthlies stopped after you gave her one of those."

Reiffen's brows arched. "Really? She never told me that."

"It's not the sort of thing you tell your son." With a firm gesture, Ferris folded Reiffen's hand around his gift. Rock and thimble clicked together. "I haven't married you just for your magic," she went on. "None of our parents will be happy if we make them wait for grandchildren. Nor will I. Hern is dying for someone to call her Mims."

"There will be plenty of time for that later, love. Once you're settled into your power, the risk will be less. It is painful, but the stone can be removed."

Ferris waggled her thimble in the air. "Less painful than this was?"

"Well, maybe not. A lot more painful, actually."

"Then I'd rather not. Babies first, immortality after. For all you know, some of the things the Living Stone changes might last even when you remove it. In the meantime, we'll work on the other part of the deal. The sooner we have a child, the sooner I'll be ready to swallow your stone."

"As if we needed any fresh incentive."

True dawn was spilling around the edges of the blanket draped over the window when Ferris asked him another question. "I don't suppose you know how to make these things," she said, rolling the Living Stone across the quilts with her finger.

"Make one? Why would I want to do that?"

"For our children, of course."

Reiffen scowled. "I know how, but it's not a spell I ever want to practice. Or teach. Nothing comes free in magic. The life in the stone has to come from somewhere. And someone."

Taking the gem from her, he cupped it in his hand, cradling the light. "No use wasting it, though, now we have it. What's done is done."

"But what about our children? I don't want to live forever only to watch them grow old."

"Giserre told me she's going to give hers up the moment she

gets a grandchild. She wants to look a proper grandmother as the child grows up."

"And our other children? You don't think we're going to be happy with just one, do you?"

Reiffen rolled his eyes. "Let's not get too far ahead of ourselves, love."

He still hadn't told her what Fornoch had said to him in his dream. He wasn't sure he would, either. There was always the chance their first child wouldn't be a daughter at all.

Some months later, and many leagues to the south, Avender danced with Wellin in the Old Palace. Other couples swept around them in swirls of skirt and stockinged calf, but Avender saw only the woman in his arms, her laughing mouth and eyes, and felt only the grip of her fingers on his sleeve.

"So?" she asked, her voice gracing the air more merrily than the music. "Is it settled? Are you staying with Brizen in Malmoret?"

"Yes."

"And the rumors are true as well? King Brannis has presented you with an estate in Wayland to help you make up your mind?"

"The estate had nothing to do with it. I tried to refuse, but the king insisted. He says no one will take me seriously at court unless I own land. It's only a small place in East Wayland called Goose Rock."

"A charming name. Have you seen it?"

"Not yet. Want to come with me when I do?"

"The king would never approve."

She smiled, all promise and perfection, even as she glanced toward the dais at the end of the hall. Avender followed her gaze, though he had seen it all before. The garlanded columns, the musicians on the balcony above, King Brannis glowering at the dancers parading on the marble floor. Except that always before the king's displeasure had been directed at Ferris and his son. This time it was Avender's turn.

Before the dance flung them away, he saw the king gesture toward Brizen, who stood at the side of his father's chair. The son bent amiably to listen to what Brannis said, but when the king was finished Brizen said one short, round word, and remained where he was. The king's scowl deepened.

"You're right," said Avender. "If he doesn't like our dancing together, your coming to Goose Rock with me would make him even angrier."

"It would. But then, if you do not value the king's gifts, I suspect you care little for his displeasure either. Unless you have been dissembling about the value of your acquisition."

Had Avender's hands not been so pleasantly occupied with Wellin's, he would have snapped his fingers. "Your company is worth far more than a dozen Goose Rocks, and a duchy beside."

She smiled. Her fair hair swirled around her shoulders as she spun in her partner's hands. Avender's heart rose. Happily he admired her throat and the ring of bare arm that showed between the tops of her long gloves and her gown's puffed sleeves.

"If you flatter the king half so well as you flatter me," she told him, "I have no doubt you will soon have that duchy to go with your farm."

The music stopped. Wellin curtsied demurely; her partner answered with a bow. A dozen young men darted up from either side, all wanting to have the next dance with the most beautiful woman in Malmoret.

Brizen was not among them.

Wellin waved her prospective partners aside, though the warmth in her apologies enflamed them all the more. "Baron Lavinier, I know I promised you a second dance, but Avender has worn me out so completely, you must forgive me if I cannot fulfill my promise now. I really do need to catch my breath. Avender, if you would be so kind as to give me your arm. I think a pass through the garden is just what I need."

"But the cold, my lady," said Baron Lavinier. "It's as bad as Rimwich."

"At least let me fetch your shawl," said another.

"I shan't need my shawl, Dosset, but thank you all the same. This dancing has heated me enough for a snowstorm in the Bavadars." Mustaches bristled as she rested her gloved fingers on Dosset's arm, but the young men calmed back down when her hand returned to Avender. Everyone knew so beautiful and ambitious a young woman would never settle for the penniless master of Goose Rock, even if he was a hero.

Collecting a cup of hot punch along the way, Avender escorted his prize out to the garden. Low shrubbery shadowed them like shrunken crones as they strolled along the paths. Above them the dark walls of the empty palace rose up against the night, unlit upper windows darker than the sky. Except for the occasional ball, the Old Palace was never used at all.

"Are you sure you don't want a shawl?" Avender asked.

"Thank you, no. The cool will clear my head."

"Baron Lavinier is right." He rubbed his hands against the cold. "This weather does feel more like a Rimwich winter than Malmoret. When I came in, I heard a man say how, now Reiffen has renounced the throne and Brannis's triumph is complete, he's even brought Wayland's weather with him to Banking."

"Nonsense." Wellin's arm tugged on his as she lifted her punch glass to her lips. Pungent spices floated past his nose. "The weather is just unusual, nothing more. Have you seen them lately? Ferris and Reiffen, that is?"

"Not since we were all in Valing for the wedding, but that was months ago. I haven't been to the castle they're building in Grangore yet." And was unlikely to go there any time soon, he thought. Let Ferris and Reiffen have Grangore; his life would be in Malmoret now. Malmoret had fewer regrets.

Wellin stopped and gazed up at the clear sky. The cold seemed to have chased away everything but the stars.

"They are very lucky," she said with a trace of what Avender thought might be wistfulness. "Everything worked out perfectly. True love overcoming all obstacles, just as the poets describe. It is too bad not everyone can be so lucky."

"It certainly is."

Wellin laughed, her voice joyful enough to make the spying shrubbery nearly turn away in shame. When she turned to face him, her dark eyes burned. "As if you would ever have any trouble on that score. Do you have any idea how marvelous it is, dancing with you? You are the handsomest man in the room."

Avender's heart quickened. Ferris had once told him that Wellin thought him handsome, but he had hardly expected to hear it from the woman herself. Especially now Brizen was back on the marriage market. But Avender wasn't someone who repeated his mistakes and, though he had never told Ferris how he felt, he had seen what had happened when Brizen had. How, despite Ferris's hating the prince the first time they met, she had almost ended up marrying him. And would have married him, too, had it not turned out that Reiffen was on their side all along in the fight against the Wizards.

Given the look in her eyes, Avender guessed he had more going for him with Wellin than Brizen had ever had with Ferris. "If I'm the best-looking man in the room," he said, "you're easily the best-looking woman. In Malmoret. In Banking. In the entire world."

She met his glance steadily, her face a pale oval in the darkness. He laid his hand on her shoulder as he bent to kiss her and found her skin smoother than Skimmer's fur. And warmer, too, despite the courtyard's cold.

Tapping him sharply with her fan, she twirled away. "I thought you understood," she said.

"You mean I don't?"

"My cap is set for Brizen. You know that." She examined him straightforwardly with the same dark eyes that had smitten him a moment before, her fan now lying against the swell of her lower lip.

"But Brizen hasn't been paying any attention to you at all. And you seemed to enjoy my compliments as much as I enjoy yours."

"I have enjoyed your compliments. Very much. And Brizen has paid attention to no one. But that will change. He is only a man, after all, just like you. If you can get over Ferris, I am certain Prince Brizen can as well. When he does, I, for one, am certainly not going to let a second chance slip away."

Avender's hands suddenly felt cold. He pushed them into his pockets. "If you've been paying me compliments you don't mean, it's cruel."

"Oh, I mean them."

Wellin smiled again, a sly, honest smile that Avender felt as keenly as the kiss he would have preferred. "I mean them very much. But I am not in love with you and, if you try too hard to make me so, I shall have to throw you over entirely. The temptation would be too much. In the meantime, I see no reason not to go on flirting with you more than anyone else—it is much more pleasant. Not to mention the fact that Brizen would not be the first man to notice a woman only after she has been noticed by someone else."

"That's hardly fair to me."

"No. But you cannot accuse me of leading you on, as I have stated my intentions plainly. If you still wish to dance with me, and promenade in moonlit gardens—"

Raising his hands in frustration, Avender gestured at the empty sky. "What moon?"

Wellin laughed, accepting his small joke as a sign he had finished his sulk. "There will be other nights, I assure you, before Brizen gets over his broken heart. He is a good man, and loves truly. I doubt I could bring myself to marry him were he not. But, as I was saying, if you continue to flirt with me, which I would like very much, what happens to you is your responsibility, not mine. And who knows? I might even fail to catch Prince

Brizen's eye a second time, at which point I will require a great deal of consoling. Though by then I should not be at all surprised if you had moved on to someone less cruel."

"At least you're aware of the damage you're doing."

"Oh, I am quite aware." She gave him another cool glance, more intense than the first. "And of the damage to myself as well. I have meant every compliment I have given you as much as you have meant yours. I hope you will forgive me if I do not permit myself to go further."

She smiled again, a different sort of smile that revealed more of conspiratorial friendship than private desire. Then she laid her hand sweetly on his chest. "Now that we have that straightened out, I think it might be time to return to the ballroom. Even if Brizen fails to notice we went outside, Brannis and the rest of the room will not. I think they would all appreciate the sight of us dancing together again, now we have both cooled."

Bold as ever, Wellin swept her skirts loudly across the floor as she led Avender back into the King's Hall. Every dowager turned to scowl at them, and Brannis showed his annoyance as well. But if Prince Brizen noticed the couple's return, he didn't show it.

For the rest of that season Wellin offered Avender as much attention as she dared. Once she went so far as to share several quick, deep, kisses with him behind a willow on a spring afternoon when the Duchess of Winkling thought an outing with boats would be fun. Perhaps it was the kissing that did it, though Avender was certain no one had seen them, but it wasn't much later that Wellin had no time for anyone but the prince. And even though Avender had thought himself prepared, the loss still hurt.

Wellin, however, had no regrets. Her wedding was even grander than Ferris's had almost been the summer before: this time the king approved of the match as much as his son. Ferris and Reiffen were unable to attend, as Ferris was due that fall, but everyone else was present, from Valing to Issinlough. Avender watched it all from Brizen's side, though he would much rather have been banished to the top of White Tooth in the Bavadars. For the last month he had been seriously considering throwing off his allegiance to the prince and seeking his fortune with the Dwarves. To have lost a second woman to a second friend seemed more than sufficient reason to vanish from the human portion of the world. But he soon discovered other advantages to serving at the royal court, especially once the other unmarried ladies understood Wellin no longer blocked their way to the handsomest man in Malmoret. And some of the married ones as well.

2

Pant and Purr

Not that one, Mother. The blue."

Following her daughter's orders, Ferris obediently caused the blue dress to pop back into view. Now there were three—blue, red, and green—hovering in the air at the center of the workroom.

"See?" said the child. "The blue has nicer sleeves."

"Can we at least get rid of the red?" asked Ferris.

"Yes," echoed Giserre. "Hubley, the red is much too brazen for a child your age. You are not even ten."

"I will be the month after Wellin's and Brizen's ball. Can't I wear it then?"

"That would mean getting two new dresses."

"Please, Mother? Please, please, please?"

Giserre held up her hands. "Do not look at me, Ferris. I already think she is too spoiled. The blue and green, perhaps—"

The door to the workroom burst open and Plum, the youngest of Ferris's and Reiffen's apprentices, rushed in.

"They're here!" he shouted, breathless from the long dash up the tower stair. "Tar's had her kittens!"

Hubley, who had been waiting days for this to happen, raced for the door. Remembering to ask permission at the last second, she skidded to a stop on the landing outside.

"Can I go, Mother? You said I could have one."

"What about the dresses?"

"You decide. But I really, really, like the blue and red best."

Hoping Queen Wellin would give her the other if her mother wouldn't let her have both, Hubley bounded away. Plum, several years her senior, caught up quickly.

"Where?" she demanded.

"The stable. I haven't seen them myself. Soon as the grooms told me it happened, I came looking for you."

Charging out of the Magicians' Tower, they dashed down the polished marble of the main gallery and onto the central stair. Shafts of morning sunlight reached out after them from the high windows on either side. Too old to climb much anymore, Sandy joined them when they reached the front hall, his paws clacking on the cobblestones outside.

They discovered a much larger crowd in the stable than they'd expected. Nearly a dozen people had gathered inside one of the stalls. Hubley pushed at everyone's backs in her haste to get through.

"Mother said I could have one, so I get first pick!"

The crowd parted. Sandy settled in the straw by the door as his mistress strained forward. Seeing Hubley coming, Trier flipped a blanket over the manger to hide what was underneath.

She was surprised to find Trier standing guard. Of all her parents' apprentices, Trier had always been the least interested in anything that didn't help her magic. Even Ahne, who had been senior apprentice until he'd gone out on his own two years before, had been known to enjoy a song and a glass of beer. Trier, however, spent all her time studying, or scolding the juniors for not following her example. What use could she have for kittens?

Hands on hips, Hubley raised her voice insistently. "Why can't I see them?" she demanded.

"Because I said so." Her father's voice jabbed like a pitchfork from the front of the stall. "Please, everyone. Step aside. I wish to see what has happened."

Hubley saw that her father's eyes were puffy as he joined them. Thin beard sprinkled his chin too, another sign of another long night spent in the workshops.

"Is it what we expected?" he asked.

Trier nodded. Hubley couldn't read a thing from the senior apprentice's face, but her father's eyes gleamed.

He waved a commanding arm. Hubley and Plum leaned forward as Trier reached for a corner of the blanket.

"Reiffen! What is going on here? Do you really think this is appropriate?"

With great impatience, the crowd stepped back once more. Ferris joined her husband and daughter beside the manger. Though Hubley knew perfectly well that both her parents had swallowed Living Stones, she was always struck by the way they looked no older than Trier.

Reiffen met his wife's glare with the gleam in his own eyes still intact. "Another such chance might never come again," he answered. "Do you really wish to deprive Hubley of this opportunity?"

The sides of Ferris's mouth curled down. "You'll just horrify her. What can possibly be the benefit?"

"There may be many benefits, if my suspicions are correct. The White Wizard used to breed such creatures to use in spells. We should be thankful such a rare occurrence has come our way naturally. Hubley and the apprentices will be able to learn a great deal about binding, which I otherwise might not have been able to teach them."

Ferris seemed about to say something more, then decided against it. On some things she stood firm but, if this really was a rare event, she was likely to make an exception. Especially if it had to do with magic.

"All right." Ferris nodded to Trier. "Let's take a look at what Tar's brought into the world."

The apprentice lifted the blanket. Ferris and Reiffen stooped, but Hubley went down on her hands and knees for a closer look. Tar stared back at her, yellow eyes bright in the shadow beneath the manger. Two of the tiny piles of fur lying in the straw beside the cat moved, their heads nuzzling up against their mother to nurse. The other lumps stayed still.

"Only two?" she asked in dismay.

"Look more closely," said her father.

The child pushed forward. Tar raised a forepaw as if to fend her off, which gave Hubley a clearer look at the cat's belly. With a shock, she saw the two nursing kittens shared a single body between them.

"Oh, that's gross," said Plum, squatting back on the straw beside her.

Hubley agreed. Then she noticed her stomach wasn't flip-flopping, and her breakfast needed no help staying down. The two-headed cat might be gross, but it was also fascinating.

The gardener muttered in disgust. "Not a good sign, that. Nothin' right can come of somethin' that unnatural."

"Actually," said Reiffen, "it is a wonderful sign. Even monsters have their purpose. There are many things a mage can do with a creature such as this."

The gardener touched his hand to his forehead. "No disrespect, Your Honor, but I wouldn't want to be the dam o' no such thing as that. Nor sire, neither."

"No one asked you, Snaps." Ferris's sharp glance cut across the others lingering in the stall. "That goes for the rest of you, as well. If none of you have anything better to do, I'm sure I can think of something. Plum, aren't you supposed to be helping Lorennin sort snails?"

The stall emptied. Sandy lifted his head to watch them leave, then decided he was more comfortable where he was.

Hubley moved a cautious hand toward the kittens. "Can I touch them?"

"Of course," said Reiffen.

Ferris consented reluctantly. "Don't pick it up, though," she warned. "The poor thing's heads don't fit at all. Picking it up might break their necks."

With one careful finger, Hubley caressed the back of the crippled kitten. A shiver creased its soft fur. One head stopped its sucking for a moment, gasping for breath as it lifted its blind eyes, but the other nursed on. Hubley hadn't been sure at first whether they were one cat with two heads, or two cats sharing a single body. Seeing them respond separately, she decided they were two.

"You said I could have one, Mother. This is the only one there is, so I guess I get to have it. Right?"

Ferris's frown deepened. "This is hardly what I had in mind."

"You said."

"If you're just going to be stubborn about it, I'll change my mind. Do you think you can take care of them?"

"Yes." With middle and forefinger, Hubley scratched both heads again. The kittens' necks wobbled weakly, but the one on the right purred. The other wheezed. "Oh please can I have them, Mother? Please?"

Ferris studied her daughter's face uncomfortably. "This is no regular kitten, sweetheart. It's not going to be up and about in a couple of weeks. It might not even last the day. And if it does, I doubt it'll ever be able to walk on its own. Those two will be dependent on you for everything. You'll have to clean their box every time they go to the bathroom, and feed them, and brush their fur. Which is more than Tar will do for them after a month. And they won't live very long, either, no matter how hard you try to keep them alive. Will you be ready for that, when the time comes?"

Though she was a little scared of all the work involved, Hubley nodded. If anyone could keep the kittens from dying, it would be her. "I can do it, Mother," she said confidently, cupping her hands around the tiny body.

"Don't get your hopes up. For them to have been born at all is miracle enough. There's a lot more wrong with them than just the heads. Do you hear the way the one on the left pants all the time?"

"Uh-huh. I'm going to name her Pant. The other I'll call Purr because she purrs when I scratch her."

Thin lines ruffled Ferris's forehead.

"I would have suggested waiting a while before you named them," said Reiffen.

"Too late for that." Ferris glanced curtly at her husband and turned back to her daughter. "Listen, darling, Pant is the way she is because she can't get enough air. See how there's no shoulder on her side, but there is on Purr's? That means Purr is the stronger of the two. I think, the more they grow, the worse it's going to get. Pant's neck and windpipe will be pinched by Purr's. Purr seems healthy enough, but if anything happens to her sister, Purr will die too. It's only a matter of time."

"Can't you use magic?" asked Hubley. "You fixed that poor Grangore girl's harelip. Can't you do something for Pant too?"

"My magic isn't strong enough for that, dear. And there's no way to save Purr without hurting Pant. You wouldn't want me to do that, would you?"

"Certainly not." Reiffen caught his daughter's gaze. "These two kittens came into the world together. Unless you want to choose one over the other, they will have to go out the same way."

Hubley nodded. "It wouldn't be fair to pick just one," she agreed.

Their fate decided, the kittens and their mother were moved to the nursery. Over the next few days Hubley did the best she could to make the poor creatures comfortable, but it was a hopeless task. Her father helped, but, as long as the kittens put on weight, he didn't seem to mind their growing worse every other way. They never learned to walk a single step, their heavy heads tipping them over onto their faces whenever they weren't propped up on pillows. When they were awake they never played; if Hubley left them alone, they mewled piteously for her to return. Once she dropped a ball of yarn into their basket to see if that would amuse them while she went off to help her mother with a potion. When she came back, both kittens were close to strangling, the yarn looped around their weak necks while they tugged feebly at the strings with teeth and claws.

By the time Tar lost interest in them, Hubley knew they weren't going to last much longer. Purr was able to eat scraps from the child's finger, but Pant was declining swiftly. As Ferris had foreseen, the larger they grew, the more trouble Pant had breathing. On the last day, Hubley spent an entire morning trying to get the weaker kitten to suck a few drops of milk from a rag. Pant did her best, but she had to stop and gasp for air so often that Hubley knew it wasn't working. So she scratched the back of the kitten's head instead, which made Purr purr. Pant lay on the pillow and gulped for air while her healthier sister licked their paws.

The late-afternoon sun had sifted through the rose leaves on the wall outside her window when Hubley realized Pant was no longer breathing. Looking down, she saw the two kittens side by side on their pillow. All four legs still moved, but only Purr's head responded when Hubley touched it. And now Purr was having a problem lifting her own neck, the weight of her dead sister anchoring her down.

The next morning Purr was gone as well. Tears streaming down her face, Hubley carried the basket to her parents' bedroom. Her mother was the only one there, and hugged Hubley tight against her robe as the child sobbed.

"But can't you do something, Mother?" she cried. "What good's magic if you can't do anything about it when someone dies?"

Her father and Giserre joined them, and Hubley clung to each of them in turn. Later, when her heartache had eased, she told them she wanted to bury the kittens under the roses in the garden. Gently Ferris explained that Sandy would dig them up before noon if she did.

"Can't we put them in a box?" Hubley pleaded. "I'm sure Snaps would make one if I ask."

Reaching over her head, her father picked up the basket. Both kittens now lay with their heads against the pillow, the life drained from their eyes.

"I am sorry, sweetheart," he said. "But Pant and Purr are too valuable for planting in the ground."

"Really, Reiffen." Giserre wrapped an arm around her granddaughter's shoulders. "I think Hubley deserves more consideration than that."

"This is not about the child, Mother. I made it clear from the start the kittens would be useful. Now we will see if I am right. Everything necessary for the spell is downstairs. I have only been waiting for the poor things to pass."

"You're going to use Pant and Purr for magic?" The quaver dropped from Hubley's voice as she realized her father's intent.

"I am." Reiffen spoke sternly. "I told you before, the White Wizard used to breed such creatures for their power."

"You can't! I won't let you!" Shrugging free of her grandmother's arm, Hubley snatched the basket out of her father's hands and clutched it to her chest.

Reiffen's eyebrows rose. "I thought you wanted to be a magician, Hubley. Being a magician requires hard choices."

"There's no need to rub her nose in it," said her mother. "Can't we let her be a child a little longer?"

"Normally, I would agree with you, dear. But we shall not get a chance like this again any time soon."

"No?" Ferris accused. "Tar reeked of magic for weeks before those poor kittens were born."

Reiffen's face pinched. "I did help the unfortunate creatures, yes. They would have been stillborn had I not interfered. The rest of the litter was in the way. But I did not cause them to be what they were."

Giserre steered the conversation back to her granddaughter. "Hubley has grown quite fond of the kittens, my son. Must you really use them?"

"Do you see any other two-headed creatures about the castle, Mother?"

"There is no need to be unpleasant. The subject is distasteful enough."

"Would it be as distasteful had it been a piglet? Or a snake?"

"The child has not loved piglets and snakes the way she has these kittens."

"No? Then what about dogs? Even Sandy was used for magic once."

"He was?" Hubley regarded her father suspiciously, her hands still covering the basket.

"Who do you think the three-legged puppy was that Fornoch gave us to escape the fall of Ussene?"

Hubley's anger weakened. "Sandy? You did that to Sandy?"

"Fornoch did it. But, as you can see, Sandy has been fine ever since. As a result, your mother and I, and your grandmother are still alive. Not to mention Avender and Redburr." The magician wiggled the little finger of his right hand in the air. Its iron cap reflected the light no better than the dead kittens' eyes. "It is just another part of magic, like my thimbles. It hurts for a while, but there are no lasting ill effects. Pant and Purr are dead. They cannot be harmed further."

"It's still different."

"Then you will have to decide whether you really want to be a magician, Hubley. Magicians have to do this sort of thing all the time. But I will let the choice of what to do with the kitten be yours. Not for the world would I force magic on my child. It is a heavy burden, after all. But it is only fair you know that, for a real mage, there is only one possible decision."

"I thought you wanted to let the child make up her own mind," said Giserre.

"What I want, Mother, is to be certain Hubley understands exactly what being a magician means."

Hubley knew what her answer would be before she even spoke. She had been four when she learned her first spell, and magic was already too much a part of her life to be turned away from now. She had heard the way the grooms and undercooks talked about her parents, especially her father. They loved Ferris and Reiffen, and would defend them against anyone, but they still gave the magic as wide a berth as they could. Once Snaps had come back from an evening in Grangore with his eye as purple as one of his best tulips. The story Hubley heard was that a blacksmith had called her father "Wizard." Now she saw why some people could say such horrible things about her parents, and why even the people who loved them could still be afraid of them.

But she was very much her parents' child. If a butcher could slaughter animals, and a tanner use their hides, why not a magician use them for other things as well? The kittens were already dead. If Sandy could do his part, then Pant and Purr could do theirs too.

"All right, Father. You can have them. But only if I get to watch you do the spell."

Giserre sniffed, as if she had known it would come to this all along. Reiffen beamed.

"I suppose you're going to want to get to work right away," sighed Ferris. "I have that session on beetles with the juniors to attend to, or I'd join you."

"I do need to get to work while the body remains fresh," said Reiffen. "Trier can handle the preserving. All I need now is the blood."

Giserre stood up abruptly, her distaste evident. "Reiffen, please."

"My apologies, Mother."

"Just be careful," Ferris added as Reiffen and their daughter got up to leave. "You know Hubley soaks up spells like a sponge. Don't let her see anything she might be able to understand."

"I already told you, most of the spell is already prepared."

"Just make sure there's nothing you do she can figure out." Ferris trained a gimlet eye on her young daughter. "And if I ever catch you playing with dead things, you'll be twenty before I teach you another spell. You know the rules. Learning magic is a reward, not a right."

Hubley rolled her eyes. That threat she had heard more than once before.

Still carrying the kittens' basket, she went with her father directly to the basement workshops. Below the house, Nolo and the Dwarves had carved almost as many chambers out of the mountain as they had built in the castle upstairs. Ferris's workroom was in the Magicians' Tower, but Reiffen preferred his investigations, which were often more dangerous than the Dwarves', to be undertaken underground, where no one else could be hurt.

"Would you care to cast the light spell, sweetheart?" he asked as they descended the stair.

Always eager to show off, Hubley raised a theatrical hand. *"Light the dark so I can see the walls on either side of me."* A thin ball of luminescence sprang up before them, hovering just above Hubley's head. The light spell was the first spell her parents had ever taught her, and she was proud of the way she could make brightness hang like a hummingbird in the air. Among the apprentices, only Trier could do the same, though Ahne had been able to do it too before he left. Hevves, Plum, and Lorennin all needed a stick or lantern on which to cast the spell.

They followed the glowing ball down the corridor. Hubley

had been on the other side of most of the doors they passed, but not all of them. She felt a certain thrill at the thought they might be going to one of the workrooms she had never visited, or maybe even one that could only be reached by magic, but her excitement fell when her father stopped at a door she had been through many times before.

Her pale light reflected from a hundred mirrors as they entered. Reaching over the long table in the middle of the room, her father inserted a Dwarf lamp into a small reflecting box in the ceiling. Hubley allowed her own light to die as the brighter illumination of the glowing gem filled the chamber. On either side, a wide hearth and a set of shelves occupied the only space not covered by reflections of the mage and his daughter. Pots and jars packed the shelves. A large tub stood in a corner away from the door. Though its top was sealed, Hubley knew the container was filled with silver paint.

Trier appeared. Reiffen instructed Hubley to hand over the basket, then light a fire. Hubley insisted on one last look at the body before the apprentice took the kittens away forever. They looked smaller, somehow, than they had when they were alive, which made it easier to let them go.

Sighing, she turned to the hearth. For some reason the fire-spell was one of the many her parents thought too dangerous for a nine-year-old, so she was left to start the fire with a dwarfstick. The small blaze caught the black firestone quickly, yellow tongues of flame growing more and more orange as they lengthened. Knowing her father probably wanted a cold pot for his brewing, she swung the iron arm of the pot holder out into the room and away from the fire.

Climbing onto a stool, she watched him sort through the mirrors. Finally he settled on an unframed pane as wide as his palm and twice as long. This wasn't the first time they had made mirrors together. Merchants in Malmoret or Mremmen were always willing to pay for the ability to talk instantly with the captains of their trading ships no matter how far away they'd sailed, and King Brannis and the barons had a never-ending interest as well.

Next Reiffen selected a heavy iron bowl for crushing herbs. Blumet for Dwarves, he liked to say, and iron for magicians. In the bowl he mixed a small handful of crumbled aspen leaves and another of fine hairs from the same tree's roots. Hubley had helped him gather both in a high meadow above the castle near Uhle's Gate, where they had trimmed the roots with a pair of silver shears. Using a mortar, the magician ground both ingredients into coarse powder in the iron bowl, his thimbles clicking on the metal, then added pared lichen, the beards of a dozen dandelions, the usual seven drops of frog sweat, and a small vial of vitriol, which caused the mixture to hiss and foam.

When the hissing subsided, Reiffen added a gallon jug of pure mist he had collected from the top of the Magicians' Tower to the cauldron Hubley had swung away from the fire. As he poured, her father chanted something Hubley didn't quite hear, then passed his hand over the rim. She peered forward, but saw only her own reflection in the still surface. The heavy odors of iron and water clung to the back of her nose.

"Swing that back over the fire," he said.

Carefully, so as not to slosh any liquid over the sides, Hubley pushed the pot into place. Flames grazed the bottom. She waited for a moment to see if her father had cast a spell to quicken the boiling, but if he had, it hadn't been by much.

Looking back, she saw him standing over the iron bowl. He held his silver knife in one hand, the one he used when he needed to draw blood. Pricking the end of his finger with the sharp point, he squeezed a drop into the mixture. A fresh hissing sputtered up and died.

Trier returned then, with a small jar. The thick red liquid within swirled so darkly as to almost look black. Hubley swallowed hard, more affected by the sight of the kittens' blood than she had been by her last glimpse of them. What had been Pant and Purr was completely gone now, melted away like spring snow.

Unscrewing the jar's cap, her father poured a short stream into his potion. The blood reddened as it fell, catching the light in a thin ribbon. Crossing to the hearth, he added a handful of fresh violets to the now boiling water. "So it won't smell so bad," he said, and followed by pouring in the potion. The brown glop sank quickly to the bottom of the pot, where it swirled heavily, refusing to mix. But, with the pot boiling, it was only a matter of time before everything blended together. Hubley watched as closely as she could, the heat beating at her face and the smell of violets tickling her nose. Gradually the mixture filled the bowl, lightening as it spread. When the liquid looked to be the same color as silt in a flooding river, Reiffen slowly dipped the mirror he had chosen into the roiling mass. For a moment Hubley thought he was going to burn his fingers, but the glass scraped the bottom of the pot with the top of the mirror less than a finger's breadth above the potion's surface. Gently Reiffen lowered the pane to one side, covering it completely.

They played concentration games while waiting for the spell to end. Taking turns, they made up long lists of things to pack in one of Mims's traveling trunks, trying to remember everything in order. Since neither of them had forgotten anything by the time the mirror had finished cooking, they declared the contest a tie. Reiffen retrieved the mirror with a pair of cloth-covered tongs and laid it dripping on the table. Carefully he dried the glass with a fresh towel. From his pocket he pulled a small jeweled ring and, slipping it over the middle finger of his right hand, used it to cut a straight line down the middle of the glass's width. Lining the cut up on the edge of the stone table, with the towel beneath it to prevent scratching, he snapped the mirror in two.

"Perfect," he said. He examined the twin sections in either hand, then gave them to his daughter to polish on a small grindstone. Hubley liked that part best because it made her feel as if she had really assisted in the casting. Plus she got to wear a pair of batskin goggles to protect her eyes. She worked diligently at her task until the edges were smooth, her feet pumping away at the treadle. Then she helped her father set both mirrors into a pair of wooden frames he had fashioned while she was busy with the grindstone. Each frame was made with wood cut from the same tree.

"Now we need a mouse," he said.

Finding mice was never a problem in the workshops. The apprentices liked having something to munch on while they worked, and the mice made a good living scooping up the crumbs. Hubley didn't know the spell, but she knew what her father was doing when he looked intently at a small crack at the back of the shelves and chanted,

> "Come out, mouse.
> The rent is due
> On your snug house."

Small claws skittered on the stone. Eyes shiny as black beads blinked in the lamplight. When Reiffen bent down beside the wall, the mouse leapt into his hands as if it was the most natural thing in the world. Feeling a bit ashamed, Hubley realized the mouse's lot was no different from the kittens', but she hadn't objected to what was going to happen to the mouse at all.

Slipping the animal into his pocket, Reiffen arranged the mirrors at opposite ends of the stone table. Glass side up, they reflected the stone ceiling and the edge of the lamp above. Shadows flickered across them every time Hubley and her father moved.

Young though she was, she still understood that a linkage of some sort had been established between the paired glasses. Pant's and Purr's blood had made the binding stronger, but how different this was from the connection needed for a set of talking mirrors, she had no idea.

The mouse's small legs wiggled as her father dangled it by the tail a few inches above the closest mirror.

"Shift," he said.

The mouse arched its back. A screen of smoke rolled across the glass. Hubley looked up, but no smoke drifted across the ceiling. Looking down, she saw the surface of the mirror nearest her clear; the reflection of the ceiling returned. Only now the lamp was reflected on the wrong side of the glass, the image in the mirror nearest her father now showing in both glasses.

The magician dropped the mouse. Claws clicked as it landed. Legs splayed, the mouse clung to the glass, trying to look as inconspicuous as possible.

"Did it work?" asked Hubley.

"No."

Her father frowned and rubbed his chin. The mouse scrabbled toward the edge of the table. The magician scooped it up while thinking of other things.

"Perhaps . . ."

Reiffen looked back and forth between the mirrors as if noticing something new. Hubley had no idea what he was seeing.

"Hubley," he said. "Please pick up the mirror closest to you. Yes, that's it. Now, hold it upside down over the table. No, not that high. A hand's breadth should be sufficient. That's it. We wouldn't want the mouse to be hurt in the fall, would we?"

Plucking it up by the tail once more, he held the creature out over his mirror a second time. Now Hubley's glass reflected the top of the stone table, rather than the ceiling above.

"Shift," he repeated.

This time there was no sound as the mouse hit the glass. In fact, it never hit the glass, but vanished straight through it. At the same time the mirror in Hubley's hand shattered with a terrific crack. Sharp shards splashed across the table and skittered to the floor. Dropping the empty frame, Hubley jumped back from the table in surprise.

The mouse crouched inside the empty square of wood, its body tensed in terror.

"It worked!" Reiffen shook his arms exultantly.

"It did?" Confused, Hubley brushed bits of glass off the sleeves of her dress.

The magician pointed at the mouse. "How else do you think it got all the way over there? Sleight-of-hand? Of course I still have to work on the mirrors' strength. We can't have them falling apart every time someone passes through, otherwise we'll be making traveling mirrors for the rest of our lives. But it did work."

Caught up in her father's excitement, Hubley found herself hoping Tar would have another two-headed kitten again soon.

The mouse, much luckier than Pant and Purr, slipped away.

3

The Duel on the Roof

wo weeks later, when it was time for Hubley to attend her first ball, she wore the blue dress, not the green. The red her mother and grandmother had discarded entirely.

The Summer Ball was a new tradition in Malmoret. Anyone who could spent the hot, humid season as far from the city as possible. But King Brannis had chosen to mark the first anniversary of his son's marriage with a ball at the beginning of fall, and Brizen and Wellin had continued the tradition after the old king's death. With the exception of the Winter Pageant, the Summer Ball was now the height of the Malmoret season, drawing even the most distant barons in from their summer estates, no matter how hot the weather.

Hubley was looking forward to the event with great excitement, especially since Queen Wellin was the person she loved most in the world outside her parents and grandparents. And the person who spoiled her the most as well. Every time Hubley visited Rimwich or Malmoret, the queen took her on boat trips and carriage rides, or bought her dresses in the fanciest shops. Sometimes they even had tea together in the garden of the New Palace, where white-gloved servants brought the child anything she asked. Had Wellin had a girl of her own, or even a boy, Hubley was sure she and the child would have been best friends.

She had hoped her mother would take her to Malmoret a few days early, but Reiffen had insisted Hubley stay with him in Castle Grangore. "She will be safer here," he said, his forehead furrowing in a way Hubley knew meant there was no use arguing.

Ferris recognized the look as well. Pushing back her daughter's cheeks with her fingers, she bent Hubley's frown into a smile. "You know how your father and I feel about keeping you safe. I'll be so busy helping Wellin prepare for the ball, I won't be able to keep an eye on you at all. Maybe we can stay a few extra days afterward."

Hubley brightened. "I can show Wellin that new spell you taught me for shelling peas."

"No," said her father. "You will cast no spells in Malmoret."

Ferris gave him a troubled look, but didn't disagree.

"Your father's right, sweetheart. No magic. It's too dangerous."

"Why not?"

"The crowds will be large," answered her father, "and you've had accidents before. Someone might get hurt."

"That wasn't my fault!" Hubley tried hard not to rub the spot where she had broken her wrist two springs before. "If Trier hadn't canceled my feather spell, I'd never have fallen."

"You weren't supposed to be casting spells during that lesson in the first place, as I recall," said her mother. "And you know it."

"If you disobey this time," added Reiffen, "your punishment will be more than just no magic for a month. We might even have to reconsider allowing your full apprenticeship to begin after your birthday."

"You might as well just leave me here!"

"Impossible. Your mother and I will both be in Malmoret. You cannot stay here alone."

"That wouldn't be safe at all," said Ferris.

Hubley folded her arms and slumped deeper into her chair. She had heard it all before. She couldn't go anywhere by herself, not to Valing to visit Mims and Berrel, or Malmoret to visit

Wellin, or even Issinlough to visit the Dwarves. And all because of the stupid Wizard.

"If you gave me a thimble," she complained, "I'd be able to escape just like you and Mother. We wouldn't have to worry about Fornoch catching me."

"I've told you before," said her father sternly. "There are ways around thimbles. Now, enough of this. Your mother has to go. If you stop sulking, I'll show you something new to do with doves this afternoon."

When Hubley finally arrived in Malmoret three days later, she'd made up her mind that the visit was more than worth giving up a day or two of magic. Spells would be a part of her life forever, but a first ball came only once.

From the window of their apartment in the New Palace, she watched the setting sun gild the river as if on command, while servants hung paper lanterns in the gardens below. Most girls her age were home eating cold porridge in their shifts, but she got to wear her new blue dress with ribbons and real pearls, and have oysters and asparagus and wine. Not that she liked oysters or wine, but there was sure to be plenty of cake and sweets as well. She knew for a fact that her grandfather Berrel had brought several pounds of maple candy with him from Valing. Not even spilling inkberry jam on her dress could ruin her good mood. Or her mother's.

Ferris removed the stain with a wave of her hand.

"There is no time to clean this mess,
  So jam get off my daughter's dress."

The dark patch dripping down Hubley's smocking puffed up into the air like the cap off a sliced mushroom. Catching it deftly in her handkerchief, Ferris tucked the stain into her pocket. Reiffen, who didn't like it when magic was used for ordinary tasks, frowned.

Ferris pinched her daughter's nose affectionately. Her thimble clicked against her wedding ring. "You be more careful. And remember, whatever else you do, *no* magic."

"Yes, Mother."

Guests had already begun to arrive when they joined Baron Backford and his mother downstairs. Lady Breeanna, out of fashion as always, wore a simple black gown and a conical hat with a thin black veil hanging from the top. Ferris, in her dark red dress with matching gloves that came higher than her elbows, looked dazzling in comparison, at least as far as Hubley was concerned. Especially with the moonstone necklace glittering at her throat.

Pulling free of his mother's hand, the baron sidled over to Hubley. "I'm bored."

Hubley rolled her eyes and tried to think of a suitably mature reply. Wilbrim might be two years older than she, but in this sort of thing he was decades behind.

"I was down by the river before," he continued hopefully. "There are a lot of frogs. Croakers and spotties and greens. I'll bet we could catch tons."

"In this dress?" she asked, aghast.

He shrugged and stuffed his big hands into his pockets. "Suit yourself. That's what I'm going to do as soon as it gets dark. Unless you want to dance."

Not if I have to dance with you, thought Hubley to herself. Though she was fond of Wilbrim, and of dancing, the thought of the two together was impossible.

Hern and Berrel joined them then, but there was no sign of Redburr, whom no one ever seemed to see anymore. He'd even missed Hubley's last birthday. Her mother said the Shaper spent all his time these days searching for the Wizard, but Hubley was sure he had found himself a cozy cave somewhere and was busy hibernating. How else to explain his absence? If he missed her birthday this year, special as it was, he was really going to be in trouble.

The crowd eddied around them. Thanes and barons nodded, but none stopped to talk to the magicians or their friends, being slightly afraid Reiffen might turn them into toads, or worse. Being the magicians' daughter had its advantages, but there were disadvantages, too.

The other guests' civility increased once Avender arrived, Durk dangling at his side. Lifting Hubley off the floor, he returned her delighted hug with equal pleasure.

"I was hoping you'd be here," she said. "You haven't visited in months!"

"Once I heard you were coming," he replied, "I wouldn't have missed this party for the world."

Unlike everyone else, who wore their most extravagant clothes, Avender was dressed in a plain vest and breeches, his light brown hair pulled back in a simple queue. His shirt bore only the slightest ruffle at collar and cuffs, and his buttons, instead of jewels or inlaid cameos, were rounded bits of shell. In that crowd he stuck out like an acorn in a bowl of strawberries.

"But that's it exactly," said the talking stone when Hern carped about Avender's being underdressed. "This way everyone notices him, the ladies most of all. They say his lack of ostentation is charming, but if you ask me he's as obvious as a fox in a henhouse."

"No one asked you, Durk."

Avender looked older than Reiffen and Ferris, though he wasn't, of course. He simply hadn't swallowed a Living Stone the way they had. Hubley thought his maturity made him look handsomer than her father, and more distinguished too, just as Wellin seemed so much more refined than her mother. Someday Hubley would get a Living Stone of her own, but she hadn't made up her mind whether she would swallow it at twenty-two, the way her mother had, or wait till she was Wellin's age. The only reason she didn't have one already was because you never changed once you swallowed a Living Stone, and who wanted to be nine forever?

The crowd grew around her parents after Avender joined them, which gave Hubley and Wilbrim the chance to slip away. Her father might want her near him at all times, but there were limits. Though it wasn't yet dark, they found a few pages and stable boys already skulking in the reeds by the river. Bullfrogs croaked loudly. Were it not for her dress, and the fact that Hubley didn't want to miss the entrance of the king and queen, she might have joined them. Even without magic, she was sure she could catch more frogs than Willy, or anyone else for that matter. She did, after all, have the most experience.

With a last warning to the baron to take off his shoes and socks, she wandered back to the ball. Accepting a piece of crusty toast from a passing servant, she wiped off the oldfish roe and gnawed at her snack while waiting for the royal couple to appear.

"Did you see what Baroness Abingale has done with her hair?" said a woman nearby, the top of whose head resembled a frozen wave crusted with starfish and barnacles.

"Oh, yes," replied her glittering neighbor, whose own curls sported an almandine boar chased by a peridot hunter. "But every one of those jewels is paste. I had it direct from my dressmaker, who's married to the brother of one of the Abingale cooks, that the baron won't let his wife near the family jewelry anymore since she lost that Dwarven brooch at the High Ball last season."

A loud voice interrupted this fascinating conversation, booming from the far end of the room. "Barons and baronesses, knights and ladies, good men and women of the lands of Wayland and Banking, guests and neighbors, Their Majesties King Brizen and Queen Wellin."

Try as she might, Hubley couldn't get past the people crowding around the edges of the room; the skirts were thick as hedges. She thought about getting down on hands and knees and crawling through, but knew she'd never hear the end of it if she were caught. Not to mention what it would do to her lovely dress. Standing on a quilted bench at the back of the room she was able to catch a glimpse of the diamonds at Wellin's throat, but all she saw of the queen's dress was a flash of dark green silk below her shoulders. When a footman who didn't know who she was shooed her down, she debated giving him warts or an itch, but doubted it would be worth the trouble she would get into. Sulking, she wandered off in the other direction, throwing over the dancers entirely.

She found Wilbrim and several older children in one of the dining rooms helping themselves to the buffet. Hubley noted approvingly that the baron's shoes and stockings were still dry despite the damp stains on his knees. Like his mother, Willy was very large, which sometimes got him in trouble when people didn't realize he wasn't as old as he looked.

"Hubley!" The young baron waved eagerly when he saw her. "This buttercake's really good. And the strawberries, too."

"Who's your friend, Wilbrim?" asked one of the boys. From the way he looked down his nose at her, Hubley wondered if her inkberry stain had reappeared.

Baron Backford's eyebrows rose. "You don't know the magicians' daughter?" Hubley could tell by his tone that Wilbrim was already entranced by his new acquaintances. One of the reasons Willy and she got along so well was because they were both only children with few friends. "Hubley, this is Fen—I mean Fenner—and Denear, and Bonder, and, um—"

A boy whose plate was heaped with slices of cold meat bowed. "Wilstoke. But everyone just calls me Stoke," he said.

"Is it true you know magic, Hubley?" asked the girl named Denear. Several others clustered behind her while the boys pretended disinterest.

Hubley nodded as she picked through the piles of jellied fish and sculpted melon for something she actually wanted to eat.

"How about a demonstration?" Fenner elbowed his nearest neighbor and winked. "Something simple, like carrying us all off to Dremen, or dumping a leviathan in one of the fountains." His friends all laughed.

"Stop it." Denear pushed the older boy away. "Pay no attention to Fenner, Hubley. He thinks that because Queen Wellin is his second cousin twice removed that makes him important. But is there something simple you can show us, like maybe making light, or conjuring an apple?"

Nothing would have made Hubley happier than to impress so many older children, but she knew better than to disobey her parents.

"I can't."

"Why not?"

"I'm not allowed. Magic is very dangerous."

Fenner rolled his eyes, but any further challenge was stopped when Denear led them all into the ballroom. The dancing was in full swing now, with only the oldest guests still standing around watching. For the first time Hubley noticed that the three great chandeliers on the ceiling glowed with lights as varied as the men and women twirling below. Instead of the usual wax candles, hundreds of colored gems glowed along the lamps' long, curving arms like fireflies courting in the horns of an enormous stag.

"Do you think they'll let us dance?" asked Wilbrim as couples swirled by like fall leaves in a brisk wind.

"You cannot be serious." Fenner gave the younger boy a withering look.

Wilbrim peered confusedly at the crowd. "Why else are we here?"

"Do you even know how to dance, Baron?" asked Denear in mock seriousness. Her friends collapsed in giggles.

Wilbrim straightened to his full height. Without the baby fat in his face he might easily have been mistaken for one of the dashing young lieutenants Hubley saw twirling across the dance floor with her cousins Pattis and Lemmel. "My mother's been teaching me dancing for a year."

Fenner took another sip from his glass of wine and leaned forward. "Does she teach you swordplay, too? Or do you only use brooms in Backford?"

Wilbrim's face crimsoned. Hubley almost whispered a spell under her breath, a good one that would have given Fenner the ass's ears he deserved, then remembered a second time she wasn't supposed to do any magic. Lady Breeanna was a heroine, renowned for the way she had beaten back a dozen sissit at the Battle of Backford with only a broom against their swords, but it wasn't the first time Hubley had heard someone ridicule the baroness because of it.

It wasn't Willy's first time, either. His fists clenched. "How would you like it if I made fun of your mother?"

"You don't even know who my mother is."

"Oh yeah? You just show me and we'll see who laughs then."

Even Hubley knew this was a terrible reply. Denear, who didn't seem normally inclined to take the older boy's side, rolled her eyes at Wilbrim's lack of wit.

"That is the trouble with these country folk," Fenner explained grandly to his friends. "They come to the city without knowing any of the really important things at all. Imagine that, not being able to pick the Duchess of Illie out of a crowd."

Hubley knew what was coming next. Trying to stop her friend from losing his temper, she grabbed his arm. "Come on, Willy. They may be older than us, but they're boring. Let's go find something else to do."

One of the other boys leaned forward. "Yes, maybe he should go looking for frogs again. That is the only company he is fit for, it would appear."

Fenner gave a honking laugh. Once again Hubley regretted not being able to make his face match his voice. "Good one, Bonder. I believe the baron thinks himself a heron, or a duck. I hear Backford is quite proud of its waterfowl."

No one could have stopped Willy then, not even his mother.

He wasn't as tall as Fenner, but he outweighed him. When he swung, his fist caught the older boy on the cheek, just below the eye. The Duchess of Illie's son tumbled to the floor, taking several friends with him. The baroness with the almandine boar turned to see what was going on, but Fenner and the others were already scrambling to their feet. Willy confronted them all, fists raised.

"I think he just challenged you, Fen," said Stoke.

Fenner adjusted his vest and swept a lock of hair from his eyes. His cheek gleamed like a polished apple.

"Come on!" Wilbrim brandished his fists menacingly.

"Oh no." Gingerly, Fenner felt his cheek. "You challenged me. I get to choose the weapons."

"Really, Fen," protested Denear. "How can you possibly take him seriously? He is just a child."

Fenner waved an angry hand. "Look at him. He's as big as I am. And heavier, too. What am I going to say for the rest of the evening when everyone asks about my face? That I walked into a door? I'll be a laughingstock. He needs to be taught a lesson. You can't just go striking people because you don't like being teased."

Fenner had a point. Hubley had tried to stop Willy herself. But she thought the older boy needed his own lesson about the difference between teasing and bullying.

"Bonder, fetch the swords. They're in the usual place in my mother's carriage." Fenner barked orders at his companions with an air of long practice. Willy looked uneasily among them, but showed no sign of backing down.

"You cannot mean to duel *here*." For the first time, Denear looked alarmed.

"In the ballroom? No, we'll go to the roof."

"The roof? You can't go there either."

"We certainly can. The duchess has been bringing me to the palace for years. I assure you, I can find my way to the roof. And, with everyone downstairs at the ball, it won't be difficult. I expect the guards will be paying hardly any attention to the servants' stair at all. Stoke, will you act as Baron Backford's second?"

"I can be his second," protested Hubley.

"Girls can't be seconds. You know none of the rules. Stoke will be as loyal to your friend as he would to me."

"More, even." Stoke bowed gracefully. "I am on your and Backford's side now, Princess."

People so seldom called Hubley "Princess," even in Malmoret, that she didn't realize Stoke was talking to her until he winked. His face close, he whispered, "Don't worry. I know all Fen's weaknesses. If Willy can handle himself at all, he'll look good before he falls."

They trooped to the back halls of the palace, the servants far too busy to interfere. Climbing a long, narrow stair, they took a shortcut through a linen closet, where they had to shift several large hampers to open the way, and emerged into a hallway with dark green towers on the wallpaper.

Hubley recognized the pattern at once. "Aren't these the royal apartments?" she whispered.

"They are," Stoke whispered back. "Fenner and I found this route years ago. Queen Wellin always had our mothers bring us along whenever they were invited to tea, so we figured out how to escape a long time ago. This is the same road, only backwards."

It was all very exciting, not the least because Hubley so rarely got to spend time with other children. Stealthily they snuck along, though the rooms were deserted. All of them had been there before, but the treat of being in the royal apartments while the king and queen were busy dancing downstairs was something new. Hubley noticed two girls slip off into the queen's dressing room when they thought no one was looking.

A final flight of stairs, and the party emerged on the roof. Though the New Palace wasn't nearly as tall as Rimwich Tower, the view from the top was impressive all the same. Edgewater and the Great River drifted along to the south and east, the lights of the villas on the southern shore bright with parties of their own. To the north and west, Malmoret gleamed as brilliantly as Issinlough. Avenues of light stretched across Brizen's and Wellin's city. Guildhalls and taverns glowed as weavers and tanners, smiths and coopers, cobblers and glaziers, tinkers and wherrymen gathered with their friends and families to celebrate the anniversary of their king's marriage. Only the Old Palace, which Brizen and Wellin had never liked, remained dark at the top of the low hill at the center of the city.

"Did we come up here to gawk or duel?"

Bonder emerged from the stair with a pair of long, thin swords. Having already removed his jacket, Fenner selected one and began practicing lunges at one of the trees. Stoke took the other and examined it in the dim light.

"What kind of sword is that?" asked Wilbrim.

"A dueling sword." Stoke slashed at the air, the supple blade bending like a schoolmaster's switch.

Willy looked nervous. "That's not the kind I'm used to."

"I admit, it is different from the short swords they use in the army. Dueling is not much thought of outside Malmoret. I suppose you see enough action in Backford in the regular way of things that there wouldn't be much fun in it."

Passing the blade to the younger boy, Stoke showed Wilbrim how to hold it. "A looser grip," he said. "And no slashing. The tip is what counts with this weapon."

He demonstrated a lunge, then encouraged Willy to do the same. Hubley watched anxiously as they practiced for a minute among the potted oranges. When they were done, the older boy gave Willy advice in a low voice. Willy concentrated, staring at his feet, and nodded.

A strip of ground was chosen on the garden side of the roof. Stoke and Hubley stood on Willy's end, while Bonder and another boy Hubley hadn't met stood with Fenner at the other. The rest of the group watched from the side. Beyond the short wall, the palace dropped straight to the riverside garden, balconies protruding at every floor.

It was a different sort of fighting from what Hubley was used to seeing the Castle Grangore guards practice in the courtyard. Instead of hacking away steadily like a pair of woodcutters, dueling was mostly short bursts of action. Fenner would feint and lunge, and Willy would parry him desperately, then Fenner would back off and wait, snakelike, for another chance to strike. Hubley could never quite tell what was going on till each brief engagement was finished. They fought to first blood and Hubley was sure the fight would end quickly, only Willy was much faster on his feet than she expected. Several times it looked like Fenner was going to touch him, only Willy would step aside and parry, and they would break apart again. Though Fenner was much smoother with these long blades, Willy had plainly had much more training with swords.

Fenner was soon panting. Their swords clashed; Hubley was amazed no one from the garden heard the noise. Fenner began to press the attack closely when he saw how Willy didn't pursue him each time they broke apart. Once he lunged suddenly after feinting a disengagement, and almost caught Willy off guard. But the next time the older boy tried that tactic, Willy was ready. Parrying Fenner's thrust, he struck for the older boy himself. His lunge missed but, rather than breaking off, he knocked Fenner down with a punch almost as heavy as the one he had thrown in the ballroom. It looked to be all over then, only both Stoke and Bonder leapt forward to pull the duelists apart.

"None of that," said the seconds.

Fenner rubbed his chin in a rage. "He cheated! The point is mine by default!"

"I didn't cheat. Everyone knows you're supposed to fight with both hands!"

"Not in dueling," cautioned Stoke. "If you do it again,

Backford, you will forfeit the match. Really, Bondurain, he did not know the rules."

"I will accept it this once, Wilstoke. But if he does it again we will claim default."

Hubley's initial fear that Willy would be hurt had vanished. Now she just chewed her fingers and hoped he'd win. The two boys fought back and forth, Fenner desperately, knowing he would never live it down if he allowed himself to be beaten by a boy three years his junior, and Willy grimly. Then Wilbrim slipped, his new shoes scuffing on a slick spot in the stone, and Fenner was on him in a moment. The baron parried the older boy with nothing more than the strength of his arm. A more skillful opponent would have had Willy then, but a more skillful opponent would never have let the fight go so long in the first place.

Gritting his teeth, Fenner charged again, more determined than ever to end the duel. Willy made a sweeping motion with his right arm and Fenner's sword flew up and over the wall.

"I won!" cried the younger boy.

"The sword!" shouted Stoke.

Hubley followed Stoke to the edge of the roof in time to see Fenner's sword bounce off the balcony below and out into the night.

Denear shrieked. "What if it hits someone!"

Without thinking, Hubley cast a spell.

"Feather swift, feather light,
   Catch the sword that falls tonight."

The sword stopped. The other children gasped as the weapon hung in the air, quivering slightly in the breeze. Just below, an un-witting baroness chatted with her neighbors.

"That was close," said Stoke.

"How do we get it back?" asked Bonder.

"Someone has to go down to the garden," Hubley told them. "Then, when no one's looking, I'll end the spell and you can catch it—"

A stern voice interrupted. "Enough. Hubley, you were told to cast no spells."

Wrapped in his long black cloak, Reiffen stood behind them. The other children, three-quarters afraid of the magician already, backed away.

"But Father." Hubley struggled hard to keep her hold on the hovering weapon as she pleaded. "If I hadn't stopped the sword, it was going to hit that baroness in the head. She could have been killed!"

The magician's voice lifted warningly. "I am not concerned with the baroness."

Ferris, Giserre, and Lady Breeanna popped into view at the top of the stair behind him. No matter how hard she practiced, Ferris was always slower than Reiffen when casting a traveling spell.

Lady Breeanna spoke first. "Wilbrim," she demanded. "What have you been up to?"

The young baron drew himself up to his full height. "It was all my fault, Mother. I struck Fenner, which meant we had to have a duel. Hubley only kept Fenner's sword from landing on someone in the garden."

"A duel?" The anger on Lady Breeanna's face almost matched Reiffen's. "With swords? Are you injured?"

"No, Mother. I won."

"Humph. That may be what you think now." Shouldering her way through the orange trees, the baroness took hold of her son's ear and pulled him toward the stairs.

Ferris glared at the other children. "It's time the rest of you returned to the party. If you wait here much longer, your parents, and the king and queen, are going to find out what you've been up to."

"What about the sword?" asked Bonder. "We can't just leave it there."

Ferris stepped to the wall. Raising her hand, she said simply, *"To me."* With great relief, Hubley felt her connection to the blade break. The sword, as if on the end of a long rope, soared upward.

Bonder accepted the weapon from Ferris, and hurried off after his friends.

"Do you know why you are being punished?" Reiffen asked Hubley when they were gone.

She pushed her lower lip out as stubbornly as she could. "No. If I hadn't stopped the sword with magic, that baroness might have been killed."

"And you would never have cast a spell again if she had. Your friends would have been punished, too. Your sacrifice has saved them. Perhaps they will remember. You did well in making certain no one was hurt. You did not, however, do so well in putting yourself into a position where you had to use magic to prevent someone from being hurt. That is what your punishment is for. Do you understand?"

She did. But that didn't mean she liked it. "It's not fair," she insisted.

"Exactly," her father answered. "Magic never is."

Ferris looked troubled by Reiffen's severe tone, but Giserre had something to say too. "Hubley, it is important you realize how your every act will always be judged by those around you, those who have not had the same benefits in life as you have had. Just as I raised your father to live according to higher standards than the rest of the world, so he and your mother are doing the same with you."

"It's the only way to learn magic, sweetheart," added Ferris in a softer voice, but her message was the same as Reiffen's and Giserre's. "You have to have control. Without control over your spells, and yourself, there's no telling what the magic might do. To you, or to the people you're trying to help."

"Maybe I don't want to learn magic, then, if all it does is get me into trouble," Hubley said, still sulking.

Her father laughed.

"Oh, yes you do. There is nothing in the world you want more."

4

Widows and Wives

Ferris and Reiffen took Hubley home, but the party didn't end when they left. The dancing continued for hours afterward in the grand ballroom, the couples twirling under the Dwarven chandeliers like riders on a carousel. Few noticed the magicians had gone, and most of those who did didn't care. Hern and Berrel, country folk to the end, retired early, leaving Durk on a velvet cushion in one of the smoking rooms to regale those present with snippets from famous plays and his own tales of derring-do during the years he had spent lying immobile in the darkness deep beneath the wizards' fortress.

Avender only learned what had happened on the balcony while chatting with Lady Breeanna. Fleeing from yet another baroness who wanted him to dance with her marriageable daughters, the sight of his old friend standing alone in the tightly packed crowd attracted him like a lighthouse on a distant shore. At the very least he and Lady Breeanna had things to talk about, which was rarely the case with the baronesses' daughters, who generally went mute in the arms of the man even their mothers considered the most eligible in the two kingdoms. But Lady Breeanna's sharp glance warned off all pursuit, along with the fact that none of the other women could get around her ample skirts and veil.

"Thank you so much for asking," she replied to his invitation to dance, "but I am a widow, you know. Dancing, no matter how enjoyable I might find it personally, would not be proper for a woman of my situation at all. However, it is good to see you young people enjoying yourselves so thoroughly."

Avender reflected that the baroness was no more than two or three years older than he, and that neither of them were even close to being among the oldest present. But he was just as glad she had declined, as the last time they had danced he had nearly broken his shins. Of course, that had been his first ball, and he was much better at it now. Lady Breeanna's feet, however, remained as large as ever.

"Really, Avender," she told him. "It is so kind of you to spend time with an aging matron like myself. Though you may not believe it," the baroness leaned close and whispered into her companion's ear in a voice that could be heard halfway to the river, "I was never particularly good at parties. Now that Ferris and Reiffen have left, I find I have almost no one to talk to."

"Ferris and Reiffen left?"

The baroness's mood switched from confidential to stern. "We found Wilbrim dueling on the roof. Can you imagine it? If my baron were still alive—"

"Wilbrim? Dueling? I hope he won. But why would Ferris and Reiffen care?"

Lady Breeanna's eyebrows arched. "Hubley was with him. Casting spells."

"Ah." Avender had heard about the ban on Hubley doing magic, and wasn't surprised it had been broken.

"Frankly, I think it a good thing Ferris and Reiffen are finally trying to rein the child in. I love Hubley dearly, but she is quite the harum-scarum. The last time she was in Backford—"

A thin woman with several strands of pearls tight as a noose around her neck made the mistake of approaching close enough to nearly interrupt. Behind her, the woman's terribly embarrassed daughter buried her face in her hands. Lady Breeanna's fierce scowl forced them both to retreat without a word. Some might sneer behind the baroness's back at her prowess with a broom, but they usually quailed when facing her directly.

Avender tried unsuccessfully to hide his smile. The baroness turned her glare on him.

"You are a fine one to complain of so much attention," she said. "I do believe you enjoy it. Their notice is complimentary, after all. It reminds me of the way the ladies used to cluster around my baron, back when I was a mere slip of a girl."

Pulling a tiny black handkerchief from her sleeve, she dabbed at the corner of her eye. Even after a dozen years, the memory of her late husband was difficult for Lady Breeanna.

"And what have you and the magicians done with your wayward children?" asked Avender, trying to change the subject.

The baroness's wide face set stern as stone. "Wilbrim is locked in his room. Nor will he be sitting comfortably for a while, I can assure you."

"And Hubley?"

"Her parents took her home. Quite a row they had about it— I heard it all through the window. Their apartment is next to ours, you know. The children insisted on it years ago."

Avender dismissed the idea of the magicians quarreling. "Ferris and Reiffen have fought since they first met. I think it's how they let each other know they care."

Lady Breeanna sniffed. "The baron and I never argued, but then we were remarkably well matched. I do not suppose marriages like ours come around more than once in a generation."

"No, I don't suppose they do." Though he had spent only a few days with them, Avender well remembered the old baron's fondness for his young wife. Looking to change the conversation a second time, he stood on tiptoe and looked out around Lady Breeanna's veil at the dance floor.

"Wellin certainly looks beautiful tonight," he said.

"She always looks beautiful." Lady Breeanna sighed sentimentally at the sight of the queen pirouetting in the arms of one of the Cuspor captains, his inky tattoos contrasting sharply with her pale skin and hair. "I do wish I could wear yellow again, though the color never became me nearly so well as it does Her Majesty. She used to snub me terribly when we were girls, you know. I suppose it is King Brizen's influence that has made her so sweet now."

"He has that effect on all of us."

Catching Avender's eye, the queen made a small signal with her hand. Then she was gone, the Cuspor captain's long pigtail lashing his coat as he jibed his partner back to the middle of the floor.

"I believe the queen just called me," said Avender.

"Really?" Lady Breeanna's broad features squeezed together in a suspicious frown. "How can you tell?"

"We have a signal. See that handkerchief in her right hand? That means she wants me for the next dance."

"Would not that sort of thing be better left to the king?"

"The king probably needs rescuing himself. I don't think either of them are enjoying the party that much. It's all work for them."

"Were it at all proper, I would volunteer for that delightful duty in a snap. As it is not, I suppose I shall have to suffer here, alone, on the outskirts of the fray."

The music stopped. Avender slipped into the crowd before the other baronesses could reassemble their blockade. At the same time, he noticed the King of Firron bearing down on the queen from the other end of the room like a log on a spring flood. Lengthening his stride, he reached Wellin just before his rival, who was left alone on the dance floor tugging at his beard in frustration.

The queen rewarded her champion with a smile. "I was beginning to think you had forgotten your promise."

"You know better than that."

Taking her hand, Avender guided Wellin across the floor as the musicians started another tune. Brizen, his own arms around the Duchess of Illie, smiled at them as they passed.

"Do I? I notice you have danced twice already with Baroness Tregillis."

"I have not. It was one long turn. I always make it a point to dance with no one more than once, except you. People talk, you know."

"But not about me."

"No, Your Majesty. Never about you."

"You remain as gallant as ever. Which is why I know you will not mind my telling you how, if I had my way, I would be having a quiet supper right now with the dearest child in the world instead of dancing here with you."

"I don't mind at all. But not tonight. Hubley's not here."

The queen frowned when he explained about the duel on the roof. "But Ferris promised me that Hubley and she would stay another week."

Avender shrugged. "Lady Breeanna said Reiffen took her home. He and Ferris had a big fight about it."

"Then I shall have to persuade him to bring her back." Wellin covered her previous concern with a playful smile. "Even though we shall see one another again at her birthday next month, I had very much set my heart on seeing her for more than a few hours on this visit."

"If anyone can persuade Reiffen to relent, it's you."

Wellin dipped her head. "Thank you. As I have already said, you are truly the most gallant man in Banking, and not just because you are the king's captain. Which is why I consider myself lucky to be dancing with you, when there are so many unmarried girls fighting for the chance."

"I'm the lucky one, Your Majesty."

"Stop calling me 'Your Majesty.' You know I hate it."

"Yes, Your Majesty."

She tried to scowl but, with her partner beaming at her, had to laugh instead. "At least I saw your potential from the first."

"And here I thought you only picked me out of the crowd in the Old Palace because Brizen picked Ferris."

Wellin laughed again. "Well, there was that, too. But you turned out to be much more than the simple bumpkin I supposed."

They danced a figure without speaking. The king and his partner passed by again. From the look of rapture on the duchess's face, Avender guessed the woman would tell the story of how she had danced with His Highness all the way to her grave. Which she would never have done with the previous king.

"Aren't you related to the Illies?" he asked.

"She is my mother's cousin by marriage. The fact she is dancing with Brizen is proof Brannis was right about some things in suggesting our match. At least I have helped heal some of the old wounds between Rimwich and Malmoret."

Something in the way Wellin made that last remark made Avender regard her more closely. Was it possible she regretted doing what she had most wished for? Ferris had told him more than once the queen was upset over her childlessness, but Wellin's face gave no sign of what she was thinking. She looked away at the other dancers, the barons and baronesses who preferred the slower pavanes, and who would be replaced soon enough by the unmarried girls and their lieutenants when the music turned quicker. Perhaps she regretted becoming one of the former, especially now she was queen.

"Why do you not marry?" she asked.

"I haven't met the right woman."

"What about Reiffen's cousin Pattis? You know she would take you in a second. She is already more than half inclined to love you, but then the same could be said of every other woman in the kingdom. The Hero of the Stoneways, and the handsomest man in the room as well."

"She's young. She'll get over it. They all do."

"I should feel insulted. There is no more attractive, and eligible, woman in Banking, now that my husband has pardoned her father's treason. Look. There she is dancing with young Veranon. Not a penny to his name. I am surprised she even condescended to do that much, but then she probably has no idea how poor he is. And all those other young fellows lined up for their turn. She would pick you in a moment, if you joined them."

"But I won't."

"Now I am insulted."

"I'd much rather dance with you."

"Of course you would. But you cannot marry me."

"I can't marry Pattis either. Can you imagine her in Valing? Herding sheep and scrubbing floors?"

"What does Valing have to do with it? My dear Avender, I cannot imagine myself in Valing either. The winters alone would be too much. I may start shivering at the very thought."

"If I do marry, it'll be back to Valing for me. I can't think of any place else I'd want to have a family."

"Nonsense. You will go where your wife takes you, and smile the entire time. Valing is behind you now. You can no more return to it than Ferris can. Besides, the king would never let you go."

"Brizen would never make me do what I don't want."

"Well then, I shall be the one to make you stay. I need you to dance with when I am supposed to be dancing with heads of state."

"Thank you, ma'am."

Wellin frowned. "I like 'ma'am' even less than 'Your Majesty.' Come, I do not want to dance with the King of Firron yet. He always steps on my toes, the way Lady Breeanna used to step on yours. Take me for another turn."

"You know I can't. If King Jursken goes back to Firron unhappy, the price of timber will rise. You and I both have our tasks tonight, you to dance with him and me to steer him toward

Nolo when you're done so they can share a few pints. You, of all people, know a queen must not shirk her duties."

"Yes, I of all people," she murmured crossly, allowing Avender to lead her away.

Like the queen, Avender did what he was supposed to for the remainder of the ball. The Duchess of Illie wasn't the only woman that night who could boast of having danced with her heart's desire. Even the daughter of the woman with the tightly wound pearls got a turn. But none of them received his full attention, not while the memory of the queen lingered in his arms and eyes. Although Avender had been able to quickly get over his feeling for Ferris, he had never been able to do the same with Wellin, perhaps because Wellin, unlike Ferris, had never really changed. Ferris had leapt off the side of the royal barge in her wedding gown and disappeared in the middle of the Great River; by the time Avender saw her again she was married and a mage. Wellin, however, had remained a princess, even after she married the prince, and the step up from princess to queen hadn't been a long one at all. Many in Rimwich and Malmoret had been surprised at how easily the laughing girl of ballrooms and riverside picnics took to the maneuvering and secrets of Brannis's court, but not Avender. To his mind the ball and council rooms were one and the same, both requiring sharp wit, subtle tact, and mulish perseverance. Wellin had shown all those graces and more in the little time Avender had spent with her. If the way she had baited the prince's trap with the Hero of the Stoneways hadn't shown the mind of a master strategist, he didn't know what would.

That was the heart of the matter, he told himself, as he handed yet another young beauty back to her mother. Wellin had been born for this role, while for Ferris it had only been a dream. Avender wished his own dreams could be as fleeting, that someone might call him back, the way Reiffen had called Ferris. But, no matter how far away her triumph carried her, he found himself as drawn to Wellin now as he had ever been.

He left the party when the dancing was done. King Jursken and Nolo had already disappeared into one of the smoking rooms to share a barrel of Firron's own tamarack and sing songs about bears and snow. In another, Brizen mediated a discussion on tariffs between a pack of Malmoret merchants and the Dremen delegation. The queen, her own duty finished for the evening, had retired.

A few footmen wobbled noticeably at their posts along the halls as Avender returned to his apartment as well, but he was hardly the sort to report them. The flagon of wine he had ordered was already in his study when he arrived, and the night from his balcony was both soft and sweet. The scent of jasmine and roses mingled with the char of the candles burning low in their paper lanterns in the garden below. Lovers lingered along the river, their whispers obscured by the rustling of the water through the reeds.

"Is that you, Avender? I really cannot get rid of you this evening, can I?"

Twisting round on the iron railing at the edge of the balcony, he looked up. A small figure smudged the stars on the terrace two stories above, wisteria and trumpet vines tangling the air between them.

"Your Majesty?"

"I see we both had the same idea. A little quiet before bed. It has been a long day."

"It certainly has. Especially for you and the king." Avender glanced toward the hall door, hoping his guest would be late. Right now he preferred the company of the queen.

"Worse for Brizen than for me. I fear it will be some time yet before he joins me. If he is able to join me at all."

Before Avender could answer the melancholy in the queen's voice, she went on.

"I enjoyed dancing with you very much. It made me remember the old days."

It had reminded Avender of the old days, too, but then he remembered the old days all the time. Rare was the ball when Wellin didn't insist on their taking at least one turn together. Her wedding had been one of the few exceptions, mostly because Avender had spent the evening consoling himself with the widow Menliss, and most of the night as well. The widow had been kind enough to teach him how much a hero could be in demand for less than heroic deeds.

"Do you ever think of what might have been?" she asked.

Startled by the directness of her question, he thought before replying. Stars streamed above her head like a veil in a high wind.

"I think about it all the time."

"I would never have made you happy."

"Perhaps not," he agreed, despite the way his heart began thumping at her unexpected boldness. "Especially after what you said earlier this evening about not liking the weather in Valing."

The queen's rich laughter hovered in the scented air. "You are, as ever, too gallant."

"I have learned never to be gallant with Your Majesty. You imbibe gallantry the way a babe quaffs its mother's milk."

"You should not tease me. I shall tell my husband to send you on a mission to Cuspor, where you will no doubt drown in a winter gale."

"As you command." He pantomimed a bow, which was difficult to do leaning backward over an iron railing.

"Stop it. I mean it. You sound as false as Mindrell."

"My apologies, Your Majesty. Neither of us want that."

Bracing her hands on the railing, the queen leaned farther out over the night-gray roses and looked east across the river. Avender, not wanting her to go back inside, spoke again.

"What about you? Do you ever think of what might have been?"

"Yes."

They stood that way for some time. Avender wondered if he would have the strength to turn away should the queen choose to look down and meet his gaze. Long years of yearning lifted in his heart, but he knew he would never say a word. Brizen was his friend. And the king was a good man, who did not deserve falseness. All the same, Avender watched and dreamed. He would remain where he was through the entire night if Wellin chose to stand on her balcony. Such moments were precious to him, and not just for their rarity.

A door whispered. Long skirts rustled across the rug.

"Avender?"

He glanced away from the queen. A slender form leaned lazily against the balcony door, one long arm raised against the jamb. Bare shoulders shimmered above a dark gown.

"One minute, love."

The queen looked down. "What was that? I did not quite make out what you said."

The lips of the woman in the doorway framed an anxious question. Avender held up a finger and looked back at the queen.

"Is there someone with you?" she asked.

"Why would you think that?" he replied.

Perhaps her face clouded, but the night was too dark to tell. Avender wondered if his own trolling in foreign waters bothered Wellin as much as hers had troubled the king before their marriage.

"Because of your reputation, sir. I have half a mind to come down there and see who it is."

"At this time of night? Please, Your Majesty. What would the castle gossips say if you were to come to my room? Even you would be talked about, then."

She leaned farther over the balcony, crushing blossoms against her robe. The woman in Avender's room stepped back into shadow, her skirts hissing. Avender couldn't tell if it was his imagination, but he was almost certain he saw the queen's eyes gleam.

"I could bring my ladies-in-waiting with me," she warned.

"You could. But then how angry with yourself would you be if you find I actually do have a guest in my room? And that my guest is a friend? With so many witnesses, it would be impossible to prevent the story from getting out."

"You are impossible," the queen replied, but her anger was gone.

"Good night, Your Majesty."

"Good night, Avender. I only wish my duties were as pleasant as yours."

Straightening, the queen disappeared. A last wisp of starlit robe waved good-bye. Avender pushed himself off the railing, the smell of roses lingering behind him, and returned to the bedroom. Baroness Tregillis came out of the darkness, her eyes wide.

"Was that really the queen?" she asked as he held her.

"Yes."

The baroness pushed him away. "Did she see me? If she did, it will be terrible for both of us. My husband will feel compelled to fight you, which will only get him killed."

Avender kissed his finger and pressed it lightly against her lips. "Hush. We're safe. The queen is not a gossip."

The baroness shook her head, her neck and shoulders straining. "I do not feel safe. It would be a great thing to love you, but not for this sort of risk. What was I thinking?" She raised a hand to her forehead, her smooth skin creasing in confusion.

Avender let his hands drop. He had been caught off guard by the queen's appearance as well and, if Her Ladyship's mood had vanished, well then so had his. "Perhaps it was the wine, Baroness. By all means leave, if that's what you want. I can well understand your change of heart."

Some of the worry softened in her eyes. "You can? You really are a lovely man. But I do think it would be better if I go. I am sorry."

"Don't be. What we might have done is difficult enough without worrying about regrets. Let me see if the passage outside is clear."

Crossing to the door, Avender stepped into the corridor as if his was the most innocent action in the world. Left and right, there was no one else in the hall. He beckoned the woman forward.

She kissed him impulsively. "I wish I had met you before I married the baron," she said.

"No you don't."

She didn't argue. From the doorway, he watched her pass down the hall. She was a charming woman, but there were many charming women in Malmoret, and a few in Rimwich, too. He tried to steer clear of the ones who were too much in earnest, but he didn't mind when those who weren't changed their minds. Sometimes they had been known to change them back again. And it would never do to enjoy the company of someone who didn't really want to be there.

Uncorking the bottle on the desk, he poured himself a glass of wine. Occasionally he was troubled by what he did, but tonight was not one of those times. The world had not offered him an alternative. No tidy cottage with sons and daughters tussling in the yard; not even Valing Manor. Who was there to share such a prize with him? He hadn't found her. Instead he accepted those who found him instead, the embrace of women who should have known better, or did and didn't mind.

But sometimes, especially when he visited Ferris and Reiffen in Grangore and watched them roll their eyes in exasperation as their daughter ordered them around, he wished he had been lucky enough to find something else. It was draining, loving other men's widows and wives.

Cup in hand, he went back out to the balcony. The night took him in again, leaves rustling and scent kissing his nose. On the other side of the river the lights of Nearside flickered at the edge of the water like beads on a child's necklace. Sipping his wine, he looked at the balcony above and dreamed of Wellin being one of those women who someday changed her mind.

5

The Manderstone

D espite the queen's pleading, Hubley was not allowed to return to Malmoret. Nor could her mother persuade her father to change his mind when they argued about it the next morning.

"Don't you think taking away magic till her birthday is punishment enough?"

Ignoring his wife's irritation, Reiffen reached for the toast. "It is not about punishment. The child is safer here. I have important work at hand, and do not intend to spend a week wasting my time in Malmoret guarding her."

"She'd be safe enough with me," said Ferris.

"She would not. What if Fornoch showed up?"

The fight ended as it always did, with Ferris storming off to her workshop or surgery, and Reiffen acting as if nothing had happened. Hubley crept away to be by herself. She always did that when her parents fought, and lately they'd been fighting more and more. Fetching her father's spyglass from the library, she retreated to the top of the Apprentices' Tower and watched the children playing in the valley below. But she was able to watch their fun for only so long before she sighed, snapped the spyglass shut, and sat grumpily with her back against the parapet for a good long bout of feeling sorry for herself.

It could have been worse. Her parents could have taken her

magic away for years. But even then she wouldn't have been al-lowed to play with the other children, for fear that the Gray Wizard would carry her off the way he had her father. Then she might end up learning magic the way he had, from Fornoch, which would be almost as bad as not learning magic at all.

Not that Hubley thought there was any real danger from the Wizard. No one had seen him in years, not since he had helped her parents escape from Ussene. There had been rumors, of course. A trader had seen an old man teaching tricks to the Keea-dini, and a Dremen merchant had brought news of a woman sell-ing love potions in the bazaar to anyone who would pay (and the secret of how to make them to anyone willing to pay more). Reif-fen and Redburr had investigated every report without ever find-ing the Wizard, though what they did find disturbed them almost as much. Plum had told her the Keeadini shamans could now cast real charms, and the Dremen woman had been taught what she knew by an old man in gray robes who came to her every night for an entire year.

Over the next few days, Hubley spent more than a little time with the spyglass. Without magic to keep her busy, it was either that, or practice needlework with her grandmother Giserre. She loved her grandmother, but her mims was a lot more fun, even when she was mad.

Her boredom finally broke when her father found her a week later.

"We're going to Malmoret," he said.

"You changed your mind?" Surprised, Hubley forgot to hide the spyglass behind her back as she scrambled to her feet.

"So that's where that got to." Taking the telescope from her hand, the magician tucked it away inside his cloak. "Trier's been looking for it for three days. And no, I haven't changed my mind. Dwvon has something to show us in Issinlough. We are only go-ing to Malmoret long enough to pick up the king and queen, who have been summoned as well. Your mother and the apprentices will meet us underground."

Without another word, he whisked them back to the New Palace, where they found Avender waiting for them in addition to Their Majesties.

"Do you know why Dwvon wants us to come to Issinlough?" Brizen asked Reiffen after Hubley had given him and Wellin much-desired hugs.

"No." Reiffen shook his head. "Only that he does not think Ferris and I, or any of our apprentices, will want to miss what he wants to show us. Something about the Nolostone, and how a Bryddin named Faffin has found another just like it."

Hubley's imagination raced. The Nolostone was the strange rock that had dropped from Fornoch's robe just before Ussene's destruction. Her mother had seen it disappear with Nolo as he tumbled into one of the cracks in the fortress's floor. Weeks later, when Dwvon and the other Bryddin had finally dug Nolo out from under the bottom of the mountain, they had found him clutching the stone. The only thing the Dwarves had been able to learn about it since was that it was a strange mixture of Inach and brittemin, and that it was growing. The latter fact had convinced everyone the Wizard had given up the stone deliberately, but they had been unable to agree why. Hubley couldn't wait to see the new one, and maybe learn more about them both.

Taking only a little more time than he had traveling to Malmoret, Reiffen carried them off again. Hubley gasped as the floor disappeared beneath her feet, replaced by the empty darkness of the Abyss. Then she noticed the glittering silver dish of the Bryddsmett hanging in the air on her left and understood why she wasn't falling. A sheet of thick glass held her up over the bottomless deep: her father had brought them to the Bryddis B'wee at the foot of the Rupiniah. Mullioned windows surrounded them, a stone bench running below the sill. Overhead stretched a roof of smooth stone. Beyond the windows' diamond facets, the lamps of Issinlough gleamed like a thousand colored stars.

The queen took a deep breath. "Reiffen, you nearly scared me to death." A slippered foot appeared from under her long blue skirt to tap delicately at the glass.

"He was just showing off," said Avender.

"And quite successfully, too," agreed the king. "A thrilling arrival. Shall we find the others?"

The queen and all three men stooped as they ascended the narrow stair at the back of the room, but the ceiling was tall enough for Hubley. They followed a winding path up into Dwvon's unneret, past galleries and balconies that looked out upon the city. Around them, Issinlough hung upside down from the bottom of the world like roots from the roof of a cave. Gleaming bridges and catwalks connected the unnerets like dew-daubed cobwebs. The gnarled trunk of the Halvanankh dangled in the center, great black parsnip jutting from the stone, the Bryddsmett just below its tip. And in the distance, circling the entire city the way the windows of the Bryddis B'wee had circled the travelers on their arrival, shimmered the thin streams of the Seven Veils.

They smelled their next stop before they saw it. Even Reiffen sniffed delightedly as they turned in to the narrow hallway that led to Mother Norra's kitchen.

"Hello, dearies," the old woman called.

They entered a room with ceilings high enough for humans, a long table and benches wedged against one wall. Seated on a low stool beside the fire, Mother Norra stirred her stewpot with a wooden spoon.

"Give us a kiss, Hubley. And is that Avender?" The old woman peered closely at her visitors. "Pippins and pie, but you haven't been to see me in ages. And who all is that with you? My eyes aren't what they used to be, but I'll tell you, when I was a girl, I could spot morels and tenpuffs at fifty paces!"

Avender waded into the full flood of the old woman's welcome. "I'm here with Reiffen. And the king and queen."

"The king and queen!" Mother Norra flapped her arms like a pair of fish on a dock. "Help me up, Avender, help me up. I have to make my curtsy."

With Avender catching her arms, the old woman creaked to her feet. Her skirts swept perilously close to the fire, but Avender saw what was happening and flipped them out of the way with the toe of his boot. Holding on to his shoulder, Mother Norra was able to bend far more deeply than Hubley thought possible. The queen answered with a curtsy of her own, while the king bowed and kissed the old cook's smoky hand.

"It is our privilege," he said, "to meet someone so renowned for her art."

"Peas and parsley, I'm just a cook."

"Redburr tells me you make the best redbrick and flinny stew he's ever tasted," said Wellin. "Not to mention your milkberry scones."

The old woman waved her hand dismissively, but there was no hiding her smile. "That Redburr. He'll say anything if he thinks it'll get him an extra bite. But if it's scones you're after, I've got some plain ones in the breadbox. That's it there, Avender, under the second shelf. And there's fresh clover honey in the pipkin, too."

"We are here to see Dwvon," said Reiffen. "Do you know where he is?"

The old woman shook her white-haired head. "Not a clue. But he'll show up soon enough. Till then, why don't you all bide your time with a bite of stew. And I do hope you'll favor an old woman with more than a how-de-do when you finish your business. . . ."

With Avender and Hubley fetching bowls, Mother Norra ladled out portions of her most famous dish. Hubley thought it delicious, almost as good as the mussel stew Mims made whenever her granddaughter visited Valing. Reiffen and Avender put theirs away with hungry familiarity, but Hubley wasn't so sure about the king and queen. Brizen at least finished his, while Wellin smiled through the occasional spoonful.

"It is delicious," she said. "If you are willing to share the recipe, I do hope you will allow me to take it back to Malmoret. My chef's accomplishments will be incomplete should he never prepare this dish."

Mother Norra covered her mouth with her apron. "Mash and mush, Your Majesty. Why, I'll bet your housemaids eat better'n this every day. Besides, I don't hold much with recipes. Mostly I put in whatever comes to hand. Redburr's told me more than once he likes my cookin' so much 'cause I always surprise him. A little of this, a little of that. That way it comes out different every time."

"Well this version is splendid. No wonder Redburr always wants thirds." Dipping the end of her spoon into her bowl, the queen savored another small portion.

The old woman squinted at the empty hallway behind her guests. "Where is Redburr, anyhow? I don't see you usually, Avender, 'less he comes along too."

"Redburr is hunting the Wizard," said Brizen.

"Good for him." Mother Norra banged her ladle vigorously on the edge of her pot. "I always knew he was good for something besides stuffing himself. Cheese and chocolate, you tell him there'll be a place for him in my kitchen if he catches the last of those villains. When I think of what they did to poor Reiffen there, it makes my blood boil hard as alder tea."

Her outburst ended as a boy not much older than Hubley entered, his mouth and nose twitching at the flavors in the air.

"Nolo says you're supposed to meet him in Dwvon's workshop," he said, his eyes on the bowls of stew.

Reiffen started for the door.

"Sorry we can't help with the dishes," said Hubley as she and the others followed.

"That's all right, dearie. You come back as soon as you can." The old woman turned her attention to the boy. "What about you, lad? Like a taste of stew? Then help yourself to one of those bowls on the table. No sense in having to wash a dish more than once. . . ."

They met Ferris on the way up, the apprentices schooling behind her. Nolo joined them at the top of the unneret soon after. "Come on," he said, hurrying them along. "It might happen any minute. You don't want to come all this way for nothing, do you?"

Hubley tagged close behind the Dwarf. "Are there really two Nolostones?" she asked.

"That's right. Only it looks like we shouldn't have been calling mine the Nolostone at all."

"What should we be calling it?"

"A manderstone."

"Manderstone?" asked Ferris.

"I'll let Faffin explain. He understands it better than I do."

"Who's Faffin?" asked Hubley.

"You'll meet him in a minute."

Refusing to answer any more questions, the Dwarf led them into Dwvon's workshop. Huge blocks of stone lay scattered around the vast chamber like cottages and small barns. Ferris and Trier fitted Dwarven lamps to the fronts of the thin silver bands they wore around their heads to hold back their hair, but with only three lights in the entire party, the enormous cave remained mostly hidden. In the distance hammers tapped on stone.

Stopping in front of a large block of olath, Nolo laced his fingers into a set of gouges in the rock. With Dwarven strength, he lifted what turned out to be a heavy slab set flush against the wall. A low passage ran straight into the rock on the other side.

"You've hidden the Nolostone more thoroughly than before," observed Reiffen as he stooped to follow the Dwarf through the low door.

"We still get a lot of pilfering," Nolo explained, "despite the punishments you humans give one another. I didn't notice it so much when I was living on the surface, but I do now. Sometimes I wonder if I'm going to have to follow Angun's example and move away. If only for the peace and quiet."

Beyond the passage, the travelers emerged into a narrow room. Pale lamplight flickered across tables set in rows down the middle of the hall. Most were empty, but some were strewn with tools—chisels and hammers, compasses and plumbs, the sort of gear Dwarves used when working with stone.

"Wait." Reiffen pointed toward something large and egg-shaped nestled in a niche in the wall as Nolo led them toward the far end. The Nolostone. It was larger than Hubley remembered, thick as Nolo and almost as tall. "Isn't that what we came to see?"

"No." The Dwarf stopped at the far door. "We've come to see Faffin's. That's why we're in such a hurry. He thinks it's about to hatch."

"Hatch?"

For the first time in her life Hubley saw her father look confused.

"That's what he says," said Nolo. "And if we don't hurry, we'll miss it."

Beyond the long hall, the passage opened into another, larger cave. Here the floor sloped down to a small lake, a dozen Dwarves standing in clusters around the edge. One of the nearest started up the stony beach to welcome the new arrivals; the rest kept their lamps on a small island three or four fathoms offshore.

As usual, Dwvon was covered in rock dust from head to toe as he greeted Reiffen and the rest of his guests. Leading them down to the shore, the eldest introduced them to the other Dwarves. Hubley recognized no one's name except Faffin's. He was smaller than most of the Dwarves she'd met, and even thinner than Findle. But unlike Findle, Faffin almost looked frail.

Perhaps it was the nervous way he pushed his spectacles up his nose, or the fact that Hubley thought he might jump if she shouted "Boo!"

Ducking his head after he was introduced to the king and queen, the small Dwarf waded straight back into the pool. When the water reached his knees, he resumed staring at the island. Hubley stared, too. Now that she had come closer, she saw the low speck of land was empty except for a smaller version of the Nolostone set on end in the sand. Lit from all sides by the lamps of the Dwarves around the pool, it cast no shadow.

"Is that it?" asked Reiffen.

"Yes," Dwvon answered.

"What makes you believe it will hatch?" Wellin lifted the bottom of her skirts as she approached the edge of the pool. "Granted, it does look very much like an egg, but is it not just a stone?"

"Faffin should explain that," said Dwvon. "He's the one who figured it out."

All eyes turned to the small Dwarf, who retreated reluctantly from the water when he realized the newcomers were waiting for him.

"I haven't met many humans before," he began shyly, "so if I say the wrong thing, please let me know. I don't mean to offend."

"You won't offend us, Faffin," Ferris reassured him.

"I hope not." The small Dwarf ran his hands nervously through his beard and glanced down at his dripping toes, which made it necessary to push back his glasses before they slipped off. "I spend so much time in wild cave, I forget what it's like to be with other people. People aren't my specialty, you know."

"Faffin's a student of natural history," explained Dwvon. "Especially manders."

Faffin nodded. His bright eyes, lighter in color than most Dwarves', shone. "That's right. The trouble with manders, though, is they're hard to find. With Findle out there killing them all, I've had to roam far astone. But it has been easier lately, after Gammit shared the airship plans with me."

"What do manders have to do with airships?" asked Hubley.

"Having an airship helps me travel far enough to find them."

"What we would really like to know," Reiffen interrupted, "is what manders have to do with the Nolostone? And why you now think it should more properly be called the Manderstone?"

"*A* manderstone," corrected Nolo. "Faffin thinks my stone and his are the same kind."

The small Dwarf frowned thoughtfully. "They do share many characteristics. The Nolostone's older and bigger, so it will be interesting to see how much it ends up having in common with the others. Not counting Nolo's, this is only the second manderstone I've ever seen, so I'm afraid it's much too early to generalize."

"Is that the other one?" Hubley pointed toward the stone on the island.

"Yes." Faffin pushed his spectacles back up his nose. "I found it almost exactly seven of your surface years ago. It was much smaller then, but the one that hatched before it was exactly the same size, which is why I expect this one to hatch any minute. That's right, I said hatch. I started my study of natural history with flickers, so I know what a hatching egg looks like as well as anyone. Even a hatching mander egg."

Warming to his subject, the small Dwarf's nervousness began to disappear. Hubley, more curious than afraid, slipped her fingers out of her mother's hand and took a few steps closer to the shore.

"I found the first one in a mander's nirrinankh. At first I didn't think it had anything to do with the mander. I thought it was just an Inach stone worn smooth by the constant bubbling and frothing of its nirrin bed. Lava, I think you humans call it. That itself was strange enough for me to want to take it back to show Dwvon. Inach usually can't be worn or cut by anything except another piece of Inach. So, after finishing my observations of the mander, I brought the stone back with me to my airship.

"You can imagine my surprise at what happened next. There I was, cranking away at the engine, when I heard a loud cracking from the hold. At first I thought it was one of the struts breaking loose. I'm not so good at building things as most of my fellow Bryddin, you know. My mind tends to wander, and sometimes I don't quite finish. But it wasn't the struts. It was the manderstone.

"I saw that right away when I went down to the hold. Two cracks, no wider than hairs, ran down the top of the stone. I was wondering what sort of instability might cause it to break in such a fashion, as there had been no external stimulation, when the stone cracked again. A third line opened halfway down the side. The stone wobbled, as if something was moving inside. That was when I finally understood what was happening. Something was trying to get out. The crack widened, and a thin tongue licked the air.

"It took a little longer than it does for flickers, probably because mander shells are so strong. But the creature broke free eventually. It was smaller than any mander I'd ever seen, no longer than I am tall. And very thin. Unlike every other mander I've come near, this one didn't attack the moment it saw me. Instead it crawled out of its egg and squeezed itself flat against the decking. A long shudder passed through it. Thinking something was wrong, I wondered if it was weak because I'd taken it away from its nirrin pool. Manders need heat, you know. I believe they even gain most of their sustenance from it. Their fierce, predatory nature is more a matter of territoriality, I believe, than hunger.

"But it wasn't the lack of heat. A final tremor passed through the creature. Something round and white rolled onto the deck. I started forward to see what it was. Could the mander have already laid another egg? Yes, it could. And had. The creature hissed, but didn't attack as I picked its egg up. Without its nirrin bath to warm it, and after all the effort of laying, it was too weak to harm me. Studying the fresh manderstone, any idea I had of bringing it to Dwvon was forgotten. Manders are my area of expertise, not his."

"Which is why this is the first time you've seen it," explained Dwvon. "Faffin only just showed it to me."

"You can have the next one." Faffin's eyes flicked back to the island once more. "I'll be busy studying the parent. Of course I'll have to move it from this lake to someplace warm."

"The water is for your sake," Dwvon told the humans, "not ours."

"I imagine a young mander is only a little less dangerous than one full grown," said Brizen.

"Oh, yes," Faffin agreed. "Manders are always dangerous. Why, I was lucky just to make it out of my airship and back home to Issinlough. It was the hissing that warned me. It hadn't stopped since I picked up the egg. But when I looked at the creature I saw it wasn't the mander hissing at all. It was the ship. The creature had poked holes in the balloons beneath the decking. The way it was scrabbling around, it looked like it was going to poke some more. What was worse, the way its sharp claws were striking the blumet, it was only a matter of time before it set off a spark. Then all the balloons were going to explode at once, and both mander and I would drop into the Abyss."

"Dwarves don't fall," muttered Avender, almost to himself.

"Yes," Faffin agreed. "But I still needed to get back to the bottom of the world as quickly as possible. Luckily I'm a very cautious flier, and prefer to cruise close to stone. Clutching the new egg, I raced up to the deck and immediately opened all the spigots to let loose the ballast. Even so, it was a close thing. When the ship finally did blow up, I was close enough to the bottom of the world to grab on with one hand. A few feet lower, and I would have gone down with the ship. And the mander."

Hubley strained her eyes for any sign of cracking in the egg as

Faffin finished his tale, but was too far away to see. Wondering how far she could wade into the lake before her parents stopped her, she began inching around the shore in search of the spot with the best view. Plum followed.

"Are you saying the Nolostone is also a mander's egg?" inquired Wellin as Hubley and the apprentice edged away.

"Not exactly." Faffin pushed nervously at his glasses. "This manderstone is seven years old. Maybe it will open now, maybe it won't. But the Nolostone is at least twelve years old, and shows no sign of cracking. It's still proportionally heavier than this one, and more solid. Which means it has more room to grow. If it is a manderstone, it's going to hatch a much bigger mander than anything I've ever seen."

"I've seen large manders," said Reiffen. "And Avender has fought them. Usseis bred them for size in Ussene. But he never showed me that particular workshop, so I don't know how he did it. Whether the Nolostone contains one of them or not, I really can't say."

"I wouldn't bet against it," said Avender.

"Nor I," agreed the king.

"Perhaps," Wellin suggested, "you should dispose of the Nolostone before it hatches."

Faffin's eyes widened in alarm. "You can't do that! We may never get a chance like this again. If Usseis bred them, there may not be any more."

"Wouldn't that be a good thing?" asked Avender.

"It is an irreplaceable chance," said Reiffen, agreeing with the Dwarves. "And I think that one mander, no matter how large, will never present any particular danger to the Bryddin. Wizards have broken Bryddin, but not manders."

"Reiffen's right." Nolo crossed his arms and looked around for anyone to contradict him. "Manders are to be respected, not feared. I'm certain we can rig up some sort of cage to keep it in. Maybe I'll open a zoo."

"Just as long as you keep it in the Stoneways," said the queen. "I would not want to find it sitting in my garden."

"If the Nolostone does open, it's going to be years," said Faffin, who had relaxed now that no one was threatening the precious object. "The proportion of weight to volume is still too high."

As if on cue, a small pop sounded from the low island. The company along the shore leaned forward to get a better view. Now Hubley easily made out the hair-thin line running down the side of the stone. Another pop, and a second crack ripped the white surface, reminding her of the way small streaks of lightning flashed across the moonstones in her mother's necklace. But on the moonstones the jagged streaks flashed and disappeared, while these remained.

The popping grew louder and more frequent. Something small pushed up out of the top of the egg, followed by a questing tongue. A fleck of white shell broke off, clattering to the ground like a dropped dinner plate. A smaller chunk arced out over the lake, hitting the water with a splash.

"Excuse me." Faffin pushed his spectacles up his nose and began wading out to the spot where the fragment had landed.

With the loudest crack yet, the top of the shell opened like a brittle flower. Claws clicked at the jagged edges, scrabbling to widen the opening. A blunt snout and scaly shoulder appeared, black and oily against the shell. Gleaming eyes reflected the lamplight from the shore. The mander stopped to study the assembly the way they were studying it, then redoubled its efforts to escape its casing. The egg toppled; the mander slithered free. Long cords of slime dripped behind. No sooner was the creature loose than it squatted flat against the ground and, shuddering exactly as Faffin had described, laid another egg.

Posterity accomplished, the mander scuttled down to the edge of the island. Its long tongue flicked out to taste the pool. But the water wasn't at all to its liking, so the creature took off around the shore in search of a dry spot to cross. It moved much more quickly than Hubley had expected, nervous as a trotting dog, its tail and body wriggling. When it found it was trapped, it hissed loudly, the sound squirting across the lake.

"I can't see a thing," said Plum, standing next to Hubley. "I think I need more light."

Pulling out a small stick he carried for just this purpose, the apprentice spoke a rhyme.

"A flame upon my stave I need,
 So I can watch the mander breed."

Plum didn't know yet how to make a light without fire; the mander's snout flicked up as soon as the tip of his stick began to glow. The water, which had so bothered the creature a moment before, now seemed no hindrance at all. With a scuttling dash, it wiggled off the side of the island into the clear pool. A ripple formed on the surface as it disappeared, widening as the creature hurtled along the bottom straight for the flame.

"Hubley!" cried Wellin. "Run!"

Avender was already dashing round the edge of the pool, his sword drawn. Ferris and Reiffen had their arms raised to cast. Nolo and several other Dwarves charged after Avender, but their stocky legs weren't nearly fast enough to keep up over so short a distance.

"Flame, wick, coal, and tinder,
 Burn the mander to a cinder."

"No, Plum!" shouted Ferris, interrupting her own spell. "You'll just make it worse!"

Hubley backed quickly toward her parents, afraid that if she took her eyes off the small wave that marked the mander's progress for even a moment its sharp claws would rake her from behind. Water sprayed everywhere as the creature burst up the bank, but Plum's fireball caught it before it was out of the pool. Thick fog ballooned across the cavern, spreading quickly under the low ceiling. Hubley tripped and fell backward on the suddenly slippery stone.

All was confusion. Lamps bobbed in the fog like glowing globes. Shadows darted back and forth. Then the mander leapt out of the shredding vapor, much larger than before. Its teeth gleamed as its black tongue snaked toward Hubley. Grabbing her ankle, its tongue tugged and burned.

She screamed. The creature stopped, its right foreleg poised above the ground.

Avender arrived then, hacking at the mander with his sword. His first cut severed its tongue, but the next skipped sideways off the creature's stony skin, ringing like a hammer on an anvil. He slashed several more times without effect, then stopped when he realized the mander was neither fighting back, nor moving. Black blood steamed on damp stone. A crowd gathered. Plum helped Hubley to her feet, just in time for Ferris to hug her child.

"Are you all right?" Kicking aside the length of twitching tongue still dangling from her daughter's ankle, her mother examined Hubley's face.

"I-I think so. What happened?"

"Plum drew the beast to you by showing it a source of heat. Then he made it worse by hitting it with a fireball."

Hubley shook her head. "Not that. What made it stop?"

Ferris looked at the mander. The creature remained standing, still as a statue, with one foot raised.

"Your father," she answered grimly. "Something Fornoch taught him, I'm sure."

Hubley let her mother lead her back to the cave's entrance. "The Dwarves can deal with the mander," Ferris said. "You and I'll go back to Mother Norra's for tea and scones. Trier. Hevves. Gather the rest of the apprentices and come with us. This lesson is over."

Plum, who had been hovering at the edge of the crowd, hurried forward.

"I'm sorry, ma'am. I didn't know manders liked heat."

"If you'd been paying attention to Faffin's tale, instead of daydreaming about itching spells, you would have."

The apprentice glanced toward Reiffen, hoping the other mage would accept his apology as well. But Reiffen was still concentrating on his charm, his body nearly as rigid as the mander's, while he waited for his daughter to leave.

Hubley shivered, the tension of the beast's attack finally draining out of her. The sting of its long, black tongue still scorched her skin. For the first time she understood why her father had built a wall around their home. Bad as the mander was, there were other things out there that were even worse.

One of which was probably sleeping in the Nolostone right now.

6

Hubley's Tenth Birthday

he morning before Hubley's tenth birthday, Ferris woke alone. She wasn't surprised. More and more, Reiffen's nightmares were proving too much for him to sleep. Often he preferred not to take the chance of dreaming at all and worked till dawn instead. Only when she slipped out from under the quilt and saw him standing by the window did she realize this time he had at least come back to their bedroom and tried.

"I wish you'd take that tonic I mixed for you," she said. "I'm sure it would help."

"And leave me groggy all day," he grumbled. "Fornoch would like that."

Knowing it was always best to curb his black moods early, Ferris threw a shawl over her shoulders and joined him, her bare feet flinching on the cold stone floor. Outside, a hard gray sky capped the woods beyond the castle, the trees waiting patiently for their last leaves to fall.

"You'll be just as groggy if you don't sleep," she said.

"Perhaps. But there are potions for that too. Fornoch needs neither. No doubt he is outside the walls right now, waiting for me to let down my guard."

Ferris pursed her lips. Patience had never been her strong suit, but she was getting better. Reiffen, however, was getting worse. Ten years ago his worry had been a vague unease. Now he was obsessed.

Hugging him from behind, she savored the smell of magic and last night's mutton on his clothes. "Trier and I can protect Hubley," she offered. "It doesn't have to just be you."

His back stiffened. "You're wrong. It does have to be me. Do you really think you and Trier have the strength to fight a Wizard?"

"I don't see why not. I've been studying magic for longer than you did before you fought Usseis. And Trier will be the king's mage in another two months."

He turned to face her, his tone both patronizing and hard. "You know better than anyone that each year I spent in Ussene was worth five here in Grangore. Did we not agree to keep the worst of what I learned hidden, even from you? That it wasn't worth the cost?"

"Yes. But really, Reiffen, it's been ten years. Don't you think, if Fornoch wanted to take Hubley, he'd have already tried?"

His jaw trembled. "Why can't you trust me on this? Don't you think I know Fornoch's mind better than anyone? Our daughter is a far greater prize to him than I ever was, especially if Brizen and Wellin remain childless. As my daughter, she is the natural heir. But the Wizard won't even bother to try and take her if he thinks he'll fail. Which means we may never see him at all, if I can just keep her safe till she knows enough magic to protect herself. But that doesn't mean we should not be prepared."

Ferris didn't argue. It wasn't that she disagreed with Reiffen about the danger the Wizard represented, but rather that she wished he'd be easier on himself. Despite what he claimed, her husband wasn't the only person who could protect Hubley. Though she might not know the most terrible kinds of magic, Ferris knew enough to be able to grab their daughter and flee if the Wizard ever came close.

"You're right," she said. Still trying to soothe him, she straightened the collar on his jacket. "It is too early to relax our guard. But will you at least promise me you'll try to be in a good mood for the party tomorrow?"

"I will be as sprightly as Plum."

"It might help if you took a nap."

He shrugged, and went back to his brooding. A little hurt, but used to her suggestions being ignored, Ferris let him go. Reiffen was never going to stop worrying about Hubley until their daughter's magic was as strong as his. And maybe not then, either.

Even without the added burden of her husband's gloom, Ferris had a long day ahead of her. The king wouldn't be arriving till tomorrow, but many of the other guests were already present, and the queen was coming that afternoon. Wellin hadn't said a word on the subject, but Ferris was certain she intended to take advantage of the king's absence for another private consultation. She and Ferris had kept the first examination secret, and Ferris guessed Wellin would want to keep this visit quiet, too. Ferris's news was good, for Wellin at least, but she wasn't at all sure how the queen was going to react when she told her.

Like most magic travelers to Castle Grangore, the queen arrived at the top of the Magicians' Tower. One moment nothing was there; the next four women had joined the small crowd awaiting their arrival: Wellin, gorgeous in a dark green traveling costume, two of her ladies with half a dozen pieces of luggage around them, and Trier.

"Are we there yet?" demanded an impatient voice from somewhere on the queen's person. "With all due respect, Your Majesty, I really can't tell that sort of thing myself."

"You brought Durk!" cried Hubley. Letting go her mother's hand, she rushed forward to greet Her Majesty. The queen handed over the small string bag that served as the talking rock's personal dispatch pouch.

"Of course she brought me," said the stone. "How else was I going to get here?"

"Usually you come with Avender."

"Avender's on official business which has very likely taken him underground. Have I told you, child, how much I detest the Underground?"

Lady Breeanna bustled forward to join the new arrivals. "I know just how you feel, Durk. My own adventures in the Stoneways were quite difficult. There was nothing to eat, and poor Marietta was scared to death, and of course there was my own delicate condition to consider. . . ."

Wilbrim stuffed his hands in his pockets and tried desperately not to be noticed.

"Hubley." Giserre attempted to pry her granddaughter away from the queen. "You do remember what I told you this morning about being more respectful of Her Majesty."

Wellin hugged the child tighter and laughed. "Let her play, Giserre. Please. I get little enough of such joy at home."

Pressing her cheek against the queen's, Hubley beamed. Ferris, thinking about what she had to tell the queen, sighed.

An hour later, Wellin appeared in the surgery as Hubley was handing a jar of ointment to the last of the day's patients. The goodwife nearly had a relapse when she came face-to-face with Her Majesty, but Hubley managed to hustle the woman off while her heart was still beating.

Left alone, the two friends sat by the garden window. A few hardy pansies blushed pink and purple from a box on the sill. Wellin, despite changing into casual clothes, still easily outshone them, and the dark red roses climbing the trellis on the side of the Magicians' Tower. Despite her own agelessness, Ferris knew she was unlikely ever to equal Wellin in beauty, even after the queen had aged another forty years.

"Avender's arriving this afternoon," she began.

"Is he?" Helping herself to an apple from the basket on the table, the queen began to peel it. "I was wondering whether he would make the party at all. The last Brizen and I heard, he was still in the Pearl Islands."

"He's coming by way of Bryddlough. Apparently the Dwarves cut a new way up to the islands, though it's still a secret. I think they're interested in the pearls. Anyway, Dwvon sent word yesterday that Avender had arrived in Issinlough by airship."

Wellin looked up from her apple, golden peel dangling like a loose lock of her hair. "He still has to ascend the Sun Road, doesn't he? The trip takes three days."

"Not anymore. Gammit finally finished the last of the new lifts. Nolo and Dwvon took the first run two days ago, and are coming back tomorrow. Now anyone can make the trip to Issinlough in hours instead of days."

"Perhaps that will inspire Reiffen to finish those traveling mirrors he keeps talking about, so the trip from Malmoret will be just as easy. That would make our consultations much more convenient."

Ferris caught the shift in the queen's tone. "Are you ready to hear what I've learned?" she asked. Wellin nodded. "The tests we did in Malmoret came out just as I thought. If there's a problem, it's with Brizen, not you. You could have a child any time."

She watched her friend carefully, but the queen showed no reaction to what she had said. Perhaps she'd been wrong about Wellin's intent.

"There is no doubt?"

"None."

The queen glanced at the window. "Are we alone? Though my experience is limited, I have heard that it is the littlest pitchers who have the largest ears."

"I can take care of that easily enough." Ferris held up her hands, palms facing window and door. *"Let no ear our speaking hear."*

The room looked and felt no different, but magic would be needed now if anyone wanted to listen in on what the queen had to say. "That was one of the first spells I made up on my own,"

Ferris confessed. "Little pitchers do have big ears and our Hubley has the biggest of all."

"She is a wonderful child."

"You'd sing a different tune if you had her for a month."

Wellin dropped her apple and laid a hand on her friend's arm. "What a brilliant idea. Do let me take her, Ferris. For a week, even."

Ferris wished she could say yes. The queen's need was palpable, like a new leaf's for the sun.

"You know Reiffen would never allow it, Wellin. He won't even let her visit Valing anymore unless all three of us go."

"Does he think Brizen and I cannot protect her? Perhaps if we persuaded Findle to join us. Fornoch would not dare attempt anything with a wizard-slayer standing guard."

No matter how fond she was of Wellin, Ferris knew she had to be firm. The queen was too adept at getting her own way. "If it were just me, it would be fine, even without Findle. But it's what Reiffen thinks that matters. He wouldn't even let us visit Valing this summer—Hern and Berrel were terribly upset."

"The New Palace is much safer than Valing Manor."

Ferris shook her head. "It's not guards that keep Castle Grangore safe. It's magic. Wards and alarms cover every inch of the house and walls. Even I don't understand half of them, and Reiffen puts new ones up all the time."

"Surely he could cast the same sorts of protection on the palace."

"Someone would have to be there to monitor them. Which is why Hubley can't go anywhere without us."

With a thoughtful air, the queen began slicing her apple. "Though I do not agree with him, I suppose we must respect Reiffen's thinking in this matter. Without his sacrifice, we would all be dead or slaves. But it is your sacrifice as well, Ferris. And Hubley's. All of us understand it. Reiffen becomes more difficult every day."

Ferris brushed aside the queen's concern. "It's no sacrifice for me. He's the one with the nightmares. Even I don't know everything that happened to him in Ussene. And I don't want to, either. The least we can do is try and make it easier for him. Though sometimes he's so obtuse I think all he really needs is a good whack on the head. That's what Avender was always so good at. Telling Reiffen when he was wrong."

Setting down her knife, the queen picked up a slice of fruit. "Avender is good at many things, which is part of what makes him such a favorite in Malmoret. Especially since he rarely asks for anything in return."

"I imagine Baroness Tregillis would disagree with you about that."

Wellin laughed, her tone implying she didn't see anything at all wrong with Avender's, or the baroness's, behavior. "Oh, that was over after the ball. Now it's Amalla Vensey."

"The merchant's widow? Well that's an improvement. A lovely woman. I tried to help her husband, but he was too far gone by the time I was called in to be of any use."

"It was a pity when Maschel died. He used to throw the most wonderful parties. But now that his wife is on a budget, evenings at the Villa Vensey are more subdued."

"Do you think there's any chance Avender might actually settle down this time? I did hope something might come of him and Pattis. But I guess that's impossible now she's engaged to Duke Aramoor."

"Pattis was never in the race." Wellin nibbled at her slice of apple. "A man of Avender's experience requires something more than youth and innocence. Pattis adored him, but Avender was far too much of a gentleman to take advantage of her."

"Well, he'd better make up his mind soon. Hern and Berrel won't wait forever." It was an open secret the only reason Ferris's parents hadn't retired was because they were hoping Avender would find a wife and succeed them. Only a married couple could run for steward in Valing, the idea being that what worked best for a household ought to work best for the entire valley as well. "And he'd better find someone young, too, if he wants children. Amalla has three of her own already, and may be too old for more."

The moment the words were out of her mouth, Ferris knew she had said the wrong thing. The queen's forehead clouded. Leaning forward, she fixed her friend with her warm brown eyes.

"Ferris," she said. "I would do anything for a child before I grow too old as well."

It was the confession Ferris had been expecting ever since she had told the queen her news. All the same, she was surprised to finally hear it. "Anything?" she asked.

"Anything," the queen repeated, her purpose as fixed as her sadness.

Ferris refused to believe it. "That's ridiculous. Think of the consequences."

"I have, ever since you first suggested I might not be the problem. Brizen has never said a word, but I know how unhappy he is. How I have let him down."

"That's just it. Now we know you're not the one letting him down."

"That is not how the world will ever see it."

Ferris was out of her seat with her arm around her friend's shoulder in an instant.

"Look at you," she said. Carefully she tucked a contrary lock of the queen's perfect hair back into place. "Look how much even thinking this sort of thing has upset you. You love Brizen. It's obvious. You know you can't do this."

"But I want a child so much." Wellin's lower lip trembled in a way that reminded Ferris of her daughter. "Everyone else gets one. Why should I be cursed?"

"You're not cursed. Why, one of the best women I ever knew never had children. She was always happiest when Avender, Reiffen, and I came to visit—she always had a treat for us, candy or a bit of pie. Avender and Reiffen abused her terribly."

"That is the last thing I want." Sitting up, the queen dabbed gently at her eyes. "Everyone pitying me. I should prefer to chance anything than end up like the woman you describe."

"You know you don't mean that."

"Do I not? Why, I think Brizen would probably forgive me if he ever found out."

"Hmph." Ferris had hardly expected Wellin to take that particular tack. But she seemed to have made up her mind. Ferris straightened the folds of her skirt. "That sounds too noble even for him."

"It is certainly not something I wish to test him on."

"All the more reason not to do what you're thinking. It's not right."

"Even if my providing a proper heir might prevent the sort of civil war that always follows a questionable succession?"

"Yes."

Wellin laughed sourly. "If I did not know you so well, I might believe the fact that Hubley is next in line colors your opinion."

Ferris held her temper, but her face hardened. Wellin's insinuation had cut more deeply than she would have supposed. "You know perfectly well Reiffen and I don't want Hubley to be queen."

"So you say. But her reign would be long and trouble free. Perhaps she would found a dynasty of mages to rule Banking and Wayland in peace and harmony for a thousand years. While my own line runs dry as the western waste."

"Stop it." Ferris held Wellin tightly by the arms. "Don't torment yourself like this. It's horrible. Reiffen and I have told you often enough Hubley can't be Brizen's heir. Someday she's going to have her own Living Stone. We're both afraid, if she's a queen as well as a magician, she'll never give it up. The temptation will be too great."

Wellin's eyebrows lifted. "Her own Stone? Where will you get it?"

"You're forgetting Giserre gave hers up after Hubley was born. Reiffen and I aren't going to keep ours forever, either. That way there'll be Stones for our other children, too."

"You have talked about other children for years."

"And meant it, too. But it won't be long now. Hubley will get her own thimble in a year or two. She'll be a lot safer then. And I'll be able to remove my stone and have another child."

"And Reiffen?"

Ferris leaned back in her chair. "He knows what I want."

"That is not what I meant. Will Reiffen also be willing to give up his Stone?"

"He's always said he would."

The queen measured her friend with a long, probing look. When she spoke, the spite in her voice had been replaced by weariness.

"For your sake," she said, "I hope you stick with your choice. I had hoped you might talk me out of mine. It seems, however, that I am not as strong as you. Just as I would doubt my own ability to give up the treasure you seem so determined to throw off, so am I also unable to deny myself the prize you love so dearly. I am sorry if you think the less of me for it. But this is something I must do. And though I pray Brizen never learns what I intend, I still believe he would understand. As he would most likely understand should you, or Reiffen, find you lack the strength to give up your Living Stones."

They talked some more, but both women were uncomfortable after what Wellin had confessed, so the queen soon left. Ferris had grave doubts about her friend's choice, and thought less of her for having made it, though she had half-expected something of the sort. Wellin was too used to having her own way. Not in the manner of a selfish child, for Wellin had worked hard to gain her rewards. And she would work hard to gain this prize, too. But at what cost? Did the queen fully understand the shame that would follow if her falseness were discovered? And what of the man involved? Whom would Wellin trust to keep such a secret, especially if his child ascended the throne?

To the last question, at least, Ferris was fairly sure she knew the answer.

Supper was already on the table by the time Avender and Nolo arrived. As Ferris had told Wellin, the new lifts made the journey from Issinlough to the surface last no longer than an afternoon. Gammit and the other Dwarves had built three, the first stopping at the road to Cammas, and the second at the Axe and Ruby and the entrance to the Upper Mines.

Without the lifts, or the airship that had carried him from the Pearl Islands to Issinlough, Avender would never have reached Castle Grangore in time for Hubley's party. Now he was a day early, a day to be savored as much as any other spent outside Malmoret. Though Ferris and Reiffen sometimes snapped at one another in ways Avender had never expected, he still enjoyed the time he spent in Castle Grangore almost as much as he enjoyed Valing. But he didn't get to Valing much anymore, so Ferris's and Reiffen's home had to do instead.

It was a cheerful meal. Hubley sat at the queen's right, and Wellin was delighted to forego the formality of the New Palace for the easy grace of Castle Grangore. Even Reiffen appeared to forget his worries long enough to relax with the wine and laughter. At the bottom of the table, the younger apprentices played small pranks on one another with whispered spells, Ferris only interfering when young Baron Backford's steadily growing hair seemed in danger of catching fire from the oil lamp overhead.

When Hubley finally fell asleep on the window seat, her shoes kicked off and her bare feet tucked up beneath her dress, it was her father who carried her off to bed. Ferris remained with their guests, but the easy mood had left with the child. Giserre and the stewards followed soon after, then Wellin with her ladies-in-waiting. Ferris chatted with Avender for a while, much more interested in the latest gossip from Malmoret than usual for her, before she finally called it an evening as well. By the time Avender left, only Lady Breeanna and her son were listening to Durk describe his latest theatrical triumph. Having actually attended the performance, which had consisted of Durk voicing all the parts while the human actors pantomimed the action on the stage, Avender had no desire to hear any of it again.

Not quite ready for bed, he took a turn around the court-yard, then ascended to the roof of the Apprentices' Tower. As usual, being so close to the queen had left him restless, but at least she appeared to be in better spirits than she'd been in some time. It was Hubley's doing, of course. If Hubley brought out the queen's loneliness and loss more than any other child, she brought out more joy as well. It really was a pity so lovely and loving a woman, who had everything else in life, had been frus-trated in her quest for the most precious, and most common, prize of all.

Footsteps scuffed softly on the stair behind him. Expecting Plum or one of the other apprentices to be sneaking up to the roof for some last trick, he was surprised by the sight of the queen.

"Your Highness," he said. The shadows shifted as he bowed.

"Stop it," she answered. "I have not come up here to renew the formality we left behind in Malmoret."

She joined him by the wall, a dark cloak fastened close around her neck to keep off the night's chill. Together they watched the twin points of the quartered moon shred the clouds in the mountain sky.

"How fared your embassy to the islands?" she asked, when Avender didn't speak.

"The headman sent a gift. I'll give it to Brizen tomorrow so he can present it to you. Another fine pearl necklace. Pink, this time. I told old Tuatu you had white and black and gray, but no pink."

"Most men do not remember such things. Even Brizen might not be able to list the number and color of my necklaces."

"Yes he would." Avender leaned forward to escape the temptation of the woman's scent. Not of her perfume, which was as delicate as uncut roses, but of the woman herself, a richness of skin and hair at the end of the day. A fragrance that would linger on her pillow in the morning and fill the sheets at night. "Brizen's not the sort to forget small things. Especially about you."

The queen leaned against the wall beside him. Moon-fair hair floated around her face. "Sometimes he remembers. Sometimes he does not. I suppose he is like most husbands in that. Though, in his defense, he does have more on his mind than most."

"I don't know much about being a husband."

"I suppose not. The passion of courtship is quite different from that of marriage."

Avender chose not to respond to the discontent hinted at in the queen's tone. "Everyone knows that," he said instead. "Everyone knows a married couple is different after ten years than they were as brand-new lovers."

"If you know so little about being a husband, perhaps I should ask your opinion on the latter. You are the expert, after all."

This time there was no way of avoiding her obvious irritation. "Is something bothering you?" he asked.

Instead of answering his question, Wellin asked one of her own. Her brown eyes deepened in the darkness even as the moonlight silvered her hair.

"Have you ever gotten over losing Ferris?"

Avender laughed. It never occurred to him the queen might have missed the mark deliberately. "Ferris? I got over Ferris long ago. She was never mine to lose. Even when I thought I was in love with her I knew it was impossible. She loved Reiffen from the moment she was old enough to fall in love, even when she was trying to persuade herself otherwise."

"Perhaps you pine for someone else, the way you once did for her. Really, Avender, you are not so inscrutable as you think. You are exactly the sort of man to fall deeply in love. I can only suppose, if that has not happened with any of your widows and other men's wives, then you must be in love with another woman entirely. The way you once were with Ferris."

In for a pennyweight, in for a pound, Avender told himself. "And who might that be, Your Majesty?"

"I believe we both know the answer to that. Though, of course, it helps your cause not at all when you insist on addressing me so formally."

Avender's heart began to pound, though more from panic than excitement. "My formality, Your Majesty, is the only protection I have."

"How much better would it be," she answered, "if it turned out you need no protection at all?"

Twisting away, she gazed at Ivismundra. The moon had slid down the mountain's northern slope and was about to disappear behind neighboring Aloslocin's gentle shoulder. Knowing it would be easier to read the waning disk's face than the queen's, Avender wondered if Wellin was playing with him deliberately, the way she had played with him years ago in order to make Brizen jealous. He had sensed, sometimes, that Wellin wasn't entirely satisfied with her marriage. She and Brizen were not the most demonstrative couple he had ever seen. But he had never supposed Wellin to be the sort of person who might do something about her dissatisfaction, no matter how much he might have dreamed she was.

"Have you ever considered you might not be the only person who's lonely?" she asked, interrupting his silence once more.

"What I might consider, and what I let myself consider, are two very different things, Your Majesty."

"If you call me 'Your Majesty' one more time, I swear I shall strike you."

"Yes, Your Majesty."

She raised her hand. For the first time he saw her expression despite the darkness. Her nose flared; her mouth pursed tight as the seams in her finest gown. Avender thought about kissing her, but couldn't make up his mind. Passion was all very well, but what the queen was offering went well beyond passion. If they were caught, the repercussions would be swift, and involve more than just the two of them.

Wellin lowered her hand. "It is not fair if you do not fight back. And I was hoping you would do something else."

"Perhaps I will. But I have to be certain you know your own mind. I can't say I've never dreamed of a moment like this, but, if it is going to happen, I want to make sure we both know what we're doing."

"I know what I am doing. I have thought about this a long time. I do not imagine we shall have many opportunities. Certainly not in Malmoret."

"No," Avender agreed. "That would be too dangerous."

"But there are other places. This is probably the best of them. We may not have another chance again soon."

"Would that bother you?"

"Yes."

He kissed her then, and knew he should have kissed her before. Her mouth fit his own perfectly. When the kiss was exhausted, she fell against him, unwilling to let go.

"We cannot go to my room," she whispered. The night leaned in closely around them. "My ladies would hear."

"Mine's just as bad. Both Reiffen and Ferris think they can barge in on me any time they want."

The queen looked down at the wall. Avender felt her reluctance to leave through the wrapping of their cloaks.

"Don't worry." He kissed her forehead and hair. "Hern told

me she made up more beds than were needed. There are several empty rooms near mine."

Taking the queen's hand, he guided her down the stairwell. His heart still pounded; he found it hard to breathe. When Wellin squeezed his fingers at the first lamp, he stopped and drew her to him. Some time passed before they broke apart. On the floor above his own they slipped quietly into an empty room. A startled dove beat its wings in the window and flew away.

Later, in the darkness, Wellin held him tightly. "I've dreamed of this," she murmured.

"So have I," he answered drowsily.

"If you asked me to run away with you, I would."

"Would you? But you know I won't ask. It would hurt too many other people."

"I know." She snuggled closer to his chest. "That is why I love you." Her hand stroked the soft muscle of his belly. "I wish I knew when we will be able to do this again."

"I'll be miserable till we can."

But Wellin hadn't become queen because of her love of pleasure. With an effort she pushed him across the bed and sat up. Running his hand gently along her spine, Avender admired the curve of her back. He didn't understand how he could think she was more beautiful than he had thought an hour before, but he did.

Quickly she pulled on her robe and cloak. "Can you make the bed?" she asked as he watched from the pale sheets.

"Of course. Hern taught me. I can sweep, and sew, and wash clothes in a tub."

Wellin laughed. "A fine hero you are."

He remembered the way she had laughed the first time they met. Rich and knowing, and full of promise. Glad she'd finally kept her pledge, he grabbed a corner of her cloak and pulled her back under the covers.

The next time she got up she was insistent. Together they

made the bed before Wellin slipped out into the passage. The queen might make any excuse she wanted for wandering the halls of Castle Grangore at night, as long as she wandered them alone. They kissed. Avender watched her disappear down the stair.

When enough time had passed that no one would connect his wandering with the queen's, he returned to his room. He missed her already. For the first time in his life he wished he knew magic. With a traveling spell he might visit Wellin whenever he wanted. The invisibility spell Reiffen had cast on him in Rimwich might prove useful, too.

He shook his head. A fine night he was having. First he cuckolded one of his closest friends, and now he was thinking of taking up magic. Perhaps he should just chuck his life so far, turn buccaneer, and take what he wanted from the world.

He knew if he could cast the traveling spell, he'd be in Wellin's bedroom right now. And every other night she was alone. Neither of them were going to be satisfied with meeting in secret once or twice a year.

He felt no different when he woke, even though his head had finally caught up with his heart. But Brizen was arriving that morning, and their lives were going to be difficult now, even when the king wasn't around.

He would have to leave Malmoret, of course. There was no way he could possibly serve Brizen any longer. Short of dying for him, there was nothing Avender could ever do to atone, and even dying would only end his own feeling of guilt. The shame of what he and Wellin had done would never fade. The selfish path he had chosen after she rejected him years ago had been bound to lead to something like this eventually. A challenge, or a gang of street toughs falling on him during the night with knives. Or, what was most likely now, a good man suffering in silence.

Before anything else, he had to get through the day. Luckily they were not in Malmoret, where business would have kept him at the king's side all morning and afternoon. Here at least everyone's attention would be focused on Hubley. He could hide behind that.

It would be worse for Wellin, he realized, and the thought shamed him even more.

Dressing, he went down to breakfast long before the sun cleared the mountains. Though none of their other guests were up, Ferris and Hern were already busy in the kitchen. They fed him cornbread with honey, and eggs and bacon. When they asked why he was up so early, he told them he was still too used to traveling to sleep late.

Later he encountered Wellin strolling with her ladies in the garden. She bowed and spoke easily to him, as if nothing had happened. Other women he had known would never have carried it off so well. He found he was able to laugh and smile too, his own practice in this sort of situation helping him a great deal, even with a woman he adored.

Habit carried him through with the king also, though this time he couldn't help but feel his shame was plain to all. And Ferris was watching him like a hawk, almost as if she knew. Ordinarily he would have said that was impossible, but in Castle Grangore he knew better. With magic, anything was possible. He would have to be more on his guard than he ever had been before.

At least it was a busy day. With no formal duties, Avender followed his original intent and kept to the background as much as possible. The worst moment was when Hubley insisted he and the queen sit on either side of her at lunch, but everyone's attention remained on the child. All Avender had to do was smile and make a fuss, like everyone else.

Hubley sniffed as they all sat down at a long table in the garden and pretended not to care that the Shaper hadn't shown up this year either. "Wait till Redburr sees what I do to him the next time he comes to visit. I'm going to transform every jar of honey in the castle into glue, only I'll make it so they still smell like honey. The first bite he takes, he's going to get stuck. He won't be able to unstick, either, until *I* release the spell."

"He should have known better," agreed Lady Breeanna.

Despite his discomfort, Avender found the child's good humor catching. In some ways she was more spoiled than her father had ever been; at least Reiffen's high opinion of himself as a child had been tempered by the knowledge that he was a guest in Valing. For Hubley, however, everything was as it was supposed to be, with the result that, unlike her father, she had no chip on her shoulder and nothing to prove. Everyone, from Queen Wellin to the stable boys peeping in on the party from the hall, adored her.

"Your punishment might be a little harsh," suggested the queen. "Perhaps the reason Redburr is not here is because he is involved in very important business."

Hubley sipped at her lemonade. "What could be more important than my tenth birthday? Now I have two numbers to my age, just like everyone else. Besides, Father promised to teach me real spells when I'm ten. Traveling, and fireballs, and how to conjure cupcakes out of toadstools. All the important things."

"Especially that last one," called Plum from the bottom of the table.

"Conjuring cupcakes from toadstools is a key skill when you're adventuring," said Durk. "Especially underground."

Hubley nodded solemnly. "I know. And then, when I've learned everything, that's what Avender and I are going to do. Isn't that right, Avender?"

Called upon to speak, Avender managed to smile and nod.

Hubley required nothing more. "And then we're going to find the Gray Wizard and slay him, just like you did with Father and Mother, and then there will be nothing bad left in the whole world. I was going to invite Redburr to come with us, only now I've changed my mind."

For luncheon they ate fresh noodles with butter and peas, and steamed crayfish from the Ambore. Hubley had a small cup of golden wine with her guests, but mostly she drank lemonade from the pitcher at her elbow so she never had to wait for the serving maid to refill her glass. Ferris and Giserre handed round a plate of fruit and cheese, then Hern emerged from the kitchen with a large tray of chocolate cupcakes, which Avender hoped were fresh baked rather than cast from toadstools.

After that it was time for presents. The apprentices went first, and for several minutes the garden was filled with every imaginable color and shape of bird and butterfly, and some flying creatures that existed only in the casters' imaginations. Hubley clapped her hands at the sight of a long green and red striped snake flying through the air on three sets of wrens' wings, and laughed at a pair of piglets who floated another foot off the grass every time they squealed. For the grand finale, Trier and Plum scooped all the strange creatures up in a pair of long butterfly nets and deposited them in a pile. Instead of magical creatures, a shower of small boxes poured out on the table. Gleefully, Hubley unwrapped each one to find a wonderful assortment of gifts: a silver thimble; several rolls of colored ribbon; a vial of sneezing powder; a pot of jellied spider's eyes.

"Thank you all so much." Standing, she dropped a curtsy.

"You're welcome," replied the grinning apprentices. "Soon you'll be one of us." Even Trier's somber face lit up with a smile as bright as the butterfly spells she had just cast.

The rest of the presents were equally enchanting. From Nolo she received a trick box made of stone. Small enough to fit in her hand, the box was carved in loops and whorls. Certain loops, if pressed in the correct order, caused drawers to open from the box's sides. Hubley memorized the order as soon as Nolo showed it to her, and opened the drawers for her parents. Uhle's present lay inside, a pair of moonstones.

Streaks of tiny lightning flashed across each jewel's milky surface as Hubley cupped them in her hands. "Just like yours, Mother. Now I can play with them whenever I want."

From Hern and Berrel she received a beautiful patchwork quilt, while Giserre gave her a lovely sweater. Avender's gift was a set of tiny porcelain bowls he had purchased in Issinlough at the last minute, the perfect size for serving tea to Hubley's dolls.

He kept his eyes on the queen's gift rather than the queen as she handed it to Hubley, a lovely dress of green Dremen silk. "Just the thing for you to wear on your next visit to the palace," said Wellin as Hubley held it up before her.

Lady Breeanna pushed Wilbrim forward, a long box in the young baron's hands. "Try to pretend you like it," he whispered as he handed it over. "Mother's not used to buying gifts for girls."

Opening the lid, Hubley found a long row of toy soldiers lying in soft cotton. Each one was a carefully painted Backford lancer, their faces different, their horses chestnut, white, and roan.

"Thank you, Lady Breeanna. And you, too, Willy. They're perfect for the shelves in my room. They look far too delicate to play with."

"How right you are." Lady Breeanna's voice boomed off the garden wall. "I cannot begin to tell you how many sets Wilbrim has gone through. The horses' legs especially are prone to breaking."

Replacing the lid, Hubley laid the box of soldiers on the table beside her other gifts. The only present left was her parents'. But her parents' present was what everyone had come to see. What her mother and father gave Hubley was always the highlight of their daughter's birthday—not only the gift itself, but the way it was given as well.

The ground trembled. Everyone looked nervously at their feet, even Nolo, whose legs were too short to reach the grass. Hubley peered under the table as a second tremor rolled in from the garden behind her, the ground rising and falling in a low wave.

"Oh my." Hern held fast to her chair as it rocked up and down.

Nolo pointed toward the middle of the garden. "It's coming from over there."

Everyone craned around for a better look. A third wave rippled across the lawn, knocking the table and chairs about like boats in a harbor. Durk was shaken off his pillow in the middle of the table; Sandy retreated to the safety of the flagstones by the door as Hubley clapped her hands and laughed.

The ground bubbled; small clods of earth burst up from the grass and tumbled to the ground. A second spurt sent the dirt almost as high as Hubley was tall, and continued until it grew into a small black fountain at the center of the garden. Sod and soil showered down. With a loud crack, the bottom of the fountain split open and something more solid than dirt shot up through the middle, rising into the air. At first Avender thought it looked like one of the lances carried by Lady Breeanna's tin soldiers but, as it kept growing, he saw it was a sapling. Three green leaves appeared at the tip even as the young tree thickened and stretched farther into the sky. The leaves grew also, broadening until they broke apart into new limbs and greenery.

The tree soared. Fresh branches sprouted from the rough brown bark, spreading beneath the crown. Soon it had turned into a full-grown tree, its wide branches shading the entire garden.

"It's a chestnut!" Berrel exclaimed.

The leaves grew dark and thick, shutting out the sky. Bright green fruits appeared beneath them. A crack sounded from above, followed by the spatter of something falling quickly through the foliage. A large nut struck the ground. The mottled husk burst open; Avender's nose twitched at the deep woodsy smell of drifting mast. Another nut fell, and this time he caught the green scent of wet bracken at the start of a fresh spring rain. Soon the air was filled with dull thuds as nut after nut hit the grass, the leaves pattering loudly. The smells of a forest deep in the Bavadars swept across the garden: a bluebird's nest when the chicks have just hatched; fresh earth outside a badger's den; henbite and buttercups blooming in a summer meadow.

The nuts stopped dropping; the leaves turned from green to yellow to brown. But then, instead of falling from the tree, they kept turning, the color draining out of them completely until they were as white as the pages of a book. Their veins showed dark and thin as print on paper.

A wind from the south snaked over the top of the castle wall. The tree rustled. The ground beneath it swelled. With a last heave like a boy spitting a melon seed, the earth shot the tree into the high blue sky. Light flooded back into the garden. The magic chestnut soared like an overfletched arrow, spinning as it tore through the air.

At the top of its arc it exploded. Green rockets burst in all directions; spinners and crackers and whizzbangs flashed across the sky. The blasts thundered against the guests' ears. The air hissed. Hubley clapped her hands over her head as a rain of cold green sparks erupted into small flame flowers wherever they touched the ground. For a moment the green expanse of the grass was turned into a field of jumbled tulips: reds and yellows, whites and purples. Quietly crackling, the flowers died. Nothing was left on the grass, not even the hole from the tree.

"What's that?"

Wilbrim pointed at the sky. Something white twirled in the air near the top of the Magicians' Tower. It descended slower than it should, as if the long blades spinning at the top were holding it up.

"What is it?" gasped Lady Breeanna.

"A rotor," answered Nolo. "Grimble used to play with them before he built the *Nightfish*. I've never seen one anywhere else before."

The rotor twirled down. As it came closer they saw something brown as bark attached to the bottom. Hubley reached up; the falling object settled into her hands. She grunted as she felt its weight, cradling it heavily. The rotor flopped to the grass, attached to the brown package by a length of string. Hastily Hubley tore the present open. Inside she found a heavy book with a red leather cover and letters of gleaming gold.

"What is it, dear?" asked Lady Breeanna. Avender's chair creaked as she leaned over the back.

"A book."

"We can see that. What's the title?"

"*Of the Nature and Manner of Things*." Hubley hefted the tome as if judging its purpose by its weight.

"It's a grammarye," said Plum.

"One of the few I took with me when I left Ussene," said Reiffen.

"Now that you're ten," said Ferris, "you can start your official apprenticeship. What you've learned so far has just been play."

Scratching his head, Berrel peered out at the empty garden and up at the sky. "But how'd you do it?" he asked. "There's not a trace of the tree or the giant chestnuts anywhere."

"All illusion, Dad," laughed Ferris. "Not a bit of it real."

"Even the waves in the ground? But we all felt them."

"Feeling is believing," Durk agreed.

"It's an easy matter to shake tables and chairs," explained Reiffen, "but the rotor and the book were real enough. I had one of the guards throw them off the top of the tower." The magician looked up. A soldier waved down at the crowd.

"Very impressive," said Nolo. "Especially the noise."

Hubley had already opened her book's first pages and was nosing through it for interesting spells. The rest of the party settled around the table, helping themselves to second cupcakes or wine. Only when a large crow settled in the middle, its wings knocking over cups and glasses as it pecked at the nearest piece of cake, did everyone realize Redburr had finally arrived.

7

The Mirror

lthough he had a good idea why the Shaper had returned, Reiffen said nothing as the crow cocked his head to the side and fixed Hubley with one bright button eye.

"Brawwk. Happy birthday. I wasn't sure I'd make it, but I guess I got here just in time."

The bird paused, his attention distracted by the shiny sparkle of Hubley's new silver thimble. Hern snapped her napkin at him. "Shoo, you."

"I've got him." Avender scooped the crow up off the table with one arm.

"Take him away," ordered Ferris. "And don't bring him back till he's changed into something more respectable."

"Brawk! There isn't time. I haven't come all this way to be locked in the barn." Unable to get at Avender with his beak, the Shaper flapped his large wings and scrabbled with his claws. Reiffen pocketed one of the large black feathers that floated through the air.

"What have you come for?" asked the king.

The crow gave Hubley another sideways look. "This isn't the place to talk about it."

Reiffen agreed. "Giserre, if you would take over as host, Ferris and I will escort Avender and the Oeinnen to her workshop. Your Majesties. Nolo."

Hubley jumped up, wrapping and ribbons flying. "I'm coming, too!"

"Not now," warned her mother. "This is for your father and me."

"But it's my party!"

Giserre's eyebrows rose. "Hubley, you are now ten. It is time you learned the meaning of duty."

"We'll have plenty of fun without them." Snapping his fingers, Plum produced another bright butterfly. It flew off across the garden before dribbling into the air like a handful of sand.

As they went inside, Avender let Redburr go. The bird flew up toward the top of the Magicians' Tower while everyone else climbed the stair.

"Not there!" Ferris leapt forward as she spotted the Shaper perched on a small table in the middle of her workshop. "Wellin gave us that for our fifth anniversary. I won't have you ruining it."

Spreading his glossy wings, the crow glided over to a stool. Unlike the basement workshops, Ferris's was an airy chamber, with a tall ceiling and wide windows facing east, south, and west. On the northern side a long bench stood against the wall, rows of books and beakers filling the shelves above.

"Well now," she asked, satisfied the damage to the table could be repaired. "What's this all about?"

The Shaper glanced bird-wise at Reiffen. "You never did tell her, did you?"

"We agreed I wouldn't," the magician replied.

"Tell me what?" Ferris demanded.

"Redburr's been watching Ahne."

"Watching Ahne? What in the world for?"

The Shaper gripped the edge of the stool with his claws. "Ever since Reiffen and I learned the Gray Wizard was teaching magic to Dremen witches and Keeadini shamans, we knew it was only a matter of time before he went after your apprentices. I've been watching Ahne for the last year."

"Ahne would never have anything to do with the Wizard," scoffed Ferris. "He's a good man. It's why Reiffen and I picked him."

"A pleasant fellow," the king agreed.

"Well, he isn't pleasant anymore." The bird snapped his beak with a sharp crack. "Remember that girl who disappeared in West Wayland last year?"

"Of course." Wellin's interest sharpened at the mention of the child. "We sent two companies of the guard to help with the search."

"Ahne has her now."

Ferris broke through the hush of everyone else's surprise. "I don't believe it."

The Shaper fixed Reiffen with one dark eye. "I'm sure your husband does. He knows the Wizard's power better than anyone."

Though he would have preferred not to, Reiffen agreed. The news that Ahne had stolen a child shook him deeply. It meant that all his worst nightmares were coming true. He and Ferris had chosen their apprentices for goodness as much as wisdom, but now, when the first of them had faced the Wizard, goodness hadn't turned out to be much good at all. He should have known he had to get rid of Fornoch first, before passing his knowledge along to anyone else. Now, in addition to the Wizard, he was going to have to deal with the apprentices too.

"But why would Ahne want to steal a child?" asked the king.

"There are many uses a magician might have for a child," Reiffen answered. "Ahne, however, knew none of them when he left Castle Grangore. Ferris and I do not teach that sort of thing."

"Fornoch does," said the bird.

"Did you see him?"

Redburr shook his beak. "I haven't even seen the girl. But I heard her. Three days ago Ahne left the door open to a secret cave in the hill behind his cottage. They talked for a while, and he called her by name. That's how I knew who she was."

"So she's still alive," said Ferris.

"We must rescue her," said Wellin.

Reiffen decided to speak up before everyone's good intentions got out of hand. "It might be a trap. Clearly, Fornoch has been corrupting Ahne for some time now, otherwise a child stolen from her parents a year ago would not be in his possession."

"Remember it's the Wizard we're after here," added Redburr. "Not the child."

"Nonsense." Wellin's look dared anyone to contradict her. "If the child is alive, rescuing her is our first concern."

Brizen pulled at his chin. "I have to agree. Redburr, I will not permit the child to be used as Wizard's bait."

The Shaper pointed his sharp beak at the king. "Even if it rids us of the Wizard once and for all? One child for many is a good trade."

"It is not," said the queen. "You are not human, Redburr. You cannot understand."

"It hardly matters anyway." Everyone turned to Reiffen as he waved their arguments aside. "Redburr just told us he has not seen Fornoch once during the entire year he's been watching Ahne. In all likelihood the Wizard has never visited Ahne in person at all. He will be using dreams or mirrors. I shall have to go see."

Ferris began untying her apron. "We can rescue the girl while we're there."

"Redburr and I will certainly rescue the child if we can," said Reiffen. "But I think it would be better if you remained behind."

"Why?"

Reiffen readied himself to catch her apron in case his wife threw it at him. "As I said, this may all be a ruse. Fornoch may be attempting to lure us away from Castle Grangore. Someone has to stay and guard Hubley."

Ferris didn't bat an eye. "Better I go, then. You're always saying how you guard Hubley better than I do."

Reiffen hadn't considered that. Hubley's safety was his first concern, but he much preferred being the one to examine Ahne's cottage. Alone, if possible. Ferris might find things there it would be better she never saw.

"No," he said, making up his mind. "Fornoch will know we've seen through his plans if you show up rather than I. Better for you to stay. You and Hubley can hide in our special place."

"If you think I'm going to cower in the basement while you go off to fight the Wizard, you're out of your mind. I'll stay here, but I won't be chased into hiding. A fine example we'd be setting for our daughter if I ran away at the first sign of danger. It's bad enough I can't go with you to see what sort of a mess Ahne's gotten himself into, but I'm not going to pretend to be afraid to stay behind."

"If you thought about it for a minute," said Reiffen, "you'd know there's no pretending as far as being afraid of Fornoch is concerned."

"Brawk!" The Shaper flew between husband and wife. Both stepped back, or his wings would have smacked each in the face. "Let it go, Reiffen. Ferris can take care of herself."

"I'll come with you," offered Avender.

"No." Reiffen shook his head. "You won't be able to keep up."

"Why not?"

"I can only travel as far as Ipwell. I've never been to Norly. After that Redburr and I will have to fly."

"You'll still need some sort of reserve. Let Ferris take me to Malmoret to fetch a company of the king's guard, then bring us along with you. That way, if it turns out you need help, we'll already be on our way."

Reiffen decided it wouldn't hurt to have a company of soldiers near at hand, provided they were properly armed. There never was any knowing the Wizard's plans.

"Fine. Have them bring crossbows. We'll arm them with Inach bolts when they arrive."

Wellin and Brizen chose to return with Ferris and Avender to

Malmoret, though their retainers had to remain behind for another trip. Reiffen spent the time they were gone preparing his spell. He had only been to Ipwell once, to speak with a Hisser who had seen Fornoch, and couldn't go there with a simple thought the way he could to more familiar places.

They were a large group when they left, about as many as Reiffen could take so far with success, five soldiers in addition to Avender and Redburr. The magician lay on the desk with his eyes closed, his companions holding his bare arms. He remembered an inn with a large beech tree standing outside the front gate, a wooden bench wrapped around the tree's wide trunk. Past the gate a whitewashed rabbit dashed across a wooden plank above the door. A small stream chattered behind the house, funneling through a narrow race to the baron's mill down the road. . . .

The soldiers gasped, though they had just traveled from Malmoret to Castle Grangore a few minutes before. But to suddenly find themselves in the middle of the road outside the Running Rabbit in Ipwell came as a shock, no matter how much they had been expecting it. Their surprise, however, was not nearly as great as that of the two farmers sitting on the bench below the beech tree. Their mouths hung open; pale smoke curled from the pipes in their hands.

"Good afternoon, gentlemen."

The magician nodded as he stood and patted the dust from his clothes. Pointing past the farmers, he showed Avender the way to Norly.

"If you march all night," he said as Redburr flew up into the tree, "you'll reach the village by dawn. Redburr and I will meet you there. By that time I imagine we will have learned everything possible from Ahne and can decide what to do next. I doubt we will find Fornoch, but, if we do, remember your Inach bolts are the only thing that will work against him. Iron, or even blumet, won't work at all."

As Avender led the soldiers away, Reiffen entered the house. Paying the innkeeper a full night's fee for an hour's use of one of his rooms, he went up the narrow stairs. After first opening the window, he sat on the bed and retrieved a small black feather and a tiny iron brooch from a leather pouch within his cloak.

"Brawwk. What's that?"

The Shaper perched on the windowsill, a bit of carrion under one sharp claw.

"A charm." Reiffen opened the brooch's clasp. "Transformation spells are not the sort of thing you can cast just anywhere. At least not at my present level of ability. So I have prepared a few in advance, like this bird, for instance."

"Looks like a bug on a pin to me." Bending over, the Shaper picked at the mouse with his heavy beak. Tearing off a long string of red flesh, he gulped it down like a robin with a worm.

"It's a bird. The feather will determine what kind."

"Is that my feather? The one you took when Avender picked me up?"

"Ah, you noticed that." Reiffen twirled the quill between his fingers. "No, this is a common crow's. The feather determines the sort of bird I shall transform into. Yours would be much too uncertain. Though it might be interesting to try sometime when our task is less urgent."

"Brawwk. Use one of mine and you might turn into a weasel instead of a crow."

"That's why I am not trying it now. Though I do wonder if it would allow me to retain the ability to speak, which this will not. Not even the language of crows."

Unbuttoning his shirt, Reiffen pinned the brooch to his chest. Two trickles of blood ran down his skin. Holding the feather in his left hand, he chanted,

> "Toe to talon, beard to bill,
>   Change my form to fit this quill."

Unlike traveling, Reiffen always felt a transformation. Not on the outside, where skin and hair and clothes merged and sprouted into beak and claws and feathers, but on the inside, where the change was most acute. Sight blurred and melted; shapes and colors spun like water spiraling round a drain. Touch and feeling disappeared. Cut loose from the world, he felt as if he were drawing in on himself, like ivy growing backward.

And then he was somewhere else. Or, in this case, something else. His sight sharpened. Weight and solidity drained away; no longer did he feel part of the earth. The air lifted his feathers and called him to the sky.

"Is that what I look like when I change?" squawked the other crow from the windowsill. "Bird and human blinking on and off, faster and faster until only the bird's left?"

Reiffen shook his head, conscious of the way his sharp beak sliced the air. Without thinking, he flapped his wings and joined the Shaper on the sill. The brooch on his breast pinched at every wingbeat, reminding him who he was. The smell of dead mouse clung sweetly to the air.

The sun was falling behind the higher peaks of the Blue Mountains as they darted out the window. Redburr led them northwest toward Norly, the hills falling away beneath their wings. They saw no sign of Avender and the soldiers, who would have to wind their way back and forth around those same hills. A trip that would take the better part of a night for men walking was going to take a pair of crows no more than an hour.

The light failed quickly. The land fell into shadow, broken only by the occasional glimmer of farmhouse or town. Despite the pull of his crow's nature to investigate each shining flicker, Reiffen enjoyed his flying very much. It was so very different from anything a human could do. Even the steady prick of the brooch against his breast did nothing to lessen the joy of racing through the sky, wings nearly brushing the early stars.

Night had come by the time they arrowed down toward a

small dot of light at the side of a hill several miles past Norly. The smell of chickens and other delightful edibles eddied through Reiffen's bill as he swooped across the yard and settled into one of the weedy flower boxes in front of the two shuttered windows. Cocking his head, he set an eye to a crack in the wood.

A single cluttered room met his gaze. Shelves of books and magical apparatus lined the opposite wall, where the stony side of the hill cut straight to the floor. On the left, a sleeping loft hung just below the rafters. Reiffen's former apprentice sat on a stool by the side of the hearth, a ladle in one hand. Fresh bread and butter lay on a plate nearby: the pot bubbling over the fire smelled more like soup than magic. A chicken and several rabbits hung from the rafters alongside bags of onions and potatoes; what looked like a tiny fox's paw lay on a large platter, several thin metal wires trailing from it to a jar of bubbling yellow liquid.

Reiffen hopped back and forth along the window box as he tried to see into every corner of the room. Stirring his pot by the fire, Ahne certainly didn't act as if anyone else was with him. Had Fornoch been present, Reiffen would have been forced to fly several miles down the road in order to change back to human, otherwise the Wizard would have sensed the burst of magic. Ahne, however, had no such sensibility.

Spreading his wings, Reiffen darted to the woods at the other end of the yard. His bird-self felt a pang at having to give up such freedom, but his human-self remained in firm control. At the base of an old silver birch, he poked at his breast until he found the hard iron of his charm. The clasp had been designed to open easily; the difficulty was in pulling it out. Bright pain seared his chest with each tug. Though he couldn't see them, he felt bits of down waft across his face. But he had done worse things to himself, and others, in the course of nearly twenty years of magic, and the bit of iron soon came free.

The night swayed. Falling on his side, Reiffen waited for the dizziness to end. When he could sit up again, he found the Shaper perched on a low stump.

"Your turn." The magician spat the brooch out into his hand.

"Any trace of the Wizard?"

"No. But I will have a better sense of whether his magic is around now I am no longer a bird."

"You'd better wait till I've shifted, too." Tiny glints of starlight glimmered in the Shaper's eyes.

"I won't need your help with an apprentice."

"No, but you will if we find the Wizard."

Spreading his wings, the Shaper flapped farther into the woods. Reiffen listened for a moment to make sure the crow had settled down for his change, then slipped back out to the yard. In the time it would take Redburr to shift, Reiffen would be able to learn whatever there was to know from Ahne.

He approached the cottage cautiously. A hen cackled in the coop; a cow shuffled inside the shed. Thin smoke drifted from the chimney, twisting upward across the stars in ghostly imitation of the leafless trees on the hill behind. Still feeling no sign of the Gray Wizard's presence, Reiffen knocked.

A stool scraped on the hearthstone inside. Reiffen caught a breath of dust and magic as Ahne opened the door.

"Reiffen!" Ahne's flower-blue eyes widened in surprise, then darted back and forth to see if the magician had come alone. "What brings you here?"

"I thought it was time to see how you were doing."

"I wish you'd given me some notice." The former apprentice stepped aside and let his master in. As usual, he wore a farmer's loose shirt and trousers, the legacy of his youth in Wayland. His sandy hair skewed unattended across his head. "I could have offered you better than soup."

"Soup is fine."

The room grew close as Ahne shut the door. The smells of fire and alchemy thickened the air. Scooping a pair of empty sacks off a chair, he wiped the seat with his hand and pulled it up to the fire.

"Sit, please."

Both men's thimbles clicked against the sides of the bowl as Reiffen accepted his helping.

"Rabbit?" Reiffen's eyebrows lifted as he caught the aroma.

Ahne nodded. "I still make my own snares."

"You catch more than rabbits with them, too."

"Pardon?" Ahne's broad face scrunched in puzzlement.

"The fox paw on the dish." Reiffen nodded back toward the table behind them.

The apprentice's face tightened further. "No one minds a fox getting trapped now and then. Certainly not my chickens."

"Or the rabbits." Reiffen blew on the broth before lifting the spoon to his lips. "Seems a little undersized, though. Was it newborn?"

Ahne had never been particularly good at lying, which was one of the reasons Reiffen had chosen him. The former apprentice changed the subject instead of answering. "I don't suppose you came all this way for rabbit soup. Wanting to know what I've been up to?"

"Yes."

Ahne rubbed his hands briskly, but the gesture fell flat under the uneasiness in his eyes. "I've been doing a bit of good here in Norly. Setting bones, easing labor. It's amazing what a little magic can do."

"And a newborn fox?" Reiffen allowed his gaze to wander back across the table. "What does that have to do with setting bones?"

The younger mage pulled the bread apart with his broad hands. "It's a solution I came up with on my own. Rock salt and eft glands. I'm trying to see whether the mixture staves off rot. I couldn't very well use a live animal, so I'm left with the paw."

"I see. You're looking into the problem of putrefaction in compound fractures."

"That's right." Ahne looked greatly relieved, as if he hadn't thought Reiffen would believe him. "Rot is the biggest danger in that kind of wound."

"So it has nothing to do with prolonging life?"

"No, nothing at all." Ahne paused slightly, then realized he might have said the wrong thing. "You mean preventing rot is one of the ways to extend life?"

"Not unless you use newborns." Reiffen pushed back a jar of grubs to make room on the table for his empty bowl. "The unborn work even better, though perhaps Fornoch has not told you that."

Understanding filled Ahne's face, followed by a splash of fear. As Reiffen knew from his own experience, the Wizard's touch was always deft enough to leave his pupils' guilt intact.

"So you know about that?" Without any prompting, Ahne began to talk, as if grateful for the chance to unburden his mind. "I won't ask how you found out. You've probably been spying on me ever since I left Grangore. All that talk about letting me go free after I'd served my apprenticeship, I knew that was all it was. You used to have me fooled, but Fornoch made it clear enough. He's the real master, yours as well as mine."

"He is an excellent teacher," Reiffen agreed. "You seem to have progressed rapidly under his hand."

"He shows me everything." The former apprentice's glance flickered toward the fox paw. "Unlike you, He doesn't keep anything to Himself."

"Was it he who took the child?"

"You know about her, too?"

"Of course."

"What He did to her is beyond me. And beyond you, too, He says."

"Has he shown you how to fashion a Living Stone?"

"No." For the first time self-pity showed in Ahne's fair blue eyes. "You know, none of this would have happened if you'd taught me the magic yourself. Then Fornoch would have had nothing to offer."

"Fornoch always has something to offer."

"You can do a lot of good with this sort of magic," Ahne insisted. "It doesn't have to be selfish. I never used any of it on myself."

"I am certain you did not. But there is still a cost. Did he help you heal someone first, to draw you in, then show you how to do it after?"

Ahne shifted uncomfortably, heavy boots scuffing the floor. For a while he said nothing, but sat looking at the fire. Red and gold shadows crawled across his hands.

"Baron Norly's daughter nearly died giving birth last year. When the midwife showed me a way to stop the bleeding, I had no way of knowing she'd learned the trick from Him. He only revealed Himself a few months later, when it was too late to go back. When I'd learned too much."

"And how does he come to you? In dreams? Or does he use a mirror?"

"A mirror. That's what the girl was for."

Reiffen's heart jumped. This he had not expected. What would Fornoch want with a girl and a mirror? Especially for a spell beyond Reiffen's power?

"Nothing in magic is free," he said, hoping to prod his former apprentice into revealing more. "What Fornoch has shown you with the girl is nothing compared to what goes into a Living Stone."

Rather than answer, Ahne reached for his thimble. The magician grabbed his old apprentice's wrist as Ahne spoke the word of return.

Reiffen recognized where they had gone at once. A small eight-sided room with a low stone shelf on one wall. Nine small gold caskets gleamed in the light of a Dwarf lamp on the ceiling. One was open and empty. Ferris and he had given a casket to each apprentice when the time had come for them to learn the thimble spell.

"You still use our sanctuary?"

Ahne shrugged. "I haven't found a safer place."

"More likely, you thought to bargain with me by trying to steal my child. Your other thimble leads back to the cottage?"

"Yes. Reiffen, I never—"

"Then take us there."

Ahne removed the second thimble. The dim light disappeared, replaced by tight darkness. Reiffen thought of light, and light appeared, hovering in the air above his head.

This time they were in a natural cave, dirty and damp, that had been turned into a magician's workshop. Reiffen guessed it was the secret cave Redburr had described in the hill behind Ahne's cabin. Glancing swiftly around the room, he found no sign of the girl. The single heavy table was covered with the same sort of apparatus as the room outside, but the shelves here were stuffed with the sorts of things that needed to be kept hidden from prying eyes. Like aphids on leaves, bubbles clung to the hearts, lungs, livers, and kidneys floating in the same thick yellow fluid as the fox's paw.

"Where is the child?" asked Reiffen as he dropped Ahne's arm. Having used both his thimbles, his old apprentice could no longer escape with a word.

"In the mirror."

Ahne nodded toward a large glass framed in carved locust wood at the back of the room. Taller than Reiffen and slightly wider, the mirror was far larger than necessary for simple talking. Like a phantom, Reiffen's reflection appeared in the glass as he stepped before it. He waved his hand, but no new reflection emerged.

"It opens if you touch the top left corner."

A new thought stopped Reiffen's hand. He had to be careful. "Where is the other? The twin to this one?"

"In Fornoch's workshop, I guess."

"If I open the mirror, Fornoch will know I am here?"

"He usually comes right away."

Reiffen removed his hand. "That might prove dangerous."

Ahne shrugged. Tricking Reiffen had been worth a try. Then his face tightened as he realized it might not have been worth it at all. Stealing children was one thing, but trying to fool Reiffen into showing himself to the Wizard was another matter entirely.

"You can only serve one master," Reiffen said, raising his right arm.

"The same goes for—"

"*Empty.*"

Ahne coughed, a long, wheezing gasp. His discomfort rose quickly to panic as the air squeezed out of his lungs. Silently he clawed at his mouth and throat but, no matter what he tried, he couldn't breathe. The tendons in his neck stretched; his eyes bulged. Catching himself on one corner, he fell across the table. Except for the scuffling of his feet and the soft scratching of his fingernails against the wood, he made no sound.

Reiffen found himself vaguely disappointed. He had hoped his apprentice would show a bit more fight. He himself had held out against Usseis for some time, though he had to admit he would have lost in the end had his friends not been there to help him. And the Living Stone, as he had learned over the years, did add potency to his spells. Someday Ferris would notice the difference, but until then he preferred not to tell her. Or anyone else. That extra edge was just the sort of advantage he liked to have in moments like these.

Ignoring Ahne's body, he turned back to the mirror. He should at least see how the child was connected to it. The Shaper had thought she was still alive. And any chance of surprising the Wizard was gone.

Carefully he ran his fingers along the edges of the wood. He found the switch where Ahne had said he would, a small whorl near the top, higher than most people would naturally touch. Pressing his thumb against the slight depression, he woke the magic in the glass.

The image of a child appeared, flickering at first like an oil lamp with a dry wick, then brightening. Nothing of her surroundings showed in the darkness behind her.

"Hello," said Reiffen. "What's your name?"

"Enna," said the girl. She looked only a little younger than Hubley.

"I knew an Enna once. She used to make maple candy."

"My mother makes maple candy." The girl's face gleamed pale and bloodless as the moon. Reiffen wondered how much the Wizard had taken from her already. "Have you come to take me home?"

"I hope so. I have a little girl just like you." If anyone did such a thing to his daughter, he would murder half the world. "Maybe you'll be friends. But first I have to ask you some questions. Do you know where you are?"

The child shook her head. She looked like she might cry, though Reiffen doubted the girl would be able to do that any more than it looked like she could bleed.

"Does anyone visit you?"

"The magicians."

"Magicians? How do you know they're magicians?"

"They're the ones who put me here."

"But you don't know where here is?"

She shook her head again.

Reiffen persisted. "Are you in a house? In a cave?"

"I don't know where I am. There was a cave, and the magicians, and a big mirror. They put me on the table, and hurt me till I fell asleep. When I woke up, I was here."

"Is there a mirror with you now?"

"No."

"Then how can you see me?"

She shrugged. "I don't know. You're just there, hanging in the air. I was scared first, but the nice magician told me not to be afraid."

"The nice magician?"

The girl nodded. "The big one. With the black eyes."

Raising his hands, Reiffen brushed the frame with his fingers and wondered what else the mirror was for. He really didn't think Fornoch would use so large a glass simply for talking.

"You are correct," said a voice. "It is not just for talking."

Reiffen stepped back. Only the Wizard had ever been able to tell so easily what he was thinking, but Enna remained the only figure in the glass. Glancing quickly around, Reiffen reaffirmed he was the only person in the cave.

"Fornoch?" he asked.

The girl in the glass nodded. "He's the one I told you about," she said. "The one with the black eyes."

"Where is he?"

"Don't you see him?" The girl appeared surprised. "He's here, just like you. You're looking right at him."

Like a nokken rising from the smooth surface of Valing Lake, the Gray Wizard stepped out of the glass. Not a ripple crossed the pane. Reiffen retreated toward the front of the cave, though the Wizard was only human-sized.

"Do you like my spell?" he asked, his hands concealed in the depths of his long gray sleeves. "I made these mirrors especially for you."

Reiffen thought about casting a spell, but doubted he would be able to harm the Wizard. Perhaps he should have waited for Redburr, and Avender's crossbowmen, after all. But, no, whether the Shaper was present or not, Fornoch would only run away if attacked. Reiffen had nothing to fear. Besides, he wanted to learn more.

"How do you know I have been trying to make traveling mirrors?" he asked.

"It was a natural development." The Wizard smiled in that way he had that made Reiffen unsure of whether he should feel proud or ashamed. Twelve years they had been apart, and still Fornoch treated him like an apprentice. "Given the direction of my teaching, it was only natural you should seek a less strenuous, and more permanent, mode of traveling. One that might be used by magicians and nonmagicians alike. Shall I show you how it is done?"

"I can guess." Enna watched listlessly as Reiffen replied. "It's the child, isn't it? She keeps the two mirrors bound. My mistake was in using subjects that had already died."

"Your approach was sound. The problem lies in the fact that two entities sharing a single corporality will always prefer to be separate. There is no ridding the spell of the inherent tension. Eventually you would have succeeded, but only for short periods of time. Five or six passages through the portal, a dozen at most, and even your best constructions would have shattered."

"But with a single person there is no tension." Reiffen finished Fornoch's line of thought. "In fact, the effect is just the opposite. The single spirit binds the two mirrors together even more tightly, no matter how far they are apart."

"An excellent interpretation. It is the binding that is paramount, not the connection." The Wizard's smile widened, which only made Reiffen angrier. He was not a child anymore, and did not appreciate Fornoch treating him as if he were. Still, he wished he had figured out this approach himself.

"What about the girl?" he demanded. "Is she alive?"

"Of course. The spell would cease to function if she died."

"Her body? Is it preserved as well?" Reiffen remembered how he had used a beaver kit to open the gate from his cabin in the northern woods to Malmoret, the day Ferris had chosen him over Brizen. But the kit had died as soon as the portal closed.

"Her body is safe. As long it lives, the spell will remain active between this mirror and its twin. Had I given her a Living Stone, the pairing could last forever. But that would mean expending a great deal of effort for something which is really quite simple."

"And if I break the mirror?"

The Wizard shrugged, his robe swaying like a curtain. "Then the connection is broken, of course. And the child dies."

The magic was vile, but Reiffen was still intrigued. Perhaps he could manage the same effect with a dog. Or maybe there were people in the world who would find such an existence more satisfying than their current lot. Cripples, perhaps. What would be done to them wasn't so different from what had been done to Durk, only here the subject was bound to glass instead of stone.

"Ahne appreciated everything I showed him as well."

"Ahne made his choice," Reiffen said.

"As you made yours. Still, you need not have killed him."

"Anyone you have taught is too dangerous to leave alive."

"Except you, of course," Fornoch agreed. "But what about your other apprentices? Will you slay them too? Will you ever let them go, now you know I am waiting for them when they leave Grangore?"

"You cannot turn them all."

"Perhaps not. But as long as you keep knowledge from them, you leave the way open for me. You have been greedy, Reiffen. You have not revealed everything I taught you."

"Much of what you taught me should never be revealed."

"Perhaps other mages, with greater imagination, will disagree."

"I doubt it."

"And yet you and your family take advantage of that knowledge all the same. For yourselves. If as good a man as Ahne can succumb, what of everyone else? What of your daughter? Really, Reiffen, I thought I taught you better than that. Surely you, of all people, understand what it means to have knowledge withheld. It only makes the desire for what is withheld the stronger. Look what you gave up, the minute you were introduced to power."

"Yes. But I got it all back. I have Ferris, and my child."

"You do." Another smile graced the Wizard's mouth and chin. "And it would be so terrible if they should ever turn out to be other than what you desire."

Fresh anger welled up in Reiffen at the second mention of his daughter. With great effort, he forced himself to retain his self-control. "I told you once never to bother my mother. The same is true for my child."

"Perhaps Hubley will seek me herself. You did." Fornoch's face narrowed greedily in a way that reminded Reiffen more of the Black Wizard than the subtle insinuation that was the Gray Wizard's special brand of malice. "Or perhaps your daughter will agree with you, that good can come from evil."

Reiffen's chest tightened further. "Touch my daughter, and you will discover how much I have learned in the dozen years since I killed your kin."

"You have shown yourself to be quite formidable, there can be no doubt of that. And unlike my brothers, I am not afraid of sharing power. But I warn you, if your daughter grows up to be anything like you, there may come a time when she welcomes my tutelage. If only to augment yours. And who knows? Maybe I shall teach her to do good. Just as I taught you."

Reiffen raised his hands. What he had to do was clear. No one could hurt his daughter. But Fornoch had not spoken without knowing what his words would bring. Wrapping his gray cloak around him, he stepped back through the mirror the same moment Reiffen's lightning bolts burst across the cave. Past the glass they crashed, smashing the walls like clumsy manders. Rocks and sand rattled from the ceiling. Several of Ahne's jars smashed against the floor.

The wooden door at the front of the cave crashed open. Roaring, the bear rushed in. He stopped short when he saw Ahne's body sprawled across the table, his claws scratching furrows in the floor.

"What's going on here?" he growled. "I thought I heard an explosion."

"Fornoch was here."

The Shaper sniffed at the body on the ground, and the insides of others littering the floor. "He killed Ahne?"

"I did that."

"Why? Did Ahne kill the cub?"

"No." Reiffen pointed wearily at the mirror. "She's in there. Fornoch has used her to fashion a portal of the sort I have been trying to make for the last five years."

The bear sniffed at his reflection in the glass.

"It's a door? To where?"

"Fornoch's workshop would be my guess. Ahne didn't know."

Rearing up on his hind legs, the Shaper brought his full weight down on top of the wooden frame. The mirror splintered under his forepaws like a box of twigs. Shards of wood and glass sprayed across the floor.

"What did you do that for?" Reiffen, startled out of his lethargy, jumped up. "I could have learned a great deal from that mirror."

"Exactly."

The Shaper dropped back to all fours, broken glass crunching under the weight of his heavy paws.

Suddenly worried about where the Wizard might have gone, Reiffen removed the thimble on his left hand and spoke the word of return.

He left the bear behind.

8

Ferris Leaves

He found his daughter safe in her own room. Ferris lay on the bed beside her, the light of the new risen moon checkering their sleeping faces through the mullioned glass. Reiffen's temper calmed somewhat when he saw they were unharmed, but, knowing he had much still to think about, he woke neither. Though he doubted he would change his mind, he wanted to be sure the decision he had come to with Ahne was the right one. Unlike a dozen years ago with the nokken, this time he really had killed a friend.

Descending to the cellars, he passed through a series of hidden doors and false walls till he reached his most private workshop. Not even Ferris had ever visited him here. Chin in hand, he settled on a stone bench beside a small stream and studied the large blue-black mussels that filled the bottom of a shallow pool.

He saw it all clearly now. Fornoch's turning of Ahne had made him understand how everything fit together. Areft and Ina, the Wizards and the Oeinnen, humans and Dwarves and everything else that lived in the world—all of them were connected in ways he had never seen before. His dream of teaching magic would have to wait, at least as long as the Gray Wizard remained outside Castle Grangore to twist his purpose away from him.

He had tried so hard to keep his art's more selfish aspects hidden. To keep at bay the sort of power Usseis and Fornoch had taken such pains to make sure he learned. Living Stones and worse. Magic that created pasties, or the sorts of things that only left something like Durk behind. Spells that urged a mage to live forever, spilling other people's lives to feed his own. It was all so tempting, to reap humanity the way other people harvested corn and hogs.

He could be just like Areft if he chose.

That had always been the danger. Fornoch had hinted at the possibility sometimes, when showing Reiffen the best way to gather gills from a mudpuppy, or an unhatched clutch from a swan. Everything in the world had its use: fish, fowl, beast, water, weed, flower, tree, tuber, rock, shell, metal, gem. But humans had the most uses of all, because only humans had been created by Areft, and Areft had fashioned the world. Everything else that lived was brought forth by the other Ina—Bavadar or Oeina or Brydds—which meant that everything else's power was separate, and smaller. Tigers could not shape rocks. Ants had no use for the sea. But humans, having been created by Areft himself, could do anything. Oeina had fashioned Redburr and the other Shapers as a way to teach humans a measure of balance and respect; to keep them from picking the world clean until it was as barren as Areft's first creation.

The relationships were so obvious, Reiffen was almost ashamed he had not seen them before. The Wizards were the humans' Shapers, masters left behind by Areft to teach humans how to be like him. Ossdonc and Usseis might have thought their rule was what mattered, but Fornoch knew better. Fornoch understood the Wizards' knowledge was supposed to be revealed. The reason he had taught Reiffen every bit of magic he could was to make sure that, even if the Three were destroyed, their knowledge would live on.

Areft's knowledge.

No, Reiffen told himself. He would not be another Areft, no matter what Fornoch planned. Nor would he allow anyone else to be Areft in his place. But not teaching what he knew was not enough. He had to make sure Fornoch did not teach it, either. Even now there might be Dremen merchants able to double the count of their coins with blood and incantations, or Cuspor astromanths summoning leviathan ashore with sacrifice and chants. Even hissers, whom Usseis had once shown him were half human, might learn to cast, slithering through the night to strike their victims numb with voice instead of venom.

He knew the best way to keep Fornoch from infecting any-one else was to kill him, but that might take a while. Just finding the Gray Wizard was difficult enough, as the last dozen years had shown. In the meantime Reiffen would work to enhance his power, and Ferris's and Hubley's as well. Anyone else Fornoch had taught, he would kill. But Fornoch was the key. Fornoch rep-resented the greatest danger.

First, however, he had to make sure the Gray Wizard turned no more apprentices the way he had turned Ahne. That he could take care of now.

Making his way back upstairs, Reiffen discovered he felt better than he had in a long time. It was good to have a settled plan to work toward again, the way he had all those years ago in Ussene. The cock was crowing as he emerged from the cellars; morning brightness swept the halls. On the second floor he found Trier guarding the entrance to the Magicians' Tower. Her narrow face tightened further in concern at the sight of her master.

"My lord, we have been terribly worried about you. Where have you been?"

Reiffen raised his hand. Not surprisingly, Trier's reaction to the spell was the same as Ahne's. Fear flooded her face even as the air was pressed from her lungs. Unable to breathe, she fell forward on hands and knees, her skirt pooling on the stone. Though Reiffen was certain he could have handled her dismay, he was glad she had not looked him in the eye. She had been his best student, after all. Which was why, if Fornoch ever got his hands on her, she would be much more dangerous than Ahne.

His concentration wavered as his mother appeared on the stair. Trier gasped.

"Reiffen!" cried Giserre. "What are you doing?"

Without waiting for an answer, Giserre hurried down the last few steps to Trier. Reiffen broke the spell at once. Though she had spent seven years with him in Ussene, his mother had never fully comprehended Fornoch's mind. She would not appreciate why he had to slay Trier, or the other apprentices either. Much better to present her with the matter over and done with, than give her the opportunity to stop him.

Trier gulped fresh air. Giserre, when she saw the young woman was out of danger, looked up at her son in fury.

"What has Trier done that you should attack her?" she accused.

"It is not what she has done, Mother, but what she may yet do."

"In that case you might as well murder us all."

"Hopefully, it will not come to that."

Fresh coughing from Trier rescued Reiffen from further argument. While Giserre's attention was turned back to the apprentice, he continued up the stairs. He could finish with Trier later.

Entering the family apartment, he decided Ferris was no more likely to agree with what needed to be done than his mother. Better to have it out with her right away. That way there was less chance of any of the apprentices escaping.

She met him outside the door to Hubley's room, her finger to her lips. For the sake of the sleeping child, Reiffen embraced her silently, and reminded himself the current difficulty was his fault, not hers. He had been the overconfident one, certain he could teach others what he had learned from the Wizards. He had misjudged what would happen when his young, impressionable mages went off on their own, the Gray Wizard ready to pluck them like feathers off a dead bird.

Not everyone was as strong as he was.

"Where have you been?" Ferris asked when their hug was finished. "We've been scared to death since Brizen told us what happened at Norly. Hern and Giserre sat up the whole night with me."

"I went to you as soon as I returned, but you and Hubley were asleep. Hern and Giserre were not there."

She frowned at his deliberate misunderstanding. "Brizen must have called right after. You should have woken me. Instead we heard the news from the king. Avender called on his mirror— he's fit to be tied after the way you ran off without him. You'll have to go back at once after you've rested. Neither Trier nor I have ever been within three days' march of Norly, or Ipwell, so we can't do it."

Reiffen shook his head. "My place is here, with Hubley. Tell Brizen Avender must make his way back to Malmoret without me."

"You took him there. You have to bring him back. You can't just abandon him."

"I will not leave the castle."

"Why not? Avender said everything was taken care of. I admit, it would have been better if you hadn't killed Ahne, but if he really was turned, you didn't have a choice."

"It is more complicated than that."

"I'm sure it is," she agreed. "What you had to do was terrible, and then you had to deal with the Wizard, too. You must be exhausted. But you really owe it to Avender and his men not to leave them in Norly. It'll be more than a week before they get back to Malmoret on their own."

Reiffen checked his temper, reminding himself that Ferris still did not know how much everything had changed. "Come with me to the top of the tower and I will explain. This is not a place we can talk alone."

While Ferris fetched a cloak, Reiffen looked in on their daughter. Hern, full of sympathy, pressed his hand, but he let the child sleep.

Together, he and Ferris climbed to the top of the Tower. A drift of gray cloud made the dawn dim and cold; the tops of the mountains pierced the rumpled sky.

Ferris laid her hand gently on her husband's shoulder. "Tell me everything that happened. It must have been horrible. And everything the Wizard said, too."

Reiffen remained staring across the dull morning. "I have been thinking about it all night. Fornoch made me realize many things he did not intend, not the least of which is that it was a mistake to start this school."

"Nonsense." Ferris rubbed her husband's back. "The whole point of your returning to Ussene was to steal the Wizard's power. You made the right choice, dear."

"I am not talking about that." As he spoke, Reiffen remembered the look on Ahne's face. Not at the moment when his former apprentice realized Reiffen was about to kill him, but earlier, when Ahne had wished bitterly that Reiffen had taught him everything he knew. "I am referring to the teaching only. The power is too great. Especially while Fornoch still lives to tempt our students with its more unpleasant aspects."

Ferris continued rubbing her husband's back. "You're just in one of your dark moods. The temptation hasn't been too much for you."

"It was for Ahne. And it will be for Trier, too, and the rest of them, when their time comes." Dropping his hands to the cold stone of the parapet, Reiffen leaned out over the wall.

Ferris leaned beside him. "That was Fornoch's doing. Our mistake was picking someone who listened to him when he should have known better."

"Will you have the strength to ignore the Wizard when he comes to you? Because he will, you know." Sadness touched Reiffen's voice, a sadness of resignation rather than despair.

"I would hope so." Straightening, Ferris faced the morning breeze. "You're a wonderful example for all of us, dear. The Wizard's offers meant nothing to you."

"After speaking to Fornoch yesterday, I am not so sure. I may have chosen my own path, but the Wizard has always controlled the larger design."

"You know better than that. That's just Fornoch's way. He always says whatever happens was his idea. As long as you keep trying to do your best, what he says doesn't matter. Right and wrong are pretty easy to tell apart, if you ask me."

"Only in the narrowest sense," said Reiffen. "Look what I did at Rimwichside."

"I keep telling you, what you did there was absolutely necessary. Rimwich was under attack. People are allowed to defend themselves, you know."

"What if I had simply stayed in Valing after you rescued me? Would it have been necessary then? Would Gerrit have raised an army against King Brannis? Would Backford have been sacked? Baron Backford killed? Or Baron Sevral?"

"Something like it, I'm sure." Reiffen noticed Ferris examining him closely as she spoke. "You don't think the Wizards would have just let you go, do you? Something else would certainly have happened. There was nothing you could do to stop it. I think you made the best and bravest choice possible. You've said it yourself more than once—it was the Wizards and their magic that were the problem. Until they were beaten, nothing else mattered. I say we've done two-thirds of the job, and the rest still has to be finished. And that's what we're doing. That's why we're teaching magic. So it won't just be the Wizards who have that kind of power, and we won't have to fight them alone."

"But that's just it. We are alone. Fornoch will turn all the apprentices. He will turn you, if you give him the chance. He will even turn Hubley, someday. We have to try a new approach. No more contact with the rest of the world. Just the three of us, here in Castle Grangore, preparing for the day we fight him. The day we can finally end the rule of Areft, which is all the rule of Wizards really is."

Ferris's face filled with sympathy. "You really are tired, dear, if you think that's what we should do. You're not thinking straight at all."

"I am not tired. My understanding has never been clearer."

Ferris shook her head. "You're just feeling bad about Ahne, but you'll get over it. You've always gotten over it before."

"I will get over it, but only when it is finished. Mark what I say—I will have to slay Trier next, and she will be far more dangerous than Ahne because she is a better magician. One by one I shall have to kill them all. Better to slay them now, and not take the chance of failing later."

Ferris gripped her husband's wrist. "You can't just kill them."

"I certainly can. The only reason Trier isn't dead already is because Giserre stopped me."

Ferris let go his arm. "You tried to kill Trier?"

"I did. The next time I will do more than try. It will be better for them all that way."

"Better?" Ferris gaped in disbelief. "How?"

"Better than if they go through what I did. Or Ahne. You cannot imagine how easily he confessed to me what he had done. How much he regretted his fall. It will only be a mercy if I prevent that from happening to the others."

"You can't punish people for what you think they might do. All this talk of not wanting to become Areft—can't you see you're acting just like him?"

Reiffen stepped back as if Ferris had slapped him. "Areft? How am I like Areft?"

"Are you listening to yourself? You're talking about murdering people. That's what Areft used to do. That's why Issing and the other Ina came into the world. To stop him."

"It's not the same at all. I'm trying to prevent greater evil.

What Areft did was wrong in and of itself. I did the exact same thing twelve years ago when I slew Ossdonc's army in Rimwich. You just said so."

"I did not. Our apprentices are not an invading army. You can't kill them just because you're afraid of what they might do. If they start acting like Ahne, I'll be the first to help you. But you have to let them have their chance. You got yours."

Reiffen rubbed his forehead wearily. Maybe Ferris was right. He really didn't want to do this. "One does not drown kittens because one wants to," he protested weakly.

"One doesn't drown kittens at all, if one knows what's good for one. Not around me."

"It's Trier I worry about the most," he admitted. "She is much stronger than Ahne. The others know too little to cause any real harm. Perhaps we could simply stop teaching them."

"First you have to get rid of this crazy idea about killing them. Then we can talk about the rest."

Reiffen shook his head. "No. There will be no more teaching, regardless of what we decide. We have to defeat Fornoch first."

She paused for a moment, looking at him. "Maybe I should take the apprentices away for a while. To Valing. We can discuss it when I come back."

"No."

Her tone became more challenging. "Maybe I'll take Hubley with me, too."

"No," Reiffen repeated more sharply. "Hubley stays here."

"Are you ordering me?"

"This is the only place any of us can be safe from Fornoch anymore. He will be sure to go after you in Valing, especially if I am not there."

Ferris pulled her cloak closer around her neck. "I don't have time for this. We'll talk about it when I get back."

Their eyes met. Reiffen could see his wife was not going to back down. She could be so stubborn sometimes, and he was doing it all for her. And Hubley. But he could not stop her from taking her own road. And she might be right; slaying the apprentices might not be a good idea until they had actually been turned. Everyone would be against him then, and that was not what he wanted. He had fought the Three alone before, and knew how hard it was.

And would do so again, if he had to.

He knew he would have to act quickly. As Ferris stalked away, he traveled to Hubley's room, surprising Hern at his sudden reappearance. She jumped back; the sock she was darning fell to the floor. Gathering his sleeping daughter in his arms, Reiffen disappeared.

When Hern told Ferris what Reiffen had done, Ferris knew she had no choice. Her husband might be showing signs of madness, but there was no way he would hurt their daughter. Besides, she had no idea where he'd gone. Angry though she was, there was nothing she could do for now to bring Hubley back.

The apprentices were another matter. The best thing would be to get them away from Castle Grangore as quickly as possible, in case Reiffen came back to finish what he had started. That he was serious about slaying them Ferris had no doubt, especially after she found Giserre tending Trier in the Apprentices' Tower.

Plum and the others were already awake and wondering what was going on. They whispered to one another in the halls, fearful and confused. Ferris hushed them with a look and told them they were going to Valing for a few days. "We've all been working too hard. A change of scene will do us all good. Everyone, go pack a bag, then meet me here."

Giserre wasn't fooled. "You are doing the right thing," she said after the apprentices left. "My son is not himself."

"He'll be all right in a few days," said Ferris, as much to reassure herself as Giserre. "You'll see. He'll come back tonight once he knows I've taken the apprentices. I'll come back too. But it may take a while. I'll need two spells to get to Valing with so many people, and I'll have to rest in Malmoret along the way."

"I will remain here," said Giserre. "Someone should be here to see to the child if you are correct."

Not fifteen minutes later they were in the New Palace. Hern took Berrel and the apprentices off in search of breakfast while Ferris went looking for the king and queen. Although by this point she was in as much need of rest as Reiffen, Ferris still felt it was important to tell their majesties what had happened.

Wellin nearly spilled her tea at the news. "He tried to kill Trier?"

Brizen reached out to steady his wife as Ferris wrapped her hands around her own cup. She had only just noticed how empty and cold she felt.

"Yes. I think he's completely overwhelmed. He worries about Fornoch all the time, and having to kill Ahne has taken him all the way to the edge."

"How long do you think it will be before he recovers?" Brizen's honest face furrowed with concern.

"Not too long, I hope. But I really can't say."

"And Avender?" asked Wellin, her composure restored.

"Reiffen refuses to bring him back. You'll have to do without him for a week."

"I can never do without Avender," said the king.

The queen swirled her tea with a spoon, careful not to touch the sides of the cup. Despite everything else on her mind, Ferris found herself wondering just what had happened between Wellin and Avender in Castle Grangore. Her talk with the queen two days ago now felt like it had happened months before. Later, perhaps, Wellin might confess what she'd done but, if anything had actually happened, Ferris didn't want to know. Especially not now. It was strange, though, the way both of their marriages appeared to be approaching a crisis at the same time. Though perhaps that was an exaggeration of her situation. Reiffen would come back to his senses soon enough. The queen, on the other hand, might well have done something from which there was no going back at all.

"He just needs a good night's sleep," Wellin advised. "Matters would be far worse had he actually killed the poor woman."

"I've already talked him out of that," said Ferris more forcefully than she actually believed.

"Perhaps if we invite him to Malmoret for a few days he will be able to relax," suggested Brizen.

"No." Ferris set her cup back down on the breakfast tray, her thimble clicking on the saucer. "Leaving Castle Grangore is the last thing to suggest to him. He'll think the Wizard put you up to it. Once I get the apprentices settled in, I'm going back to Castle Grangore to look after him."

Her duty done, Ferris excused herself. Brizen went with her, his manner plainly showing he had something he wanted to say. The fact he didn't get around to saying it until they were outside her door suggested it was personal.

"Please pardon me for bothering you with this now," he finally began, tugging at his ear. "But, when things in Castle Grangore settle down a bit, I wonder if you might come back to Malmoret. In your capacity as a physician, of course."

"Is something wrong? You look fine."

"No, nothing like that. Nor is it anything that needs looking into right away. Whenever you have time. Only I'd just as soon you not say anything to Wellin. No need to bother her with what will probably turn out to be nothing at all."

She forgot Brizen's request as soon as he was out of sight. Although her mind was racing, and she was more worried about Hubley than she cared to admit, she still fell into a deep sleep that lasted well into the afternoon. She woke suddenly, not remembering where she was and feeling as if she had forgotten something important. Thin rain spattered on the windows; the curtains veiling the room made the day seem later than it was. Jumping up, she found her parents waiting for her outside.

Gathering the apprentices, she cast the second spell. With such a large crowd, Ferris took them to the Tear, where there was less chance of running into someone. Finding the strain of the second spell even greater than the first, she lay back on the musty cushions as Hern hustled everyone else off to the Manor for hot chocolate and making beds. What she really wanted was to just go home. Her uneasiness had been growing all day, and wouldn't be quelled until she spoke to her husband and child. With any luck, they had probably returned the moment Reiffen learned Ferris and the apprentices had left. It might be a good idea if she went up to the house and tried calling them on her parents' mirror. But the Tear, though cold, was comfortable once the dust on the pillows had settled. The thrum of the gorge rushing below lulled her.

Still, she grew cold without a fire. She had almost made up her mind to move on to the house when the double doors at the top of the room opened and a tall man stooped to enter the room.

Not a man at all, she saw, but Fornoch.

9

A Hundred Arefts

T here is no need for magic," counseled the Wizard as Ferris reached for a thimble. "I have only come to talk."

"You and I have nothing to talk about," she answered, not letting go her finger.

"Oh, but we do." Warmth filled the room as the Wizard spoke, one giant breath seemingly enough to replace the Tear's cold air. Unless it was Ferris's dread that warmed her. "Reiffen is about to embark on a most dangerous course. I fear you are the only one who can stop him."

"Why would you care?"

"I have always cared about Reiffen. My brothers would have killed him more than once had I not been present to intervene on his behalf."

"That was only because you wanted Reiffen to kill them instead."

The Wizard smiled, his black eyes empty. "All families have their disagreements," he acknowledged. "I expect you know that. And I do sometimes feel like a father to him."

He lifted his broad hands in a gesture of resignation, his back still bent uncomfortably beneath the ceiling. "Would you mind if I came down to the center of the room? I am quite cramped here. You could retire up and around to the entrance as I descend. Unless, of course, you do not mind being so close to me."

Ferris thought about pulling off her thimble then, but her curiosity about what the Wizard had to say overcame her apprehension. For twelve years there had been no sign of him, and now here he had shown up twice in two days. Careful to face him the entire time, she retreated up the broad ledges that ringed the Tear as the Wizard made his way down.

"Excellent," he said when she was standing by the door. His head was now on the same level as hers. "Is this not much better?"

"Reiffen said you'd come looking for me if I left the castle. I should tell you right off, there's nothing you can tempt me with I'd possibly want."

"Really? Not even another child?"

The fact that Fornoch had hit the mark on the first try stunned her. Reiffen had often described the uncanny way the Wizard appeared to understand his deepest thoughts, but this was the first time Ferris had felt that insight herself.

"What is it you want?" she demanded.

Fornoch slipped his large hands into his gray sleeves. He looked much less threatening that way, more like a scholar than a Wizard. "As I said, only to help your husband. He has not been himself, lately, has he? All those dreams, and his increasing distress about your daughter. I would speak to him myself, but he is unlikely to listen to me. So I have come to you instead. I imagine your concern is even greater than mine."

"You know about his dreams?"

"Certainly. They are the natural recoiling of his better nature against everything Usseis forced him to do to prove his loyalty."

"Usseis? What about you?"

"I played my part," Fornoch confessed.

"And now you want to help him."

The Wizard regarded Ferris closely. "Are you certain there is nothing with which I can tempt you?"

Ferris gripped her thimble a second time. Twice now the

Wizard had offered her something she wanted very much. She hoped she could resist the third.

"Unfortunately," he continued, "there is no easy solution to your husband's difficulty. Magic is not an art that is particularly accepting of half measures. Reiffen must either accept what he has learned and everything with it, or renounce the craft altogether. Otherwise it will tear him apart. This teaching only what he thinks fit for you and your apprentices will never work. Ahne knew there was something missing. I imagine you feel it yourself."

"Reiffen and I have no secrets."

"Are you aware he knows how to fashion Living Stones?"

"Yes."

"And that he once made one?"

Ten years of small doubts came together as Ferris wondered why Reiffen had never told her there was a fourth Stone in addition to the three Fornoch had fashioned. Had he never intended to give his up at all? Had he meant to replace it with the one no one else knew existed? Or was the Wizard just lying?

"I thought not." Fornoch smiled sympathetically, but it was hard to find the kindness in his all-black eyes. Like mirrors, they revealed nothing of what lay behind them. "Some things Reiffen prefers not to discuss. With anyone. The Living Stone was his masterwork, the task that marked the end of his schooling, just as yours was the healing of that carter who nearly crushed himself to death trying to emulate Nolo on the Sun Road."

"I've told Reiffen more than once I don't want to know about the Stones. Their cost is too high."

"Your self-control is admirable, but then you already have one. Ahne was much weaker. All I had to do was point out to him how many more people he could help, were he to delve a little deeper into his art. From there it was a short, quick step from taking what he wanted from a fox or squirrel to helping me take it from a child."

"You only want Reiffen to give up magic so you can turn our apprentices without him getting in the way."

"Are you saying you would not want him to give up his magic, even if it might be for the best?"

"It isn't for the best. Magic is part of Reiffen now, good or bad. He can't be just one thing or another. All this talk of what's good for him is just you trying to confuse us. It's not the magic that's bad, it's what you do with it. Swords or spells, it's what you do that matters, not what you know."

"You see the issue precisely. Unlike your husband, who thinks on a grander scale. But mark what I say. If Reiffen does not give up his magic, he will only get worse. He might even become so obsessed as to cut you off and seal himself up in his workshops in order to work unceasingly on my demise."

Ferris reached for her thimble a third time. "I've heard enough. Everyone knows all you ever do is lie."

The Gray Wizard smiled. "Actually, I rarely lie. Has Reiffen not told you? Since you humans tend not to trust me anyway, I find it much easier to tell the truth. That way your mistakes can always be your own."

"There's more than one kind of lying. Your kind is to tell just enough truth to lead people the wrong way. That's what you did with King Brioss years ago, and I'm sure you did the same to Reiffen in Ussene. No wonder he's confused. Don't think I won't tell him everything you've said."

"By all means, tell him," the Wizard agreed. "That would be best. It is always better to confess to people like Reiffen what they already suspect. Otherwise they end up mistrusting even more. Believe me, he will know we have spoken, whether you tell him or not. As Ahne unfortunately learned, my mark is difficult to conceal. But do make sure you explain to him that he cannot escape the consequences of what he has learned unless he does as I suggest. Killing my brothers changed nothing. Nor, I imagine, will killing me."

Ferris knew Fornoch was trying to trick her, playing games with her mind. He had done it before, sending Mennon off to be slaughtered by Cuhurran and the Banking army in the Udrun fens, and he had done it again when he had persuaded Reiffen that his only choice was to return to Ussene and learn what he could of magic. But both times Fornoch's cunning had proven too sly by half. Mennon had survived Cuhurran's arrow and ended up discovering the Dwarves; Reiffen's learning magic had led to the death of the White and Black Wizards. As long as Ferris followed her own mind, she was certain Fornoch's trickery would trip him up again.

"Not everyone is as easily led as Ahne," she said.

"I do hope so. Your husband was a most excellent pupil. It would be a pity if he had to give up what he has sacrificed so much for."

"I'll tell him that."

"Thank you. I can ask no more."

The Wizard disappeared.

Ferris knew she had to return to Castle Grangore as quickly as possible. The more time Reiffen thought she'd spent with the Gray Wizard, the less he was going to believe that nothing had happened. He'd gotten that difficult about Fornoch, almost like a jealous husband. Finding her mother in the Manor kitchen, she explained her plans without saying anything about the Wizard, then climbed the pantry steps to her old room. Still exhausted from all the traveling she had done, she would have liked nothing more than to take another long nap. But there wasn't time.

Twisting the thimble on her left little finger she said, in a small, soft voice, "Return." The thimble dropped to the floor.

Her airy bedroom disappeared. The rag rug vanished, replaced by a mosaic of dark and light stones forming an eight-sided star. A stone shelf protruded from the nearest of the chamber's eight walls, nine small gold boxes arranged in a neat row on the top. Three were empty: Ahne's, Reiffen's, and hers. Pocketing the last two, she rested briefly, then concentrated on another chamber in the rock overhead. This traveling spell she had practiced so many times it took little effort. A moment passed, and then she was exiting one of the cellar workshops and on her way up into the castle, her finger itching where the fingertip had reattached at the last knuckle. She rubbed it ruefully, not looking forward to having to cut it off again.

She thought about how much everything had changed since she'd become a magician as she climbed the stairs. She couldn't remember the last time she and Reiffen had spent a day together. Now they were too busy with their own projects, she with mending and healing the broken and sick, Reiffen with the intricate connections of every place and thing. In the first whirl of their marriage everything had been new, the magic and the love. Now both felt worn as favorite shoes. Not less loved for all the wearing, but less exciting than before. Her parents' lives had been dull as dishrags for as long as she had known them, yet their feeling for one another had never dimmed. Ferris had been certain her life with Reiffen would have both excitement and contentment, but lately she wasn't so sure. Now she was learning that even dullness had its charm.

She found her husband and child in the sitting room in the Magicians' Tower. Giserre was with them, knitting by the window in the fading light while Hubley and Reiffen played checkers at a small table nearby. Reiffen seemed to have put aside his morning's distress, but the sharpness in his mother's glance as she watched her son showed she had not yet forgiven him for his attack on Trier. If Hubley hadn't been there, Ferris was sure she would have arrived to an entirely different scene.

With a loud whoop, Hubley moved what looked like a wiggling worm to one of her father's squares.

"King me!" she cried.

"All right. But you have to do the spell yourself."

Chest swelling with pride and a deep breath, the child pro-claimed,

> *"Caterpillar, caterpillar, crossing the board,*
> *Caterpillar, caterpillar, here's your reward!"*

Almost as excited as she was, Hubley's piece pulled its head and tail together and arched its back in the air. Frail wings sprouted from the top of the hump, black with red edging and white spots on the tips. The body shortened and thinned. In a matter of sec-onds, a Red Admiral emerged, skipping its cocoon entirely.

"That was well done," said Reiffen. Hubley beamed.

Giserre noticed her daughter-in-law standing at the door. "Ferris," she said. "I am glad you have returned. Are the appren-tices settled?"

"Hern's got them all in hand."

Hubley waved. "Hello, Mother. Father and I are playing checkers. Do you like our pieces?"

Wings twitched; the butterflies that had already been trans-formed flew in wavering figures around Ferris's head before re-settling on the board, one Red Admiral and a pair of Nightflys that must have been Reiffen's.

"They're lovely, sweetheart." Ferris wasn't sure she could master a dozen caterpillars so easily, let alone have strength left over to turn them into butterflies as well. The ease with which Hubley learned new spells was already much greater than any-thing Ferris had ever managed. Or Reiffen, either. "Are they real?"

"Of course." Reiffen greeted his wife amiably but, before he had half-crossed the room, the happiness in his face shifted to a scowl. "Where have you been?"

"Malmoret and Valing." Though she knew why her husband had snapped at her, she couldn't help but feel annoyed at his sud-den change of mood. And at the Wizard too, for having caused the problem in the first place.

"You reek of Wizardry," he said.

"That's because Fornoch paid me a visit. In the Tear."

Hubley's eyes went wide, in envy more than worry. "You saw the Wizard, too?"

"Yes." Ferris plopped down in the nearest chair. "It's been a long day."

Reiffen's ease vanished. "Did he threaten you? What did he want?"

"To talk. To give me warnings."

"About what?"

"This isn't the place to discuss it."

"Whatever he said, he said just to confuse you."

"I'm well aware of that, Reiffen. But again, this isn't the place to talk about it. If you really want to continue this conversation, I'll be in the bedroom. As I already told you, it's been a long day."

Reiffen shut the door behind them, his mood at least as sour as hers. Ferris stalked straight to the window, upset that they had already gotten off on the wrong foot.

"I told you this would happen," he said.

Hoping to end the argument before it started, Ferris turned to embrace her husband. Instead Reiffen took her head in his hands and, locking her face close to his, examined her eyes. Ferris was too surprised to wiggle away or fight back; by the time her astonishment had passed he had already let her go.

"He does not seem to have done anything to you," he said.

"I could've told you that." Ferris stretched her neck to make sure it still worked. "You didn't have to attack me."

"That was hardly an attack."

"It was closer to an attack than anything else. Really, Reiffen. No matter what's happened, you can't push me around like that."

But Reiffen wasn't listening. "So what did Fornoch want?" he asked.

"He wanted me to tell you to give up magic."

"Really? After all the time he spent making sure I learned everything I could? He must be worried about how easily I disposed of Ahne."

"Mostly he's concerned about how you aren't sleeping, and how being a magician is preying on your mind. He didn't say a thing about Ahne."

"His concern is for himself, not me," Reiffen scoffed. "Ahne's death means one less person on his side. That is what this is all about, you know. Trying to get me to stop hunting him. He knows I'll catch him some day, just as I caught his brothers."

"That's what I think, too."

"Good. I am glad you are finally seeing it my way." He rubbed his hands together, his mood brightening. "You were right about my needing a rest, you know. Well, I napped all day, and see things even more clearly now."

"That's not what I meant." Ferris tried again to say what needed saying without setting her husband off. "We have to talk about the apprentices. We're going to need them, you know. We can't fight Fornoch alone. And we already know he can't turn everyone."

"We do?"

"He didn't turn you."

Reiffen waved her compliment aside. "I knew what I was getting into. They do not."

"We could tell them."

"Tell them? Tell them what?"

"Everything. All the magic you've been holding back. I'm not interested in it because I've seen how hard it is for you, but it's not the same for the apprentices. As long as the Wizard can teach them what you won't, he'll have an appeal that some of them will find hard to resist."

"We already decided we would only pick apprentices who would not want to learn that sort of thing."

"Yes, and we were wrong. The very first time. I think we're going to have to go on with this in an entirely different way."

Scowling, Reiffen made no reply. Instead he turned to the window and looked out at the darkening day.

When he neither agreed nor disagreed with her, Ferris went on. "Is it true you made a Living Stone?"

"Yes."

"Why didn't you tell me?"

"You never asked. It is not something I am proud of."

"Where is it?"

"Hidden."

"Why?"

"Living Stones are not easily destroyed. Had it fallen into the wrong hands, it would have been very bad. You can't make them for yourself, you know. Someone else has to make them for you. The process requires something from you, as well as from others."

Reiffen's mouth tightened, as if even the memory of what he had done was painful. Unable to see her husband so distressed, Ferris hugged him fiercely. He squeezed her in return, but his embrace was weaker, almost hesitant. She led him to the bed, where they sat side by side.

"Fornoch didn't tell you that part, did he?"

"No."

"The magician may not use his spell himself, but anyone else can. I almost gave the Stone to Avender in Backford when he was wounded, but I was able to heal him without it. I don't believe he would have forgiven me if I had. When Hubley was born, my thought was to give it to her when she was old enough, on her twenty-first birthday, perhaps. But Giserre had already asked me to remove hers, so I kept the fourth Stone hidden."

"You should have told me. We're going to have to teach the apprentices everything, even about Living Stones. Otherwise Fornoch's going to say you're keeping the best magic to yourself."

"No." Reiffen stiffened under Ferris's arm. "That is a temptation I will reveal to no one. A mage may not be able to fashion his own Living Stones, but two mages could make them for each other."

She saw the problem at once. If they taught this art to the apprentices, sooner or later one would be tempted to use it. As Fornoch had suggested, she might have been tempted herself had she not already had a Stone of her own. And one for her daughter. But what would Trier think when she realized Reiffen had this power? It was one thing to believe only Wizards could fashion Living Stones, but quite another to learn magicians could do it, too.

"This is the real secret Fornoch wants to give to the world," she realized.

"Yes. Can you imagine humans living forever? You and I already understand it, which is why we have no thought of Hubley ever being queen, despite the fact that Brizen's crown is hers by right. But a dozen, or a hundred such, would be even worse."

"They'd fight among themselves for control. Not to mention that everybody else would resent the people who could live forever."

"Exactly. We would have replaced three Wizards with a hundred more. A hundred Arefts. As you said, that is Fornoch's real intent. I'm sure of it. For all we know, he is talking to Trier in Valing right now."

"She won't follow him if he is. Not that I'd blame her if she did, after what you tried this morning. Really, Reiffen. What were you thinking?"

"That we can trust no one but ourselves. You believe she will resist the Wizard this time, but what about the next? Or the time after that? And what if he offers her a Stone?" Angrily, Reiffen clenched his fists. "I should never have let her go. I should have slain her while I had the chance."

"You must stop thinking so poorly of people. Everyone has to take their chance. You did. I have."

"Not Hubley. Our daughter will not go through what I did. Not if I have to lock her up till the day I kill the last Wizard."

"That day's never going to come if you keep talking like that."

Reiffen stood, his arms shaking. "You don't understand. You never have, and never will. No one will. I killed Molio, and Mindrell's wife and child. And all those men at Rimwichside, and mothers and fathers you've never heard of. And then I stole the children they never even knew they had. If there is anything, anything I can do to keep Hubley from having to do such things, I will."

Ferris laid a hand on her husband's arm. Despite her best efforts, the conversation was going exactly the way Fornoch had predicted.

Reiffen shrugged her angrily away. "As long as you continue to be willing to expose our daughter to the Wizard, you prove you don't understand."

"If you mean I'm not willing to lock Hubley up in this castle, you're right. I don't understand."

He took her by the shoulders then, his fingers biting her arms. Spit flecked the corners of his mouth.

"Let go," said Ferris. "You're hurting me."

"You have to understand!" he exclaimed. His eyes bulged. "If you don't, I can never trust you! I'll know that he'll get around you some day, just as he gets around everyone. The only alternative is to wait, gaining power, till we have enough to destroy him."

"Stop shaking me, Reiffen! Have you lost your mind?"

He stared at her for a moment, then dropped his hands. Ferris backed away, rubbing her arms. She had never seen him so out of control. He had lost his temper before, especially when Hubley was concerned, but never like this. For the first time she had a sense of how much bigger he was, how easily he could hurt her. She didn't like the feeling at all.

"I can't talk to you about this now," she said. "Not while you're like this. I'm going back to Valing. When you've calmed down you can come apologize."

She left him standing in the middle of the room, face flushed and panting. Outside, the sitting room was empty. Evidently Giserre, at the first hint of raised voices, had taken Hubley somewhere else.

She found them mixing cookie batter in the kitchen. Giserre's eyebrows rose at the look on Ferris's face, but she made no comment. Ignoring her mother, Hubley picked up a great hunk of golden dough and mushed it through her fingers. Small dabs rained into the wooden bowl.

Snatching a dish towel from the counter, Ferris grabbed her daughter's hands and wiped them clean.

"Mother!" Hubley scolded. "I was going to lick those!"

"Not now, Hubley. Giserre, we're going to Valing. Do you want to come, too?"

Giserre shook her head. "Not until I have told him what he needs to hear. I have been waiting for Hubley to be out of the way all day."

Still holding her daughter's hand, Ferris seized her remaining thimble. A quick twist and a firm "Return," and she found herself in darkness.

"Mother!" Hubley tried to pull her arm away but Ferris's grip was firm. "Now I won't be able to eat Grandmother's cookies."

"Mims will make you better ones when we get upstairs."

Washing the batter from her hands, Giserre went in search of Reiffen.

She found him slumped in a chair in the bedroom, his head thrown back, his eyes staring at the ceiling. Her heart ached at the hurt and listlessness in his face, but now was no time for softness. What he had done to Trier was inexcusable; she hoped he had not crossed the line with Ferris as well. But it would be hard to talk to him. He was older than he had been the day he dragged her back to the Wizards' fortress, and more confident in what he believed. Which made him more difficult than ever to reason with.

He did not look up when she came in.

"Ferris has gone back to Valing," she said. "Judging from the way you have behaved today, she has my sympathy."

"It is this business with Fornoch, Mother," he answered. The tone of her voice had not affected him at all. "I am afraid it will come between us."

"Only if you allow it."

"What Ferris asks is impossible. Hubley's danger is greater than ever, now the Wizard has reappeared. I could refuse him nothing should he ever steal her the way he stole me. The way he twists things, I would probably even think I was doing what I wanted."

"I remained with you in Ussene to help make you strong, Reiffen, not to shelter you. You must help Hubley in the same way."

"I cannot. The risk is too great."

"Then you are wrong, and Ferris is right. I am not surprised she took the child with her."

"She what?"

Reiffen sat up. Giserre hardly recognized the wildness in his eyes.

"She took Hubley home with her to her mother," she scolded. "It is what a woman does when her husband starts acting the way you have."

He flung himself across the room, reminding Giserre of his temper as a child. "She did this deliberately! Fornoch was just there! For all I know he's already taken her!"

"Ferris will allow no harm to come to your daughter. She can guard the child as well as you."

"If that is what you think, you might as well go with them.

You understand the situation no better than she does. You, at least, will be in no danger."

With some effort, Giserre kept an even tone. "Your behavior is appalling. There is no excuse for it, no matter what else is pressing on your mind. Ahne's death should not weigh so heavily on your conscience that it should make you behave badly to those you love."

"What is important, Mother, is the safety of my child."

He disappeared without another word. Giserre was stunned. And she was angry, too. Not at the way he had treated her, but at the way he seemed to be treating everyone. She had known he was distraught when he had returned from Norly, but she had assumed he would soon recover. He had always recovered before, and his trials in Ussene had been much harsher. It was fear for his daughter that had done this to him.

Briefly she wondered if the Wizard had cast some spell. But, though Giserre understood little about magic, she did not believe Fornoch had laid an enchantment on her son. That was not the Wizard's way.

Driving a husband and wife to fight with one another was.

Leaving the bedroom, she selected a small mirror from the collection on the sitting-room mantel. When she passed her hand across the glass, a view of Valing Manor's kitchen emerged.

"Is anyone there?" she asked.

Sally Veale appeared in the glass.

"Has Ferris arrived yet?"

"She's been and gone, milady. More than an hour ago."

"She is on her way back now. When she arrives, please have her call me. I think I shall be going to Valing, too."

But it was Trier who returned to Castle Grangore for Giserre. After all her recent traveling, Ferris was too tired to make another trip. And so it was that Giserre was not in Valing when Reiffen came striding out of the orchard to grab Hubley by the hand as she stood with her mother and the other apprentices at the top of the Neck. Daughter in tow, he walked straight off the edge of the cliff.

Lorennin screamed. Ferris and Plum raced to the edge, but Reiffen and Hubley had disappeared. No splash marked the dark blue surface of the lake forty fathoms below.

Ferris's eyes narrowed, but she didn't say a word.

10

Avender in Malmoret

fter his and Reiffen's failure in Norly, Redburr disappeared into the mountains without telling anyone where he was going. Avender waited a day for Reiffen to come back for him, then gave up and marched south with the soldiers to Maarend. Maples and willows edged the riverbank in red and yellow as they boarded the last schooner of the year bound for Malmoret.

Wellin and Brizen met them at the pier. Avender braced himself for the worst, but soon saw that what had happened between him and the queen wasn't the source of the unease he felt as soon as he stepped ashore. Nine days had passed since Ferris and Reiffen had dragged Hubley back and forth between Valing and Castle Grangore, but, as far as anyone in Malmoret knew, there had been no change since.

"It has already lasted far longer than anyone expected," explained Wellin as the three of them walked toward the wharf. Avender wondered what it was about women like Wellin and Giserre that allowed them to face any situation with complete composure.

"They are too similar in temperament not to reconcile," the queen continued.

Brizen rubbed a finger across his chin. "Their similarity is exactly what worries me. Both are so stiff-necked that neither is likely to give in."

"Reiffen has always liked getting his own way," Avender admitted. "Since he came back from Ussene, it's only gotten worse. If Ferris doesn't go to him, this could last forever. He certainly won't give in first."

The queen paused to allow one of the footmen to clear a way for her wide skirts through the apple crates blocking the pier. "He tried to kill Trier," she declared.

Avender stopped in mid-stride.

"He does not deny it," she continued. "He claimed it was necessary to prevent the apprentices from being turned by the Wizard. It is all rubbish, if you ask me. If not for the child, Ferris would be perfectly justified in never going back to him."

"We should keep in mind," cautioned Brizen, "that we all thought Reiffen was in the wrong once before. I cannot help but wonder if he might be right this time as well, horrible though that sounds."

"It is horrible," Wellin scolded. "Taking the law into his own hands with Ahne was bad enough, but at least Ahne had committed a crime." She shuddered at the thought of what that crime was. "The apprentices have done nothing."

"What does Giserre say?" Avender started forward again, though he hadn't fully recovered from the news that Reiffen had tried to kill Trier.

"Giserre is with Ferris. Not even she will take her son's side in this."

"What we really need is someone Reiffen will listen to," said Brizen. "Someone to talk to him."

Avender raised his hands. "Don't look at me. The only time Reiffen ever listened to what I had to say was when I used to knock him down, and I can't do that anymore."

"Please try," begged Wellin. "You cannot have any less success than we have had."

"This quarrel between Reiffen and Ferris could cause all sorts of complications," the king added. "The situation regarding the succession is already delicate enough."

Avender deliberately kept his eyes on the men unloading the schooner. Now was not the time to be sharing glances with the queen.

"You think Ferris and Reiffen might fight over that, too?" he asked. "They've both always been dead set against you naming Hubley your heir."

"If their disagreement worsens," replied Wellin, "who knows what might happen?"

"I suppose I can try."

Avender did his best not to flinch as the king clapped him on the shoulder.

"It is good to have you back." The worry in Brizen's face had already begun to ease. "You know the magicians better than anyone. With you here, I am sure this will all blow over soon."

At the queen's carriage, another footman held the horses steady as Brizen helped his wife up into her seat. Avender turned away as Wellin's skirts ruffled across the door and cushions. Here was Brizen, so glad to have him back, and Avender was only bringing more trouble. During the entire trip from Norly he had debated whether he should be returning to Malmoret at all, but the lure of the queen had been too strong. Now that he was here, he felt like a traitor.

Even Reiffen couldn't claim that.

At the palace, Avender left the king and queen and went immediately to the mirror room. If he was going to talk to Reiffen, he wanted to do it as soon as possible. And he wanted to talk to Ferris, too. His old friends were both known for stubbornness, and he could just see them digging in their heels. Ferris, if she thought she was right, would never give in. But telling Reiffen he was wrong wasn't easy, and had only gotten worse after his great successes in the last war.

With a crisp salute, the guard outside the mirror room allowed Avender to pass. A pair of clerks at desks set against the walls looked up as he entered. Nearly two dozen mirrors covered the sides of their small closet, quills and bottles of ink close at hand. One clerk's pen scratched busily across the page, the feather waving back and forth beside the writer's cheek like the tail of an attentive cat. A man Avender recognized as the harbormaster in Mremmen was reporting from one of the mirrors on the arrival of several Banking ships. Other faces waited to speak from other silvered panes.

"May I?" Avender reached for two empty mirrors.

"Of course, Sir Avender. Let me just make a note of the time, and which ones you're taking away." The second clerk glanced at the wenwick above the door and added two small notes to his ledger.

Rather than go to his own room on the other side of the palace, Avender found an empty study and, seating himself in a comfortable chair by the window, addressed the first glass. Smoke swirled, reminding him of a dark night years before when Reiffen had first revealed what he was able to do with magic and mirrors. At the time, Avender had wondered at Reiffen's purpose, but he had made the right choice in the end and had supported his friend even before Reiffen proved he was the enemy of the Three. Avender wondered if he was going to have to make the same choice again.

"Hello," he called as the smoke cleared. "Is anyone there?"

The Valing kitchen appeared in the mirror. Out of sight, dishes clattered faintly. Avender imagined he could smell the bread that was certainly baking in the ovens beyond his view.

It took a while, with Hern sending Lorennin scurrying to find her mistress, but Ferris finally appeared in the glass. "Made it back at last, have you? I'm sorry Reiffen left you behind like that."

"Is it true he tried to kill Trier?"

Ferris's face clouded further. "He wanted to kill all the apprentices, but I think I talked him out of it. At least he hasn't tried since."

"What about Hubley? Will he still not let her leave Grangore?"

"No. That I can't talk him out of at all."

"Do you think I'd have any luck?"

"I doubt it. He's being very difficult."

"Do you think Fornoch did something to him?"

Weariness showed in Ferris's eyes. For a moment she actually looked her age. "I don't know. I don't think so. At least nothing that wasn't already done a long time ago."

"Have you gone to see him?"

"No, and I don't intend to, either. He has to know he can't just order me around."

"Even if that's the only way you can see Hubley?"

Ferris's mouth tightened. "That won't last long. He can't keep her locked up forever."

"This is Reiffen we're talking about."

"I know. But with everyone against him, he has to give in eventually. I'm not the one who's wrong."

"Do you really think that matters? Reiffen probably doesn't think he's wrong, either. Hubley's the one you have to think about. What's best for her."

Crossing her arms, Ferris cocked her head to one side and gave Avender a stubborn look. "I know you're trying to help, but really, Avender, this is between Reiffen and me. If you'd ever been married, you'd understand."

His conversation with the other magician went no better. Asking Reiffen to think of what might be best for Hubley was no use at all.

"What can matter more than the child's safety?" he declared after answering Avender's call. "Ferris's and my feelings are of no consequence."

"But you tried to kill Trier," argued Avender. "Don't you understand how that might make everyone suspicious about what you're up to? At least take Hubley to Valing to prove your good intentions."

"My intentions need no confirmation. And Valing is no longer safe. Fornoch was just there. Who knows what sorts of traps and temptations he left behind?"

"Even with you there to protect her?"

"I would not take Hubley into the High Bavadars in snowslide season, either, though I believe my magic would keep us safe enough. Ferris must come to me. That is what is best for our child."

Avender stared at his reflection for a long time after the smoke cleared in the Castle Grangore glass. It was at times like these he was glad he'd never married, but that thought soon passed. He was certain the good in having someone to share a life with was far greater than the bad. Ferris and Reiffen would get over their quarrel eventually. In the meantime, Avender was reduced to wandering around the New Palace in love with the king's wife. Worst of all, he couldn't even be noble and self-sacrificing about it, because he knew she loved him, too.

Despite his better judgment, he tried several times over the next week to visit Wellin when the king was away from the palace. She was more than glad to see him, but always kept two or three of her ladies in attendance.

He knew she was right. Such things were paid more attention to in Malmoret than they were in Castle Grangore. As long as nothing had happened between them, neither he nor Wellin had ever given a single thought to meeting alone. But, now that something had, they thought about it all the time.

He considered hiring rooms somewhere outside the palace, but couldn't picture either of them doing that sort of thing. Such secrets had a way of always coming out anyway. Furtive meetings were for the stage, with husbands and lovers inevitably dueling by the fourth act. As Durk liked to point out, it was always the lover who died. Avender was certain, should such a duel ever come about, he'd slit his own throat before he'd murder a man he'd already wronged.

By the end of the first week he knew he couldn't stay. It wasn't his guilt that made him want to leave, or the feeling he might accidentally do or say something to hurt the queen. The problem was he couldn't do or say anything at all. Every day he and Wellin came together, at audiences and council meetings and formal dinners, and every day it hurt more that he couldn't go to her, couldn't take her in his arms. He had known that would be the case, but at least before there had been the prospect of future visits to Castle Grangore. That was impossible now, at least until Ferris and Reiffen reconciled. How perfect, he told himself, that his friends' troubles had afflicted him as well.

Even if he did leave, he didn't know what excuse he could give. No one would believe him if he claimed he was retiring to Goose Rock, especially not the farmer who rented the land from him. Perhaps Brizen would give him a ship and crew to sail east to look for the other side of the ocean. Everyone would blame his wandering on some misbegotten love; he wouldn't be the first to flee Malmoret because of a broken heart. No doubt the poets would sing of his sorrow for generations. Mindrell could write a masterwork of melancholy and sarcasm.

Then one afternoon, about a month after his return, a lady-in-waiting intercepted him as he was on his way to the College to look at their collection of ancient maps. The woman flirted terribly as she told Avender her mistress wished to see him, but he was too busy wondering why Wellin had sent for him to pay attention. Had the queen's desire finally overcome her caution? Had she summoned him to tell him the affair was over? His heart tumbled between joy and despair as he rolled their last several meetings back and forth in his mind in search of clues.

"Thank you, Fanning," said the queen as the messenger showed Avender into one of the cozier sitting rooms. "Sir Avender and I wish to converse alone. If you would, come to me an hour before dinner. I shall need at least that much time to prepare for the duke and duchess."

Bowing, Lady Fanning backed out of the room. For the first time since the night they had spent together, Avender and Wellin were alone.

He couldn't say how often he had been in that room before, but this time it all seemed different. He noticed everything, from the small portraits of the queen's mother and father hanging beside the door, to the edging of the lace draped over the side tables. Outside, the bare branches of the rose bushes rattled in the gusting wind.

When she held out her hand to him, he went to her at once. Allowing a single kiss, she pushed him away.

"Fanning will notice every wrinkle in my dress," she said. "She intends to be your next conquest, you know. It was all I could do not to dismiss her on the spot when she told me, but I fear that would have caused too much notice. Especially as you have taken no new lover since your return."

"You know, as long as I love you, there can be no one else."

The queen rolled her eyes. "You sound like something written by Durk."

"That's because I'm out of practice." Bracing his hands on Wellin's chair, he leaned down to kiss her without rumpling. This time it was a while before the queen pushed him away.

"I have missed you, too," she told him. "But I fear I have some difficult news. Ferris has been with the king. We have been very foolish. I should have known Brizen would ask her the same questions I did."

"What do you mean?" Sitting on the edge of the chair, Avender took the queen's hand. She did not pull away.

"I mean the king has had the magician examine him as if he were someone's prize bull. As I once had Ferris examine me like a common heifer."

"And?" asked Avender, still not comprehending.

"Now the king knows that he is the one to blame, not me. At least in the matter of public concern. Privately, the matter is entirely reversed."

"You're saying Brizen can't father a child."

"So Ferris has told me. She thought it best I know."

"But then . . ."

The queen nodded. "Yes. Only it is too late to start worrying about that now. When I heard she was in the palace, I asked Ferris to see me also, to confirm what I have only just begun to suspect. She did confirm it, which was why she felt obliged to tell me what she had already told my husband. Unfortunately, that news has taken nearly all my own joy away."

"You're pregnant?"

"Yes."

"Well, that's just great," he said, appreciating the queen's predicament at last. His own satisfaction at the idea of becoming a father passed quickly. "Will you keep it?"

He wanted to bite his tongue the moment he asked the question, thinking he sounded terribly cruel. But Wellin didn't seem to mind.

"At first, I thought not. Ferris would help me easily enough. I believe it is what she wishes me to do. But the thought itself is terrible to me. I have wanted a child more than anything else in the world, more even than I wanted to be queen, or I would never have risked it all to be with you. If I have to, I will certainly give up the one for the other. Being queen, that is."

From unhappiness at the queen's distress, Avender's mood switched to sudden joy. Wellin would give up her throne for the sake of the child they would have together? What could be more perfect!

"We could go to Grangore," he said at once. "Or Valing. Or Far Mouthing if you want, to your family's estates. I hardly think Brizen is the sort who will start a war to get you back. Look how easily he gave up Ferris." At the thought of the king's failed first wedding, Avender's elation dimmed. This time his friend's unhappiness would be his fault.

"I will not run away," said Wellin. "I cannot be so base. I will ask him to forgive me first. Then we can both live honestly, released from our pledges to his side and service."

"We'll live quietly somewhere," Avender agreed. "You and I and the child."

"Perhaps," said Wellin. "If we are lucky."

He caressed her cheek with the back of his hand. "I'm usually the one who distrusts the future, not you. Yet here I am, thinking everything's going to work out for once."

Wellin rubbed her lover's fingers against her soft skin. "Right now I am not sure I can believe that we can be happy after what we have done. It would not seem right. Perhaps our child will be happy, but I cannot imagine the same for us."

"I can," said Avender. "It's what I've been waiting for my whole life."

She kissed his hand. "Leave now. I will talk with you again after I speak with the king."

For the rest of the day Avender roamed the streets of Malmoret, his face muffled. Cold showers came and went, sweeping across the city like a damp broom, but Avender paid them no mind. His skin remained warm and flushed despite the weather, his long stride propelling him along. As he had said to Wellin, he had been waiting for this his whole life. At last he could settle down. His dozen years in Malmoret had been a long pause, an extended lull while he waited for what he really wanted. What he thought he would never get, not since he had first realized that Ferris didn't love him. Even Wellin he had only loved in the way that a man dying in the desert loves a mirage. He had never imagined actually winning her.

His ears burned at the thought of what he had done to Brizen, what he had yet to do. Even so, he would not change any of it. At some point he had to look to himself. He had had enough of being a guest in his friends' lives. It was time he had his own.

Night had fallen by the time he returned to the castle. When his servant told him there had been no messages, Avender had to fight back the urge to find Wellin. Brizen wasn't the sort to make trouble, no matter how sore his own hurt; Wellin would handle the king easily enough herself. Stripping off his wet clothes, Avender ordered supper and a hot bath. Packing he ignored. When he and Wellin left, it would be to start a new life, fresh and clean. None of the possessions he had collected during his years in Malmoret meant enough to take with him, not even his sword.

He was finishing a last glass of wine when he began to wonder what was taking her so long. Had the king finally shown some temper? Avender found that hard to believe. He knew the king as well as anyone, except Wellin. He had seen Brizen sorely provoked by his father, by greedy barons, by merchants and guildsmen who thought to take advantage of his openhandedness, but he had never seen him actually lose his temper. Always Brizen tried to see things from the other person's point of view. Even when Ferris had left him on their wedding day, he had kept his composure. But there were limits to everything, and Avender imagined losing a well-loved wife might be one of them. Maybe he should go see if anything was the matter. Not that he could do anything if there was. The king's guard were loyal only to the king; Avender had made sure of that when he chose them.

He was pacing his room, his eye on his sword where it hung over the back of a chair, when a firm knock sounded at his door.

He knew something was wrong the moment Wellin slipped inside. Instead of coming straight to his arms, she crossed to his desk. Nor did she throw back the hood of the light cloak she wore, but left it up, concealing her face.

"What's wrong?" he asked. "Did he threaten you?"

"No." Wearily she settled into an uncushioned chair. In the

faint light of the two oil lamps on the walls, Avender couldn't see her face at all. "Brizen would never do that."

"Then what has he done?" Kneeling beside her, Avender took the queen's hand.

She drew her arm away. "He has forgiven me."

"Forgiven you?" Bending forward, Avender tried to see her face around the edge of her hood.

She dropped her chin still farther. "Yes. He said he understood my concerns entirely, that my wanting a child overcame any other consideration. Oh, Avender, he is too good. Too good for either of us."

"We've known that for a long time. Maybe someday he'll forgive me, too."

"He does not know it is you."

"You didn't tell him?"

"He does not want to know. He says knowing would make it worse."

The shame that had troubled Avender since his return to Malmoret tightened around him. He should have known Brizen would take this tack. The king was too good for even himself. "He'll find out eventually. It's not like we'll be able to keep it secret."

"He knows that. But he said he does not want to hear it from me. That way, if I go back to him, it will not matter."

"Go back to him?" Until now, Avender had thought Brizen's forgiveness was a blessing. He hadn't seen the threat.

Wellin nodded, her gesture as feeble as Avender's voice. "He has understood it all. He has even apologized for not seeing my need sooner. He says I have done nothing wrong, that it is my right to have a child."

She began to sob, her racking tears swallowed by the folds of her hood. Avender laid his arm around her shoulders, hugging her close. This time she didn't pull away. Instead she turned and buried her face in his chest. Her small, fine hands pulled at his shirt. Wrapping his other arm around her, he rested his chin on top of her head and felt her sobs.

"I cannot leave him, Avender," she whispered when her crying eased. "He is too good."

"But you love me."

"I love you both. And I owe him so much. He has said he will love the child as his own. Boy or girl, the babe will be his heir."

Avender saw what had happened then. Brizen or Reiffen, it was always the same. The women he managed to fall in love with were always interested in more than he could give. Wellin had gotten everything she needed from him that night in Grangore. Now she could move on, back into the life she had always dreamed of. Everything had worked out for her far better than she could have imagined.

He dropped his arms. She threw back her cowl and looked at him, sensing he had finally understood.

"I am sorry," she said.

Her apology was more than he could bear.

"You do understand?" she pleaded. "If he is so good as to forgive me, after what I have done, how can I leave him?"

"I understand." His voice was cold. "You get it all this way. You can be queen, you can have an heir. It's just the way it would have been if you'd never been caught. Would you have gone away with me had the king believed the child was his from the start?"

Her manner chilled to match his. "You know I would not. We discussed it that night. My need was for more than love. Though love was most certainly a part of it."

"Well, you got what you wanted. No need for you to stay."

He turned his back. The queen took him by the arm and pulled him around to face her.

"You know that is not true," she said. "There is more to it than that. I adore you, Avender. If things had been different, you would have been more to me than Brizen can ever be. But things are not different. I have a duty to Brizen, and to the lands we rule. It will mean much more to the world if I can give the king an heir than it ever will that another Wayland baron has a wife and child. Surely you understand it."

"Please don't try to tell me you are doing this solely out of duty."

She would not lie. "You know I cannot make that claim. I have already said I love you both. The Brizen I love is very much the king. Just as the Avender I love is very much the Hero of the Stoneways. Were you a Valing shepherd, no matter how handsome, none of this would ever have happened. Allow Brizen to be who he is."

She kissed him below the ear. "Good-bye, Avender. I will not mind if you stay in Malmoret, but I doubt you have the strength for it. Even with all the hearts you have broken, you are too single-minded. Perhaps it will comfort you to know, for all that I am staying with my husband, you have a part of me that he can never share."

He refused to turn around as she left. The last he heard was the rustle of her cloak against the door and the click of the latch. The last chance at the life he wanted disappeared.

For a long time he sat in darkness. Stray bursts of rain pattered on the windowpanes like crows pecking at corn. Too numb to think, he watched the pieces of his life shuffle through his mind: Ferris's engagement to Brizen, Wellin asking him to dance at his very first ball. Fragments that, if different, might have meant all the world to him. Better now if the queen had never come to him at all, in Malmoret or Grangore. Then he could have gone on as he had before, watching her life from the outside. Her husband's friend.

But none of that was possible now. Brizen might not know the father of his child, but Avender did. Better to go someplace far away, someplace where every day wasn't a reminder of what might have been his.

He didn't think he'd wanted so very much. Just a wife and children, and a bit of land to live on. His sword at the king's command, but the rest of his life his own. Most men got such things, but not him.

He knew it was his own fault. Had he chosen to do so, he could have walked into any town in the lands east of the Blue Mountains and had his pick of wives. He still could. Good or bad, maid or matron, nearly all would marry him if he asked. The problem was, he couldn't bring himself to ask. Like Ferris, he had been spoiled. He had met kings and princesses, fallen in love with them, and become their friend. If Reiffen had never come to Valing, Ferris might have married him instead.

And none of this with Wellin would ever have happened.

11

The Return of Mindrell

By morning, Avender had decided he couldn't leave right away. If he disappeared too suddenly, even Brizen would figure out he was the father of Wellin's child. But the king had been urging him to have another talk with the magicians for some time and, though Avender still doubted he could help them patch up their quarrel, now seemed the perfect time to do as the king asked.

He only had to wait two days before Brizen mentioned the matter again. This time Avender gave in reluctantly. Although he would have preferred to make the journey on his own, he asked Ferris to come get him. The first snow had already fallen on Firron Pass, and no one was going to get through to Valing without magic till spring.

Trier came instead, leaving Avender to guess Ferris didn't want to take the chance of being away in case Reiffen finally decided to come to Valing. Hern and Sally Veale gave him enormous hugs when he arrived, their aprons smelling of apple sausage and fresh-brewed beer.

"This is a surprise!" said the steward, embracing Avender a second time. "Berrel'll be that mad he missed your arrival, but he's gone over to Bracken to help with the mill. The stone cracked in the middle of Dub's grinding, and Dub's just the one to raise a fuss. Will you be here long?"

"Not this time." Avender scraped his muddy boots on the door-mat. "A quick talk with Ferris, and then I'll probably be off again."

The lines in Hern's face deepened as she sensed his visit's pur-pose. "She's in the orchard with the apprentices. They'll be com-ing in soon for lunch, if you want to wait for them."

But, now that he had come home, Avender found he was anxious to move on. There was nothing for him in Valing either. One more stop in Castle Grangore and he would be free to find something new, away from all the places that reminded him of what would never be his.

He found Ferris and the apprentices practicing levitation spells on the cliff beyond the apple trees. A piglet squealed, its legs kicking at empty air as Plum raised it magically off the ground and sent it gliding over the edge of the cliff. The poor an-imal nearly dropped out of sight on the other side before Plum managed to catch it again and hold it steady.

"I'm showing them how to focus properly over shifting ground," Ferris explained when Avender asked whether she was teaching magic, or how to terrify pigs. "If the apprentices can handle a sudden change like a cliff, they can handle anything."

"And if they can't?"

"So far I've caught all the pigs myself before they hit the water. Otherwise Hern and Sally will just have to make more sausage."

She led him up to the Map Room when the lesson was over, leaving Trier in charge of the apprentices. A switch in the wind sent the mist from the gorge across the pines, masking the back of the house in a white fog that reminded them both of the Tear.

She looked older than the last time he had seen her. At her daughter's birthday Ferris had still been the same twenty-two-year-old he had known for the last ten years. But now her eyes were darker and more deep-set, the care and worry clearly visible despite her smooth, unlined face. Apparently Living Stones pre-served only a body's appearance, and could do nothing about the drift of memory inside.

"You've been an idiot, you know," she said, settling into a chair by the window.

"Pardon me?"

"Having an affair with the queen. What were you thinking?"

"I don't see how it's any business of yours," he grumbled. Magicians had too many ways of knowing what they weren't supposed to for Avender to bother pretending her accusation wasn't true.

"I'm your friend. And Wellin's and Brizen's, too. I don't like seeing any of you unhappy."

"Wellin and Brizen'll be fine."

"I wouldn't be so sure of that."

"I would. Brizen's overjoyed he's finally going to have an heir. He doesn't care who the father is."

"So Wellin told me. But that doesn't mean he won't figure it out eventually. He's not as innocent as he used to be."

"I'll be far away when he does."

Ferris nodded. "I suppose that's best. Have you decided where you'll go?"

"Not yet. Maybe the Pearl Islands. I hear winter's the best time there. I was thinking I might hire a ship in the spring and go looking for the other side of the ocean."

"Don't you think that's a bit extreme?"

He shrugged. "I'll worry about that when the time comes. But I didn't come here to talk about me. What's the news with you and Reiffen?"

Some of the stiffness went out of Ferris's shoulders at Avender's show of concern. "It's sweet of you to ask, but nothing's changed."

"Do you want me to try and talk to him?"

"Do you really think you can bring him to his senses any more than I can? Or Giserre?"

"It's worth a try. I don't imagine you're enjoying things the way they are. You must miss Hubley terribly."

Anguish weakened Ferris's face. "It's not just Hubley. I miss Reiffen, too."

"All the more reason to go back to Grangore. Leave him alone and he'll just think you've deserted him."

"I know. To tell the truth, he frightens me. I thought he was going to hit me the last time we fought."

Avender was about to say he didn't think Reiffen was the sort of man to hit his wife until he realized that wasn't true. If Reiffen thought he was right, he was capable of anything. How else had he managed to survive all those years in Ussene?

"You agree, don't you," she said, guessing his thoughts.

"I can see it," he confessed. "And I can understand why that might make it hard to go back to him. But don't you think your fear is a bit like Reiffen's attitude toward the apprentices? He hasn't hit you yet. Until he does, I think you have to trust him."

"There are worse things than being hit." Ferris folded her arms across her chest. "If I give in to him on this, he'll be even worse the next time. He'll think I've surrendered completely. And there are the apprentices to think about, too. The next time he tries to kill one of them it might not be so easy to stop him."

"What does Giserre think?"

"She agrees with me. And you. But she also thinks the longer I wait before going back, the better. Reiffen needs to know he's wrong. I'll tell you right now, neither of us is going to be happy if I'm the one who gives in."

"So I'll talk to him then. It can't hurt."

"I should warn you, Giserre's been to the castle twice and hasn't been able to budge him either time. What he really needs is for you to knock him down the way you used to do when we were children."

"I'd probably get myself turned into a toad if I did."

"Or something worse. Which is why, if you do go, I want to make sure you have a way to leave quickly. You'll have to watch out for Mindrell, too."

"Mindrell's at Castle Grangore?"

"He showed up here first. About two weeks ago."

"Hern must have had something to say about that."

"She did. But Mindrell left soon enough. He came to offer Giserre his service."

Avender shook his head. This was getting much too confusing.

"So why is he in Valing if he wants to serve Giserre?"

"Giserre didn't want him around any more than the rest of us did, so she sent him to Castle Grangore to guard Hubley."

"Guard Hubley? Guard her from what?"

"From her father."

"And Reiffen allowed it?"

Ferris shrugged. "We haven't heard from either of them since he left. For all we know Reiffen killed him."

"No loss there. But why would Mindrell want to serve Giserre?"

Ferris looked at her old friend curiously. "I guess there's no reason you'd know. Mindrell's been in love with Giserre ever since Ussene."

"You can't be serious. Does he really think Giserre could ever do anything but despise him? He was the one who stole Reiffen for the Three in the first place."

"Giserre's forgiven him a great deal, after all the time they spent together."

"Not enough to fall in love with him, I hope."

"Of course not. That's why she sent him off to Castle Grangore, to get killed for all we know, instead of letting him stay here. And why he was willing to go."

They said no more about Mindrell, or Reiffen, when they went down to lunch. Even so, it was a much gloomier meal than Avender was used to in Valing, or even Castle Grangore. Giserre and Hern tried to keep the conversation going by asking everyone questions, but even they had given up by the time Hern passed around slices of maple cake for dessert. Avender had the feeling his presence didn't help. Probably his arrival had re-minded everyone even more of the way things used to be. One more example of how he really didn't fit in anywhere.

The tops of the High Bavadars were the only part of Valing still catching any sunlight when Ferris finally led him up to a long garret under the Manor roof. Avender remembered the room as having been used for storage when he and Ferris were young; now all the old furniture and unhung paintings had been piled against the back wall to make room for a long table. An assortment of jars and other magical equipment lay stacked at one end.

Ferris retrieved a small gold box from a chest under the window. "I was preparing this for myself, but I think you might need it sooner than I will."

"What do I need a reliquary for?"

"To hold your finger."

"You think I'm going to let you use magic on me after all these years?"

"Yes." From a second drawer in the same chest she removed a thimble and a small silver knife. "I'm not about to let you visit Reiffen without a way to make a quick escape. Just in case."

Restraining the urge to hide his hands behind his back, Aven-der shook his head. "You know I hate magic. Look at what it's done to you and Reiffen."

"If it hadn't been for the magic, Reiffen and I would never have gotten together in the first place. Now hold still. It's not half as bad if you don't have to do it to yourself."

When she was done, Avender had to admit he'd been through worse. The iron thimble wasn't as heavy as he'd expected. In time, he probably wouldn't even notice it. Not that he wanted to wear it long enough for that to happen.

"You're sure you don't want to spend the night?" she asked as she stuffed the last of the bloody towels into a hamper. "Hern's making cabbage and leek pie for supper."

Avender shook his head. Valing was already making him feel sad. More than any other place in the world, this was the life he missed most.

"Let's go." Wiggling his new thimble in the air, he added, "I can come back any time I want after I'm done."

His nose wrinkled as Ferris set a pair of smoking smudges at either end of the table. Holding hands, they sat between the pots on a pair of tall stools. The usual echo of the caster's memory seeped across his mind as Ferris composed herself for traveling: town and forest, lake and mountain. Sooner than he expected, his stool vanished and he tumbled to the ground. Their thimbles clicked faintly as Ferris let go his hand.

Back on his feet, he brushed the damp leaves from his trousers. Gloomy trees arched through the dusk around them, the patter of a small waterfall somewhere close by. Avender guessed they were near Nolo's Glen.

She gave him a hug. "Good luck."

He left her seated at the base of a tall beech, her eyes closed as she concentrated on her return. Except for the brush of his boots through the wet leaves, he walked in silence. What little light still clung to the sky was just enough to allow him to see the trail. Above his head bare branches framed the first stars sprinkling the sky.

He stopped when the narrow path he was following ran into the Grangore Road. Ahead of him, an old woman hurried toward the castle.

"It's a little late for you to be out, isn't it, grandmother?" he asked, his long strides bringing him quickly up beside her.

The old woman nearly jumped off the road. "Oh, what a fright, sir! Coming up on me like that in the middle of the forest. And so close to the castle, too!"

"Sorry. I didn't mean to scare you. Didn't you hear my feet in the leaves?"

"My hearin' ain't what it used to be, sir."

"Are you going to the castle?"

"I am." She showed him the basket on her arm. "I only just found out Widow Notte didn't go up today, so I thought I'd come myself. No reason my vegetables aren't as good for his honor as hers."

"You're not with the castle?"

"Lands, no, sir. He's given 'em all the sack, he has. Cooks, grooms, maids—even the soldiers. Widow Notte comes up twice a week with truck from her garden, but no one else. Don't see why I shouldn't be gettin' some o' the business myself."

"I don't see why you shouldn't, either." Lifting the cloth, Avender made out what looked like beets and butternut squash filling the old woman's basket. The smell of black earth drifted past his nose.

They paused at the edge of the woods. A few lights shone in the Magicians' Tower, but the rest of the castle was dark. More stars had come out in the sky above Aloslomin, though Ivis-mundra's shoulders still carried the faint glow of evening.

Crossing the meadow, Avender hammered on the front gate several times without an answer.

"They expectin' you?" asked the woman.

"No."

"They must be in the dungeon then."

"Dungeon?"

"Castles always has dungeons," she said with the firm authority of someone who'd never seen one.

Avender pounded at the entrance again. Finally a voice snapped out at them from somewhere in the air above their heads. The old woman shrunk even closer to the ground.

"Visitors are no longer permitted at Castle Grangore. Or peddlers. Off with you!"

"Reiffen, is that you? It's Avender. I'm here with a woman from town. She's brought vegetables, but I've come on business of my own. Will you let us in?"

A long pause. "No."

"Why not?"

"I have no guarantee you were not sent by Fornoch."

Avender checked his impatience. Ferris was right, Reiffen did need wrestling in the dirt.

"Maybe I'll just leave my basket on the stoop," suggested the woman.

"And trudge all the way back to town without getting paid?" Avender addressed the air once more. "Really, Reiffen. How can either of us hurt Hubley? We're not mages. Even if we are under the Wizard's control, do you think we can steal her away from under your nose?"

Another long pause, then the post-door opened. At first Avender thought Reiffen had done it magically, until Mindrell stepped out from behind the gate.

"Welcome to Castle Grangore," he said.

The bard's easy manner vanished at the sight of the old woman. "Do I know you?" he asked, bending forward to inspect her face suspiciously in the fading light.

She looked him straight in the eye. "I don't know, do you? I never been to the castle before. Maybe you seen me at the market in town."

"I've never been to Grangore on market day. But you bear more than a passing resemblance to someone I used to know."

"Well, it don't matter to me none whether you know me or not. Unless it makes you more likely to buy what I brung. I don't see why Widow Notte should be gettin' all your custom."

Mindrell's self-assurance returned as he decided he didn't know the woman after all. "I don't see why she should either, but then I'm not the one in charge. Don't try it again, though. Next time the mage might fry you. Here."

With a flick of his thumb, he launched a copper into the air. Dropping her basket, the old woman scrambled along the road after her payment.

"Who'd you think she was?" asked Avender as he entered the castle.

"Someone I used to know in Ussene." Shutting the post-door, Mindrell rebarred the gate. "But it couldn't have been her. She'd have to be a lot older, for one. And she didn't act the same at all."

Crossing the courtyard, he opened the door into the house. Clear light spilled across the step, allowing Avender his first good look at Mindrell in years. The bard may have become as famous for his songs and ballads as he was for slaying Usseis, but Avender had always tried to avoid him. Mindrell had tried to murder him once, after all. The bard was middle-aged now, thicker through the chest and shoulders, with strings of gray in his hair, but his mocking smile remained the same.

"Come to see if I'm still alive?" he asked.

"No."

"Sorry to disappoint you."

They entered a small library off the front hall. Finding the room empty except for a desk and pair of chairs, Avender asked where Reiffen was, only to discover Mindrell had left. Trying the door, he found it still unlocked.

"Leaving so soon? I thought you came to see me."

Turning around, Avender discovered Reiffen seated behind the desk. Good as Ferris had become at casting the traveling spell, Reiffen was always going to be better.

"I can't say I approve of your friends," said Avender as he sat down in the empty chair.

"Mindrell is hardly a friend. But he provides good service."

"As good as he gave Fornoch?"

"Better, I hope."

"Why's he here?"

"To help me guard Hubley."

"I thought that was your job."

"It is. But who is going to guard Hubley from me? At first I was going to send the harper away but, when he put it that way, I had to let him stay. But I do not suppose it is Mindrell you came to talk to me about."

"No."

"I hope you are not here to persuade me to let Hubley visit her mother. Giserre has already come twice on the same mission. If I refused her, what chance do you think you have?"

"I still have to try. Ferris misses you, you know. It's not just about Hubley."

"And I miss Ferris. We will be much happier when we are back together. Believe me, I understand it all."

"No you don't. You don't understand anything. You're acting just like you used to when we were children, a spoiled brat who had to have his own way about everything."

"Not everything. Just Hubley. It is unfortunate my decision is causing so much discomfort to my family, but it cannot be helped. Any other choice would lead to misfortune of the worst sort."

"Worse than sending Ferris away?"

"I have not sent Ferris away. She is free to return whenever she wants."

Avender grunted. "Only if she does whatever you say once she's here. Do you really think you can make Ferris live like this, completely cut off from the rest of the world? And for what, some fear you have the Wizard's going to steal your daughter? Has he ever even tried?"

The magician laid his hands patiently on the desk, the long sleeves of his cloak nearly covering the surface. "He threatened Hubley quite plainly in Norly. That is why I made such a hasty return."

"If you ask me, what he really wanted was for you to come back here and hide just like this."

Reiffen shrugged. "It is the correct decision, regardless of Fornoch's wishes. In the meantime, once Ferris returns, she and I, and Hubley also, will study and learn. And although we do not know enough now, some day we will know enough magic to bring Fornoch down. Until then, I refuse to allow Hubley outside these walls."

"And how long do you think that'll take?"

"As long as it has to."

"I see. And after that you'll be the new Three."

"No." Reiffen drew the word out with condescending patience. "After that we will be free. Free to present Fornoch's gift to the rest of the world without fear of Fornoch's interference."

"Right. Just like Fornoch's done with you."

Reiffen's face hardened. "Do not compare me to Fornoch again, Avender. It is true I have done things I regret, but I am no Wizard. The fact I turned down Brizen's crown proves that. Unlike the Three, I seek to rule no one."

"Except your wife," Avender reminded him. "Ferris is afraid of you, you know. She said you nearly hit her."

"I did no such thing. Such an act would be monstrous."

"That's not what she thinks. And it's why she gave me this, in case you got angry with me too." Avender held up his thimble.

"I was wondering why you finally allowed Ferris to do that. But it was not my intent to scare her. Please apologize for me the next time you see her. All the same, I cannot promise to always hold back my anger when provoked. But she should know I would never hurt her."

"Well, she doesn't. Which is your fault, not hers. Every one of your friends thinks you're the one in the wrong about this, Reiffen. Wellin, Brizen, even Giserre. How arrogant can you be that you won't even listen to us?"

"I have listened. I may not show it, but do not doubt that I am as hurt as Ferris by the course I have chosen. I am just more used to this sort of thing than she is. Castle Grangore is not nearly as horrible as Ussene."

Avender reminded himself he had come here as an excuse for leaving Malmoret, and not with the hope of changing Reiffen's mind.

"Can I at least see Hubley before I go?" he asked.

"No. She is asleep. Unless you want to wait till morning."

"What about Durk?"

"Durk's with Hubley."

"Are you going to keep him here, too?"

Reiffen opened his hands generously. "The stone has asked when he might return to Malmoret. I have no objection. Hubley is bound to grow as weary of him as I have eventually."

"Then I guess I'll spend the night. That way I can see Hubley, and take Durk back with me in the morning."

"As you wish. You know the way to your apartment. There is food in the kitchen. If you will excuse me, I am working on a spell that will require my attention for the remainder of the night."

The magician left as he had arrived, in an instant. Avender went off to the kitchen to see if there really was anything to eat. Half-expecting the cabinets to be filled with imaginary food, he was surprised to find fresh eggs in the larder, and bread on the counter that tasted no more than a day old. Dust covered Ferris's spice rack, and the evidence in the flour bin was that the mice were making themselves quite at home. But there was bacon and onions to go with the eggs, and a jug of milk, and Avender found more than enough for a quick meal without having to poke through the contents of the old woman's basket.

Afterward he went to his room. The autumn wind knocked against the window as he lay on the bed and thought about what had happened in the six weeks since he and Wellin had spent an hour together on the floor above. He might have felt out of place in Valing but now, as he watched the clouds skid across the icy stars, he knew there was no place he'd rather be. Sailing off into an unknown ocean didn't sound nearly so interesting as it had in Malmoret the day before. Maybe he should just forget the last dozen years, lay them aside as if they had never happened. It wasn't too late to learn to farm.

He, at least, could do what he wanted. Hubley had to live

with her parents' quarrel. Who knew what Reiffen had given as the reason she couldn't see her mother. Or worse, perhaps the magician had cast some sort of spell on her. For all Avender knew, Hubley was sleeping in a glass casket out of some fairy tale. Maybe that was why Reiffen hadn't let him see her, and not because she'd gone to bed.

The thought made him sit up. Surely it wouldn't hurt if he peeked in on Hubley while she slept. How would that harm Reiffen, unless he really did have something to hide? The least Avender could do was bring Ferris news about her daughter. And if Reiffen caught him and did something rash, Avender could always whisk himself back to Valing. For that matter, he could bring Hubley with him, too.

He stopped with his hand on the door. Did he really want to stir the pot that much? Checking to see if Hubley was all right when Reiffen wasn't around was one thing, but carrying her off to her mother was another matter entirely. Ferris had already tried that once, and had only made things worse.

Putting on a bold front, he crossed the castle from the east to the west tower. No sense acting as if he was doing anything wrong. Even outside the family apartment he made no attempt to move cautiously, and pushed open the door to the sitting room as if he had as much right to be there as Reiffen himself. But he found no one inside. A single Dwarven lamp lay uncovered on the table in the middle of the chamber, its yellow light casting soft shadows across the walls.

Hubley's room was the second on the right, beyond Giserre's. A pair of eyes glimmered in the lamplight as Avender entered: Sandy's yellow face and shoulders soon followed. The old dog recognized Avender at once and came out from under the bed to lick his hand. Avender scratched the animal behind the ears, feeling suddenly silly about his suspicions. Sandy would only be in Hubley's room if Hubley were there. Maybe he ought to turn around and go back to bed.

But he didn't. His hand still on the doorknob, he peered inside. Though the back of the room remained dark, enough light seeped in from the sitting room to reveal Hubley asleep in her bed, a small mound among the rumpled covers.

He leaned forward. The child breathed softly, fast asleep. No, he really should let her be. Her parents would figure everything out eventually. Meddling would only make things worse. Gently he brushed his hand along the dark fan of her hair. Maybe, if he were lucky, he'd have a daughter he could call his own someday.

A second light came on. Startled, Avender looked up. His thimble scuffed against the quilt, catching on a tear. Mindrell came forward from the back of the room, setting the new lamp on top of the chest by the door. A sharp, heavy axe gleamed in his other hand.

"I wouldn't try it," said the bard.

Avender realized Mindrell thought he was trying to steal the child.

"It's not what you think," he said.

"It's exactly what I think." Mindrell pointed with his chin. "Reiffen expected you'd try something like this. I've been guarding her ever since you arrived. It's what Ferris sent you here to do."

"No it isn't."

But even as he spoke, Avender wondered if he should just do it. What did he have to lose? It couldn't be good for Hubley to be living here alone with Mindrell and her father. The one was a thief and a murderer, no matter what Giserre thought of him, and the other seemed to have fallen back into all his worst habits. Children were better off with their mothers, anyway. If Reiffen had turned into such a suspicious ass as this, maybe Avender should just do what they expected of him.

"I say." Durk spoke from the tangle atop the chest. "Avender, is that you?"

Thinking to take advantage of the stone's interruption, Avender grabbed Hubley's wrist in his left hand and reached for his thimble with his right. Sandy, fearing for his mistress, jumped up from his place below the bed and began to bark. But Mindrell wasn't distracted. His arm swept forward, the axe a bright blur. A burst of pain shot up Avender's arm, much worse than Ferris's severing of his finger that very afternoon.

"Return!" he shouted, fighting off the agony long enough to twist the thimble free.

Nothing happened. Numb with shock, both from the pain in his arm and the fact the magic hadn't worked, Avender dropped the empty cap. Looking down, he saw a pool of dark blood thickening on the bed. Hubley, half-awakened by the noise, rubbed her eyes as she pushed herself up from the pillows.

There was no sign at all of his hand.

12

Something Worse

hen Avender woke, he found himself in a low cave. Magical light hovered near the walls and roof; he had seen drawing rooms in Malmoret less well lit on winter evenings. Beneath his back a dirt floor ground itself into his hair whenever he moved.

He didn't move much. His left side, from the shoulder down, felt numb. Evidently Reiffen had seen fit to heal him once again, and had brought him to one of his underground workshops to do it. Lifting his arm, Avender saw it was tightly bandaged from wrist to elbow. He should have known better than to depend on magic to get him out of Castle Grangore.

"Feeling better?"

Rolling onto his right side, Avender looked behind him. Reiffen and Mindrell stood there, the magician cradling something small in his hand. It was Reiffen who had spoken. For once the bard's smirk had fallen from his face: he almost looked uncomfortable.

"How's Hubley?" asked Avender.

His reply rasped through the cave. Then his head went faint with the effort of sitting up and he curled onto his side, his cheek resting on the cold earth.

"Thank you for inquiring," Reiffen answered. "She is fine. I have no wish to murder you but, had you not shown some concern for my daughter after what you put her through, I might not have been able to control my anger. You do understand, though, that because of your rash actions, I shall have to tamper slightly with her memory. It really would not do for her last recollection of you to be that you tried to kill her."

Furious at Reiffen's lying, Avender forced himself to speak again, though his mouth was dry as the dirt under his cheek. "That's not true."

"No? How do I know where you were going when Mindrell stopped you?"

"I was going back to Valing. I told you, Ferris gave me that thimble."

"So you say. And so I think you believe, too. But can you be absolutely sure it was Ferris, and not the Wizard pretending to be Ferris?"

"It was Ferris." Though, as Avender spoke, the tiniest suspicion that maybe it wasn't wiggled into his mind.

"Perhaps it was." Reiffen stepped forward, still cupping whatever it was in his hand. "You understand that I cannot afford to take that chance. Should the Gray Wizard ever succeed in extracting Hubley from my care, I would be hard-pressed to regain her. Even if I could enlist Nolo and Redburr to help, the way you did for me once upon a time."

Avender wished he had more strength. His worst imaginings had come true. Reiffen was either completely mad, or had been turned by Fornoch. Either way, he seemed more Wizard than human now.

Reiffen waved a hand in front of Avender's face to catch his weakening attention. "Do you know what this is?" he asked.

Like a conjurer, the magician rolled his fingers in the air. A small green stone appeared between thumb and forefinger. Though Avender had never seen such a stone before, he knew what it was at once. Dark as jade, the large pebble began to pulse with slow light as the magician brought it closer to his prisoner's face.

"It's a Living Stone, isn't it?" said Avender.

"Yes. Yours."

"I don't want it."

"Are you sure? Without it, your hand will never heal. But you must be quick. Once your body accustoms itself to what you have lost, nothing can ever be regained."

"Why should I care if my hand heals? You're just going to kill me anyway."

"Am I?" Slowly, Reiffen closed his fingers around the dark gem. "If that were my wish, I would have done so already. Dumped you in the privy until you bled to death. This is the second time you and I have been through this. I have no more wish to kill you now than I did twelve years ago in Backford. No, I only want to punish you."

His bad arm tucked against his chest, Avender pushed himself up onto his knees. A second attack of light-headedness kept him from rising farther. Chest heaving, he took several deep breaths, then looked up again at his old friend.

"If you're not going to kill me, what are you going to do?"

"I am not going to let you go, if that is what you hope. At least not right now. This matter with Hubley must be resolved first. And I must send a message to the world that I do not wish to be bothered by future rescue attempts. All the same, I assure you, you will be safe enough."

Avender glanced around at the walls of the low cave. "Your prison has little to recommend it."

"You will grow used to it very quickly. And how much easier to dig through this soft dirt," Reiffen scuffed the earth with the toe of his boot, "if you have both hands."

"How do I know it will work? Ferris's thimble didn't."

"That was because I instructed Mindrell to cut it off you. The magic worked, regardless. Your hand and fingers are now complete, wherever it was that Ferris stored your reliquary. They are, however, of little use without the rest of you."

In the end it was an easy choice. Much as he hated magic, Reiffen knew Avender would hate being a cripple even more.

"Very well," he said. "What do I have to do?"

"Only swallow the Stone. The magic will start to work at once."

Again the magician offered Avender the small green gem. Like an emerald heart, the Living Stone began to pulse once more. With great effort, Avender balanced himself on his knees and raised his good hand off the ground. Reiffen dropped the Stone into Avender's palm. Avender expected the rock to shift to a strong and rapid pulse, which was what Ferris had told him had happened to hers, but his continued feebly, its light erratic. The stone was only reflecting his own weakness, he thought, as his heart and body struggled to adapt to the loss of his hand. Maybe he would even die if he didn't accept the magician's offer.

He put the stone to his lips. Too dry, his mouth and tongue failed to swallow it. He lacked the strength to make them, his stomach recoiling at the magic.

"Mindrell, a cup of wine for Avender."

The bard produced a wineskin and a small clay cup. Spitting the stone into his hand, Avender accepted the drink. Stone and cup clicked together as he lifted them to his mouth, the dark wine rich and satisfying to his dry lips. With a third of the liquid left in the cup, he pulled his mouth away. Only after he had swung his right arm up to take hold of the cup did he remember his hand was gone. Stifling the urge to hurl both cup and stone across the cave, he managed to grasp the clay container by crooking his maimed arm against his chest. Stone in mouth, he brought the drink back to his lips and swallowed the last of the wine.

His throat still resisted, but this time he had better

self-command. The need to retch retreated. Like a gobbet of meat, the stone descended. He felt it all the way to his stomach, his throat swollen, but it went down easily enough despite its size because of its smoothness.

He felt better at once. Warmth flooded his belly; his light-headedness lifted. Around him the room came into sharper focus. Reiffen and Mindrell weren't so very far away. One quick burst, and he ought to be able to get past both of them, though he didn't see a way out in any of the walls. He was bigger and stronger than they were, and his hand didn't hurt nearly as much as it had. Perhaps he could even get Mindrell's dagger away from him before the bard knew what was happening.

As if he could see Avender's thoughts in his eyes, Reiffen took two steps backward. The bard, finding himself exposed, followed. Wiping the last of the wine off his lips, Avender stood.

"You had better unwrap your bandages," said the magician. "Otherwise the new hand will be unable to grow."

"Will it happen quickly, Your Majesty?" The bard watched Avender's hand closely, with what Avender thought was a hint of jealousy.

"Not fast enough for you to notice, harper," Reiffen replied. "But the spell does work. You will receive your own reward soon enough."

"Was that what he offered you to do his dirty work?" Avender shifted his gaze to the bard. "A Stone of your own?"

"Something like that. And my lady Giserre didn't ask me to start a war between magicians, just guard her granddaughter. Which is what I was doing."

"An excellent idea of my mother's," added Reiffen, "sending Mindrell to me. We know from past experience that he does good work. All the same, I shall have to prepare something extra to protect Hubley with, something special, to convince Ferris not to try sending another champion."

"Ferris didn't ask me to do anything except talk to you. But now that I see how much you've lost control, I wish I had been trying to steal her. If that was what I'd really come here to do, I'd never have botched the job."

A sudden perverse itching at the end of his right arm distracted Avender from saying more. Quickly he stripped the stained wrappings from his wrist, expecting to find fresh fingers growing out of the stump at the very least. Instead he saw what he had seen once or twice on battlefields, a raw and blackened wound. Thin strips of skin hung off the end of his wrist like threads on a ratty sleeve. Most of the flesh was seared black as a burnt roast where a heated blade had been pressed against the stump to seal the wound. But was that his imagination, or did the outside edge of his wrist look pinker, swollen like a healing scar?

"Enough. I have healed you as I said I would. It is time you began your imprisonment."

Looking up, Avender discovered Reiffen had half-raised his hands. Behind him the bard was picking up a shovel.

"*Back,*" intoned the magician.

Avender stumbled backward, his feet moving on their own. But they hadn't thought to coordinate with the rest of his body, and he soon found himself falling. Reaching out with his good hand, he twisted around to catch himself as he tumbled. A dark ditch loomed in front of him, the air suddenly thick with the scent of fresh digging. Avender fell directly into it, his hand scrabbling at the edge. Though he held his bad arm close against his chest, the pain of landing on his shoulder shook his entire body. Clods of earth knocked loose by his clawing hand fell across his cheek and ear.

Ignoring the pain, he braced his forearms on either side of the narrow grave and pushed himself back toward his feet. Reiffen and Mindrell appeared on the lip above.

"*Freeze,*" said Reiffen.

No longer able to move, Avender fell back. His arms and legs hung crabwise in the air as he settled on his back at the bottom.

"Bury him," said Reiffen.

The top of the bard's figure bent briefly out of sight. Avender heard the crunch of the shovel biting dirt. Then all of Mindrell reappeared and Avender watched as the first load of earth was dumped on his face. Several clumps struck him painfully in the eye, while others dropped straight into his gaping mouth. He tried to cough and shut his eyes: the cough stuck in his throat like an unscratched itch. His eyelids wouldn't close. Another shovelful followed the first, and a third. Avender realized he wasn't breathing.

Reiffen's cloak swayed over the edges of the grave. Another load of dirt and small stones showered across Avender's vision. When it was clear again he saw his old friend was gone.

It took a long time before Mindrell had shoveled enough dirt into the hole to cover Avender's face. Avender tried to curse both bard and mage, but his voice stuck in his throat the same as his cough. Dirt swaddled him like a blanket, tucking him tight against his earthen mattress. Unable even to scream, he boiled away inside, every inch of skin and bone ringing with Reiffen's treachery. Let him live? The magician was burying him alive! Avender would smother beneath his six feet of Grangore earth, buried where no one would ever find him. Already his lungs ached for air, but still his muscles wouldn't move. Dirt filled his mouth, packed as tight as that around his shoulders. Grit scratched his open eyes.

Only after he stopped feeling the soft thud of fresh earth laid on top of old did Avender realize he had held his breath far longer than was possible. And only then did he realize that Reiffen's magic was working after all.

And that he wasn't even going to be permitted the comfort of dying.

In the deeper warrens of his workshop, Reiffen returned to his daughter. Much as he would have liked to keep her away from this sort of thing, she couldn't very well remain alone in the castle. But she was a brave child, as well as bright, which made him proud. Not for her the night terrors of ordinary ten-year-olds. Nor, if he could help it, the nightmares of the more than ordinary either.

He had known Avender was up to something. It had been too long since the two of them had had any sort of serious talk; he had not been convinced that Avender had come all this way, and given up his deepest beliefs about magic, just to try and patch things up between Reiffen and his wife. Avender had to have had a different goal, and it had not been difficult for Reiffen to understand what it was. Ferris had sent their old friend to try and rescue Hubley. Unless the fool had come up with the idea on his own.

The thimble had given it all away, of course. Why else would Avender, who still had not come to grips with the presence of magic in the world, allow Ferris to give him so powerful a charm? He needed a way to make a quick escape, of course. That was why Reiffen had sent Mindrell up to the room with an axe and precise instructions about what he would have to do with it. And then he had been forced to offer certain gifts to Mindrell in order to persuade the bard to do what was needed. "Why," Mindrell had asked, "isn't letting Brizen's captain get away with the child just what my lady would want me to do?" "Not if it would lead me to lay waste to Valing to get the child back," Reiffen had answered. "Let her be, and Ferris and I will work our quarreling out." And then he had offered Mindrell the gift he was certain the bard would accept, and the thing had been done. Not that Mindrell would ever get the other prize he wanted, no matter how long he waited.

He found Hubley had fallen asleep on the cot in the small workroom where he had left her. Sandy looked up hopefully from the foot of the bed as the door opened, then settled his head back on his paws when he saw who it was.

"Wake up, dear heart," said the magician, using no magic.

Scrunching her small face, Hubley opened her eyes. "Did you finish your business, Father?"

"Yes."

"And Avender's okay?"

"Yes. The accident has been fixed."

"Did you punish the man who hurt him?"

"I did. He's doing his penance right now, filling a hole for me in one of the workrooms." Reiffen reminded himself that he would have to fetch Mindrell back to the castle when the work was done. No path led from that particular spot to any other.

"That's good." Hubley shuddered and shrank back against her pillows. "Whoever he is, he's lucky he didn't do anything to Avender you couldn't fix. Otherwise you'd have had to hang him."

"Or worse," added Reiffen. "When people hurt your friends and family, you have to make sure they never do it again."

"Avender is family," said Hubley confidently.

"Yes," her father agreed.

The child shivered. Some of Reiffen's anger returned as Hubley showed how much Avender's foolishness had frightened her. All that blood in her bed when the poor child woke up. Well, Reiffen knew how to take care of that particular memory. It was time he got started.

"Come, child. I want to show you something."

She took her father's hand. In nightgown and slippers she went with him into the wide stone passages Nolo and the other Bryddin had carved a dozen years before. Dwarf lamps shone palely on the walls, the darkness deep between them. Reiffen prided himself on using no more lamps in his workshops than the Dwarves would have used themselves. At the end of several chambers and passages Hubley had never seen before, they came to a wooden door. Opening it, Reiffen sent a small ball of illumination forward to reveal a low cave, completely natural, that the Dwarves had used as a focal point for their delving. Even before the rock was opened up, they had known it would be there. The roof of the cave was not much higher than Reiffen's head, but narrowed distantly to the floor on either side. The tallest space was toward the middle of the room, where the stream that trickled across the cave widened into a clear pool. Reiffen's magical light hovered over the pool, lighting its bottom.

Letting go his hand, Hubley ran toward the water. "Father! Why have you never brought me here before?"

"Careful. The water is cold."

"What are those black things?" Hubley bent over the pool, her slippers at the very edge, her hands on her knees.

"Mussels," said her father.

"Like the ones in Valing?"

"No, sweetheart. These aren't good to eat."

"What are they good for?"

"Other things."

Unused to the light, the mussels had closed up tight. Each was nearly as long as one of Reiffen's hands, their shells black as night. Clustered across the bottom of the pool, they resembled nothing so much as a bunch of upside-down bananas.

"What sorts of things?"

"I will show you."

Reiffen raised one hand to cast the spell.

MIMS

Oh Father, my father, I do love him so,
From the Deep of Vonn Kurr to the Bavadars' snow.
But if you do wish it I will let him go,
Though it end all my rapture and quicken my woe.

Oh Daughter, my daughter, that's not what I said,
It's not that you love him that fills me with dread.
But will he protect you the way that I can?
There's death in the world and he's only a man.

Oh Father, my father, that chance I must take,
Or else you might find, on some morn when you wake,
My flesh turned to marble, my bones never break,
My heart hard as stone for my true lover's sake.

—MINDRELL THE BARD

13

Hubley's Tenth Birthday Again

urk? Do you think Mother will be able to come to my birthday this year?"

Hubley took her eyes off the mirror long enough to look at the stone. Her hairbrush, however, continued to brush her hair. Neither hands nor eyes were necessary to keep that particular spell going, though there might be a problem if she tried to walk around.

"Is it your birthday again so soon?" asked Durk from his comfortable pillow.

"Don't tell me you forgot! This one's special. I'm going to be ten."

"Weren't you ten last year?"

"Last year I was nine."

"Really? I could have sworn you were ten."

"How would you know? You weren't even there."

"I wasn't? No wonder I'm confused. I suppose this old cobble of mine is wearing out at last. Ever since your father left me in that box for all those years I haven't been able to tell an iamb from a dactyl."

"You know it was only a month before Father found you, and it was only an accident he put you there anyway."

"Well it felt like a year," the stone grumbled. "Or maybe three or four. Though I do suppose it's hard to tell time when you're buried like that. Either way, I'm getting so old now, soon I won't even be able to remember the soliloquy from *The Anguished Knight*."

"You sound the same as ever to me."

Durk sniffed, despite the fact he didn't have a nose. "That's because this unassuming pebble that fate has vouchsafed me bears no mark of the countless sorrows I have endured. As the poet says:

"*So plain a face no other fact can tell;*
Both grief and joy lost within its homely shell."

Hubley snorted. "If you ask me, it's easy to tell what you're feeling. All I have to do is listen."

"Hmph. I don't always say what I think, you know."

Rolling her eyes, Hubley turned back to the mirror and shifted her brush to a more tangled section of hair.

"I had another dream last night," she said.

"You did? Was it as bad as the others?"

"No. This one was about my birthday."

"That's not so scary."

"It wasn't. But it felt like the others, like it was something that had already happened. Everyone was there, Mother and Giserre and Mims and Grandpa Berrel, and Avender and the king and queen. And Redburr, too, though I think he came later. And he was a bird, not a bear. We ate noodles with butter and green peas and Father made a tree grow in the middle of the garden and it shot up in the air. And when it came down all the leaves turned into my very own grammarye."

"Oh, yes. I remember that one quite well. Lots of explosions. The best birthday surprise your father ever cast. For once I had some idea what was going on."

"No you didn't. I told you, it was just a dream." Her exasperation caused Hubley's brush to tug harder at her hair, and she grimaced as it caught a tangle. Focusing her eyes on the mirror, she forced both herself and the brush to calm down.

"This time," she said when she was done, "the best birthday surprise would be if Mother and Grandmother came."

"Yes, it would," Durk agreed. "We haven't seen either of them in a long time."

"Father says I shouldn't get my hopes up. Mother's at a very important point in her experiment."

"That shouldn't stop Giserre."

"Don't you remember? Giserre's helping. And all the apprentices, too."

"Oh, right. I'd forgotten. It must be some spell they're working on, to take so many of them. I hope someone tells me about it when it's done. But what about Hern and Berrel?"

"Father says there's scrapie in Valing, so they can't leave either."

"Everyone's just so busy, aren't they? All the same, it's too bad they can't make time to visit you. I never had a family of my own, you know, until I was lucky enough to be gathered into the bosom of the acting community. So I know exactly how you feel."

"I know. You've told me lots of times."

"At least you still have your father. You should consider yourself lucky."

Her brushing finished, Hubley sat down on the couch. Durk meant well, but what he said often made her feel worse. After all, it wasn't like losing his family had ended up all right for him in the end, unless you thought being stuck as a rock better than being dead. Her father said that Mother's and his being apart was all the Gray Wizard's fault and, until they were strong enough to find a way to slay him, her parents were unlikely to be able to spend much time together. Castle Grangore was safer than Valing, which was why Hubley had to stay with her father. All the same, it didn't seem fair her mother couldn't visit them at least sometimes.

Her father arrived a few minutes later, already dressed for the party in Hubley's favorite cloak, the one with the manders embroidered across the chest. Sometimes, depending on how he moved, the manders seemed to slither and slide across the dark blue fabric on their own.

"Father!" Hubley bounced up from the couch and darted forward.

"Hello, sweetheart." Reiffen swept his daughter up in a glad hug. "I see you've been getting ready for the party. Are you done?"

"Oh, yes. Has Mother said she's coming?"

Carefully Reiffen lowered Hubley to the ground. His eyes scrunched in sympathy. "Sadly, no. The enchantment she is fashioning is far too delicate to be interrupted. They have reached a critical point."

Hubley tried hard not to cry. "It isn't fair. She could have at least come for my birthday."

"I think she should have come, too, but you know defeating the Wizard is the most important thing now. More important than birthdays, I'm sorry to say, even your tenth. However, she did tell me she would be coming for a visit soon."

"When?" Hubley crossed her arms stubbornly.

"She didn't give me a date. But she did send several presents. The first one is for right now."

Standing, the magician held out his arm. Hubley stepped back to give him room, her hands held expectantly beneath her chin. A dark red dress appeared draped across her father's arm.

"Oh, Father, it's beautiful!"

"It's from the best shop in Malmoret, your mother says."

"What's it look like?" asked Durk.

Taking the dress from her father, Hubley held it at arms' length. "Well, it's dark red, like roses, with ribbons on the shoulders and a belt to hold the waist. There's smocking on the top, and long skirts on the bottom."

"Sounds very grown up."

"May I see you in it?" asked Reiffen.

Hubley folded her arms across her chest and frowned in concentration.

"Change, change the dress I wear
To the one I throw up in the air."

As she spoke, she flung the lovely gown toward the ceiling,
but it was the plain gray robe she was wearing that floated to the
ground. From her shoulders to her ankles the red dress took its
place, with only a little tugging and wriggling to make it fit.

Her father stepped back for a better view. "I don't know which
is better, sweetheart, the dress or the spell you used to put it on."

"Thank you, Father."

"I wish I could see it," complained the stone.

"Shall we go down to the party?"

Grabbing a hair ribbon from the top of her dresser, Hubley
scooped up Durk, pillow and all, and followed her father downstairs.

Her heart sank all over again when they reached the dining
room. Only three places were set at the table. She had hoped at
least Nolo or Redburr would come, or even Wilbrim and his
mother. With just her father, Mindrell, and Durk, the day wasn't
going to be anything special at all. Even cake and presents
couldn't make it anything more than another long, boring evening in Castle Grangore.

Mindrell, who was already standing at the table, gallantly
pulled out her chair. "You look enchanting, Princess," he said as
he tucked the seat back in beneath her skirts. "A most becoming
shade. Your mother has a dress of nearly the same color, I recall."

Lifting the silver pitcher from the sideboard, he poured
lemonade into her cup. Outside, the sun had finally set, but in the
dining room of Castle Grangore magelight flooded from the
lamps and chandelier.

"Welcome, Princess." Her father bowed from the seat on her right. "The party is ready for your delectation."

They ate fresh noodles with butter and peas, just like in her dream. It was her favorite meal. Durk, whose cushion took the place of the table's centerpiece, did most of the talking. With Mindrell's occasional assistance, the stone sang songs and cracked jokes that Hubley generally didn't understand.

When it was time for cake, Reiffen cleared the table with a wave of his hand. Hubley had never actually seen her father wash dishes, but they always reappeared in the pantry cabinets after meals as spotless as if Mims herself had performed the cleanup. Whether it was the magic that did it, or some dishwasher in town her father used spells to send the crockery to and from, Hubley had never discovered. That he was in touch with people in town she had no doubt. He certainly didn't know how to bake a chocolate cake, and one of the first things she had learned about magic was that you had to know how to do things the slow way before you could use spells to do them quickly. The cake appeared at the second wave of the magician's hand, a massive concoction dripping with butter frosting and red sugar roses, hovering just above the table until Hubley blew out the ten sparkling candles.

She unwrapped her grandparents' gifts first. As usual, Giserre had knit her a beautiful sweater of the softest Valing wool. Lifting it from its wrapper, Hubley rubbed the soft yarn against her cheek and imagined she was hugging her grandmother. The smell of lavender and cedar tickled her nose.

Mims and Berrel gave her a patchwork quilt, which she hugged just as tightly as Giserre's sweater. From the apprentices she received the usual magical knickknacks: a silver thimble, several rolls of colored ribbon, a vial of sneezing powder, and a pot of jellied spider's eyes.

Last, before his own present, her father handed her a second gift from her mother. A small box, neatly tied in ribbon to match her red dress. Hubley shook it once, but nothing rattled. Her father's eyes danced as if he had been the one to outwit her rather than her mother. Bursting with curiosity, the child tore the ribbon off and pulled the box open. Inside, two moonstones lay swaddled in a paper nest. Small, jagged lines of red and yellow snaked across their pale surfaces.

Gently, Hubley picked them up. "Just like Mother's!"

"Yes." Reiffen smiled indulgently. "Uhle said he would make them into a pendant for you, if you want."

"Oh, yes!" Hubley cupped the stone pearls in front of her face and watched the streaks of tiny lightning dash back and forth.

"Would you like my present now?"

Hubley nodded. Her father always gave her the best presents, wrapped in magic. For her ninth birthday it had been nine golden finches that looked and sang like regular birds, only much prettier. Darting around the high-ceilinged library, they had looked like sunshine set loose inside the house until her father clapped his hands and each bird swooped down to drop a bit of jewelry into her hand, rings and pins and even a pair of brilliant earrings.

She wondered what he would give her this year.

Her father spread his arms wide. The manders on his robe flicked their tails like lazy fish. Throughout the room the magelight flickered and died. As evening darkened the hall, a last ray of light abruptly pierced the middle window, some trick of the sun reflecting off the castle towers. Its thin beam revealed something curved and fluted lying beside Hubley's glass of lemonade. Pale pink and alabaster, the shell gleamed as Reiffen picked it up.

"Choose a sound," he said.

"A sound?" asked Hubley.

"Yes. Your favorite."

Hubley frowned. "I don't know. A purring cat?"

A purr swept thickly through the room. Though not loud, everyone heard it clearly.

"When did Mittens come in?" asked the stone nervously. "Remember, it took a week to find me the last time that sly creature knocked me off my pillow."

"It's just magic," said Hubley. She watched her father sweep the shell through the air around him, scooping up a draft of sound.

"What sort of magic?" the stone went on.

"We don't know yet," said Hubley.

"You'll find out soon enough," said Reiffen. "Another sound, please."

"Thunder?" suggested Durk.

The room rocked with the blast, though there was no flash of light. Hubley grabbed the edge of the table to steady herself, but it was only the noise that had startled her. The room remained undisturbed.

"What about the wind in the trees?" asked Mindrell. "Can you do that?"

"Yes."

This time Hubley reached up to hold her hair in place, but there was no wind, despite the rustle of leaves from the ceiling. As if the sky were breathing, the whispering rose and fell, a sighing tickle to the air.

"Valing Falls," she said, beginning to get into the spirit of the game.

The hall filled with a second rumble, this one steady as pouring rain. Hubley was sure the floor was trembling beneath her feet. Instead of fading, the sound grew stronger, pressing against her chest and nose and ears. Only when Reiffen had finished waving the shell slowly back and forth did the sound finally vanish.

"Apples falling."

"Surf."

"A barking nokken."

The magician caught them all. Snow falling on firs, a dog greeting its master, songbirds in the morning, and a score or so more filtered into the shell. Hubley listened, enthralled, as each noise cascaded through the room, solemn or loud, creaking or gay. Closing her eyes, she imagined herself in a whirling storm that whipped from place to place across the world. A deep forest. An evening beach. The lip of a well.

"My soliloquy from the *The Anguished Knight*."

Hubley frowned. Durk, unaware of her annoyance, explained himself further. "It's my very best, you know. Always moves an audience to tears. As long as we're picking our favorite sounds, there's no reason not to mention it."

"I've never heard it," said the mage. "Perhaps if you recite it."

"My pleasure." With a sound like someone drawing a deep breath, the stone began.

> *"As time, like jagged stones falls tumbling down*
> *Life's steep, uneven cliffs, my fumbling frown*
> *Doth journey onward, ceaseless as the sea.*
> *Unstopped, it like unstoppered wine doth seep*
> *Away despite my wretched reach to keep*
> *My heart's desire ever close to me . . ."*

Mindrell coughed into his hand but the stone, unstopped as his verse, decanted on. Hubley didn't mind. If the seashell was, as she guessed, a way to hold a few chosen sounds forever, she didn't mind at all if the voice of a friend mingled with the singing birds and tumbling waves.

"Can you do Mother?" she asked when the stone was finished.

Mindrell's eyebrows rose.

"I can," said Reiffen.

For the first time in what felt like years and years, Ferris's voice filled the library.

> *"Swim, little pup,*
> *The lake is deep,*

The fish are tasty,
The cliffs are steep.
Tomorrow's for fishing,
Tonight's for sleep.
So swim little pup
And you'll never weep."

Images of her mother singing that song danced at the edge of Hubley's memory like nokken racing beside a Valing canoe. Eagerly she reached for them, but none would stay. Only the nasty dreams, which she'd been having more and more of lately, lasted long enough to linger these days.

"I think we have enough now," said her father.

The lights returned, their soft illumination suddenly bright. Reiffen offered his present to his daughter. Hubley accepted the gift with both hands, surprised at how heavy the shell was though it looked so delicate. The outer surface was rough and worn, the inner curve smooth as glass.

"To hear what is inside, you must hold it close to your ear," her father told her.

She lifted the shell to her cheek. Faintly, as if from the other side of Grangore Vale, she heard geese honking.

"If you want everyone to hear, press the large knob."

"This one?" Holding the shell in front of her, Hubley raised her thumb over one of the stubby bumps at the closed end of the shell. Her father nodded.

The throbbing drum of Valing Falls flooded the room once more. Hubley wondered what had happened to the geese. Pressing the knob again only made the sound of the waterfall cease.

"How do I make it play what I want?" she asked impatiently.

Her father smiled in that way she knew meant he wasn't going to tell. "That is for you to discover on your own. If you're ever going to be a real magician, you will need to learn how to unlock magic's secrets. What I have given you is more than a toy, Daughter."

"Thank you, Father." Hubley curtsied, the way her Grandmother Giserre had taught her. When she looked up she was already fiddling with the shell again, poking at the various knobs and ridges, her mouth fixed in concentration.

"I wish I had one of those," said Durk. "I wouldn't need actors anymore if I did. I could just store all the parts myself, then play them back like a piper on his flute."

"You'd still need someone to push the buttons for you," said Mindrell.

The party moved on from cake to fruit and cheese. Taking his lute from his shoulder, Mindrell sang a lovely ballad about a little girl who loved her father so much she turned into a stone statue when a prince wished to marry her. Only after the prince had saved her father's kingdom from the civil war started by the king's uncle, did the princess's cold mantle fall away so she could marry her prince. Hubley thought it a rather silly song but, since Mindrell had composed it especially for her birthday, she clapped politely when he was done.

A crescent moon joined the stars in the wide window above the hall. Hubley yawned, concealing her sleepiness behind chocolaty fingers. As with all her birthdays, she didn't want this one to end, even if there were so few guests to share it with. But being ten was special all the same. A shiver of delight passed through her, and not just because of all the chocolate she had eaten. Her parents had always said her magical training would begin in earnest once she was ten. And her mother was coming home soon.

Wiping her fingers, she raised the shell back to her ear. This time the sound was the jingling of sleigh bells from sleds racing across the snow. Holding the shell close in front of her, she shook it vigorously while concentrating on her mother. So much of magic was about forcing things to do what you wanted, maybe that was all she needed to do here. Instead she heard her father say,

"Hubley, we have one last thing to do to finish your birthday."

Looking up, she saw the bard and the stone were gone. More time had passed than she thought since Mindrell had finished his song. As usual, she had gotten so absorbed in what she was doing she had forgotten about everyone else in the room.

Happily, she took her father's hand. They crossed the castle from east to west, magelight hovering in the air before them. At the base of the Magicians' Tower, Reiffen unlocked the door that led down to the workrooms. Hubley shivered with delight: her lessons were going to start right away! And maybe now that she was ten her father would start teaching her entire spells rather than just parts of them.

At the bottom of the stair, Reiffen opened a second door with a wave of his hand. Following the passage beyond to its end, Hubley was delighted when they stopped outside a room she had never entered. Being ten was already as good she had ever imagined.

The third door slid open as silently as the previous two, revealing an ordinary workroom. With a flick of his wrist, the magician sent his magelight arrowing across the chamber to fasten itself to a cresset on the far wall. Plucking a large key from the air, he inserted it into the lock of the door beside the lamp.

The key turned with a heavy click. Releasing it, the magician twisted his long, thin fingers to set the key spinning slowly in the lock on its own. Left, right, left again. Each time the tumblers clicked, the large key sank deeper into the mechanism and reversed direction. Hubley counted each revolution, wondering if her father was going to test her on it later.

The door opened. The magician stepped back and gestured for his daughter to go first. Hubley stopped as soon as she was inside. A memory she didn't recognize flashed across her mind, bright as lightning at midnight. Her father steadied her with a touch; the memory faded.

Pointing his finger here and there, Reiffen anchored mage-lights to several knobs in the stone. Hubley saw at once they had reached a cave unlike the others. This chamber was too rough for Dwarven work: in truth, it looked more natural than carved. Though the room was wide, only in the very center was it tall enough for her father to stand. A stream ran out of the darkness on the right, pooling in the center, before disappearing again into the gloom on the other side.

She began to feel afraid, though she didn't know why. Her father led her forward. Near the pool, her memory attacked her again. This time she nearly fell as the blaring images blasted through her mind too quickly to understand. Reiffen laid his hand lightly on her shoulder once more and the memories retreated, though not quite as far as before.

She was sure it was the pool causing her unease. The closer she came to it, the worse the memories grew. A clump of large, black mussels fed in the thin current along the bottom.

"Father. I don't like this place."

"It's all right, sweetheart. You've been here before. Nothing will harm you."

"I don't remember being here before." Her lower lip trembled. Not even in the strange dreams now clamoring for her attention had she ever visited this place, or anything resembling it.

"Of course you don't. The magic wouldn't have worked if you had."

Trusting her father, she took another step. Perhaps if he had held her hand she might have done better, but he was already examining the pool. The pressure building in her head burst: her dream of the night before came rushing back, only this time it was a nightmare. The smiling faces of her parents turned to howling skulls. Redburr grabbed at her with talons and bloody beak. The moonstones blinked like bloodshot eyes. Then all the sense she had of what was happening dissolved. Her memories, real and imagined, swirled together in a frightening, snapping mass, devouring one another like hawks tearing at pigeons in the sky.

She screamed. Her father's face loomed against the low ceiling, concern in his eyes.

"Here now, Hubley. Don't be afraid."

He reached for her with a hand like Redburr's claws. Unable to stand the whirlwind in her head any longer, Hubley turned and fled. Back through the small door she ran, through the next room and into the corridor beyond. Her footsteps rattled against the stone like dry bones. Already her head felt lighter, as if she had left all those troubling memories in the cave. She knew her father wouldn't harm her, but she wanted nothing more to do with that pool. Perhaps if she ran all the way back to the bottom of the stair he would pick her up and carry her in his arms the way he had when she was small. And maybe they could go back to the dining room and he would show her how to call her mother's voice from her brand-new shell.

A side door opened. Pale light spilled down the passage in either direction. A tall man wearing a Dwarven lamp at the center of his forehead followed the light into the hall.

"This way, Hubley."

Grabbing her wrist, he pulled her inside. The door slammed shut behind her.

14

Mims the Magician

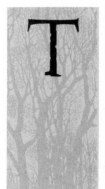

The man with the lamp kept a firm hold on Hubley's wrist as he pulled her into the workroom. His face was grim, but he didn't look like he meant to hurt her.

"Let me go!" she shouted. "Don't you know who my parents are?"

Instead of answering, the man pulled her closer. In the thin light from the lamp at his forehead, Hubley saw he was as old as Mims and Hern, with gray in his hair and crinkles at the corners of his eyes.

Something hard and cold scraped her wrist as she tried to pull free. A thimble. So, he was a magician. Pinning her arm tightly under his, the man gripped the iron charm with his other hand.

Her father's voice floated down the hall.

"Hubley? Where are you? There's no need to be afraid."

"Father, help! There's a man—!"

She found herself somewhere else. Instead of stone, the walls around her changed to rough wooden logs; the floor under her red dress turned to dirt. On either side, shuttered windows blocked out what Hubley assumed was the night. Unless they were underground.

Her captor let her go. Whirling, she cried out, "Take me home at once! My father is so going to turn you into a slug when he catches you. And my mother, too!"

Still paying no attention to her, the man unscrewed the lamp from the circlet around his head, dropped the gem into a pouch hanging from his neck, and proceeded to rub his little finger where the end had reattached itself to his hand. Hubley noticed a reliquary glittering in the firelight on top of the table between her and the hearth. If her parents had only trusted her with a thimble, she would be home now, instead of waiting for them to rescue her.

That they would rescue her, she had no doubt at all.

"Are you going to answer me?" she demanded, stamping her foot.

The man smiled. "You haven't changed."

Hubley scowled. Whoever he was, he didn't seem at all concerned about what was going to happen to him when her parents arrived. And why did he think she hadn't changed? She'd never even met him.

"My father's going to put you in the deepest dungeon he can find when he catches you," she said.

"I'll just escape again if he does."

Her discomfort increased. Though she couldn't put her finger on it, there was something familiar about him.

"Who are you?" she asked, curiosity finally elbowing her anger aside.

"Don't you recognize me?" The man spread his arms so she could get a good look at him. "I know I've changed, but I wouldn't think it'd be so much you'd have forgotten me."

He smiled again. This time Hubley nearly recognized him. His smile was so nice she almost wished he was a friend.

"Well I did forget," she insisted, "so you're going to have to tell me."

"I'm Avender."

"No you're not. You're too old." But even as she spoke, Hubley realized that was exactly who the man reminded her of. An older Avender, who'd gone away and come back after many years. The smile was the same, warm and friendly, with just the slightest hint of sadness.

But Avender hadn't gone away.

"Avender's not a magician," she added.

"You're right, I'm not."

"Oh, yes you are. Only magicians have thimbles."

The man glanced at the iron cap still remaining on his left hand. "That's not true. Your father gave one to Mindrell once."

"Well, I'm sure he didn't give you yours."

"You're right. He didn't."

"Then who did? Four people know how to cast that spell, unless Plum's learned it since he went to Valing."

"The person who did should be coming back any minute now. I think she's milking the cow."

"You know, you're being really silly pretending to be Avender. Avender would never take me from my parents. He's one of my father's best friends."

"I'm afraid the last time we saw each other, your father and I didn't part on very good company." The man claiming to be Avender flexed his left hand. "And I didn't take you from your parents, just your father. It's time you spent some time with your mother."

Hubley's heart jumped. "You're taking me to Mother?"

"Not right now. But soon."

"Why not right now?"

"Because your mother's the first place your father's going to look for you."

"So? That's even better. We'll all be together."

Before the man could answer, the door behind Hubley swung open. An old woman entered carrying a pail of milk, her thimble clicking against the bucket's handle. If the man calling himself Avender wasn't a magician, the old woman certainly was. Like Hubley's mother and Trier, she wore a plain, brown dress with bulging pockets, and more pockets in her apron as well.

Handing Avender her pail, the old woman smiled at her prisoner in a welcoming sort of way, as if kidnapping was one of the nicest things you could do for someone instead of one of the meanest.

"Hello, Hubley."

"Are you the magician?" Hubley asked suspiciously.

"I am."

"Who taught you your spells?"

"Your father and mother."

"When? I know all my parents' apprentices."

"No you don't. Your mother's taken on a few new ones since she left Castle Grangore. It's been a long time."

"But you're so old! Mother and Father only have young apprentices."

"I am old," the woman admitted. "But it doesn't seem to affect my spell casting at all."

"What's your name?"

"Mims."

"That's not a name." Hubley stamped her foot again. "That's what people call their grandmothers in Valing."

"If Mims is good enough for grandmothers, it's good enough for me." Her long, gray braid swinging behind her, the old woman pulled an iron pan and three plump stickles, already cleaned, from the cabinet built into the side of the hearth.

"Is it true you're taking me to see my mother?"

"Yes." Scooping a little milk out of the pail with a small cup, the woman filled the bottom of the pan and laid it on the grill over the fire.

Hubley flopped into the nearest chair. She hadn't liked that place her father had taken her to, so it would serve him right if she stayed away. "Then I suppose I'll stay here with you till you do. I don't care who you are or how you know magic, as long as I get to see my mother."

"Don't worry," the woman soothed. "You'll understand it all

eventually. Avender, fetch me an onion. Hubley likes a little flavor with her fish."

Despite her recent feast of noodles and chocolate cake, Hubley's mouth watered at the thought of fresh fish. Still, she did wonder how the old woman knew fish with milk and onions was one of her favorite meals.

The milk in the pan began to bubble, so Mims added the stickles. "Was there any trouble getting away?" she asked her companion.

The man tossed the onion peel into the fire. "It worked just as you said. I didn't set off a single alarm."

"And Reiffen didn't see you?"

"No."

"Good. If he had, everything might have been spoiled."

"You're sure he can't follow us?"

Mims shook her head. "He knows where we are, but he's never been anywhere near here. He can't travel closer than a day away, even if he flies. All the same, we'll have to move soon. If we stay in one place too long, he'll catch us eventually."

"Of course he will," said Hubley. "My father's the best magician there is."

"Yes. And he cast a spell on you so he would always know where you are."

"He did? Then why did he—" Hubley pointed her chin accusingly at Avender. "Why'd he say Father's going to look for me with Mother if he already knows I'm here?"

"Your father's going to think it was your mother who brought you here. And it's easier for him to get to your mother in Valing than to get to us here. Once your mother tells him she has nothing to do with what we've done, he'll come after us. That's when we'll leave."

"And go to Valing?"

"No. Your father can get back to Valing any time he wants. We have to find someplace he can't get to quickly, then bring your mother there. I haven't decided where yet." The old woman flipped the fish thoughtfully. "Maybe some place in the Stoneways."

Hubley was dreaming about seeing her mother for the first time in a year when Mims served up the fish. She didn't quite trust these two yet, but she was fairly sure they weren't going to hurt her. Besides, her parents would find her eventually even if the old woman was lying. And it wasn't as if she was being badly treated. While Mims served out the fish, the man brought out a loaf of bread from the cupboard and sliced it into thirds.

"Thank you, Avender," said Mims.

Hubley looked from her fish. "Why do you keep calling him Avender?"

"Because that's his name."

"It is not. He's too old."

The man sopped up the milk on his plate with a piece of bread and looked at Mims. The magician's mouth curled thoughtfully. "You're right, Hubley," she said. "He is too old, but that doesn't mean he isn't Avender. I'd answer your questions if I could, but it's still too soon. You'll understand it all better in a few days. Once you start remembering things, everything will make a lot more sense."

"Remembering things? What things?"

"The things you've been dreaming about."

"How do you know about my dreams?"

"I know about more than just your dreams. For example, I know your father gave you a shell today for your birthday. And that Mindrell sang that dreadful song about the girl turning into a statue."

Hubley's spoon clattered against her plate. Had she fallen into some trap of the Wizard's after all? How could Mims know what had happened in Castle Grangore? But these people seemed so nice, and their cottage was so cozy. From what she'd heard about her father's time in Ussene, there had been nothing nice about the Wizards, or their fortress.

"Who are you?" she asked.

"I already told you. Mims the magician. And I don't work for Fornoch, if that's what you're thinking. Soon I'll take you to see your mother, but we have a few things to take care of first. You're going to have an exciting few days. You might even learn a few spells."

Hubley had an idea that, even if all she did was see her mother, being stolen from Castle Grangore was going to prove worth the trouble. She just hoped her father wouldn't be too worried while she was gone.

By the time the meal was finished, Hubley had grown sleepy. Yawning, she wondered if Mims had put something in the fish. It was just the sort of thing she'd have done if she wanted to keep a prisoner from escaping. But it had been a long day, too, and she might really just be tired.

At her second yawn, Mims left Avender to do the dishes and led Hubley up a ladder to the sleeping loft above the hearth. A pair of soft beds framed the space behind the chimney, the upstairs warmer than the room below. Hubley found she was so tired she got into the nearest bed without bothering to take off her dress or shoes.

"Sleep well." Mims covered her with a bright quilt that looked a good deal like one of Hern's. Come to think of it, the old woman looked a little like Hern, too. Maybe that was why she called herself Mims. "When you wake, you'll be on your way to see your mother."

"Good. But why are you being so stubborn about Father coming too? Don't you like him?"

"On the contrary, I like him nearly as much as you do." The old woman frowned. "The truth is, Hubley, your mother isn't in Valing because of some spell she's working on. She's there because she and your father had a fight and haven't been able to sort things out since. Your father won't let you visit her, and he won't let your mother visit you, either."

"That's not true! Mother can come home any time she wants."

"That might have been true at first, though she really didn't want to because of the way your father was behaving. But, after the problem with Avender, your father wouldn't let anyone come to Castle Grangore at all."

"What problem with Avender?"

"He tried to rescue you once before."

"He did? I don't remember that. All I remember is that I was very angry with him, because the last time he was here he went away without saying good-bye."

With a shock, Hubley stopped speaking. A moment ago she hadn't thought there was anything special about Avender's having been away, but now she remembered something about a crow, and Avender and her father leaving in the middle of her birthday. It almost felt like one of her dreams. Hubley knew magic had a habit of mixing things up, but, until now, she had never known herself to be the one who got muddled by the mixing.

A vision of mussels feeding at the bottom of a pool paraded suddenly through her mind. "Has Father done something to my memory?" she asked.

Mims nodded solemnly. "But it's not that simple. A lot more is going on than just the fight between your parents. Your mother doesn't know anything about what Avender and I have done, and it's better it stay that way until after your father visits her. And there's Fornoch to think about, too. Things are happening right now that will finally make it possible for your parents to fight him. And you, too."

"Me?" Her father had always told Hubley she'd help when they fought the Gray Wizard, but she had thought she'd be allowed to grow up first.

"Don't worry." Mims pulled the quilt up under Hubley's chin. "You won't have to do much. Most of the burden will be on your father and mother."

"But I'll help them, right?"

"Yes. More than they'll ever know. What's important now is, if you want to see your mother, you're better off with Avender and me than with your father."

The magician left. Hubley tried hard to listen to what she and the man were discussing in the room below, but their voices were too low. She wondered if she ought to cast an invisibility spell and sneak outside. There was always the chance Mims and the man who called himself Avender weren't really going to take her to see her mother. But no, she preferred to hope they were telling the truth. Asking herself what her parents would have done in her place, she decided they would have stayed. After all, her father had chosen to go back to the Wizards and learn magic, even after Redburr and her mother had rescued him.

She finally slept, weariness overcoming everything else she had been through that evening. But her worry remained, which made her rest fitful. Scraps of dreams flitted in and out of her thoughts; bits of memory and spell jumbled together like toys in a messy toy box, so crammed she couldn't tell which was which, or what was real. Spells she might have known, friends she might have missed for years and years. And some of the bits seemed to come together while she slept, like pieces from the wooden puzzles she liked to work on with her father: long evenings with him and Mindrell she'd never remembered, and halves of spells that fit together for the first time.

She heard Mims and Avender talking, though she had no idea if their voices were real, or part of her dreaming.

"Should I go up now?" Avender said.

"No. Nothing's going to happen for a while."

"But she's really going to remember the spell?"

"Yes."

"What if she starts asking questions?"

"You can tell her whatever she wants to know once the two of you have left. Though you might find you're going to be in way too much of a hurry to talk about anything for a while."

"Can't you at least tell me what to expect? What's going to happen once we get there?"

"No. Just remember not to use your other thimble until it's absolutely necessary. It'll take you straight to Fornoch if you do."

"You've already told me that three times. Believe me, I understand. But can't you tell me anything else? It might save a lot of trouble."

"Or make everything worse. Believe me, nothing is as bad as knowing more than you're supposed to. Especially when there's nothing you can do about it."

"I'd feel a lot better if you were coming with us."

"I've told you a hundred times, I can't. There's too much else to do. I have to be in a dozen places at once."

"If anyone can do it, you can."

The voices paused for a moment, as if Mims and the man who called himself Avender were sipping tea.

"How's your hand?" she asked.

"Fine. Reattaching a finger hurt a whole lot less than reattaching the whole thing."

Certain the entire conversation was only part of her dream, Hubley snuggled deeper under the quilt. Who'd ever heard of anything as silly as reattaching hands, anyway?

15

The College

In the ballroom of the New Palace, a thousand Wilbrims flexed their narrow swords in a thousand mirrors. A thousand Stokes bent close to show them how to hold their blades. And, at the other end of the hall, a thousand Fenners sliced the air with long, thin weapons of their own.

Willy handed Hubley his sword. "You should be doing this," he said. "You're the know-it-all."

Knowing he was right, Hubley accepted the weapon and spread her skirts. But what were they thinking? Her long red dress was sure to trip her at the first lunge. Besides, her parents had never taught her how to fence, not even with magic.

Her father whispered in her ear. "Fear not, sweetheart. Nothing can harm you now."

She looked up, but her father was nowhere in sight. At the same moment the thousand Fenners lunged at her with a thousand laughing grins. Hubley didn't even know they'd attacked until she felt the sharp pressure of their swords' point entering her shoulder. Dark blood welled up through her beautiful gown like juice from a bruised strawberry.

"Say," called Stoke. "That's not fair. She wasn't even looking."

"She was when I started," said Fenner. "Only an idiot turns away in the middle of a duel."

Hubley gasped a second time as the thousand Fenners pulled

their swords out of her shoulder. Her skin crawled. Really. Wriggling and puckering, it groped its way back together from either side of the wound. The stain on her dress turned green.

Horrified, her friends backed away. Even Fenner recognized magic when he saw it. No wonder her father had told her not to be afraid. He had given her a Living Stone. But that was awful; she wasn't supposed to have a Stone of her own until she was grown up. Every magician knew you couldn't give Living Stones to children, not unless you wanted them to stay children forever.

She ran. A thousand other Hubleys ran beside her. Slashing out with Willy's sword, she smashed the first mirror she came to. The other Hubleys cascaded to the floor, eyes and elbows and long brown hair winking from the shards. A stair emerged from the dark on the other side. Grabbing the railing, she began to climb.

Her father followed. But how could it be her father? He loved her. It had to be the Wizard, pretending to be someone he wasn't. He had done it often enough before. Looking back, she saw she was right. Fornoch's long strides ate the stairway five and six steps at a time as he closed the gap behind her. His black eyes gleamed.

Bursting with terror, Hubley rushed on. Somewhere above was the palace roof, with its potted orange trees and stars. Her mother was waiting for her there. If Hubley could just reach her in time, she'd be safe. From Wizards, and everything else.

The stair went on and on. Hubley clenched her jaw. She knew she was dreaming: there had never been mirrors in the palace ballroom. Her nightmare was doing the usual job of trying to fool her into thinking she was never going to get where she wanted, only this time it was an endless stair rather than the usual boot-eating mud, or sewing that was never done. The trick was to make the dream give way. Although she didn't remember the exact number of floors in the New Palace, she knew it wasn't more than five or six. She really should be at the top by now, and she would be, if she just concentrated hard enough. Perhaps if she focused very, very hard, the way she did with her magic, she would find the end around the very next turn.

Her plan worked. The top of the stair appeared. Outside, leafless orange trees showed stars instead of fruit hanging from their branches. Before the Wizard could grab her, Hubley bolted through the door.

Chill wind flicked her face and hair. With a shock, she realized the dream was over. Dream wind was never this cold, or dream stars so bright. Dream branches never creaked quite so realistically, as if they might break at any minute. In fact, she didn't think she'd ever heard anything creak in her dreams at all. But how had she gotten from the warm cottage to a freezing orange grove high above Malmoret?

And who was holding her hand?

"Mims was right." Letting go her fingers, the man who called himself Avender looked around. "The traveling spell has come back to you. It looks like you've taken us to the roof of the New Palace."

Hubley saw at once he was right. The view was exactly as she remembered it.

"The only place worse," he went on, "would be Castle Grangore. We have to get out of here. If your father shows up, you'll never see your mother."

The thought of never seeing her mother was more than enough to convince Hubley to do what the man said.

"How did we get here?" she asked as he pulled her toward the entrance to the stair.

"I already told you, you cast a traveling spell. Don't ask me how. All Mims said is that those mussels in that cave your father took you to have a tendency to leak."

Hubley swallowed hard, but the uneasiness creeping up her spine didn't settle back down. "She knows about the mussels, too?"

"Yes. She said there's a lot of magic stored in them, and that you probably picked some of it up when your father brought you to the cave. From what just happened, I'd say it was a traveling spell. Which must have been why Mims told me to make sure I kept hold of your hand after you fell asleep. I certainly didn't bring us here."

They tore around the first and second turns in the stair. "But I don't know the traveling spell," Hubley said. "Father told me he wouldn't teach it to me till I was ten."

"Well, you're ten now. Can you remember how you did it?"

Hubley poked around in her head for some clue as to how she'd brought them to the New Palace, but found nothing.

"Uh-uh."

"That's too bad." Avender frowned as they rounded another turn. "We could get out of here a lot quicker if you did. Now we'll have to find another way."

They met a guard on the ground floor. The man was staring up at them as they came down the last few steps, their thumping descent having given them away. Although he made no real effort to stop them, he didn't move aside either, so Avender knocked him down. Hubley's throat tightened at the sound of Avender cracking the man's head with the pommel of his sword; the guard slumped to the floor.

"Why'd you do that?" she asked.

"So he can't sound the alarm before we get away."

Still running, he led Hubley through several hallways and down another short flight of steps. A door opened to the kitchen; they stepped carefully over the grubby boy sleeping on the floor just beyond. From a countertop along the way, Avender took the opportunity to stuff his rucksack with two leftover loaves of bread and several carrots.

Beyond the kitchen, they followed another short passage to a small courtyard separated from the street by an iron fence. Motioning for Hubley to wait, Avender tiptoed to the sentry box at the side of the gate. Peering inside, he turned and waved her forward. The gate squeaked as Avender opened it; the sleeping sentry snuffled at his post but didn't wake. Hubley and Avender slipped outside, closing the gate behind them as softly as they could.

"What was that?"

The sentry stumbled out of his box. Avender dragged Hubley into the shadows on the other side of the street. Confused, the sentry opened the gate and looked up and down the avenue, but neither the stars nor the few lights still on in the palace revealed Hubley and Avender's hiding place. Scratching his head, the guard shut the gate with a clang and went back to his box.

"If I called out," Hubley whispered, "that guard would come rescue me."

"He'd have to fight me first," Avender replied. "Then, if I didn't kill him, he'd take you to the king, who'd just give you back to your father. Is that what you want?"

"Wouldn't Brizen take me to Mother if I asked? Queen Wellin would."

"Your father's probably here already. He wouldn't let him."

Still set on seeing her mother, Hubley decided to keep following Avender along the starlit road. Through crooked alleys and back lanes they wound their way toward the center of town. Only when they reached the Kingsway did she recognize where they were, the unlit bulk of the Old Palace looming against the sky on their left. But, instead of following the Kingsway out of town, Avender led them back into the narrow streets on the other side.

When they came out onto a wider avenue a second time, Hubley guessed they were at the back of the Old Palace. On one side of the street rose the palace's tall, dark wall; on the other loomed the slightly shorter but equally dark barrier of some ancient baron's residence. Halfway along the shorter wall a deep entranceway opened like the mouth of a gaping carp.

Roosting pigeons fluttered in fright as Avender led Hubley

into the opening and up a flight of steps. Overhead, an iron clapper boomed. Reaching out, she felt the smoothness of old, worn wood beneath the tips of her fingers. Her heart's thumping grew.

"Is Mother inside?" she asked.

"Your mother?" The man who called himself Avender sounded surprised. And, for the first time, he sounded exactly like Avender, too. Unable to see him in the dark, Hubley was no longer distracted by his odd age. With a sigh of relief, she decided he really was her old friend. But how had he gotten so old?

"Don't you recognize the College?" he asked.

"The College? Why would I recognize that? I've never been there. No girl has."

"That's not true. Mothers come to pick up their sons all the time."

The door opened abruptly in the middle of Avender's second knock. The light of a single candle revealed a narrow, pinched face peering out from the darkness. Shadows like tiny caves wavered beneath the crusty ridges of eyebrow, lip, and nose.

"Come back tomorrow," said the face crossly. The eyes flicked dismissively over Hubley, not noticing the cut and color of her gown. "New pupils are only admitted in the morning."

Avender held the door open with his hand. "This isn't a new student, Nouse. We're just passing through."

The porter lifted his candle to get a better look at the pair on his doorstep. "Here, who d'you think you are, anyway? And how do you know my name?"

"I knew you, Nouse, when old Ulbrich first let you sweep the floors. Don't you recognize me?"

Nouse, whom Hubley thought looked even older than Avender, squawked loudly. "I never set eyes on you in my life. And even if I had, I still wouldn't be letting you in, not in the middle of the night. Albwin's Chief Fellow now, not Ulbrich. Say, that isn't a girl you got with you, is it?"

The porter's voice rose to a high-pitched squeak as he got his first good look at Hubley.

Avender forced his way inside, dragging Hubley with him. Eyes goggling in dismay, Nouse scurried off in search of his master. Without the porter's lamp to show them the way, Avender was obliged to stop and pull out his Dwarf lamp.

"We'll need this where we're going," he said. Like a drop of morning sunlight, the jewel glowed in his palm.

Wondering why he didn't screw the lamp into his silver headband, Hubley followed him down the hall.

They descended at the first stair. The rough stone, carved long ago by men, felt much heavier than the Dwarven work Hubley was used to in Castle Grangore. She found herself stooping, though there was plenty of room overhead, half afraid the roof would collapse at any moment.

They passed more than a few side passages, but Avender seemed sure of the way. Soon they reached a musty storeroom. Rats squeaked as Avender cleared aside a tumbled pile of schoolboy slates from the back wall, revealing a low door. Producing a heavy key from his pocket, he unlocked the door and pushed it open with a long creak like bones breaking.

Shadows stalked behind them as they entered the next room. Raising his hand, Avender shone his lamp on a section of the far wall. A barrel of broken fencing masks glittered in the light like silver shrouds, the black tears in the fabric looming emptily.

Behind the masks, a thin line appeared in the stone.

Hubley had heard of secret Dwarf doors before, but she'd never seen one. Fascinated, she watched the pale line extend upward. When it reached a spot nearly level with Avender's head, it turned sharply to the right. Another few feet, and it made a second turn toward the floor. Pushing the barrel out of the way, Avender exposed the wall completely. The line grew downward until the door's outline had been traced in soft silver across the stone. A moment later a small, glowing dimple appeared in the center. Avender slipped his lamp into the spot with a low click.

"Let's hope I'm strong enough to open it by myself," he said, putting his back to the wall. "Some of these Dwarf doors are heavy."

The room darkened as he covered the lamp with his shoulders and began to push. Only the pale glow of the door's outline remained. Hubley heard grunts and feet scuffing on the floor, and a slow, hollow scraping.

The thin light returned when he was done. The stone had pushed backward to reveal a black tunnel. Retrieving his lamp, Avender rolled his broad shoulders to get the cricks out of his neck.

"Come on." He beckoned Hubley forward.

A new, brighter light suddenly flooded the cramped space from behind them.

"No farther, sir, if you please," said a voice.

A stranger in long robes and with a snow-white beard stood in the entrance to the room, a crossbow trained on Avender. Behind him crouched Nouse with a lantern.

"Albwin?" asked Avender, still sitting on the floor.

The stranger's eyes narrowed. "You have the advantage of me, sir. Have we met?"

Nouse peered curiously out from behind the scholar and tsked loudly.

"I'm Avender, Albwin. And this, if you haven't figured it out already, is Hubley. The magicians' daughter. Hubley, say hello to the Chief Fellow."

"Hello."

The Chief Fellow's gaze shifted to the child. "Hello," he answered. "May I ask what you're doing here?"

"Trying to get to my mother."

Albwin's eyes darted quickly to Avender before returning to

Hubley. "Your mother's in Valing. Why would you seek her in the Underground?"

"Avender says we have to meet her somewhere Father can't get to, otherwise he says Father won't let me see her. Is that true?"

It had just occurred to her that the Chief Fellow might be a good person to ask if what Avender and Mims had told her about her parents was correct. As far as she knew, he wasn't on either of her father's side or her mother's.

The Chief Fellow's eyes bored straight through her. Hubley guessed he had years of practice at figuring out when boys were telling the truth or not. She hoped his experience would help with girls, too. Otherwise she had a feeling he was going to hold them there until either her father arrived or Avender decided to fight. And, even though the Chief Fellow was supposed to be a man of books rather than action, Hubley had the impression he knew how to use his crossbow.

"Yes," he said, finally reaching a decision. "Your father has been keeping your mother from seeing you for some time. Perhaps if you explained what this is all about, I might see my way to letting you go."

"There isn't time," said Avender. "He's already after us."

"The child's father?" Albwin's crossbow didn't waver.

"Yes. And maybe half the guards in the New Palace with him, for all I know. Matters set in motion years ago are finally coming to a head. I'm sure you understand."

"You do know no one is supposed to use this way without permission from the king."

"And you know I was the king's right hand once. The very fact I know this way exists suggests I already have that permission."

"True." The Chief Fellow lowered his crossbow.

"But Your Lordship—"

His master cut Nouse off with a look. Hubley heard the porter mutter something about tavern girls and laundresses before Albwin raised his bushy eyebrows a second time.

The Chief Fellow's permission secured, Avender wasted no more time. Screwing his lamp back into the socket on his headband, he led Hubley into the narrow tunnel, put his shoulder to the door, and shoved it closed.

"Now no one can follow us unless they have a lamp, too," he said. "As I recall, your father never carries one, preferring to use magic when he wants light. By the time he finds one, hopefully we'll be well on our way."

They started off down the emptiest tunnel Hubley had ever seen. She had been to Issinlough often, and had even gone with Nolo and Findle on trips into wild cave, but no part of the Stoneways she had ever visited before had been as desolate as this. Always there had been the trickle of water in the distance, or bats squeaking, or, in the Dwarven cities, the clank of machinery and the rumble of voices along the walls. Here there was nothing but the sound of hers and Avender's footsteps. And, after a time, their panting.

"A secret way has to be just that," Avender explained when she asked why the stair was so empty. "So hidden, not even an ant can find its way in."

The passage turned quickly to a long flight of stairs. Like everything built by Dwarves, there was little accommodation for humans. Avender had to be careful not to bump his head on the low ceiling, and there was never any place to stop, no widening of the steps or niches carved out of the walls, just a steady descent, one step after the other in an endless, winding spiral. Whenever they rested, Hubley and Avender were forced to sit at the edge of the long drop, staring at the twenty or so steps they could see in front of them before the light from Avender's lamp faded into the stronger darkness.

It was a long journey. Hubley's thighs began to ache after the first hour, but she didn't complain. Her parents and Avender had gone through much worse when they were only a little older than she was now. Determined to prove she was at least as strong and courageous as they had been, she didn't complain at all, but kept up with Avender step for step. Luckily, he wasn't descending too quickly, or she would never have managed it. Only when she finally stumbled wearily, catching herself on Avender's shoulder as she pitched forward, did he understand how tired she was.

"Here now, we can't have this." He pulled a water bottle from his pack.

Hubley accepted it gratefully, her mouth as dry as the cave. "I'm all right," she said, tucking her hair back behind her ears.

"No you're not." Avender studied her closely. She blinked at the glare of the lamp so close to her face. "I should have realized you're not up for this sort of thing. Picnicking on Aloslocin isn't the same as marching through the Stoneways. And you haven't done any picnicking in a while, either. Here. I'll carry you."

"You can't do that. You already have the pack."

"That's not a problem."

Avender swung his knapsack around so that it hung across his chest. "Plenty of room for you on my back now. I'll be balanced."

Hubley shook her head doubtfully. "I'm too heavy."

"No you aren't. Come on. I don't want you knocking me over the next time you fall. We'd tumble all the way to the Lamp if that happened."

They'd gone perhaps a hundred steps when Hubley, who knew even Avender couldn't carry her all the way to the Abyss, or wherever it was the stair ended, had a bright idea. "Put me down for a second," she said, already sliding down his back.

"What for?"

"You'll see."

Grumbling, he turned around. "If you're going to cast a spell—"

"It'll help."

Still frowning, Avender descended a few more steps to give her room.

"As soon as I have said these words,
Make me lighter than the birds."

Laughing, Hubley leapt forward as soon as she finished. Panic surging in his eyes, Avender braced himself to catch her. Instead she brushed against him as lightly as a cloud.

"I could have carried you," he said, hoisting her higher onto his back. "You didn't have to cast a spell."

Not bothering to tell him he was wrong, she soon fell asleep. Avender's strides rocked her as gentle as a cradle.

Her dreams, however, weren't so peaceful. Instead her mind played over and over again the scene of her father in the cave at the bottom of the castle. The mussels, rather than lying still against the rocks, wriggled like stubby eels. The current rippled cold as ice and clear as air. Her father wanted her to touch one, pushing her face down till it almost brushed the water. The mussels opened their dark mouths; bits of floating silt disappeared inside.

"No!" she cried. "No!"

Jerking back, she woke to find herself seated on the narrow stone steps. Avender stood in front of her, worry deepening his face. His hands gripped her shoulders to keep her from falling forward.

"It's all right," he said. "Everything's all right. You were just having another dream."

Hubley snuffled and wiped her nose on her sleeve.

Avender dropped his hands. "You didn't sleep very long. Do you want me to keep carrying you? The spell hasn't worn off yet, so I can."

Shaking her head, Hubley said, "I think I want to walk now. My legs aren't so sore any more."

"Can you walk when you're so light?"

She narrowed her eyes in concentration. Swaying at the sudden return of weight, she steadied herself on Avender's arm. "I can now. I just ended the spell."

"You're sure you're all right?" he asked one last time.

She was, for a while. She spent the rest of that long descent alternating between Avender carrying her and walking on her own. With no day or night or scenery to change around them, time didn't seem to move forward at all. Nothing changed except the color of the stone in the walls. Otherwise each step was the same as every other; the shape and size of the tunnel never varied. Sometimes minerals in the rock flashed as they caught the light from Avender's lamp, but even that blurred into sameness eventually. Avender himself seemed as changeless as the stone, slogging downward. Long before they were done Hubley had memorized every bulge in the back of his knapsack and every strand of gray in his hair.

The only time they rested was when he picked her up or put her back down. When Hubley asked him how he could walk so long without getting tired, he replied he was used to it.

"I used to spend a lot of time in the Stoneways," he said. "And don't forget, your parents and I grew up in the mountains. Climbing in the Bavadars isn't much different from hiking through Bryddlough. Both have a lot of up and down."

"I'm glad this is just down." Hubley sighed. "I'm too tired for any up."

It was Avender who recognized when they neared the end. For the first time in hours, his pace quickened. Hubley, who had been riding heavily on his back for a while, too tired even to cast her lightening spell, looked up wearily. As far as she could see, there was nothing different about the passage at all.

"Can't you hear it?" he asked. "There's open tunnel ahead. Our footsteps don't echo as loudly as they did before."

Hubley listened, but couldn't tell the difference. All the same, she insisted on walking the rest of the way herself. Soon the stairs ended and they passed through a short passage that led to a larger room, where a wide Dwarven well took up most of the floor. A solitary bat flew out through the opening as they approached.

Neither Hubley nor Avender came too close to the edge, but even from a few feet back they could see the well ended about six feet below the level of the floor. Beyond that the blackness of the Abyss swallowed Avender's lamplight as thoroughly as the sea swallows a raindrop.

Hubley looked around. "Where do we go from here?"

Avender pointed to the far side. A thin blumet ladder descended from the lip of the well down the stone. Lamplight skipped around the walls of the cavern as he turned his head.

"Down there? What if we fall?"

"We won't fall," he assured her. "The Malmoret Lamp is right below, but we can't see it because it's focused out toward the Abyss and not up here."

Hubley found herself unable to come any closer to the opening. The thought of falling through the hole overwhelmed her, regardless of what Avender said. And then there would be nothing but falling, forever and ever, until she finally died of hunger and thirst. Much worse than the time she had fallen off the Magicians' Tower and broken her wrist. That had been terrifying enough, but had only lasted a few seconds. Here the terror would go on and on.

"Come on, Hubley." Avender smiled patiently. "You'll be fine. It's just a ladder."

"But what's beyond the ladder?" she whimpered. "Are we going to crawl along the bottom of the world like flies?"

"No, there's something better than that. A small airship—"

He stopped before finishing his sentence. Hubley had heard it, too. An echo of voices from the long stair above.

"Come on." This time Avender's voice had real urgency. "Whoever's following us has almost caught up. We have to go."

Hubley looked back the way they'd come. Footsteps echoed distantly. The hole in the floor in front of her was just as dark, but somehow it looked a lot more inviting than it had moments before.

"I'll go first." Avender sat on the edge of the well beside the ladder. "That way, if you slip, I'll catch you. But you won't slip. Your mother's been down ladders like these a hundred times."

Hubley sat beside him. Below was not the emptiness she had expected, but a maze of girders. Beyond the unneret they formed, the Abyss looked a lighter shade of gray. Hubley guessed that was from the Lamp. Halfway between the gray bottom and her feet, an airship hung moored bow and stern to the side of the metal frame.

Clasping the blumet firmly in his hands, Avender lowered himself to the ladder. Hubley took a deep breath and followed. With her eyes focused tightly on the stone wall in front of her, she pretended she was climbing down from the hayloft in the castle stables. But that didn't work once she had descended below the lip of the world. Shutting her eyes even more tightly than she gripped the blumet bars, she kept going. At every step she expected the ladder to come to an end, her feet waving frantically in the air. Or maybe the ladder would break off from the stone to send her and Avender plunging into the darkness.

The awful descent stopped sooner than she expected. "Here we are." Avender's voice sounded from somewhere close beside her. "You first. I'll help get you aboard."

Forcing her eyes open, Hubley found herself staring at a patch of light brown canvas. An airship floated in the air in front of her, much smaller than any ship she'd ever flown on before. From stem to stern it wasn't much longer than the table in Castle Grangore's great hall, which seated fifteen people comfortably on a side. It wasn't very tall, either, maybe half again Avender's height. It hovered beside the ladder, rope rigging looped across the fabric.

"You there!" A loud voice called from the well above. "In the name of the king and Prince Merannon, stop!"

Avender's head jerked upward at the prince's name. Hubley wondered who he was. Looking up, she saw only a single Dwarf lamp shining out of the rock like a solitary star.

Avender's attention snapped back to the matter at hand. "No time to waste," he said. "Get on aboard."

With her friend pushing on her shoulders and then her back and legs, Hubley heaved herself up the ropes. The airship quivered. She banged her hand and elbow on something thin and hard as she rolled into the cockpit, then fell again and bumped her knee as Avender tumbled in behind her, tangling them both in the heavy ropes coiled on the deck.

The airship began to fall. Not quickly, but fast enough so that the metal unneret they had just clambered down was clearly moving past them.

"Stop!" cried the voice from above.

Avender drew his sword. With a pair of slashing cuts that reminded Hubley of Fenner in her dream, he severed the cables tying the airship to the upside-down tower.

The ship fell a little faster.

Looking up again, Hubley finally made out several figures clambering down the ladder. Already they were halfway to the ship. And they were gaining, too, as they climbed faster than the craft fell.

From under the airship's canvas hull, Avender produced a long pole. Placing one end on the nearest blumet girder, he began to push. He strained, muscles bunching in his neck, but for a moment nothing happened. Then the ship began to drift out as well as down. Not very quickly, but fast enough that the side of the unneret was soon two or three feet away. Avender kept pushing until he reached the end of the pole, then brought it back inside.

It was going to be a close thing, whether the airship would drift far enough away from the tower before any of the men climbing down were close enough to leap across the gap.

Avender looked down. "Careful," he said. "Make sure you close your eyes if we fall below the light."

The first of their pursuers reached a level just above the

falling ship, but the gap between it and the tower had grown too wide for a safe jump. Hubley saw him measuring the distance with his eyes, trying to gauge whether the attempt was worth the risk.

A second man appeared, the one wearing the lamp. Without hesitating, he wrapped the end of the rope that had moored the ship around his right arm and leg and, taking a few steps backward along one of the girders, raced forward and launched himself across the narrow gulf. Hubley's heart popped into her mouth as the man reached out with one hand to grasp the airship's rigging. Like Avender, he had a face she thought she recognized, though he didn't look like Avender at all. For one thing, his hair was blond.

Avender raised his sword.

"Prince Merannon! Look out!" cried the man on the tower.

Looking up, the blond man let go the rigging just in time. Avender didn't even have to swing his sword, though the prince might still have lost his hand if he had. As it was, Merannon swung heavily back against the unneret, which rang like a sour gong as he struck it. The first man, and several more besides, grabbed the prince quickly to make sure he didn't fall.

With their help, Merannon climbed back onto the tower, but Hubley and Avender had drifted too far away now for a second try.

"We will come after you, you know!" the blond man called. "A ship from Issinlough is already on the way!"

Turning his back on the prince, Avender snapped a pair of tinted goggles over his head, climbed onto the seat of the airship's engine, and began to pedal furiously. Slowly the propeller at the stern began to spin.

16

Thirty-one Years

ubley's hair fluttered at her shoulders as the airship picked up speed.

"Who's Prince Merannon?" she asked.

Avender gasped for breath, his legs pumping furiously at the pedals of the engine. Gears clicked as he worked the levers on the handlebar. Beneath the blumet decking, the drive shaft whirred.

"Tell you later. . . . Let's get out of here first."

Pressing herself flat against the canvas hull, Hubley looked to see what was happening astern. The propeller whirred a couple of fathoms from her face, but, the faster it moved, the less it obscured her view. They'd already moved far enough away from the Lamp that the only thing visible in the darkness was the prince's light, a tiny spark above the beacon's brilliance.

The broad fins set lengthwise along the propeller tilted, causing the ship to nose downward. Small, and still too bright to look at directly, the Lamp sent Hubley's and Avender's long shadows stretching across the canvas to melt into the darkness ahead. Out of sight above their heads hung the bottom of the world.

Rubbing her arms against the breeze, she turned back to the cockpit. Avender's chest swelled as he prepared for another burst of conversation. "If you're cold, Mims packed some warmer clothes."

Opening the knapsack, Hubley found socks and a pair of boots, a brown wool dress, and a warm cloak, all plainer than anything she'd ever worn. But her beautiful red gown was already torn in several places, and the wind was whipping right through it, so she took it off and shoved it into the pack. Perhaps her mother could mend it later on. Pulling the woolen dress over her head, she found it itched terribly against her bare skin, but the scratching was much better than the cold.

Avender was still pedaling hard when she finished; her cloak snapped in the galloping breeze as she stood beside him. Eager to know where they were going, she peppered him with questions, but he only panted and shook his head. Though she'd never flown one herself, Hubley knew the hard part about airships was getting them started. Once you reached the speed you wanted, the pedaling got a lot easier. Then only the air slowed you down. Which was why no one had ever tried using airships on the surface, where even a medium breeze would blow you off course. The Abyss, vast and deep though it was, never felt a breath of wind. Unless you were riding in an airship.

When the Malmoret Lamp had dimmed to the glow of a distant town, Avender finally stopped pedaling. Huffing and puffing, he stripped the goggles from his face and slid down from the engine's saddle. The airship coasted along, barely losing speed.

"Are we going to find my mother?" Hubley demanded.

Avender held up a tired hand. "Hold on a minute, will you?"

Despite the cold and wind, his forehead glistened with sweat as he reached beneath the hull and pulled out a small cask wedged in among the gasbags. Grabbing a small cup from his pack, he unstopped the cask and poured himself several gulping drinks. Thirst quenched, he passed the cup to Hubley and retrieved two sacks from the same hiding place as the cask. Opening the first, he brought out a pair of apples.

The sight of food reminded Hubley she hadn't eaten since they'd finished the bread and carrots on the stone stair, but that didn't stop her questions. "It's a good thing you found this air-ship," she said through a mouthful of what tasted like a Bavadar Gold. "Those men would have caught us for sure."

"Luck had nothing to do with it." Unsheathing his knife, Avender cut them both large slabs from a fat sausage. "Mims and I left the ship there three days ago."

Hubley's jaw dropped. "You mean you knew we were coming here all along? Even before I did the traveling spell?"

"No. Mims didn't tell me anything. All we did was drop off the ship, then travel back to the cabin. It was only after you brought us to the New Palace that I figured out we could use it."

"But how could Mims have known we were coming here?"

Shrugging, Avender kept his eyes on the sausage as he cut himself another slice. "Don't ask me. You're the magician."

Hubley frowned. It was almost like Avender was being stupid on purpose. "You can't tell the future with magic," she told him. "Everyone knows that."

"I don't."

"Well, we magicians do. Trying to tell the future was one of the first things Father tried when he learned magic, but it didn't work. Not even Fornoch can do it."

"Then I guess Mims can't tell the future. And she isn't Fornoch, if that's what you're thinking. I've spent enough time with her to know that much. Maybe she left ships at all the Lamps, and I just happened to help her with this one. Either way, she seems to know exactly what she's doing. She's a very power-ful magician."

"Not as powerful as my father."

When Avender didn't argue, Hubley asked again where they were going.

"Don't know yet," he replied, his mouth full of apple.

"You don't know? I thought you had a plan."

"My plan was to get us somewhere your father couldn't fol-low. We've done that. Now we have to decide what to do next."

As he spoke, he pulled a small, flat bundle from his pack. Certain it was a talking mirror, Hubley moved around to look over his shoulder as he unwrapped it. Smoke followed his fingers as he brushed them lightly across the surface. When the smoke cleared, the mirror showed the inside of the cabin they had left the day before, rather than the cramped cockpit of the airship.

"Mims," called Avender. "Are you there?"

The old woman appeared almost at once, anxiety and relief reflected in her face. "Finally. I've been scared to death Reiffen caught up with you. Where are you? Are you safe?"

"We're in the ship you left at the Malmoret Lamp."

"Are you still there? At the Lamp?"

"No. Prince Merannon almost caught us, so we had to leave. I've been pedaling hard for at least an hour, though it's hard to tell time down here without the sun."

The old woman's lips pursed. "That's too bad. If you were still at the Lamp I could fetch Ferris and bring her right to you. But I can't travel to a ship that's floating around in the middle of the Abyss."

"Neither can Reiffen. Which is what gave me the idea to come down here in the first place. He'll have to find an airship of his own if he wants to follow us."

"The last I saw," said Mims, "he'd gone back to Grangore. Before that, he was in Valing, though he spent some time chasing you in Malmoret, too. Don't worry, Hubley, Ferris is fine. For once your father believed her when she said she had nothing to do with taking you."

"Have you seen her?"

The old magician smiled. "No. I wanted to hear from you and Avender first."

"Well, you've heard from us now," said Avender. "The only thing left is to get Hubley back to her mother."

"I agree." Mims tapped a finger on her chin. "The question is, where's the best place to do it?"

"Somewhere Reiffen's never been, so he can't travel there before we have time to even take a breath."

"You could go back to the Malmoret Lamp. As far as I know, he's never been there. Otherwise he'd have been waiting for you when you got to the end of the stair. I could have Ferris there in no time."

Avender shook his head. "That's no good. Prince Merannon might still be there. He said something about a ship already being on the way."

"True." The old woman tapped her chin again, her eyes turned thoughtfully toward the bottom of the glass.

"What about Backford?"

Hubley jumped up before Avender had hardly finished making the suggestion. The ship shuddered slightly. "That's perfect! Willy and Lady Breeanna are my friends! I'm sure they'll help."

"I didn't mean Backford itself," Avender cautioned. "Reiffen knows Backford almost as well as he knows Valing—he'd be on us in no time. But has he ever been to the Lamp?"

"I don't think so," said Mims. "He travels everywhere, so there's no reason for him ever to use the lamps to get to the airships. Unfortunately, I've never been there, either."

Avender looked surprised. "You haven't? But what about—?"

Mims cut him off by raising her eyebrows. "Are you saying you know where I've been better than I do?"

He shook his head. "No. Hubley and I just thought you'd left airships at all the Lamps."

"That's right," said Hubley. "You couldn't have known we were going to be in Malmoret."

"And I didn't. I brought that airship to the Malmoret Lamp for an entirely different purpose. Which I won't be able to use it for, now. It really was just luck Avender knew it was there. I'm sure, Hubley, that if your spell had taken you to Valing or Issinlough or someplace else, Avender would have come up with a different way to escape."

"I suppose," Avender agreed.

Hubley didn't think he looked too convinced. And there was something else, too. "How'd you know I was going to cast a traveling spell, anyway? I didn't even know I could do that."

The magician raised her hands. "When we see your mother, Hubley, I'll explain it all. Until then, be patient, though I know how hard that is for you. In the meantime, I think Avender's made a good choice. I'll fetch Ferris, then she and I will start down the Way. It's going to take you at least a day of hard pedaling to get there."

"I'll need some sleep first."

Mims nodded, appearing to like the plan the more she thought about it. "And I'll need time to convince Ferris she should come with me. If we're not at the Lamp when you arrive, start up the road. We can meet halfway. Once we do, I can take us all somewhere Reiffen will never find us. At least not till we want him to."

Avender was about to ask another question, then thought better of it. Mims took advantage of his silence to ask one of her own.

"Is there any sign you're being pursued?"

"Not that I've seen. We're flying without lights. They can guess, but they won't know where we've gone."

"Then we're all set. You've got your mirror in case you have to change the plan. Ferris and I may not be able to get to you right away, but at least we'll know where you are."

Mims's hand swept close across the glass as she ended the connection. Smoke swirled, then Hubley and Avender were looking at their own reflections. Carefully rewrapping the mirror, Avender slipped it back inside his shirt.

"Which light is Backford?" Hubley asked when he was done.

Avender pointed into the darkness on their right. Two other lights gleamed in the distance, Blue Mountain nearly dead ahead, and Malmoret to the rear.

The airship had slowed considerably during the time they had been eating and talking, and Hubley expected Avender to climb back into the saddle at once. Instead he pulled blankets out from the same place where the food had been stored and began making up a small bed on the narrow deck behind the engine. "It'll be cramped," he said, laying the first blanket across the grating, "but we'll be warmer if we keep together. Besides, now that we know you can travel in your sleep, I can't risk letting you disappear."

"But shouldn't we keep going?" Hubley protested. "I want to see Mother now."

"I haven't slept in a day and half. And I doubt you have, either, with the dreams you've been having. Better we both get some rest. We're safe enough here in the middle of nowhere."

Side by side, they lay down on the metal grate. At their feet, the engine loomed like a giant insect in the dim light, its levers and pedals so many legs and antennae. Above them, the endless darkness welled away.

To make sure he kept hold of Hubley no matter what, Avender wrapped his belt around their hands, then fell asleep almost as soon as he hung his lamp and headband over the engine. For Hubley, it wasn't so easy. She lay on her back for a long time, her mind revolving around everything that had happened since the party. Of one thing she was sure: she wanted to see her mother. But everything else that had happened had left her completely confused. Avender much older than he should be? Her father not letting her see her mother? And who was Mims? Her parents' apprentices had always been older than Hubley, but not that much older. Mims had to have learned her magic from someone else. But the only other person who might have taught her was the Wizard. If that were the case, how could Hubley ever trust her? Then she remembered that her father had been taught by the Wizard, and he'd come out fine. Maybe Mims had been Fornoch's apprentice before her father, and had escaped after the fall of Ussene.

She was sure her mother would know the answers to everything, which was one more reason to find her. In the meantime, Avender was her parents' best friend, and she was just going to have to trust him.

Giving his hand a little squeeze, she settled more comfortably in the blankets. He answered with a snort and a snore.

Of course she dreamed when she finally did fall asleep. Knowing she would had been one of the things keeping her awake. For a while the chase from the New Palace to the Malmoret Lamp tumbled through her mind; over and over she and Avender fled down stairs and ladders, always with Prince Merannon and his soldiers close behind, always with the long, dark drop of the Abyss looming beneath their feet. But gradually her dreaming delved a little deeper, and she found herself once more in her father's cave. Blue-black shells rippled beneath the current of the shallow pool.

"Go to them, dear heart," her father whispered. His voice was tender in her ear. "My mussels are a fine magic, and will only make you stronger."

Again the cold pierced Hubley as she slipped into the water. The current tugged at her gown, black velvet this time instead of the ruined red, with white lace at cuffs and collar. Taking a deep breath, she ducked beneath the surface. The frigid water squeezed her chest and eyes. At her feet the mussels waited, alert as soldiers. Her cheeks bulging, she felt along the bottom with her fingers until they grazed the nearest shell. She saw herself wearing a different dress, plum-colored with a lavender sash, and knew at once this mussel had already been used. But the vision disappeared as soon as she touched another; now her frock was periwinkle with dark blue smocking. Obviously this mussel was full, too. One by one she reached for as many of the nearer shells as she could. Five, ten, a dozen: her birthday dress changed at every touch. And then she found an empty one. Seizing it with both hands, she sighed. Bubbles cascaded past her nose and ears.

The mussel opened. One by one it gobbled the bubbles from

her sigh, drawing them into its shell. She found she couldn't stop sighing; the mussel pulled air from her like a milkmaid draining a cow. Her lungs emptied. Memories from the last year spun away along with the bubbles: parts of spells her father had taught her, breakfasts they had shared, Mindrell's clever songs. Her mind felt thinned. The memories rose up one by one, and then they were gone. Vaguely, she recalled the taking, and then even that memory was gathered in as well.

Still, she knew she had lost something. As the last few scraps of breath were scoured from her lungs, fear took the place of air. Why had her father made her do this? Was she going to drown? Desperately she tried to let go of the black shell, but her hand was stuck fast. Her body began settling toward the bottom like an airship leaking gas. The mussels gaped wide.

She woke to find Avender shaking her shoulders with his free hand. Worry pinched his eyes.

"Are you all right? That looked like the worst one yet."

Shuddering, Hubley wrapped her arms around her shoulders and tried to shrink back into herself. She didn't want to think about what her dream seemed to be telling her at all. But, however terrifying it might prove to be, maybe now was the time to find out what had really been happening in the world while her father had locked her up in Castle Grangore.

Swallowing her fear, she looked Avender in the eye.

"How old am I?"

He blinked twice before he replied, but this time he didn't look away. "Why do you ask?"

"Because the dream I just had was all about those mussels. How father made me touch one and it took away all my memories. And how there were lots of others there just like it that were already full."

"Which means . . . ? Remember, I'm not a mage."

"I think it was telling me I'd been in that cave lots of times before. After lots and lots of birthdays, only I don't remember any of them. And since the mussel in my dream was stealing my memories, who knows how many years there might be in the others. There were lots of mussels in that pool. And then there's the way you look like you're sixty instead of thirty-three, and how Mims is too old to have been taught by my parents like she said."

"I'm not thirty-three," Avender admitted.

"I didn't think so. How old are you?"

"I'm not sure."

"How old am I? Sixteen?"

"You're forty-one."

Hubley felt as if Avender had sliced off her head. Nineteen or twenty, maybe. But forty-one? She'd lost her whole life!

"Mims told me the mussels in your father's cave each hold a full year from your past," he explained gently. "He's been making you live the year from nine to ten over and over again for the last thirty-one years."

Hubley tried to swallow, but her throat felt too swollen. Her bones felt hollow and cold. "How come I haven't gotten old?"

"Your father gave you a Living Stone."

She knew it was true. She had dreamed about that as well. A sudden feeling of power crept into her fingers and hands, as if the Stone was informing her it knew she finally knew it was there. The sense of newly discovered strength was pleasant, but Hubley was repelled all the same. She didn't want to be forty-one.

"But why would Father do such a thing? It can't be true!"

Avender reached to comfort her. She shied away.

"To protect you from Fornoch," he said, letting his arms drop back to his sides. "When the Wizard threatened to take you away like he did your father, Reiffen's answer was to hide you in Castle Grangore and not let anyone near you. Not even Ferris."

Hubley's voice dropped to a whisper. "You mean I haven't seen Mother in thirty-one years?"

He nodded. Loneliness poured over her in wretched waves.

Flinging herself onto the blankets, she burst into years of tears. Sobs filled the darkness.

She felt better when she woke. Avender sat sleeping beside her, his hand still bound to hers. Despite everything he'd told her, she still felt like she was only ten. The other years remained something from her dreams. Not that she doubted what he'd said. Too much of what she'd thought strange about him and Mims made sense only if those thirty-one years really had happened.

The hardest part was knowing what her father had done to her. Except for the mussels, her memories of him were only good. Picnics on Aloslocin, and presents on her birthday, and him putting salve on her fingers when she first tried to cast a light spell without using a staff. And all the magic he had taught her, too.

But against that happiness Hubley knew she had to weigh the fact her father hadn't allowed her mother to see her in a very long time. Even if Avender were lying, it had still been at least a year. And to think her father had said that her mother hadn't come to her birthday because she was working on a spell! She couldn't believe he'd done that, though he had always been the one most likely to forget the little things, breakfasts and good-night kisses and trips to town, because he was always so busy with magic. Her mother, however, had always been there. And her grandmother, too.

Hubley gripped the rough canvas side of the ship tightly at the thought. She hadn't seen her Grandmother Giserre in all that time either, even though Giserre loved her son so much she'd braved the Wizards in Ussene for him. The fact Giserre had disappeared as well was even more proof that Avender was telling the truth.

Tears gathered in her eyes. Sniffing mightily, she rubbed them away with her free hand. Now was not the time to cry. Her parents had been in worse places when they were young: she was only being chased by a magician, not a Wizard. She'd always dreamed of having adventures the same as her parents, and now that she had her chance she wasn't going to ruin it. So what if it was her father she was running away from rather than the last of the Three. She still had to get to her mother before he found her. Otherwise she might never see her mother again. Ever.

Brushing away a last tear, she nudged Avender in the ribs. He leapt up, his sword half drawn.

"What's wrong?" Swiftly, he scanned the dark around them. "Did you see something?"

"I want to see my mother," she said. "You've been asleep too long. Can't we go?"

He rubbed the spot where she'd poked him. "All right. Did you sleep well? No dreams?"

"No."

"That's an improvement." Rooting around in their supplies, he passed out another pair of apples. "Maybe, now you know the truth, and you won't have them anymore."

"Maybe." Hubley polished her apple on the rough wool dress. "Why do you think he did it? Father, that is."

Avender shrugged. "I've no idea. Mims thinks he was saving all those memories so you'd be much more powerful than Fornoch suspected if he actually did capture you. How she thought your father was going to release them, though, she didn't say."

"He could've just taught me the spells. I'd have been just as strong then. Stronger, even, if he'd let Mother help, too."

"Don't ask me to explain why your father does what he does. I've never known."

Hubley guessed a lot had happened in the years since she'd been hidden away. "Is Brizen still king?"

"Yes."

"And Prince Merannon? Is he Brizen and Wellin's son?"

Avender searched his sack for another apple. "I think so. I've never met him."

"Wellin must be so happy. I'm just sorry he's already grown up. I'm sure we'd have been best friends if he wasn't."

"I'm sure you'll be friends anyway."

"Does he have any brothers or sisters?"

"No."

Hubley thought there was something suspicious about the way Avender wasn't looking up, as if there was something more he didn't want to tell her.

"Is there something wrong?" she asked. "Wellin is happy, isn't she, now that she has a son?"

"I'm sorry, Hubley. Wellin's dead."

Despite her resolve, Hubley burst into tears once more. This time, instead of refusing her friend's comfort, she threw herself into his arms. Of all the things Avender had told her, this was far and away the worst.

"How?" she stammered when her sobs had dropped off to hiccups and sore eyes.

"I don't know. I wasn't there." Looking off into the darkness, Avender blinked a couple of times before going on. "Maybe she just got old."

"It's not right, Father not telling me about things like that. He should have let me see her."

"You're right. He should have."

"Has anyone else died?"

"I only know what Mims has told me. To tell the truth, I've been away nearly as long as you."

"You have? Where?"

"Underground."

Hubley assumed that meant Avender had been spending his time in the Stoneways. "I wish I'd been as lucky as you. Bryddlough's a lot more fun than Castle Grangore. At least you got to spend time with the Dwarves. Is that when you lost your hand?"

Avender looked at her sharply. "How do you know about that?"

"I heard you talking last night when you thought I was asleep. Mims said she put it back on."

Holding up his left hand, Avender flexed his fingers. The remaining thimble gleamed.

"She did a good job," he said.

"It was my father who did it, wasn't it," said Hubley, the thought coming to her in a flash.

"Close enough. Mindrell did it on your father's orders. Do you remember that, too?"

"You mean I was there?"

Avender nodded.

Hubley wondered if there were other memories from the last thirty-one years she hoped she never recalled.

"Are you mad at him?" she asked.

"Who, Mindrell?"

"Him too, but are you mad at my father?"

"Yes."

"Good, because I'm really, really mad at him."

Later, after they had finished eating, Hubley stood awkwardly for a moment, grimacing and hopping from one foot to the other. Avender understood her need at once.

"I think I'll go astern to check on the drive shaft," he said. "You'll find the chamber pot in the bow."

He returned after she'd flung the contents of the shallow bowl far out into the dark. Now the Abyss wasn't quite so empty as it had been before.

With Avender climbing back into the driver's saddle, they set off. This time he didn't have to pedal quite so hard, so Hubley could question him to her heart's content about everything that had happened in the years she'd been hidden from the world. Avender answered as best he could, but he seemed to know very little. Hubley guessed that was because he'd spent his time wandering deep in wild cave during his years underground, otherwise he'd have known a lot more. With magic mirrors everywhere, even Issinlough heard the latest news. Meanwhile, the leagues passed. The Backford Lamp grew brighter. After they stopped for another meal and rest, it began to grow larger, too.

"We're going to need some light now," said Avender as the shadow of the unneret emerged above the Lamp. "I'll never be able to moor the ship without being able to see what I'm doing."

Crawling into the forward hold, Hubley found the small switch box right where Avender had told her she would, mounted on the blumet struts in the nose. Flipping the switch, she crawled back to the cockpit, but even on the outside it was hard to tell the bow light had been turned on. Only by squinting directly into the wind was she able to see that the air in front of the ship's prow was no longer quite as dark as it was everywhere else around them.

Not much later they glided up beneath the bottom of the world: Avender had brought the ship in as high as he could to keep the Lamp from blinding them. Dark stone loomed just above their heads like frozen clouds. With both tail fins out, the ship slowed quickly, coasting toward the middle of an inverted tower that looked just like the one they had left behind in Malmoret, a skeleton of girders and beams suspended beneath a hole in the rock above. Seeing their approach was slightly off, Avender fiddled with one of the levers on the engine handle. The tail flap on the side of the ship farthest from the tower closed; the ship swung toward the Lamp. Avender toggled the lever again to re-open the flap; their course straightened.

Picking up a long coil of rope with a small anchor at one end, he went to the bow. The unneret grew bigger quickly; Hubley hadn't thought they were still moving that fast. As Avender began to swing the rope and anchor in a long loop around his head, she crouched at the edge of the cockpit. The tower loomed closer on the starboard side. When it was almost beside them, he threw his rope. The anchor flashed in the bow light, then struck one of the tower struts with a loud clank. At the same time Avender tied off the other end of the line on a cleat along the edge of the cockpit, then jumped back to the engine to close the tail flaps. The anchor rattled around inside the open tower, tangling the rope on the beams and girders. The line pulled taut. Metal groaned. Hubley stumbled as the airship swayed to starboard.

"Not much of a landing," said Avender as the ship shuddered to a stop. "But it's a lot harder when you have to do it all alone."

"I could've helped."

"With magic?"

"No. I know more than just magic, you know."

Mooring the ship securely to the tower, they rolled what was left of the food into Avender's knapsack and one of the blankets, then tied the blanket around Hubley. Avender shouldered his pack and the water cask as well.

"You can never tell how far it is between water holes on a loway," he said as he tied the cask firmly to the top of his pack. "Dwarves rarely think of humans when they delve."

Hubley reminded herself that Lady Breeanna had come this way when she'd escaped from the Battle of Backford. If someone as silly as Lady Breeanna could do it, then so could she.

Finding no sign of Mims or Ferris at the Lamp, they ate another quick meal, then headed up into the stone. This time Hubley didn't find climbing the narrow ladder in the side of the well nearly as bad as she had before. Perhaps it was easier to look up than down. Or maybe she was getting used to endless drops after the long flight over the Abyss. Reaching the top, she found herself in another cave, the walls wavering in and out of shadow as Avender helped her up. But one shadow stayed still no matter how many times Avender swung his headlamp across it: the entrance to the Backford Way.

For a long time they followed the tunnel beyond, clambering up through rough tubes that twisted and turned through the rock. When Hubley asked Avender why the Dwarves hadn't cut a straight stair the way they had in Malmoret, he replied that this was a different sort of passage.

"The Backford Way is more secret than the ones you're used to. As secret as the one in Valing, or the one Nolo has always talked about digging to the Inner Sea."

"There's a Dwarf Way to the Inner Sea?"

"They hadn't finished it the last I heard, but I wouldn't be surprised to find out it's done now."

"But how do they keep all the water from draining out?"

Avender ducked around a knob of stone. "The same way they build lifts. Dwarves can build doors so tight, water can't seep through at all. So they build a room with watertight doors on either side, and open them one at a time depending which way they want to go. Nolo calls it an air lock."

"But why would they want to have a way to the Inner Sea?"

"To hunt for pearls. And to look around. Nolo's always wanted to have a way to explore the bottom of the ocean. Didn't your mother ever tell you about the time she and Nolo met those pirates in the Pearl Islands?"

Dimly, as if she were dredging the memory up from the same sea bottom Nolo wanted to explore, Hubley remembered the tale.

They rested once along the way, in a relatively flat cave where a low ridge of stone served as a bench on the side of the wall, and ate another meal. Hubley's legs were already sore from all the climbing but, not being in as much of a hurry this time, she hadn't asked Avender to carry her. But the thought that each step was bringing her closer to her mother made her jump up again after a very short rest, despite her tender thighs.

Not much later, Hubley noticed a change in the path. Sniffing cautiously, she thought the air seemed thicker than before.

"Water," she announced the minute she figured it out. "Can you smell it?"

"I can. Look. The walls are wet."

The darker patches on the rock glistened as Avender swung his lamp round to examine them.

"If you stop and listen for a moment," he went on, "you'll hear running water."

Hubley held her breath. Sure enough, water muttered somewhere in the distance ahead.

The stream, or whatever it was, took longer to reach than she thought. Or maybe she was expecting it so much that every footstep seemed to last half an hour. But the sound of the water grew louder, the ceiling of the cave began to drip, and the floor grew slippery underfoot, until at last they reached the end of the tunnel and came out into a narrow chasm in the rock.

A stream rushed by at their feet, the water boiling along like the Ambore where it poured out of Grangore through Eggdrop and Tappet Flume. But where the Ambore boiled white and pale green, here the water was dark as ink. Even Avender's lamp couldn't pierce the surface: the gem's light was too thin for the surging flood. Hubley imagined coiling serpents and large, file-toothed fish lurking just out of sight, ready to drag her in the moment she tried to cross.

"Here's a good spot."

She looked up to find Avender working his way carefully along the slippery bank to a place where the floor of the cave came down to the level of the water. Several large rocks marked a passage across the stream, the last set under an opening in the wall on the other side that Hubley suspected was the next section of the loway. Beyond the stones the river burst out from under a shallow rock shelf which Hubley could just make out in the dim light of Avender's lamp. Where the current led downstream, it was too dark to tell. But the fact that there were other openings into the cave was plain from several thin trickles that spattered down from holes in the ceiling. Two crashed into the stream before and behind Avender, while another splashed against the stone directly across from her. With a few ferns and some green moss to cover the rocks, the spot would make an enchanting glen. But underground it was only damp and bare.

Kneeling on the flattest of the rocks that crossed the stream, Avender unstopped the cask and dipped it in the water.

"Boy, that's cold. Cold as the Hart—"

Something pale and enormous landed on his back. With a cry, Avender pitched forward into the icy stream. A second pallid figure brought a large rock down sharply on the back of his head.

A cold hand wrapped around Hubley's mouth as the cave went dark. Strong arms yanked her away.

17

Reiffen

eiffen looked around. Precious minutes had passed since Hubley had been taken and all he had done was rage. Shapeless specimens oozed down the workshop walls; splinters of wood and glass littered the floor. Despite the blood and bruises covering his hands, he felt no pain. His Living Stone was already healing him.

He reminded himself he had been preparing for this day for years. Smashing workrooms had never been part of the plan. He needed to curb his temper and get on with it. Still, his fear and anger were worse than anything he had ever felt before: losing a daughter was much worse than slaughtering armies. What if he failed to bring her back? For years he had hoped this day would never come, that he would be able to defeat the Wizard by other means. But he had also known there was never really any choice. There never was, with Fornoch.

His breathing eased. The mess in the workshop was unimportant. The first thing he had to do was find Hubley. Then he could confirm who had taken her, her mother or the Wizard, before deciding what to do next. Although he was certain Ferris could never have entered the castle without his knowledge, he still had to make sure. Springing his trap on the wrong target would ruin everything.

From inside his shirt he pulled out a small pouch at the end of a blumet chain. Opening it, he poured a single moonstone into his palm. In the dimly lit workroom its surface flashed red and yellow, like carp feeding in a chalky stream. Wrapping his long fingers around the orb, he held it up before his face. The spell was old, but he remembered it easily.

> "Moon and stars that light this stone,
> Let it now to me be known:
> Under rock or under sky,
> Bare my daughter to my eye."

The charm began to glow as its hidden magic came to life. Knives of light slashed out from between his fingers. One stabbed his forehead, the other two jabbed his eyes. Dust stirred up earlier by his temper drifted in and out of the glowing shafts, but the magician didn't move. More slowly than the jagged lights careening across the surface of the moonstone, the world rolled before his eyes, from Grangore to the Blue Mountains, past Banking's western baronies, through the Wetting and the Waste, finally stopping in the depths of the Great Forest.

He hurled the gem to the floor. It rattled off the walls, but did not break. Even combining it with the other spells he had prepared, he would never be able to reach his daughter quickly. He had expected as much, but it was still hard to swallow his disappointment. Whoever had stolen her had planned their hiding place well. Reiffen had seldom visited the Great Forest, and had always stayed close to the river when he had. Even if he changed to bird form and flew from the river to the edge of the Bavadars, it would take more than a day to reach her. Whoever had taken Hubley undoubtedly knew that, and would move somewhere else just before the time he expected Reiffen to arrive.

But first he had to make sure that person wasn't Ferris. If his wife was the one who had taken Hubley, she would be with the child. After thirty-one years she would never have the patience to stay away, not even to throw Reiffen off the track.

Picking up the moonstone, he brushed bits of glass and small jellied carcasses off the table and lay down. He would visit Valing by dream travel, as he had done on his first trips from Ussene years ago. Dreaming required less effort than a full conjuring, and chances were he was going to need to conserve his strength over the next few days. But he had not traveled to Valing, by any means, in some time, so it took him a moment to gather enough memory for the spell. His breathing lengthened; his heartbeat slowed. His body rested even though he was wide awake. He was magician enough now that he no longer needed to put himself to sleep in order to dream. Now he could separate wakefulness and sleep as easily as if they were his right and left hands.

He opened his eyes in the Tear. Even dream travel required real memory and, having only visited Tower Dale while dreaming, his memories of Ferris's current home were not real. The Tear was the closest he could come. Mist buffeted the windows; the gorge drummed through the stone at his feet as he climbed the steps and passed through the heavy oak doors into the half arch that connected his mother's old home to the Neck. Drifts of unswept leaves huddled against the wall. Quickly he ascended to the flat spit of land that housed Valing Manor, the buildings quiet and dark beneath a star-filled sky. No need to disturb the stewards or anyone else. This was not their quarrel. Not that he had ever met Hern's and Berrel's successors anyway.

Reaching the edge of the cliff beyond the orchard, he stepped off into the empty air. Ghosts required firm footing even less than birds. Below him the lake lay dark as night. With the stars and moon covered by clouds he could not even see the islands. Drifting like a puff of fog himself, he sailed south. Halfway to the Narrows the western cliffs parted to form a tapering dell, the Smaller Fall tumbling in a narrow plume to the lake below.

Passing the northern cliffs, he drifted toward a solitary tower standing in the middle of the vale. Sheds and barns clustered at its base. Behind it, fields and orchards led to a small patch of woods at the back of the cleft, where the Small Fall dropped from higher crags. Lights showed in a few of the tower's windows, but none were Ferris's. Or Giserre's. Floating downward, he stopped with his hands resting on his wife's windowsill. The shutters were open; the curtains hung motionless in the still night air.

Unhampered by the stone, he drifted through the wall. Since he was not really there, and could not do anything if he were, none of the alarms Ferris had placed around her home were alerted to his presence. Gliding across the floor, he approached her bed. Someone was sleeping there, but he had to make sure it was Ferris. Enough years had passed that he no longer recognized her sleeping form.

He whispered her name.

She woke. At first she only rubbed her eyes and looked around. Unlike those times years ago, no moonlight shimmered in his clear shadow.

"Ferris," he repeated from close beside the bed. "Do you know where our daughter is?"

Her eyes widened as she came fully awake. "Get out!" she hissed, searching the room for him. "You have no right!"

Though he had known she would, she looked the same as ever. Dark hair of a woman a third her age, skin unmarked save for a few wrinkles in the corners of her eyes. Sleek arms not yet gone to flesh. All the same, his heart beat no faster. He had trained away his sentiment years before.

"Not until I tell you what has happened," he answered.

"Then tell me." Her face stopped moving as she found his shade in the darkness. In this light he was no more than a transparency, a shape of clear glass laid across her view. He saw her hatred plainly.

"Hubley is gone," he told her. "I came to see if you were the one who took her. Obviously you did not, so it must have been Fornoch."

"Fornoch has Hubley?" Ferris's hand went to her mouth. Then most of her bitterness returned. "But you can't be sure, or you wouldn't have come here. How do you know she hasn't run away?"

"Someone took her. She called for help before she left."

His wife sneered. "So, despite everything you've done, you couldn't keep her safe after all."

"Had you been there to help me, it might not have happened."

Ferris covered her nightgown with a dark robe as she left the bed. "Do you know where she is? You were able to tell that sort of thing thirty years ago. You're probably even better at it now."

"She's in the Great Forest, close to the back of the Bavadars. A day's flight from anywhere I have ever been."

"Show me. Maybe I can get closer."

"Do you have a map?"

Lighting the way with a wave of her hand, she led him out of her bedroom and up the tower's curving stair. Although this workroom was more cluttered than the one she had had at the castle, it was otherwise much the same. Wide windows looked out on the night in three directions; books and magical ingredients filled the cabinets and shelves between. Pulling a large scroll from one of the former, Ferris unrolled it across the table at the center of the room.

"There." The spot Reiffen pointed to showed plainly inside the outline of his finger. "Have you ever been anywhere near?"

"No. Except for once with you, I've never been to the Great Forest at all. But some of my former apprentices go there all the time. Maybe one of them can get me close."

"Good."

"It will take a while to talk to them all."

"I do not expect we shall be able to rescue her quickly. Fornoch has had many years to prepare for this day. I have assembled some surprises for him in turn, but it will take me some time to ready them."

"If I find her first," Ferris declared, "you won't get her back."

"Defeat Fornoch, and you can have her whenever you please. This has always been about him, not us. That is as true now as it was thirty years ago. What Hubley chooses to do with her freedom, however, might be something else entirely."

Ferris stiffened. "Once she learns what you've been doing to her, I'm sure she'll come with me. Don't think I haven't visited Grangore the way you're visiting me now. You may have stolen her memories, but I'll be more than happy to fill Hubley in on everything you've done to her over the last thirty years."

Reiffen did not reply. Someday, Ferris would understand. And, now that the Wizard had finally acted, that day was likely to be close at hand. Too much time had passed, however, for Reiffen to have any hope that he and Ferris might regain what they had once had. Stone, living or dead, rarely changed, but people always did.

"Use your mirror to let me know if you are close," he said, "and I will try to help. As I will let you know when I am close as well."

His apparition vanished. Back in Castle Grangore, he swung up and off the table. In Valing, he assumed Ferris would already be calling her apprentices to see which one could get her closest to their child. Given what Fornoch had done to Ahne, Reiffen would never trust an apprentice with that sort of responsibility, but Ferris had made her own decisions. Let her put pressure on the Wizard by going after their daughter. Reiffen would take other measures.

Returning to the mussel cave, he began his preparations. There was much to do, all of which would take time. He may have been too softhearted to have given his daughter a thimble, but there were other ways. From a hidden shelf he brought out a small vial filled with dark red dust. Not enough for him to travel, even when mixed with his own blood, but enough to send something much more immaterial.

He was readying the knife for the final part of the spell when he felt a pulse of heat from the moonstone. Knowing Fornoch had to move Hubley regularly to make sure neither Ferris nor Reiffen caught up with him, he brought out the gem to see where they had gone. South the moonstone took him this time, across the Bavadars, through Wayland and into Banking. He guessed Fornoch and Hubley were on their way to the Toes when the moonstone surprised him by stopping at Malmoret.

Laying his knife aside, he considered this new development. Had Hubley escaped? The Wizard could not possibly have taken her to the New Palace deliberately. Ferris and he could both get there with barely a thought. Seepage was possible in the memory spell, he knew, especially if the subject came close to the vessels, as Hubley had that evening. Had enough of the traveling spell slipped out that his daughter had cast it on her own? But, if she had, why had she gone to the New Palace rather than Grangore or Valing?

There was only one way to find out. Canceling his enchantment, Reiffen concentrated on the New Palace. The smells around him slipped from firestone and lime to lavender and roses. Arriving at his old apartment, he began infusing the moonstone with fresh magic at once, but was interrupted by a shout from the servants' stair. Following the sound, he discovered a guard aiding an injured companion on the landing three floors below. The two soldiers looked up in surprise as he silently joined them.

"What has happened here?" Raising his hand, Reiffen added a touch of compulsion to the question.

"I don't know, sir," answered the soldier still on his feet. "I came to relieve Del here, and found him on the floor. Looks like he got a good conkin'."

The other soldier looked up, too dazed to have been affected by Reiffen's spell. Knowing every second meant his daughter was getting farther away, the magician took the soldier's hand and allowed a small part of his Stone to leak into the woozy man. The soldier's eyes cleared.

"Tell me who did this to you."

The soldier blinked and rubbed his temple. The magic had cured his dizziness, but not his headache. "I never saw him before, but he looked like an officer. Tall and strong."

"Was anyone with him?"

"A little girl in a red dress. I never saw her before, either."

Reiffen turned back to the first man, his suspicions confirmed. "Which is the quickest way out of the palace from here?"

The soldier scratched his head. "Through the kitchens, I guess. There's a gate just outside. Say, who are you, anyway?"

His question was put to Reiffen's back. The magician, remembering the way, was off through the kitchens at once. In the courtyard beyond, he found another sentry who told him no one had passed, though the soldier did think he had heard something in the street a few minutes earlier. Reiffen rushed out through the gate, but there was no sign of which way his daughter had gone.

Several more guards, alerted by the commotion on the stair, joined the sentry. None of them interfered as Reiffen consulted the moonstone's magic. Shouts sounded in the palace; lights came on in the lower floors. Reiffen discovered that his daughter and whoever she was with were headed toward the heart of the city. If the fool guards had been able to delay them even briefly, he would have had them before they left the palace.

Taking a deep breath to keep from losing his temper, he considered what to do next. The inner keep of the Old Palace was the highest point in Malmoret, and Hubley was headed straight toward it. From there he should be able to track her anywhere in the city. Eventually whoever had taken her would have to go to ground, at which point Reiffen would be able to rescue her whenever he wanted. Unless it was Fornoch himself who had her, in which case he would have to go back to his original plan.

Knowing that help from the palace might prove welcome, he commanded the guards to send someone after him to the Old Palace. Then, collecting his thoughts, he shifted. Not ten minutes after arriving at the New Palace, he stood at the top of the Old.

Breathing hard, he looked out across the sleeping city. Streets and alleys etched dark shadows between the buildings. A light moved slowly through Breva Market: the city watch. According to the moonstone, his daughter and her captor were hurrying through Coinside but, studying the streets themselves, he saw nothing. Still, they continued to head straight for him. He looked for them as they crossed the Kingsway, but even that broad avenue was too dark to see. Checking his charm again, he saw they had crossed into the old Baron's Quarter and were creeping closer through the back streets. If they actually were headed for the Old Palace, that would make things much easier.

Lights flickered outside the palace he had just left. With any luck, whomever Brizen had dispatched to help him would arrive not much later than Hubley. Briefly Reiffen wondered if perhaps the Wizard was doing this deliberately, trying to trap him into an ill-considered move, or wear him out with shifting. Even so, the chance to get Hubley back so quickly was worth the risk. His other plan, after all, was something he had only intended as a last resort. If he were lucky, he would not have to use it at all.

He was surprised, then, when Hubley and her escort turned aside at the base of the Old Palace wall and entered the College. Why would they want to go there? Girls and women were never allowed inside; the College was a terrible place for them to hide.

Only after he had shifted back down to the Great Hall did he realize they were making for the Malmoret Way. Like the back of the Great Forest, or the College, for that matter, Reiffen had never been in that part of the Stoneways. He was not going to be able to trap Fornoch at all. The wild-goose chase the Wizard was leading him on was just going to continue until he was exhausted.

But he was still too close to give up, even if he had no idea where in the College the Bryddin had hidden the entrance to the way. Guards challenged him as he raced toward the Old Palace gate; a wave of his hand had them opening the wicket without his having to break stride.

Outside, he ran straight into a mounted troop. Hooves clattered on the cobblestones as the riders wheeled their horses to a stop. Light from a hand lantern flashed across his face.

"That's him, Your Highness."

"The first one?"

"No, sire. The one who asked all the questions."

Reiffen considered sending the entire troop tumbling with a word, then decided he might want their help at the College.

"Who are you, sir?" demanded the second voice.

"Prince Reiffen," he replied.

"The mage!"

The lantern drew back. Reiffen counted nine men facing him on horseback, the soldiers muttering nervously among themselves. The leader looked vaguely familiar.

"What are you doing running about my father's palace in the middle of the night?" the leader asked.

"Rescuing my daughter."

"Your daughter?"

"Yes. She has been taken to the College. They are headed for the Malmoret Way."

"The Way?" The leader looked astonished. "The entrance to the Way is one of the most closely guarded secrets in Banking."

"Not closely guarded enough, it would seem."

"Since you are so certain, I suppose we should see if you are right. Trooper, dismount so that Prince Reiffen may ride your horse. You can follow on foot."

It had been years since Reiffen had ridden, but he climbed into the saddle quickly for all his awkwardness.

"It is a pleasure to finally meet you, cousin." The man who had questioned him bowed slightly, his blond hair catching the lamplight. "You match your portrait in my father's hall exactly."

"And you look a great deal like your mother, Prince Merannon." Spurring his mount as hard as he could with the house slippers he had not thought to change before he left Castle Grangore, Reiffen led the troop down the Kingsway and around the palace wall to the College.

"May I ask who has taken her?" inquired the prince as they dismounted outside the front door.

"Fornoch, I believe. Though I am not sure."

Apprehension filled the prince's handsome face, replaced at once by resolve.

The door, though locked, gave Reiffen little trouble. Inside, Merannon led the way through several passages to a stone stair. The Chief Fellow and the porter were just emerging.

"You are too late, Your Highness." The Chief Fellow bowed before the prince; the porter went down on one knee.

"You fought?" Merannon nodded at the crossbow in Albwin's hands.

"Of course not," scoffed Reiffen. "Otherwise these two would be dead. You cannot fight Fornoch with weapons."

"Fornoch?" Albwin looked confused. "There was no Wizard here. Just Avender and your daughter."

"Avender?" Reiffen found himself bewildered in turn. "That's impossible. Avender vanished years ago."

Albwin shrugged. "I have no idea if the man was lying or not, of course, but that is what he told us. He did look like Avender. Older, but otherwise the same. Tall and strong."

Though the injured guard at the New Palace had described Hubley's captor the same way, Reiffen knew it could not be true. He and Mindrell had dealt with Avender years before. "Some servant of Fornoch's tricked up to look like Avender perhaps, but not Avender."

The Chief Fellow raised a hand as Reiffen made to hurry on. "Have you brought a Dwarf lamp with you?" he asked.

"No, but I can fetch one easily enough."

"No need for that. I have several in my chambers."

The Chief Fellow began shuffling down the hall. Nouse slid through the crowd to lead the way with his lantern. Reiffen chafed at the slow pace, but there was nothing he could do. Albwin was an old man, as old as Reiffen himself, though without the benefit of a Living Stone, and could go no faster. So he was almost grateful when Merannon, sensing his impatience, offered to lead them on ahead to fetch the lamps.

"You will find them in a pouch in my desk," the Chief Fellow directed. "In the bottom left drawer. Or maybe the right. I have not used them in a while. Go with them, Nouse, and help them look."

The porter, not much younger than his master, could not keep up as the prince and the magician bolted ahead. By the time he joined them, Albwin's desk was already a shambles.

"See here, sir!" he cried when he saw Reiffen shaking a vase. "Put that down!"

"Easy, Nouse," soothed the prince. "When a man's child is endangered, a broken vase is a small thing. Come and help us search."

Nouse was pulling at his hair by the time the Chief Fellow arrived, but Albwin did not seem at all put out by the mess.

"Ah!" he exclaimed, after stroking his beard for a moment in the doorway. "Now I remember. Young Wilstoke was playing with them during his last detention. I believe he hid them under the cushions on the window seat when he thought I was not looking."

Reiffen flicked a finger. Nouse flinched. The cushions flew across the room, revealing a small leather bag. Merannon scooped it up at once.

This time Albwin remained behind as the rest of them hurried downstairs. Arriving in the storeroom at the back of the cellar, Merannon held a lamp to the wall. Slowly the outline of a door formed in the stone.

"Open it, Sergeant," ordered the prince as he fit the lamp into the keyhole in the center.

The sergeant and another soldier put their shoulders to the slab. Reiffen consulted his moonstone. Slowly the secret door slid backward to reveal a black tunnel on the other side, but Reiffen had learned that Hubley and her captor were already far down the stair. Had he brought a bat charm with him, it would have been an easy matter to fly on ahead and trap whoever had taken her. Without that advantage, however, it would be hours before he caught them on foot. Already he had wasted too much time following them through Malmoret and, if anything, was farther away from rescuing his daughter than he had been when he arrived. No doubt that was the Wizard's plan. Even if he got close again, Fornoch would merely travel somewhere else. Sooner or later Reiffen would exhaust himself if he kept insisting on following them, which was probably what the Wizard hoped. Better if he returned to Grangore and resumed his casting.

Stepping to the door, Merannon removed the Dwarf lamp and screwed it into the circlet he wore round his head. Lamplight shone a few steps down the dark path, but the rest remained as dark as ever.

"You are not coming with us?" he asked in surprise as Reiffen made no move to follow.

"No. I have other means of rescuing my daughter. But it would be helpful to me if you continued on. Should you find that Fornoch has taken her, do not fight him. You will only get in the way."

"And if we do rescue her?"

"Bring her back to me."

Alarms were sounding as Reiffen returned to Castle Grangore.

Cursing, he realized his suspicions were correct. Fornoch had deliberately lured him away. The ringing alarms proved Hubley's flight to Malmoret had been designed solely to draw him out of the castle. He should have known she could not have remembered the traveling spell so quickly, that it was all a ruse. Misdirection was the Gray Wizard's favorite ploy. With Reiffen out of the castle, Fornoch would have easy access to everything he had prepared. Everything Reiffen had been working on for all these years might already lie in ruins. Fornoch had depended on him to be rash where his daughter was concerned and, as was so often the case, Reiffen had done just what the Gray Wizard expected.

Angrily he raced downstairs. Mindrell was waiting for him in the courtyard, sword drawn. The front gate stood wide open.

"She's gone!" cried the bard. "I went to her room as soon as the alarm went off, but there was no sign of her. Where were you?"

"In Malmoret. She was already gone when this happened."

"Already gone? How? And why would the Wizard come back if he already had her?"

"To ruin my plans."

Reiffen explained what had happened as they searched the castle. How Fornoch had somehow gotten in without setting off the alarms and had stolen Hubley, then sent someone who looked like Avender to Malmoret with her to lead Reiffen on a wild-goose chase. Then, while Reiffen was gone, the Wizard had doubled back to the castle.

"But that doesn't make sense." Mindrell shook his head, trying to figure it out. "Why lure you away if he already knows how to get in without setting off the alarms? Why not do everything he needed before taking the child?"

"Are you arguing with me?"

Mindrell raised his hands. "Not arguing, Reiffen. Just trying to help."

Reiffen checked his temper. He so wished he had the luxury

to lash out at something. "There is no other explanation. I found Ferris in bed in Valing, and no other mage has sufficient power for this sort of magic. The key is how Fornoch managed to get in here in the first place."

They found no sign of the Wizard anywhere in the castle. Nothing had been disturbed, not even the mussels in the workshop downstairs. Nor was anything changed in the last cave they checked, where no one had visited in more than thirty years. Reiffen had expected that, but still, after what Albwin had said, he had to make sure.

"You think the Wizard might be here?" Mindrell eyed the shovel still lying beside Avender's grave.

"No. But some in Malmoret believe they saw Avender with my daughter, so I thought we should check."

"You want me to dig him up?"

"That is not necessary."

Kneeling, Reiffen placed his hand on the bare dirt. Avender was still there. His Living Stone sensed the other quite clearly. And the other stone still pulsed, though very slowly, to prove Avender was there as well.

Traveling back to the mussel cave, he told Mindrell to go upstairs. "Not unless Hubley or Fornoch show up am I to be disturbed. Not even if Ferris tries to reach me on the mirrors."

The door closed. The vial of Hubley's dried blood lay where Reiffen had left it, but the spell itself had to be completely recast.

Hours later, the small, pinkish gray cloud he had created gathered itself like a cat and disappeared. Wherever Hubley was, it would find her. Not immediately, perhaps, but soon. A day or two at most.

Then the Gray Wizard came swirling out of the wall.

18

Sissit Hospitality

ithout thinking, Hubley kicked hard in the darkness at the thing that grabbed her. Her heel ground against flesh and bone.

A hand almost as cold and hard as a Dwarf's clamped across her face. "None o' that, missy," hissed a voice even icier than the hand. "I don' wanna hurt ya."

Having seen just enough of their attackers to know they were only sissit, she kicked him again, harder this time, and cracked her elbow against his stony gut. Although she wasn't quite able to squirm free, the sissit's grip loosened.

"Avender, help!" she called, hoping the current hadn't swept him away.

Something hard smashed against the side of her head. Pain worse than anything she had ever imagined flashed from her skull to her toes. Dimly she felt the sissit catch her as she went limp, and sling her across his shoulder.

"What about the one I killed?" rasped another voice. "What if he wakes up?"

"He can't wake up if ya killed him, ya geep," answered the sissit carrying Hubley.

"That's right, ya killed him, Obo," said a third.

"But what if there's more?" whined the one called Obo.

"We'd o' heard 'em by now if there was," answered the first.

"Can we eat this one?" Obo pleaded. "I'm hungry."

"No." The first sissit's voice spat through the dark like a snapping goose. "Back to camp. We'll have our fun when we got more time."

"Right, Corns," the second agreed. "It's just like the boss said. Ship's gotta come t' the light, with humans on 'em, an' this is the place t' catch 'em. Too bad the river took the big un, but at least we got yours."

Somehow Hubley managed not to pass out as the sissit splashed across the stream. Her head throbbed; she felt almost too weak to breathe. Briefly the creatures debated who would carry her, before she ended up dangling like a doll from the arm of a much larger and fatter sissit than the one who had captured her. Her head lolled and her feet dragged on the tunnel floor, which sent fresh waves of nausea rolling over her. The sissit had said Avender was dead, but maybe if Hubley did something she could save him. She was a magician, after all. But she had to act quickly. All that cold water would drown him if she didn't do whatever it was she was supposed to do soon. She pictured herself sliding out from under the sissit's doughy arm and creeping back to the stream. Her mother would be there, and together they would find Avender, and everything would be fine.

She came fully awake to the slap of the sissits' soft, fat feet against the stone. The clothes on the one carrying her smelled like laundry that had been left wet and unwashed for a month; what was underneath smelled even worse. In the thin light that trickled back from the sissit in the front, she saw the one carrying her was the last in line. She had no idea how far they had come from the stream, but knew she had to get back. Even if Avender couldn't help her, her mother and Mims were somewhere close on the Backford Way.

Her head throbbed again as she pushed against the sissit's heavy arm. Her throat thickened, and she lay back down.

"Corns." The sissit carrying her stopped in the middle of the path. "The human's movin'."

"Put her down, then, ya cob. Let her do her own walkin'."

"That's right. Let her walk."

The sissit carrying Hubley set her on the ground. Her head still throbbed, and her legs weren't strong enough for sitting, let alone standing up and walking. With her back to the tunnel wall, she regarded the sissit who had captured her for the first time.

The one who'd been carrying her was the biggest. An immense, fat creature, he stood taller and wider than Redburr in human form. Rather than looking like a shaggy bear, however, he looked more like a two-legged pig. Not a single hair glossed the pale dome of his head, which was covered with fresh cuts and old scabs, purple bumps and bruises. His great, flat nose took up half his face, a pair of tiny eyes set close above. Without the benefit of eyebrows or even much of a forehead, those eyes looked like a pair of pale buttons glued to a fat man's belly. Arms as long as his legs hung nearly to the ground, the fingers on his hands turned back instead of in toward his tree-thick thighs. One broken tusk curling up along the side of his mouth gave him an oddly thoughtful air.

His fellows were different. One of them had eyes set slantwise across his face, above and beside his nose, and two right hands. The one called Corns carried a small candle lantern, the holes in the lantern's sides as oddly spaced and jagged as the holes an idle child might poke in a piece of paper with a penknife. Odd sprays of light shone across his bony body, which was as different from the two fat sissit as a string bean from a pair of pumpkins. His knees and elbows stood out from his arms and legs as thick as knots on a piece of string.

"Here." Corns came back down the path, his lantern swinging from a gnarled hand. His toes looked even worse. "Yer walkin' now, see? No more shirkin'. Even cows walks t' the slaughterhouse."

"That's right." The one with two right hands nodded his head. Given the arrangement of his eyes and her own wooziness, Hubley wasn't exactly sure whether he was agreeing or disagreeing with the leader. Either way, it made her dizzy just looking at him.

"Wish I had a cow," said the large sissit.

"You are a cow."

As he spoke, Corns grabbed Hubley and pulled her sharply to her feet. His grip was hard and dry as bone, much different from the large sissit's moist, spongy hands.

Her head spun. After a couple of wobbly steps she would have sat down again had Corns not still had hold of her arm.

"None o' that, missy. I'll knock yer head again, if ya don't do what I say." Corns raised his fist menacingly. Up close it looked more like a misshapen mace than a hand.

Hubley swallowed and made an effort to stand straight. She had already made up her mind what she was going to do. Her head still ached, but she found it was starting to clear. When it did, she knew which spell she was going to cast. One she had known for years. Fooling a bunch of stupid sissit wouldn't be hard at all.

Surprisingly, she wasn't afraid. The sissit were almost comic, creatures out of one of Hern's bedtime tales. Hubley had never taken those stories seriously, not even the ones where they ate careless children, because Hubley knew she wasn't like other children. Or most adults, either.

They set off again down the passage, Hubley walking between Righty, as she decided to call him, and the one she guessed was Obo. Corns still led the way. Sparks of light fluttered like moths across the rock walls from the swinging lantern. Though her head still hurt terribly, Hubley had recovered enough so she could walk without too much weaving back and forth.

When she thought she had recovered enough to run, she whispered her spell.

"Make me dark as caves at night,
Keep me from the sissits' sight."

She stepped to one side. Righty lumbered past her before he noticed the change.

"Hey?" The awkward sissit stopped in the middle of the passage and scratched his head with both right hands. "Where'd she go?"

"What d'you mean, where'd she go?" Glaring at his companion's stupidity, Corns turned around.

"Don't blame me," said the giant. "I didn' touch her."

He might have, though, as Hubley scooted past him along the side of the wall. Obo was wide, but not so wide that he took up the entire tunnel, no matter how much he stooped.

Past the sissit, Hubley's footsteps echoed loudly off the walls as she raced up the passage.

"What's that!" Corns's voice rattled along the tunnel like an avalanche of marbles.

"What's what?" asked Righty.

"I don' see nothin'," grumbled the giant.

"She's gone 'visible! Quick! We gotta catch her! If she gets back t' the ship, the Boss'll have our skins for boots!"

"I still don' see nothin'."

Hubley ran as fast as she could but found she couldn't run very far. Her head hurt worse than ever, and she soon caught a stitch in her side. Looking back over her shoulder, she found the three sissit already in pursuit. Corns, especially, was flying down the tunnel. Like a spider missing half its legs, he scrabbled along on all fours, running high up the side of the outer wall every time he rounded a turn, the lantern rattling as he carried it between his teeth like a dog.

Shrinking down to the floor of the tunnel, Hubley hoped they would pass her by. Normally no one ever found her when she turned invisible. But things were different here in the Stoneways. With no place else to go, the sissit knew she couldn't be anywhere but ahead of them. Unless they ran right past her. Then she might actually have a chance to get away.

Corns, however, had already figured that out. Stopping his reckless rush, he called back to his fellows, "Righty. You take the right side of the tunnel. Obo, you go left. Whatever ya do, don' let her get past ya." A thin smile creased his face until his cheeks looked as knobby as his knees. "I'll take the middle. And I'm gonna turn out the light, too. Let's see how the little lady does in the dark."

The sissit's cheeks bulged as he blew out the candle in the lamp. The tunnel dipped back into darkness. Hubley, huddled as small as she could on one side of the passage, tried not to breathe. She couldn't think of a single spell that would help. Most would only give her away. What she really needed was the traveling spell. How many times had she heard her mother say the ability to travel was the best thing about magic? Well, that was certainly true now. It would serve her parents right if she ended up in some sissit's stew pot.

Bare feet scuffed close by. A nose sniffed. Screwing her eyes tight, Hubley tried to remember how she had made the spell that had taken her to Malmoret. She had been scared then, and she was scared now. But that wasn't the trick. She had been asleep then, asleep and dreaming of the place she would rather have been. If that was the secret, she was never going to be able to use it now. No way was she going to fall asleep with three ugly sissit hunting for her in a pitch-black tunnel.

"Gotcha!"

Knobbed fingers tightened around her shoulder. The sissit jerked Hubley roughly to her feet. "Little witch." Cold spit spattered her face. The smell of spoiled fish lingered on Corns's clammy breath. "No more tricks."

Blinding light burst behind her eyes as the sissit's clublike fist smashed against her cheek. Her jaw stung; warm blood trickled down her chin.

"Any more witchin' from you and you'll get a lot worse than that. Unnerstand?"

"Yes."

"How'd she do that?" Obo's voice sounded querulously from the air above her head. "How'd she disappear?"

Steel and flint cracked in the darkness as Corns struck a light. A brief flame arced evilly below his face as he used his glowing tinder to relight the lantern. "With a spell, dummy. How d'ya think?"

"Only big humans do magic. Ain't that right?" Obo's tiny eyes squeezed even smaller as he tried to figure things out.

"Guess that's diff'rent, now. This one ain't full grown."

"That's right. Not full grown," Righty agreed.

"Here. Gimme your belt."

The knobby sissit reached toward his larger companion.

"What's gonna hold up my pants?"

"Yer hand. Come on, we're late gettin' back already."

"That's right. Don' wanna be late. Might miss grub." The giant untied the rope around his waist and handed it to Corns. His pants, stretched up and over the widest part of his belly, looked in no danger of falling down. All the same, he gripped the top firmly.

"You got a belt," he complained. "Ya coulda used yours."

"Mine ain't big enough."

Fashioning a quick noose, the sissit looped the rope around Hubley's neck and jerked it tight.

"Ow." The girl loosened the greasy coil with her hand.

Grinning, Corns tried to pull the knot tight once more, but Hubley stopped him by keeping her hand inside the noose.

"Let's see you try and get away now, missy," he said with a nasty grin.

Hubley had half a mind to turn the rope into a snake, just to see the look on the creature's ugly face. Only her jaw still ached, and the cuts on her cheek stung every time she spoke. She'd get him later, when she had a better chance. Plum had taught her an interesting spell once. Her mother had sent her to her room for an entire day the last time she used it, but this time there would be no objection at all.

With Corns leading the prisoner at the end of her leash, the party continued on. Hubley soon noticed that, whenever they encountered a branch in the road, the sissit chose the one that led down. No longer was she headed toward the surface. Apparently the secret camp the sissit kept mentioning was closer to the bottom of the world than it was to the top.

Corns kept the pace brisk. Righty trudged along easily enough behind them, but the giant often found the going tough, especially when the roof of the tunnel dipped. Though he slouched, and spent most of the time leaning on his knuckles, he still knocked his head against every uneven spot in the ceiling. Each time that happened he grunted and winced, his tiny eyes nearly disappearing inside his enormous face. Hubley started cringing herself at each hollow knock on the stone behind her.

By the time they came to another stream, Hubley had started to believe Avender really had been killed. Otherwise, she was sure he would have caught up with them long before. And where were her mother and Mims? The fact that no one had rescued her yet scared her more than all Corns's threats and blows. Despite appearances, the sissit might not be as pathetic as they seemed.

Following the water upstream, they reached an apparent dead end. A small waterfall poured loudly out of the rock into a shallow pool. Moisture glistened on the cavern walls. Hubley wondered if they had come here to rest before continuing on.

Instead of stopping, Corns walked straight into the small cascade. Stumbling a bit as she tried to keep from being soaked, Hubley followed at the end of the rope. Beyond the curtaining water another small tunnel narrowed down into the darkness. The smell of wet sissit filled the cramped space as the last two members of the party squeezed into the passage. Obo squirmed along on his belly as the way became so tight that even Hubley had to crawl. The loop of rope hung slack between her and Corns, who had gone back to creeping on all fours like a spider, knotty elbows and knees rising above his skinny back.

He stopped before a large rock that blocked the way. Using his swollen knuckles as a knocker, he rapped on the stone. One, two, three. One, two, three. It wasn't a complicated signal.

There was no immediate answer. Righty crowded behind Hubley, his flesh as cold and flabby as Obo's, who huffed and puffed as he squeezed through the passage behind them.

Rocks scraped. The blocking stone slid slightly to the side, exposing a dark opening above one corner. A pale, two-fingered hand wiggled through the gap to get a better grip on the rock. From the other side a voice barked orders; with a great deal of grunting and scraping, the stone was pushed aside.

As soon as she entered the new cave, Hubley started coughing. Thin smoke from an oil lamp on the far wall filmed the air. Its hissing light revealed half a dozen figures slumped around the low room, and, standing in front of a hole in the floor, a sissit whom Hubley almost mistook for human. Beneath a felt cap, dark hair dangled over his pale forehead. His eyes were both in the right place, and his nose, though large, was not horribly so. A few black teeth lurked behind his flabby lips, the lower of which glistened like the walls in the cave outside. If not for his hands, which boasted a pair of thumbs and four fingers between them, Hubley might even have been fooled.

"It's about time, Corns."

The knobby lieutenant ducked as his dark-haired chief raised a hand to strike him. The blow was checked, however, as he caught sight of Hubley. The chief's watery eyes widened. Like his fellows, he lacked eyelashes or brows, despite the hair on his head.

"What's this? A human? You found a human? An' a female, too. I don' believe it. Did my ship come in?"

"Yup. It's tied up on the Lamp jus' like ya said. Two humans on it, an' we caught 'em at the river." Corns, no longer fearful of being struck, pulled Hubley forward by the rope. "We had to kill th' other, though."

"Why didn't you bring it back so we could eat it?"

"We lost it in the water. Obo hit it too hard. But this one oughta taste just fine. It's young and tender."

"That's right. Young and tender." Pushing into the crowded room, Righty pinched the prisoner with one of his right hands.

Hubley recoiled, but not before stamping hard on one of the sissit's broad, flat feet. Laughter like strangled hiccups popped out among the others.

"Yeah," said the chief. "It is young and tender. But ya shoulda brought the dead one. We coulda eaten it first. This one'll have t' squeal some before there's any chewin'."

Reaching for his cap, the chief bowed to his prisoner. Only, instead of lifting his hat in salutation, he clapped it firmly to his head.

"Welcome, human," he said. "I'm Locks. Before we eat ya, please be my guest. And don' worry, there's plenty o' fish, so we prob'ly won' be eatin' ya for a while."

Hubley didn't find this the most welcoming invitation she had ever received. All the same, she remained less terrified than she might have been, despite the sting of Corns's blow on her cheek. There was something hapless about the sissit, for all their fierce hunger. And she still had a trick or two up her sleeve before she was really going to start worrying about the stew pot.

"It needs watchin', that one." Corns nodded in Hubley's direction. "It knows magic."

Locks's face twisted like kneaded dough. "Magic? It's not old enough to know magic."

"That's right. That's what we thought." Righty's head bobbed up and down.

"She went away an' we couldn' see her at all." Obo popped through the entrance like a cork pushed into a bottle, then single-handedly rolled the stone gate back into place.

"I don't believe it," said Locks. "None o' you was payin' attention. She's not big enough to cast no spells. Are ya?"

The chief turned on Hubley with a savage eye.

"I can too do magic," she said before she had time to think better of it.

"Ya turned invisible?"

Locks's tone suggested he might be interested in a demonstration, but Corns didn't like the idea at all.

"Don' let her do it again!" The gnarled sissit sprang forward, pulling the noose tight around Hubley's neck at the same time. "She almost got away, first time she tried that trick."

"What else ya know how t' do?" Locks cocked his head sideways, his watery eyes glittering slyly.

"Not much." Something in the chief sissit's look made Hubley more cautious. "Adults don't trust children with magic, you know. I only know a few spells."

"Show me."

Hubley glanced around the room. She needed to show them the simplest conjuring she knew, the sort of magic her father had taught her as soon as she could speak. Anything more powerful would only make them warier of what she might be able to do. Spotting a ratty knapsack lying on the floor, she pointed a finger at it and said, *"Fly."*

The knapsack lifted off the floor. The sissit scrabbled as far away from it as they could. Waving her hand, Hubley made the pack float back and forth across the room before lowering it to the ground.

"Told ya," said Corns.

"That's right. He did."

"I believed ya. I just wanted to test ya t' make sure ya was tellin' me the whole truth. Make sure ya know better'n t' hold anythin' back." The chief nudged the knapsack with his toes. "Is it still goin'?"

Hubley ended the connection in her mind. "No."

The bag toppled on its side. Satisfied the magic was gone, Locks gave it a second, more scornful kick, and turned back to his prize.

"Ya don't scare me, human. As long as we got the front door blocked with that stone, there's no way ya can escape, no matter how much ya disappear. I'll keep my eyes on ya, but don' go ex-pectin' anything special. Corns, what else ya find out there?"

"Nothin'." The gangly sissit spat into a wide opening in the center of the floor.

"Any stoneboys with the ship?"

"Nope. Jus' the two humans we caught at the ford."

"That's right," piped up Righty. "No stoneboys."

Apparently satisfied with this news, Locks nodded in ap-proval. Corns and Righty slouched off to join their fellows, while Obo began scrounging through the refuse surrounding the hole in the floor. Finding nothing to eat other than a few glassy-eyed fish heads, he checked the fishing line tied to his nearest neigh-bor's toe. Drawing it up through the hole, he found nothing there either, and turned plaintively to his chief.

"Can we eat the human soon?" he asked.

"No. I told ya, ya shoulda brought back the other one. I wanna ask her questions first."

Sighing, Obo picked up one of the fish heads and swallowed it whole, bones and all, without even bothering to chew.

Locks picked up Hubley's halter and led her off to the back of the cave. A ragged curtain separated a small alcove from the rest of the cavern; behind it Locks had furnished his private apartment with several dirty pillows, blankets, and a lamp as marks of his senior status. Hubley, noting the small things crawling among the folds of the blankets, demurred when he offered her a seat.

"I'll sit then." Grunting, the sissit settled on the nearest pillow. Vermin streamed out from under him. "No use both of us standin'."

He poked at a plate on the floor. More insects scuttled off to safety. Dark brown stains coated the chipped dish, but there didn't appear to be anything on it even a sissit might eat. Snuffling unhappily, he knocked it away.

"So," he said, looking back up at his prisoner. "Where'd ya learn magic?"

Hubley, never having met anyone who didn't know who her parents were, saw no reason not to answer the sissit's question.

"From my parents."

"Yer parents are magicians? Which ones? Cannapt? Weidel?"

"My father's Reiffen and my mother's Ferris."

"The Wizardsbane? The one who killed the White an' Black Wizards?"

"Uh-huh." Hubley nodded proudly. All her life she had been accustomed to people behaving especially nicely toward her once they learned she was the magicians' daughter. Maybe the sissit would be the same.

Locks's eyes nearly disappeared into his doughy cheeks as he looked at his prisoner suspiciously.

"An' ya came down here without 'em? Why'd ya do a fool thing like that?"

"I'm meeting my mother."

"Where?"

"Along the Backford Way."

"Yer ma lives here in the Stoneways?"

"No."

"So why ya meetin' her here?"

Hubley shrugged. Her parents' problems were none of the sissit's business.

"Don't ya live with her?" Locks went on.

"Not right now."

"I thought all ya humans stayed with yer dams till ya was full-growed. Maybe yer gettin' smart now an' doin' it our way. No sense in havin' extra mouths t' feed when brats can rummage fine on their own. Well, it's yer tough luck, then, runnin' in t' me."

Hubley almost blurted out that her mother was somewhere nearby and sure to find her, then decided it might be better to keep the sissit in the dark. That way he'd be unprepared when her mother and Mims finally showed up.

"Ya fly th' airship ya come in yerself?" he asked.

"No. Avender flew it."

"Avender? Who's Avender?"

"The man your friends killed."

"Bet ya miss him now." Licking his fingers, the sissit rubbed them across the crusted plate, then sucked them thoughtfully. "But don't worry. I'm not gonna let the boys eat ya, least not till ya show me how t' fly yer ship. Ya do know how t' fly it, don't ya?"

Certain that if she didn't say yes she might not last long enough for her mother to arrive, Hubley nodded. The more the sissit chief thought Hubley could teach him, the longer she'd keep out of his gang's stew pot.

Which gave Hubley an idea.

"I can teach you magic, too, if you want."

The sissit's eyes gleamed under hairless lids.

"Yer a smart little missy, ain't ya. I see the two of us're gonna get along like bats an' bugs."

Bounding up from the bed, he seized Hubley by the hand and threw back the curtain that cut off his part of the cave. "This ain't food!" he called out loudly to his lolling troop, dragging his captive before him. "You all get that? Anyone touches her, it's straight to the stew pot for ya."

Scowls answered Locks's fresh order. Obo, another fish head poised at his slobbery chin, said, "We ain't got no stew pot, boss."

"That's right," his droop-eyed companion agreed. "Can't go into a stew pot if we ain't got one."

"Quiet, both o' ya." Locks glared at them. "Ya know what I mean. This one's goin' t' teach me everythin' she knows. With a ship an' my own magician, I'll be king o' the Stoneways by the time we get back north. Ol' Leadlegs ain't gonna be able to touch us, ya hear?"

"Sure, boss." Corns squatted near the fishing hole, his bulging knees nearly as large as his head. "But it's gonna be hard, sittin' here wi' such a tender piece o' veal just lyin' there beggin' for it. How's about ya give us a little taste, jus' so we knows what we're missin'."

"No tastin'. And no lickin' neither." Locks stared hard at Corns till the bony sissit looked away. "Go back to your fishin'. I'll take care o' the prisoner."

Just how Locks intended to take care of her, Hubley never learned. Instead a loud explosion rocked the cave, filling the air with bits of flying rock. Several hit Hubley on her shoulder and side, the ones that missed ricocheting off the walls around her. Behind the splintered stone three figures burst into the room, the first short and the second two tall. Dwarf lamps pierced the oily gloom.

"Findle!" she cried in joy and surprise, recognizing the Dwarf at once. And was one of the two men Avender?

"Stoneboys!" warned Locks. "Get 'em, Obo!"

Tossing aside his fish heads, the giant sissit stepped in front of the Dwarf. With one upward stroke, Findle ran his blade deep into the creature's chest. Ignoring the stroke, Obo picked Findle up in a massive hand and tossed him against the wall. Avender and the other human advanced cautiously, ducking under and around the giant's sweeping attempts to grab them.

Two other sissit seized their clubs and attacked the Dwarf before he could rise. The stranger rushed to Findle's aid. Unlike Obo, regular sissit were no match for either Dwarf or man, who cut them down immediately.

"There's no fightin' stoneboys!" shouted Locks. Grabbing Hubley around the waist, he carried her to the hole in the floor. "Everybody out the back door. Obo, hold 'em as long as ya can!"

Like a farmer stuffing a kitten into a sack, the chief thrust Hubley down the well. Scrabbling at the stone, she plunged into darkness. It wasn't fair! Avender and Findle had been about to rescue her! And where was her mother?

The stone around her disappeared, and she fell through empty air. With a shock that almost knocked the wind from her, she hit water. Bubbles foamed in the gripping cold. Frantically she kicked out with her legs and clawed for the surface, until something heavy fell on top of her and drove her deeper. She thought she was going to die then, her lungs bursting, the water clutching coldly at her clothes.

19

Mouse in a Drainpipe

I t took Avender a while to remember he wasn't outside, and that what looked like stars spinning in the clear night overhead were actually drops of water shining on the roof of a small cave.

And it wasn't the roof that was spinning, it was him.

He enjoyed a moment's peace, something he hadn't had in a while, before the cold of the water he was floating in finally roused him. Remembering the struggle by the stream, he scrambled ashore. He'd lost his pack and sword, but at least he'd kept his lamp. In its pale light he studied the cuts and bruises still healing on his hands, and decided the only thing that had kept him alive after the sissit had knocked him into the water was his Living Stone. How long it had been, and how many flumes and falls his battered body had tumbled through during the descent to this new cave, he had no idea.

He wondered what had happened to Hubley. Had the sissit captured her? He didn't see how she could possibly have escaped. Mims had told him the child wouldn't remember any more magic than the traveling spell for some time. He frowned at the thought of how easily the sissit had ambushed him but, knowing there wasn't any time for guilt, forced himself to think the matter through. As long as Mims was alive, Hubley would be, too. With any luck, Ferris and the old magician were rescuing her right now. Or at least they would be, once Avender called them on his magic mirror and told them what had happened.

His already cold skin chilled even more when he pulled the mirror out of his shirt and discovered it was broken. Although he was sure Mims would find Hubley before it was too late, hungry sissit had been known to bite off bits of their captives before they killed them. And even her Living Stone wouldn't help if they had time to actually cook and eat her.

He had to help the old magician find her.

Jumping to his feet, he examined the source and outlet of the stream. Neither looked promising. The water entered through a gap in the far wall near the ceiling before dropping to the pool in a small and noisy fall, then left by way of a larger opening in the bottom at the other end. Avender saw at once the current coming out of the wall was much too strong for him to be able to force his way back up it. He supposed if worse came to worst he could always let the drain suck him out and away, and trust in the Stone to revive him wherever he came out. Even if he fell into the Abyss, his thimble would always bring him back. Bad as the Gray Wizard was, he was still better than an endless fall through darkness.

But he refused to believe that Mims had rescued him from Castle Grangore just to get him trapped all over again in an even deeper cave, and began to search the chamber more thoroughly. It took some time, with a lot of clambering up and down the slippery walls, but eventually he discovered a hole in the ceiling over the deep end of the pool. Unfortunately, it was a good bit farther than he could reach from the wall, and Avender was no Dwarf that he could hang from the rock by his fingers and toes. He tried jumping for it several times from a tall pile of broken stones near that edge of the cave, but there was no ledge to catch onto even when he did manage to reach the opening. All he got for his trouble was a fresh wetting each time he fell into the pool.

On his last try he landed on his pack. Apparently it had come loose from whatever had caught it upstream. The sight of it swirling lazily in the slow current above the drain, the same way he'd spun when he'd first arrived, gave him an idea. What if he blocked the drain?

He would never be able to dam it completely, but what if he could clog it enough for the water to start filling the cave? Raise it high enough and he'd be able to swim right up to the hole, if he didn't freeze first. Of course it would help if the opening actually led somewhere, otherwise he'd just get stuck. In which case he really would have to use his thimble.

Grabbing the pack, he scrambled back up onto the rocks he'd been using as a diving platform and began kicking them into the stream. At first only a few fell, but it wasn't long before he managed to overweight one side of the pile. A section rolled into the water like a single slab with a roar loud enough to drown out the rumble of the fall at the other end.

When the dust cleared, Avender saw the rocks had partly filled the drain. Taking the blanket out of his pack, he waded back into the water. Cold clamped his trousers fast against his legs. Bracing himself for the freezing plunge, he ducked his head under the surface. With heavy rocks to anchor the corners, the blanket covered the opening completely. The little current still flowing sucked the material down till it settled over the rocks like a dark brown crust on a pie.

Returning to the surface several times for air, he piled more stones on top. Finally, when his hands were so cold even large rocks were slipping out of them, he stopped. The water in the pool had risen nearly to his neck. Now his only hope was for the water to rise fast enough that he would still have some strength left to climb the passage in the ceiling.

Back at the top of the pile, he clapped his hands and slapped his arms on his chest to keep warm. Already the water had risen two-thirds of the way up the fallen stone, the thunder of the waterfall lightening as the pool rose. He tried not to think about how horrible things must be for Hubley while he waited. Sissit prodding her in the darkness, their lips smacking as they talked about munching her legs and arms; better to assume Ferris and Mims had already saved her. Turning his mind to something else, he thought about Brizen and Wellin's son. His son. Mims had told him how the people of Banking and Wayland loved Prince Merannon even more than they loved his parents, which was hard to imagine. He only hoped Merannon wouldn't hold his attack at the Malmoret Lamp against him. Even if Avender still planned to keep the secret to himself, trying to cut off the prince's hand was hardly the best way to meet his long-lost son.

The water rose to his knees. Climbing faster as it approached the roof, the surface was soon above his hips. Already the front of the cave was completely submerged. Shadows rippled against the ceiling as small waves rocked the surface of the pool.

Filling his knapsack with air, Avender turned it upside down to use as a float. At least the pool was rising quickly enough he didn't think he would have to tread water long. Waves chilled his chest. A last few stones skittered beneath his feet as the dark water swirled up and over his chin.

Kicking out from the wall, he swam till he was under the high point of the roof. The weight of his boots threatened to drag him down, but he was a strong swimmer and the pack helped. Soon he was grasping the edge of the overhang. His head scraped the ceiling, so he ducked down beneath the water, the cold embracing him from head to toe, and swam to a spot with more room.

Surfacing, he found himself directly beneath the hole. He could see a little further into it now, but still couldn't tell how far it went. Deciding there wasn't enough room in the passage for both him and his knapsack, he kicked it off into the cold darkness. Without the pack, staying afloat was much harder; his arms and legs felt heavy as blocks of ice. But, if he didn't keep himself under the center of the opening, he was likely to be smashed against the rock. And what if the hole was too small? If his shoulders didn't fit, he was likely to get stuck like a mouse in a drainpipe.

The hole rushed toward him. As fast as the water was going, there would be no need to climb. Grasping his thimble with his right hand, he dropped his arms in front of him and narrowed his shoulders. With one last deep breath, he shot up into the opening. Water rushed past his face, surging bubbles tickling his eyes and nose. He was reminded of how Silverback had carried him out of the rookery the last time someone had tried to drown him, and how he'd thought he'd never make it to the surface then, either. Hopefully his lungful of air would be enough to carry him to the top of the tube. Clamping his jaw shut as tightly as he could, he held on.

His head burst above the surface. Wet rock gleamed in front of his face, then disappeared back into the foaming water as he sank back down. Bracing himself with his legs, he scrabbled to bring his nose and mouth back above the surface. His grip held. The water stopped rising. For a long time he clung to the stone, gasping for breath. His chest ached even more than his frozen fingers and toes, but it seemed he had gone as far as the water would take him.

He looked up. Tunnel darkness stretched above. Somewhere at the other end of the stream, perhaps at the cave where the sissit had attacked him, the water had risen high enough to find a new way down. Which meant it had taken him as far as it was going to here. Now he had to climb.

Carefully he worked his hands up along the rock till they were in front of his face. Though the stone was rough, his fingers felt no handholds. They were just too numb. He found, however, that by pressing his forearms and knees against the stone in front of him, and his back against the wall behind, he could inch his way upward.

He concentrated on nothing else. Water poured off him. His jacket ripped at the elbows and along the back; the knees of his trousers shredded. His skin was probably shredding, too, but he was still too numb to feel it. The Living Stone would heal his cuts soon enough anyway, whether or not he made it to the top of the tunnel.

The passage curved. With a sigh of relief, Avender rolled onto his stomach. After that it was a much easier climb. He could even rest occasionally, his legs braced against the sides of the passage. Eventually he reached a place where he could stand and walk until the tunnel narrowed again and he had to crawl forward on hands and knees.

He came to another cave. After staring at it for some time, he realized he was back at the place where the sissit had attacked him, in one of the openings above the stream. Although he still had a long way to go to find Hubley, a wave of relief washed over him. At least he knew where he was again.

He looked for a way down. As he had guessed, the river was higher than it had been before. The stepping-stones had disappeared, and a steady stream poured over the lip of the passage through which he and Hubley had arrived. By a combination of weary climbing and sliding he lowered himself to the passage he had originally intended to cross to on the other side.

"So," said a voice. "You're not dead after all."

Two more lamps joined Avender's, one in the passage and the other on the far side of the swollen stream.

Avender recognized the Dwarf on his side first. "Findle!"

The Dwarf stepped closer, his sword at Avender's chest. "You know me?"

Unlike his brothers, Findle was slender enough to resemble a short human, if you ignored the full beard and shaggy eyebrows.

"Of course I know you," answered Avender. "Don't you recognize me?"

The Dwarf called across to his companion on the other side of the stream. "It's like Albwin says, Merannon. He does look like Avender. But not enough to convince me that's who he is."

"I can hardly imagine Fornoch going to all the trouble of creating a double without making the copy exact."

Avender recognized Prince Merannon as the other man splashed across the stream. Filthy though he was, he still looked very much like his mother.

"I'm Avender. Not a copy."

"Can you prove it?" asked the prince.

"There isn't enough time. Have you seen Ferris?"

Merannon frowned suspiciously. "Ferris? Why would she be here?"

"Hubley and I were going to meet her." Avender saw no need to mention Mims yet. Explaining who she was would take too much time. "That's why I brought Hubley."

"You were bringing the child to her mother?"

"That's right."

Findle pointed back up the tunnel. "We found her footprints there. We'd have been after them already if we hadn't noticed your light. They're already more than an hour ahead."

The prince turned to the Dwarf. "Do you think we can trust him?"

"Either we take him with us," said Findle, "or we have to kill him here."

"No need for hasty judgment. The situation with Reiffen is quite complicated. If you really are Avender, sir, my father will want very much to see you."

Avender was struck again by how much Merannon looked like his mother. The same blond hair and blue eyes, on a face that was almost too pretty for a man. Perhaps if he saw the prince in broad daylight he'd find something of himself in him as well.

They set off with Findle in front and the prince guarding Avender from the rear. As the Dwarf led them along the sissits' trail, Merannon explained how, after Avender had gotten away, he had called his father for suggestions about what to do next.

His father had sent his court magician to the Malmoret Lamp, and then she and Merannon had traveled on to Issinlough. There it had been an easy matter to persuade the Dwarves to lend him their fastest airship. Trier, who turned out to be the court magician, would have been no use on an airship, so Merannon had brought Findle instead.

"How'd you think to come to Backford?" asked Avender.

"It's what I would have done," replied the prince. "After Malmoret, Backford is the place you and Hubley know best. You have friends there. Had I been thinking more clearly, I would have called Trier while we were still pursuing you on the Malmoret Way. Then again, I had no idea she had been to the Lamp before and could travel there at will. We would have cut you off before you could escape, if I had."

"Just as well you didn't." Avender stooped as they hurried along under the tunnel's low ceiling. "Reiffen would have killed me and taken Hubley straight back to Grangore."

He told his own story then, or at least part of it, about how Reiffen had buried him at the bottom of the castle until a magician named Mims had dug him up, given him back his hand, and set him the task of rescuing Hubley. How Hubley had then managed to remember the traveling spell at the worst possible time, which had left him scrambling to keep her out of her father's hands until they could meet with Mims, who had gone to fetch Ferris.

"But who is Mims?" asked Merannon. "I know no magician by that name."

"I've no idea who she is," Avender lied, "or where she comes from. But one thing's sure, if she's not as powerful as Reiffen, she's close."

"Could she be Fornoch?" suggested the prince. "The Wizard has been known to take other forms before."

"Even if she was, I'd still have helped her rescue Hubley. You and I both know that what Reiffen's been doing to that child all these years is wrong. Not to mention what he did to me. The man's as bad as a Wizard."

"Do not say such a thing," Merannon cautioned. "No one is as bad as a Wizard. He could have killed you, but chose to keep you alive for some reason instead. This would not be the first time Reiffen's choices have turned out better than expected. You should know that better than anyone."

Merannon might look like his mother, but he sounded exactly like Brizen. "Which is why you need to listen to me," Avender told him, "when I say this time he's gone too far."

They hurried on. Avender kept hoping to meet Ferris and Mims along the way, but they had no such luck. For a while there was only the one passage to follow, and they made excellent progress, but eventually they came to a spot where another tunnel crossed their path. Motioning for the humans to be still, Findle pressed his bare toes against the rock like a stubby hound nosing at a trail and felt for the faintest echo of footsteps in the stone.

"That way," he said, pointing to the right.

They encountered two more turnings, with Findle feeling for the sissit at each one. Avender believed they were still moving much faster than their quarry, and was glad they found no sign the sissit had stopped to eat. The only question now was how hungry the creatures would be by the time they reached their den.

Arriving at a stream, they splashed up its course to a cave with a small pool. A waterfall veiled the far end, its thin mist drifting through the pale lamplight. Without hesitating, Findle strode straight up to the glittering curtain and disappeared through to the other side.

The prince motioned for Avender to follow. "Were it merely a question of bravery," he said, "I would go first. But until you have proven we can trust you, I must insist you lead the way."

Beyond the waterfall the passage became low enough that even Findle had to crawl. Not much farther, they ran into a flat stone blocking the way. Pushing up beside the Dwarf, Avender reached for possible handholds to shove it out of the way. Stony fingers circled his wrist.

"Don't touch. Someone may be listening on the other side."

"We'll have to touch it, if we want to get it open."

"Not with our hands, we won't."

Unhooking his pack from his shoulders, Findle pulled out a small sack. Silently he removed a long spike and a heavy, short-handled hammer, then studied the rock. The surface was flat but not smooth. Neither Avender nor Prince Merannon saw anything different about any part of the stone, but then they weren't Dwarves.

"You'd better cover your eyes," said Findle as he raised hammer and spike to strike. "I rarely cut stone as cleanly as my brothers."

The humans turned their backs and did as they were told. The passage erupted in a ringing explosion; gravel peppered their shoulders. When it stopped, Avender and the prince found Findle already leaping into the cave beyond. Startled sissit rolled around in the dust-filled dimness, shouting in dismay.

"Findle!" Avender heard Hubley's glad cry as he and Merannon followed the Dwarf inside.

"Stoneboys! Get 'em, Obo!"

The largest sissit Avender had ever seen lumbered up to the front of the cave. Findle drove his sword deep into the creature's flabby chest. But a stroke that would have felled a spitting mander had no effect at all on the massive sissit. With one meaty hand the giant grabbed Findle by the throat and tossed him back across the rubble of the broken door.

Knowing the Dwarf could take care of himself, Avender tried to go around the giant in order to reach Hubley, who was struggling in a normal-sized sissit's arms on the far side of the cave. But the giant was quicker than he looked, and Avender found himself dodging its clumsy attempts to grab him instead. Snatching up their clubs, two other sissit attacked Findle and the prince, who cut both the creatures down with the first flash of their swords.

"There's no fightin' stoneboys!" cried the sissit holding Hubley. "Everybody out the back door. Obo, hold 'em as long as you can before you come after us!"

Pushing Hubley through a hole in the middle of the floor, the sissit chief jumped in behind her. Avender lunged after them, but another swing of the giant's huge fists forced him away from the hole. Merannon tried the same thing on the other side with no better luck. The sissit had arms long enough to reach either side of the cave.

Three more sissit followed Hubley and their leader down the bolt hole, the last scuttling sideways like a crab. Merannon skewered a fourth as he tried to follow, then jumped back out of the way of another swipe of the enormous swinging arms.

With no more normal-sized sissit left in the cave, Findle and Merannon advanced on the giant at the same time. Avender, lacking a sword, could do little more than throw rocks. But the sissit, instead of fighting them, took a quick step backward, turned, and followed his companions down the hole.

Only he didn't. Like a cork in a wine bottle, he stuck fast about halfway down. Utter confusion wrinkled the flabby flesh around his tiny eyes.

Darting forward, Findle stabbed the giant deeply in the chest a second time, then leapt out of the way. Blood trickled down the creature's pale skin to match the Dwarf's first strike, but neither wound looked particularly severe.

Hands on hips, Findle stepped back and studied the chubby thing. "By Inach," he complained, "how do I kill you?"

The giant sissit shrugged. "I dunno. Nobody ever done it."

"Your heart should be right here." As he spoke, Findle drove his sword deep into doughy flesh once more. The sissit only grunted, not bothering to try and catch his opponent this time.

"Maybe he lacks that particular organ," observed Merannon.

"The question is," said Avender, "if we can't kill him, how are we going to get down the hole?"

"Oh, you don't have to go this way." Despite his predicament, the sissit didn't seem afraid of his enemies at all. "There's other ways down to the fish."

"Fish?" Merannon, who was barely as tall as the giant even with the creature stuck to his waist in the floor, cocked his head curiously.

"You, know. Fish." One of the sissit's long arms flopped across the stone. Merannon and Findle took cautious steps backward, but there was no need. Grabbing the nearest pile of garbage, the giant waved a fish head in the air. "See? Fish."

"There must be a pool below," said Avender, guessing at the sissit's meaning.

The creature nodded, then shoved the snack into his mouth. Loud crunching filled the cave.

"How do we get there?"

The sissit pointed toward the front door as he chewed and swallowed. "Follow th' water. That's what I do."

Stepping over the bodies of two dead sissit, Avender started for the door.

"What about him?" Findle jerked his head toward the giant.

"Leave him," said Merannon. "It is Hubley we are after."

"Ya just gonna leave me here?"

The large sissit's look of confusion deepened into mournful alarm. His long arms pushed nervously at the floor, but he remained stuck fast.

"You don't expect us to set you free, do you?" said the prince.

"If we weren't in such a hurry," added Findle, "you wouldn't be alive."

They left the giant doggedly trying to squeeze out of his trap. Splashing through the waterfall and around the edges of the pool, they followed the stream back into the twisting tunnels.

It wasn't an easy trip. By the time they had crawled through a third damp passage, wondering how the giant had ever been able to pass this way, the three of them had realized the other sissit must be long gone from wherever the hole in the floor had led. Cold, and soaked to the skin, the weary rescuers at last came to the top of another pool, the stream pouring out beneath their feet in another short cascade. The thin light of their lamps swept from side to side, revealing nothing but dark, wet rock and a hole in the ceiling.

Findle pointed toward a shallow shelf of rock running up to a tunnel on the other side. "That's the only other way out."

They set off once more, following the sissit down. Only when they reached a window at the bottom of the world and saw the Lamp did anyone realize what the creatures were up to.

"If they get to the airships before we do," said Merannon, "we will never catch them."

They all but sprinted the last stretch of tunnel. The only thing holding Avender and Merannon back was that Findle couldn't run as fast as they could, and Findle had to lead. Bursting into the cave at the top of the unneret, they paused at the lip of the well to check what was happening below. Outlined against the dark gray glow of the Lamp, five figures clambered around the two airships. One sawed frantically at the mooring rope of the smaller craft, while the other four were already climbing into the one Hubley and Avender had brought from Malmoret.

"Good," said Findle. "They're taking the slower ship."

"They're taking both." Grimly Avender leaped for the ladder that led down the side of the tower. "If we don't hold on to at least one, we may never find Hubley again."

Feet flying from rung to rung, Avender descended as fast as he could. Findle and Merannon followed. At the sight of them, the sissit gave up their attempt to steal both ships. The mooring rope of Merannon's craft parted; the creature who had cut it loose kicked it away with one clumsy leg, then scuttled across the unneret like a spider on its web as another of the creatures slashed the closer ship free. Not wanting to be left behind, the one on the tower jumped, but missed his target. With a long, dying cry, he vanished into the darkness. The airship, which had been dangling steeply at the end of its tether, followed him down, but much more slowly.

"Idiots," scoffed Findle. "They've overloaded the ship completely. It'll never fly."

"Can we catch them?" asked Avender.

"Only if they figure out how to operate the ballast. Knowing sissit, they're just as likely to open the balloons as the water cocks."

"Can we catch them with the other ship if they get it wrong?" Avender glanced at the other craft as it floated serenely up toward the bottom of the world, just out of reach. It might take a while to reel it back in, by which time the bigger ship might be long gone.

"If they don't get too far away," answered the Dwarf. "But we can only go so deep without bleeding gas, and if we bleed gas we can't come back. At least not all of us."

"Then I guess one of us has to get on that ship down there and make sure no one opens the gas."

Findle measured the distance to the falling craft with his eyes, then flexed his knees. "Easy as cracking stone."

"No." Avender shook his head. "Your ship's already floated too far away for Merannon or me to get to it. You'll have to crawl across the ceiling. I'll make the jump."

His heart pounded. Already the leap was longer than he liked, six or seven fathoms at least. Longer than any cliff he had ever jumped off in Valing as a child. And he might very well break a leg on the landing, if he managed to hit the ship at all. But the ship was sinking, and would give a little when he landed, so at least he had a chance.

"Don't." Findle lowered himself onto the strut beside Avender.

"It's the only way."

"You might miss. I'll throw you."

"All right. But you have to do it now."

The Dwarf grabbed Avender below the shoulders as Meran-non joined them. "What in the world?"

Avender held out his hand. "Give me your sword."

The prince obeyed. Like a gambler pitching coppers, the Dwarf hurled Avender into the Abyss.

20

A Lullaby

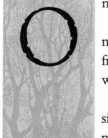On your feet, grubs. We gotta keep movin'."

Locks's voice spat harshly out of the darkness close by Hubley's ear. Her scalp still ached from where he'd dragged her from the freezing water by the hair.

"Why?" Corns grumbled from her other side. "Ain't no one followin' us. An' not likely to, neither, with Obo pluggin' up the back door."

"You think Obo pluggin' up holes is gonna stop stoneboys?" Locks sneered. "They'll carve him up like the grunter he is, push the pieces down the hole, and hotfoot it after us. That's what I'd do."

"Obo'd be good eatin'," said a wistful voice Hubley didn't recognize.

"When the chops come rainin' down we ain't gonna have no time t' eat 'em. Stoneboy's'll be right behind. Who brought the light?"

"Not me."

"That's right, boss. Not me, neither."

"Ya worthless nicks."

"You're the chief," snorted Corns. "Light's your job."

"Ya think so?" Locks's voice curled like a snake about to strike. "Well, it ain't no more. Not when I got my own magician. You, witch. Snap us up some light."

A soft hand cuffed Hubley hard in the dark, banging her head to the side. Despairing, she fell back onto the stone. Her head hurt, and her hands and fingers had been rubbed raw scrabbling at the rock as she fell through the hole. The fact that Avender and Findle hadn't been able to rescue her had frightened her thoroughly.

Locks used Hubley's hair again to pull her back upright. "Answer me, witch, or I'll do ya a lot worse 'n that."

"That's right, boss. A lot worse."

Shivering, Hubley let out a long, choking cough. "A-all right. B-but you have to stop hitting me, or I can't concentrate enough to do the spell."

"You do the spell, or it's th' end o' ya," Locks warned. "My knife's ready for stickin' in yer gut any time."

Hubley's heart shrank as the sharp point pressed against her stomach. Her wet clothes provided hardly any padding against the blade at all.

Normally, light was a spell she could cast in a moment. However a knife to the ribs changed her state of mind considerably. Her father had often told her she needed to be able to cast spells regardless of what was happening around her, and now she understood why.

It was a moment before she could think of the appropriate words to give her magic focus.

"Give me light so I can see the sissit standing over me."

A small brilliance burst forth above her head and a little bit in front of her. Startled, the sissit jumped back. Righty held up both right hands as if warding off a flame.

The chief nodded approvingly. "That's the first spell yer gonna teach me," he cackled.

She started at the sight of him. His hat had disappeared, and his hair along with it. Now he was as bald as the others, water glistening off his pale skin.

The other sissits' jaws dropped.

"Where's yer hair?" asked Corns.

The chief flushed and groped his naked pate. His eyes narrowed. "None o' yer nosy business. You boys wanna get outta here or what?"

"That's right, boss. We wanna get outta here."

"Then crack a leg."

Corns leaned forward warily. "Where ya takin' us?"

"Down." Locks pointed his thumb at the stone beneath their feet. "We can't outrun them stoneboys. They'll sniff us out like hungry toads. But if we beat 'em down to the Lamp there's an airship just waitin' fer us t' steal. Then you'll be kings o' the Stoneways, an' I'll be emper'r."

"That's right, boss. Kings."

"Ain't I always said to stick with me?" Locks sneered wickedly. "Always good eatin' when I'm boss."

Tired, frightened, and sore, Hubley trotted with the sissit through the tunnels and caves. There were four of the creatures now, including one named Dinge whose left arm and leg were considerably longer than his right. Although he hopped at the back of the column like a bird with a broken wing, he still made better time than Hubley, who found herself nearly overwhelmed with fear and fatigue. Corns prodded her from behind every time she faltered, his knotted knuckles jabbing her in the back, but it was only fear that kept her going now. Her legs blundered on like leaden stumps; her plain wet dress weighed her down like a pack full of stones. The long, weary climb down the stair from the College seemed like a picnic on Aloslocin compared to this horrible trek.

She stumbled once, catching herself on her hands just before she hit the ground. As her mind jerked away from the spell, the light went out, ending as suddenly as if doused in a pool. The sissit called out in surprise.

"What's that?"

"Right. What's that?"

Corns pressed a knobby knee hard against Hubley's back. Gritting her teeth, she forced herself to think about nothing but light. To her great surprise, fresh brightness swelled out near the roof of the cave though she hadn't said a word.

Locks slapped her hard across the face. "Don't do that again," he warned.

"I fell!"

"I don't care if ya die. Jus' keep that light on. I might o' run into a wall."

They trotted off again. Hubley thought miserably about all the people hunting for her in the caves and tunnels nearby: her mother, Avender, Mims. But none of them seemed any closer to rescuing her now than they'd been when she was first caught. What had seemed almost a lark at the beginning had become a nightmare. Findle might be the greatest hunter in all the Stoneways, scourge of Wizards and manders, but Hubley was afraid that, by the time he or anyone else found her, the sissit would already have stolen the airship and taken her off with them to plunder the bottom of the world.

What felt like hours later, a call came up to douse her light. Hubley didn't understand at first, having focused so hard on not letting go of her spell no matter what. Corns made sure to remind her by cracking her hard across the back of the head. Once again, the brightness died. Dimly, she realized the pale radiance ahead was not an afterimage of the blow she had just received, but something new.

Arriving at a place where the tunnel branched in two, the sissit and Hubley crowded into the lower opening. Hubley found herself looking out through a narrow window at the bottom of the world. The Backford Lamp filled most of the view, its bright light making the sissits' pale bodies gleam like moonlit snow. But nothing was visible of the unneret above as the Lamp's glow pointed only out and down. Hubley couldn't help but feel the Abyss crouching like a cat just beyond the veil of light, waiting to pounce on them all should the brightness ever falter.

"Ya hear any guards?" Locks demanded, his round head shining like an egg.

Corns, who clung to the edges of the window like a folded bat, shook his head. "Nah. 'Less they ain't movin'. Looks like we beat the stoneboys here."

"Do you want me to make another light?" asked Hubley as Locks led them back into the stone.

"You'd like that, wouldn't ya?" The sissit chief whacked her between the shoulders, sending her stumbling into Corns's hard back. "Let the stoneboys see us if they're anywhere near by. I ain't gonna let ya louse up my chance t' be emper'r that easy."

Unhappy that Locks had seen so easily through her plan, Hubley plodded on through the blackness. Her arms brushed the rock on either side but, with her hands in front of her, she managed not to run into any walls. At one point she knew they had entered a larger cave by the way the sissits' feet slapped less harshly against the stone. After that, they were hurrying down smooth steps in another tunnel until they emerged into what felt like another large chamber.

"Hold her," Locks told Righty. "If she says anything, crack her head."

His extra right hand feeling very odd on her left arm, Righty grabbed Hubley from behind. The other three sissit slithered away. Hubley strained to see what was happening, but she might just as well have had no eyes. The creatures whispered together somewhere in front of her, but she had no idea what they were doing.

What they weren't doing, she realized, was watching her. Now was her chance to get away. If she could just get Righty to let go of her. She remembered the spell she had intended to use on Corns, an itching spell Plum had taught her that didn't need words. If she cast it on Righty, he'd be so desperate to scratch himself he'd have to let her go.

Her chance passed as Locks hissed across the darkness. "You, witch. Cast that light spell o' yers again. We gotta see what we gotta do."

Righty pushed her forward without letting go his grip. Afraid that Corns and Locks would hit her again if she didn't do as they asked, she cast the spell. This time she didn't even notice she did it without words.

She recognized where they were as soon as the soft light appeared: the bottom of the Backford Way. The other three sissit crouched at the edge of the well a few feet in front of her like frogs skulking at the side of a pond.

"No one down there," whispered Corns.

"Better make sure," countered Locks. "Go take a look."

Arms and legs poking out above his back like fenceposts, Corns vanished over the edge. At the same time, the spell Hubley had been concentrating on came completely to her mind. Surprised, she cast it without thinking. Her light spell didn't even waver. With all the nasty things still crawling around Righty's clothing despite his plunge in the freezing pool, she didn't think it would take long for the magic to take effect. She only hoped the bugs didn't take a fancy to her as well.

Righty twitched, but didn't let go her arms. Another shudder followed, more violent than the first. Unable to stop himself, he let go with his right hand and scratched behind his shoulder. Hubley tensed herself to run the moment his other hand let go. But Righty showed more control than Hubley would have thought possible, and managed to keep tight hold of her with one hand or the other no matter how much he scratched and squirmed.

Locks waved them forward. "We need yer light."

Still clawing at his sides, Righty brought Hubley to the side of the well. Looking down, she saw not one, but two airships hovering at the edges of the unneret. Startled at first, Hubley guessed Findle must have brought the second.

Scrambling headfirst down one of the larger supports, Corns

disappeared for a moment beyond the arc of Hubley's light, then reappeared to wave them down.

"C'mon." Locks hooked both legs over the edge of the well and reached for the blumet ladder.

"Right, boss." Righty shuffled forward, one hand still gripping Hubley tightly. His free arm jerked out in another twitch, nearly knocking his chief over.

"Watch it! Y'almost shoved me over the side!"

"Right, boss. But I got the itches. Ya know how it is when I gets the itches."

Locks conked him in the head. Hubley felt Righty nearly drop her at the blow.

"Dinge, you take the witch. Quick, now, before the stoneboys get here."

Passed from one sissit to the other, Hubley found herself hanging lengthwise from Dinge's long left arm. Face-on to the glowing depths beyond the bottom of the Lamp, she was certain she was going to fall. But Dinge, like most sissit, was stronger than he looked. They proceeded down the ladder in a series of steady jerks, Hubley with her eyes tightly closed till they stopped descending.

"Corns!" shouted Locks as the knobby sissit reached the airship that had brought Hubley and Avender. "Grab that one, ya gangle! Righty, ya go down an' cut th' other free so we can tie it t' the first."

The first airship quivered as Corns and Locks climbed aboard. When Dinge and Hubley followed, it began sinking noticeably.

"Look, boss!" Corns pointed back toward the stone ceiling. "Lights! Stoneboys is comin'!"

Hubley looked up with the others; three lights had appeared at the top of the well. Her heart leapt with fresh hope. Her friends might save her yet. Already one was climbing down the ladder, his lamp bobbing in the darkness.

"Cut that rope, Righty!" Locks hissed. "No time to take 'em both now. But give it a good shove before ya go, so the stoneboys can't use it."

Drawing his knife, the chief sissit turned on Hubley. "Now, missy, ya better tell me how t' fly this thing or I'll kick ya over the side. Yer friends may catch me an' mine, but they ain't never gonna catch you."

Knowing the sissit meant what he said, Hubley pointed to the engine. "Sit on the seat there and work the pedals with your feet. Th-that's how you make it go."

Calling back to his fellows, Locks climbed into the saddle. "Dinge, start cuttin' us free. If that gimp Righty don't get back in time, it's his lookout."

But Righty saw what Dinge was up to and, after giving the other ship a push to send it floating up and away, hurried back. Scrambling awkwardly among the girders, he reached the other ship just as it floated free. The Abyss opened up between them. He jumped but, just as he did so, a savage twitch jerked him off balance. Trying to scratch his shoulder, he missed the ship completely. For a moment his high, horrible scream hung in the air behind him, then followed him down.

Hubley covered her mouth with her hands. She'd killed Righty, as sure as if she'd stabbed him with a knife. She'd cast a spell she hadn't thought was dangerous at all and killed him. Even though he'd wanted to eat her, that wasn't what she'd intended at all.

Knowing Locks would do the same to her if he found out what she'd done, she looked up at her friends. They'd covered half the distance down the tower, but seemed to have given up getting any closer. Standing on a girder, Avender and Findle argued in a bubble of light. Hubley's heart nearly stopped as the Dwarf grabbed the human and looked like he was about to throw him off the tower. Then the other man arrived and gave Avender his sword.

Findle threw Avender off the tower anyway. His lamp shining at his forehead, her old friend shot down toward the airship like a falling star.

"Look," said Dinge. "We're goin' right past the Lamp. What ya think it looks li—"

All four sissit screamed. Hubley closed her eyes just in time, or she would have been blinded by the Lamp as well. A moment later there was a heavy thud and bodies falling all around her. Something heavy and fat knocked her down, but she still had enough sense to shout a warning.

"Avender! Close your eyes! Don't let the Lamp blind you!"

Her old friend didn't reply. Bodies thumped, interrupted by grunts and curses. Wrapping her fingers through the mesh, Hubley clung to the floor of the cockpit and hoped no one knocked her over the side. Twice she heard dying wails like Righty's. In between, feet stepped all over her, though none of their owners took any more notice of her than they would a rug.

Quiet followed, along with one person's heavy breathing.

"It's all right, Hubley. You can open your eyes now. Just don't look up."

Peering out through her hands, she saw Avender leaning against the engine, his sword dripping. Around him the ship was awash in light. Every scuff and dent on the metal catwalk gleamed bright as day. The balloons, usually lost in the dimness beneath the deck, bulged like gigantic brown eggs, every seam plain.

"There's only one sissit left," he said. "The one that looks like a spider."

Keeping her eyes down, Hubley searched the well-lit nooks and crannies on either side of the catwalk. "I don't see him."

"He's in the stern. Hey, you!" Cupping his hands around his mouth, Avender yelled aft. His gray hair gleamed in the lamplight.

"His name is Corns," said Hubley.

"Corns! Listen to me! I've thrown your friends overboard. If you give up now, I'll let you go when we get back to the Lamp. The ship's stopped falling, so we're safe. Do you hear me?"

The hidden sissit made no reply. Knowing how well Corns climbed, Hubley shaded her eyes and peered over the airship's side.

"Go up in the bow," Avender ordered after a few more unsuccessful attempts to coax the sissit out. "You can watch while I pedal. If you see so much as a finger come out of the stern, tell me. Meanwhile we have to get going."

He was just working the ship up to cruising speed when the stern began to droop. Hubley found herself leaning backward on her heels to stand up straight.

"That's funny." Avender pumped away on the engine. "I haven't started heading us up yet."

Wondering what was wrong, he stopped pedaling and looked over his shoulder. Now that the chain no longer rattled beneath the deck, he and Hubley both heard a soft hiss.

His face went pale. Seeing Avender as frightened as any adult she'd ever seen terrified Hubley as well. Handing her his sword, he placed his knife between his teeth and crawled back into the narrow tunnel between the stern balloons.

The deck dipped farther. The hissing increased. A breeze lifted Hubley's hair. The ship was falling again, despite having lost the weight of two sissit. Already the deck was canted more steeply than any part of the road up Aloslocin. Hubley's boots slipped on the blumet, making her grab the engine in alarm. Casting through her small catalog of spells, she wondered how she could help her friend.

Movement on the port side caught her eye. A hand grabbed one of the lines running over the canvas hull. A second hand, then Corns's face came into view as the sissit crawled up onto the top of the ship like a crab on the side of a rock.

"Avender!" Hubley shouted, hoping he could hear her inside the ship. "He's outside!"

Shivers ran along her back as the creature crept toward her. She could almost feel Corns's spindly fingers gripping her spine instead of the airship's cables. The angle of the deck steepened as the craft settled farther onto its stern, but the sissit caught himself quickly with both feet and hands. Above him on the catwalk, Hubley looped her hand in the rigging. If this tilting kept up the airship would soon be standing on end.

Making sure he had at least three of his hands and feet holding onto something at all times, Corns scrabbled around the edge of the deck and into the cockpit. Overhead, the still-bright Lamp shone nearly straight down, forcing the sissit's eyes into cruel slits as he climbed up toward her. Hubley pointed the sword Avender had given her at the creature's face, but she knew she wasn't nearly strong enough to use it. If her father had planted any other special spells in her mind, now was the time for them to spring up and be useful. Light or invisibility or itching would never do the trick.

Reaching suddenly up out of the stern, Avender grabbed Corns's ankle and heaved himself up the nearly vertical deck. Snarling, the sissit turned and slashed at him. Avender let go and reached for his own knife. The sissit twisted away, stabbing blindly as the human crawled up the deck after him. Avender jabbed upward. The sissit scrambled out of the cockpit and onto the side of the hull, where his strong fingers and toes gave him a better grip than Avender's boots.

The airship tilted farther. Avender just managed to get a hand around one of the engine pedals, otherwise he might have fallen over the side.

"Corns!" he cried. "Can't you see what's happening! We're falling! Unless we lighten the ship, we'll never get back!"

In answer, Corns launched himself at the human, who had no choice but to let go his hold. Soaring across the deck, the sissit missed his mark entirely as Avender fell back into the stern. Desperately the creature grabbed at the rigging, then disappeared into the darkness. Like his companions, his screams faded quickly.

"Are you all right?" Hubley's heart spun as fast as the engine's whirling pedals.

"I'm fine."

Carefully Avender climbed back up the blumet deck toward her. The airship had tilted almost completely onto its stern. What had once been the back wall of the catwalk was now the floor. Hubley started to disentangle herself from the rigging in order to climb down, but Avender held up a warning hand.

"Wait." Using his knife, he cut free a section of the rigging. "We can't be too careful. Tie one end of this around your waist."

It took three tries, but Hubley eventually caught the end of the cable Avender threw up at her. She had some difficulty fashioning a knot out of the thick rope but, after some cheerful coaxing, eventually got it right. Avender tied his end off on one of the catwalk's blumet struts, then caught Hubley as she lowered herself down to the bottom of the deck. His steady arms and calm strength reassured her much more than any rope.

"What happened?" she asked.

He shook his head. "I should have known better than to leave a sissit alone in an airship. He had no idea what he was doing."

"Did he cut the balloons?" Hubley slumped down until she was sitting on the mesh bulkhead. Above her head the Backford Lamp had dwindled to the point where she could almost look at it without blinking, but the slight wind blowing past their faces hadn't let up at all.

"He did," Avender answered. "He found the access hatch down to the drive shaft, then cut his way through every bag until he reached the hull. Half the stern balloons are gone."

"Would it help if we made the ship lighter? The first time I ever rode in an airship Nolo let out some water because we were too heavy."

"I already did that. But this ship is built for speed, not cargo, so there isn't a lot of ballast. If I could cut off some of this blumet, that would do it, but I can't cut blumet without tools. Grimble and Gammit once blew up an airship in midair and managed to get back to Bryddlough all the same. But I'm not Grimble or Gammit."

"Maybe I can cast a feather spell on us."

Avender thought for a moment. "Can you do it to the whole ship?"

Hubley shook her head. "No. It's too big."

"Better we stay with the ship, then. Otherwise we might get lost. Even feathers fall. But it was a good idea."

"What about your thimble?"

Avender looked briefly at his hand. "Mims told me not to use it unless I absolutely had to. She said it'd take us to Fornoch."

The Wizard was the last person Hubley wanted to see just then. Thinking hard, she peered out over the edge of the deck. "Maybe if I go up into the bow and switch on the light, Findle will come get us in the other ship."

"We should definitely do that," Avender agreed. "But it might take a long time for Findle to reach us. We're falling faster than he can fly. I don't know about you, but I'd just as soon not waste all that time just waiting. Your mother wants to see you, you know."

"And I want to see her." Hubley felt a tear tickling at the edge of her eye. "But how?"

"You got us to Malmoret, didn't you? Maybe you can cast the traveling spell again."

"I don't know." Hubley looked down at one of the balloons that was still full beneath her feet. The light from the Lamp was dimmer now and she could no longer make out every dimple in the fabric. She didn't want their escape to have to depend on her, but Avender, though he was very good at things like fighting and scouting, wasn't the one who was a magician.

"You've already cast the spell once," he went on encouragingly. "I don't see why you can't do it again. I think you're far stronger than you know. Don't you remember how you cast it the first time?"

"No." Hubley's lower lip edged forward. "I was asleep."

"Then maybe you should try sleeping again. I'm tired enough myself." Avender yawned widely. "All that fighting wore me out."

Knowing full well that yawns were catching, Hubley clamped her jaw shut. The idea of trying to cast the travel spell again without knowing what she was doing frightened her much more than sissit. Who knew where they might end up this time? "What if I can't do it?"

"Then we'll just have to wait for Findle." Settling his hands behind his head, Avender yawned again.

This time Hubley couldn't help herself, though she was certain Avender was more concerned about their situation than he was letting on.

Together they climbed up to the forward hold. While Hubley switched on the light, Avender built a small bed on what had once been the stern bulkhead with the last blanket that had been left in the ship, then lashed their hands together once again.

Of course, the moment Hubley lay down all thought of sleep disappeared. Her wind-dried dress scratched her chest and chin, and the torn canvas fluttering in the wind was much less soothing than the steady rattle of the chain. She tossed and turned, but it was no use. Despite her every effort to think of something else, she kept seeing Righty's missed jump and hearing his fading scream.

"Avender," she asked, turning to look at him in the pale light. "Why'd you never get married?"

"Hmm?" He yawned again, sleepier than she. "I don't know. Not as lucky as your mom and dad, I guess."

"Did you ever love someone?"

"Of course. I love you."

"That's not what I mean." Snuggling closer, Hubley settled under Avender's arm. "I mean did you ever love anyone like my mother and father love each other?"

Avender looked past Hubley, though not at anything she could see.

"I did," he said.

"Didn't they love you, too?"

"Yes."

"Then why didn't you get married?"

"Sometimes you can't get married. Sometimes it's too complicated."

"Who was it?"

"Hmm?" Blinking, Avender looked back at Hubley. "Who was who?"

"The person you loved."

He put a finger to his lips. "It's a secret."

"You can tell me. I won't tell anyone."

"I'm sure you wouldn't. Maybe I will, someday. But not now. Now it's time to go to sleep."

He brushed her tangled hair back behind her ears.

"All right," she murmured, closing her eyes. "But you have to sing me a song."

Avender thought quietly for a moment before beginning.

"Hush little baby, don't you cry,
Mamma's gonna sing you a lullaby.
And if that lullaby don't suit,
Mamma's gonna give you a golden lute.
And if that golden lute don't play,
She'll kiss you awake at the break of day."

"I like that one," Hubley said, her eyes still closed. "I never heard it before."

"It's from very far away."

"Where?"

"A place I went."

"When?"

"When I was buried in your father's cave. That's what he did, you know, after he cut off my hand."

Hubley wouldn't have believed him if she hadn't been to the mussel cave herself. If her father could do something as awful as that, he could do anything.

"But how could you visit somewhere else if you're buried?"

"I don't know, but I did. Maybe I was just dreaming."

"Can you tell me where you went?"

"Someday. But not now."

"Then you have to sing the song again. Please."

They were both asleep when he finished.

SPIT

—— — — ——

And then one day it came to pass
That even his bard, the stupid ass,
Refused to sing for the prince, alas,
Because of the lives they'd led.

—MINDRELL THE BARD

21

The Queen's Bedchamber

etermined to find Hubley before Reiffen did, Ferris hurried downstairs the moment he left her workroom. She didn't think she could last another day without holding her daughter in her arms, even if Fornoch was the one who had taken her.

She had spent years searching for a way to rescue Hubley, even after she guessed why Avender had disappeared. Only when Plum also died helping her had she stopped. After that she had allowed no one else to take the risk, though there were many who thought rescuing the magicians' daughter a gallant quest. Instead she had permitted herself only dream visits, and even those had grown less frequent once she realized Reiffen was stealing Hubley's memories of her each morning when the child woke. It was just too painful to relive over and over her daughter's joy at seeing her mother for the first time in months, when the last visit had been the night before.

Arriving in the mirror room, she decided Ham was the magician most likely to get her closest to her child. Of all her former apprentices, or her apprentices' apprentices, Ham was the only one who had much to do with the Great Forest. Sweeping her hand across his mirror, she called into it several times. Receiving no response, she went on to the next most likely candidate. There was, of course, the possibility Ham had been turned by

Fornoch since the last time she had seen him. The Gray Wizard visited every magician from time to time, but Ahne's example, and that of a few others Ferris and Redburr had caught taking advantage of their position, was usually enough for any of them to summon her immediately whenever the Wizard dropped by.

One by one, she made the calls. Those she spoke with agreed to come to Tower Dale at once, but none of them had ever been any closer to the place Hubley had been taken than Ferris herself. Those she didn't reach on the first try called her back as soon as they heard she wanted to speak with them. Only Ham was enough of a hermit to have no one ready to take a message when he couldn't answer himself.

"Is this about what's happening at the palace?" asked Trier when she returned Ferris's call.

"I don't think so," said Ferris. "What's happening at the palace?"

"Reiffen has been here, or at least we think it was Reiffen. He was chasing someone, but we are not sure who that was, either."

Ferris stiffened at the idea that Reiffen had gone to Malmoret after Tower Dale. Had he been telling her the truth, or was he trying to distract her from his real purpose? Perhaps he had found something in the New Palace that would help him get to Hubley first.

"I'm asking the other magicians to join me here," she said, "in case we have to fight the Wizard. But maybe you should stay in Malmoret. Let me know what Reiffen's up to as soon as you learn anything more."

"Prince Merannon and Findle have already gone after him. I shall let you know what they learn the moment they return."

It was dawn before Ferris finally got hold of Ham. "Looks like the place is close to Grays Pond," he said when she showed him the spot Reiffen had pointed out to her on the map. "I've been there a few times. Was there about a year ago, in fact, to look into reports of a witch."

"Did you find her?"

"Yep. Just an old woman brewing love charms and wart potions. No real magic at all."

"Can you take me there?"

The other magician pulled thoughtfully at his chin. "I might have to rest a bit in Tower Dale, but I remember the place well enough. I've been up casting all night and probably don't have more than a spell or two left in me. Even then I might not be able to carry more'n two or three."

Ferris made a quick decision. "I'll come to you."

She could only take one or two people, but the decision of who to bring was easy. Grabbing her current senior apprentice, she went looking for Redburr in the kitchen.

She found him with his snout in a bucket of porridge. Giserre whacked his backside with an oversized baking peel to attract his attention. Gruel covered his mouth and chin as the bear looked up and growled.

"Would it not be preferable to take one of the more experienced magicians with you instead of an apprentice?" Giserre asked as she handed round a platter of bacon and eggs to the magicians who were breakfasting as well. Though she had grown old and gray, Giserre still insisted on doing her full share of the housework in Tower Dale.

Ferris shook her head. "Not yet. Ham can't bring that many. Jodes can bring them with her on the second trip. At this point all we need is someone who can travel."

With Ferris casting the traveling spell, they met Ham in his workshop. His smudges were already burning. Ferris and Jodes took the man's right hand while Redburr seized the other softly between his jaws. A hermit thrush fluted sorrowfully beyond the window as forests flashed through Ferris's mind, brown and bare except for the dark green firs. Lakes shone between the trees like raindrops beading on a nokken's fur.

When the smell of wood mold and leaves replaced the

slightly stale odor of Ham's workroom, Ferris let go his hand. Standing at the edge of the trees, she found herself looking at a small farm. Honking geese rushed them from across the yard, wings flapping; a pair of dogs scrambled around the corner of the house at breakneck speed. Still irritated that his breakfast had been interrupted, Redburr sent the creatures running with a growl.

"Is this where the witch lives?" asked Ferris.

Ham pointed into the forest behind them. "There's a path over there that leads north out of town. The old woman lives on a small pond about twenty minutes' walk away."

Ferris turned to Jodes. "Memorize this place, take Ham back to the tower with your thimble, then return with as many magicians as you can. Redburr and I will be at the pond."

Walking fast, they arrived sooner than Ham had said. A dusty yard led from the water's edge to a cottage tucked back among the trees. Masked by a row of cedars between them and the house, Ferris and the Shaper watched an old woman hang washing on a line.

"This can't be where Hubley is," Redburr rumbled.

Ferris agreed. Unless Ham had guided them to the wrong spot, her suspicion that Reiffen had sent her on a wild-goose chase was nearly confirmed. But why? Was there some reason he wanted her out of Valing?

"Maybe someone in the village can give us a better lead," the bear went on. "If there's anything around here, they'll know. We can search the area thoroughly once the rest of the mages arrive."

The woman hanging laundry turned around as if she'd heard them, though Ferris was sure they'd been whispering much too softly.

"Ferris," she called. "I can't see you or Redburr, but I know you're there. Hubley's gone, but you still ought to come up anyway, so we can talk. There's no need to be afraid. Reiffen sent you to the right place."

Afraid was the last thing Ferris was feeling, but she was still cautious. How had the woman known they were there, or that it was Reiffen who had sent them? Or was she simply lying, and Hubley was still in the house? Ferris certainly wasn't going to leave this place until she had learned everything the old woman could tell her about her daughter.

The woman waved an insistent hand. "Really, there's no reason to hide. You can search the whole cottage. I won't get in your way."

"What do you think?" Ferris whispered to the bear.

"It's a trap."

"Of course it's a trap. But what choice do we have? She already knows we're here. Either we do as she asks, or we go back to the village for reinforcements."

"I vote for reinforcements."

Ferris shook her head. "Not me. I've waited long enough."

Firebolts ready on her fingertips and tongue, she walked toward the cottage. She was almost at the door before the woman, who was hanging the last of her sheets, noticed her.

"Have you had breakfast? I was going to make pancakes for Hubley, but she left too early to eat."

Ferris pointed all ten fingers at the woman. "If you don't tell me where Hubley is right now, I'll kill you."

The woman looked as if Ferris had hurt her feelings. She was older than Ferris, or, more correctly, older than Ferris looked, with gray hair and a sturdy frame. In truth, she was probably close to Ferris's real age.

"Of course I'll tell you where she is. She's in Malmoret. Or, more precisely, below Malmoret by now."

"Below Malmoret?"

"That's right. Trier told you about the disturbance at the New Palace, didn't she? That was Hubley, trying to get away. She's almost reached the Lamp by now. I'd tell you to travel there to meet her, only I don't think you've ever been."

"I can get to the College fast enough and follow them from there."

"No, no. Don't do that. It would take you hours, and they'll be gone by the time you get there. Besides, Merranon and Findle are already after them. It'll be much easier if we wait for Hubley and Avender to make their way back on their own."

"Avender?"

"It's a long story. Come inside, have some breakfast, and I'll tell you all about it."

"I'm not hungry."

"I'll bet Redburr is."

Cupping her hands to her mouth, the woman called back to where the Shaper was still lurking behind the trees. "Redburr! You're being silly. I've a cask of that Upper Nutting you like so much. Brought it here myself a week ago when I knew you were coming, and it's just going to go to waste if you don't drink it. I'll leave the door open, in case you change your mind."

Knew they were coming? The strangeness of the remark, combined with the woman's earlier mention of Avender and the fact she knew Reiffen had sent them, made Ferris nearly forget why she was there.

"Who are you?" she demanded as she followed the woman inside the cottage. The scent of the same sort of smudges Ham had used lingered in the air. "And why are you acting as if this is all some sort of picnic?"

"Oh, it's no picnic, Ferris."

"You don't seem particularly concerned."

"That's probably because I've been through it all before."

Leaving Ferris openmouthed in the center of the room, the older woman called into the woods one more time. "Redburr, I'm only going to explain myself once. If you want to know what's going on, you'd better come in now."

"Don't wait for him," said Ferris. "Too much is at stake. I

want you to start explaining everything now. You can start by telling me who you are."

"I'd rather wait for Redburr."

Taking a large wooden bowl from the table in the middle of the room, the older woman filled it with beer from a small cask behind the door. Redburr poked his massive head in as she set it on the floor. Sniffing the bowl suspiciously, he glanced at Ferris.

"She's about to introduce herself," she said.

"That's right, I was." Chair legs scratched the dirt as the woman sat down at the other side of the table. "I told Hubley to call me Mims. A lot of people think that's my name, but the ones who know me best call me Hubley."

Hands on hips, Ferris glared at the other woman. "Is this some kind of joke? You and my daughter share the same name?"

"We share more than just a name. Mother."

Ferris's hands dropped to her sides. "What?"

"I'm Hubley. *Your* Hubley."

"No you aren't. I've seen Hubley enough over the last thirty years to know she's still only ten years old. Reiffen's been keeping her that way all this time."

As surprised as Ferris, Redburr actually stopped sniffing at his beer. "She is about the right age," he said. "Maybe the Hubley you've been seeing is a fake, to throw you off the scent. That would explain why she never remembers your visits."

The old woman smiled firmly. "No, that's the real Hubley, and I am, too. I'm older than I look, a lot older than the Hubley I sent Avender to rescue last night. I have a Living Stone, Mother."

"If you had a Living Stone," Ferris argued, "you'd still be ten."

"You know that's not true. Grandmother Giserre made you take hers out years ago. I've removed mine more than once, and not just so I could grow up, either. There have been a few occasions when I couldn't afford to be caught with it. Would you like to see the scars?"

"That won't be necessary. Scars can be faked as easily as anything else."

A little overwhelmed by what the woman was telling her, even if she didn't believe it, Ferris sat down. The woman had to be some trick of Fornoch's. Or Reiffen's. But, for the life of her, Ferris couldn't imagine what advantage either of them thought they could gain from having someone pretend to be a fifty-year-old Hubley.

"Can you prove you're my daughter?" she asked.

The woman held out her arm. Reluctantly, Ferris took the offered wrist. The lump was there, but proved nothing. A good magician could fake broken bones as easily as mend them.

Mims met Ferris's skeptical gaze. "Plum and I were floating back and forth across the top of the Magicians' Tower when it happened. Trier was supposed to be teaching us about the stars, remember? Only Trier got mad because Plum and I weren't paying attention, and I fell into the rose bushes when she cut off our magic. You weren't so good at setting bones then, so my wrist is a little crooked. It convinced Avender."

"That's the second time you've mentioned Avender," growled Redburr, still unable to make up his mind about his bowl of beer. "What's he got to do with this?"

"I had to rescue him first, before I could rescue myself. Father's had him buried alive in the castle all these years, which is why he's the only one who could get in without setting off the alarms. I couldn't take the risk of doing it myself. He might have recognized me."

"Recognized you?" asked Ferris.

"Father's seen me this way before, Mother, though I didn't tell him who I was. You don't think he survived all those years in Ussene on his own, do you? He'd unravel the mystery soon enough if he saw me again. The person I was then couldn't possibly still be alive."

Ferris raised her hands. "Hold on. Are you trying to tell us that, not only are you Hubley, but you're a Hubley who can go back and forth through time?"

"I am." Mims beamed. "Aren't you proud of me, Mother? Even Father never figured out the Timespell."

Ferris snorted. The whole thing was impossible.

Unable to restrain himself any further, the Shaper took a cautious lick at his beer. Ferris didn't really expect it to be poisoned, but she waited to see what happened anyway. After another slurp, the bear looked up.

"She smells like Hubley," he offered. "I'd be surprised if the Wizard thought of giving her the same scent if she's a fake."

"I'm more worried that she's part of some plot of Reiffen's than I am of the Wizard being involved."

"Perhaps if I gave you some proofs of my ability to travel through time." Mims held up a small silver coin. "Mindrell gave me this thirty-one years ago. Well, thirty-one years in his time, but only a couple of days ago in mine. Ask him about it the next time you see him. It's how Avender was able to travel to Grangore without me."

"That proves nothing," Ferris scoffed.

"Maybe if I gave you a more immediate demonstration."

"The only demonstration I'd believe is if you actually took me somewhere I'd already been."

"All right. I can do that."

Before Ferris could react, Mims reached across the table to touch her hand. The world shifted, just as it did for a regular traveling spell. Ferris recognized where they had gone at once, Hubley's old bedroom in the apartment Ferris still used in the New Palace. It looked no different from the last time she had visited Malmoret, a few weeks before.

She jerked her arm away. "This proves nothing. A traveling spell to the New Palace? I don't have time for this. You're some trick of Reiffen's to keep me from finding Hubley so he can find her on his own."

"You have all the time you want," said Mims. "I'm the chronothurge, remember?"

Turning away from Ferris, the mistress of the Timespell poked her head into the next room. "You can never be too careful going back and forth in time," she said. "For one thing, it makes people extremely uncomfortable to see two versions of the same person at once. And for another, the more people who know about the spell, the more likely Fornoch will hear about it."

"Since you've yet to prove to me we've actually gone anywhere in time, that's not really much of a concern."

"Patience, Mother. You'll see I'm telling the truth in a minute. Maybe you should cast the invisibility spell, so you won't have to worry if I'm just making a few illusions."

"Why do we want to cast an invisibility spell?"

"So we won't be seen. I just explained it to you."

Ferris's temper rose. She was the second most powerful magician in the world, and didn't like being condescended to one bit. Recovering her composure, she chanted:

"Sunlight, moonlight, or the stars,
Lights in gemstones or in jars,
Magefire, woodfire, cold or hot.
Show the world where we are not."

The women disappeared. Ferris had cast a very formidable version of the spell. Nothing, not even more magic, would make them visible again until she released it.

Fingers wrapped around her wrist. Mims's voice came out of the clear air. "We have to stay together, Mother. And don't be surprised when you see yourself."

"And just where are we supposed to have gone? Or should I say when?"

" 'When' is correct. A little less than two years ago."

They went out into the corridor. The halls were full of servants, all of whom moved silently with their eyes on the floor. Not the typical mood in Brizen's palace, where everyone was used to kindness and plenty. Ferris remembered the last time she had seen the New Palace so somber, which, exactly as Mims had said, had been a little less than two years before.

"Is this when—?"

"Sssh." Mims voice whispered close beside her. "We have to be quiet. If someone hears us, I may not be able to get us out before we're caught. Trier is a very good magician."

They made their way carefully to the royal apartment. The higher they went, the fewer people they saw. If Mims really had mastered the Timespell, it seemed she had brought them to a point in the past Ferris remembered well. The queen had died not two weeks after the onset of her illness, and Ferris had been with her almost the entire time.

Following a pair of servants carrying tea and broth into the royal bedchamber, they slipped into a corner of the room where no one was likely to bump into them. Ferris recognized the scene at once; they had arrived very close to the end. Her younger self was there, standing close to the queen's sickbed, along with the king and the prince and Trier. Quietly the servants set their trays on a table and left, closing the door behind them.

Ferris was stunned. Mims really did know the Timespell. Which meant she really could be her daughter, an older version of Hubley who had probably seen many things that would prove very useful to know. For a moment Ferris thought about using the travel spell to take them both away, but stopped when it occurred to her she didn't know whether her spell would take her back to the Valing of her own time, or this.

The king spoke to the Ferris near the bed. "Are you certain there is nothing you can do? Could you not give her a Living Stone?"

The younger Ferris shook her head. Her older self hoped the scene that was about to play out wouldn't be as difficult to live through the second time as it had been the first.

"Even if I had one, Brizen," she heard her younger self answering, "a Living Stone would do nothing. In order to work, the Stone must be inside the subject before the illness strikes. To give Wellin one now would only leave her like this forever."

"I have heard there are other spells."

The Ferris beside the bed looked Brizen full in the face. "Yes, but they have costs. Would you be willing to pay them?"

The king stepped forward. "Of course. You can take me."

"You're too old. Your blood is thin and wouldn't work at all."

The prince advanced beside his father. "Take me then."

Gently, the king restrained him.

"You see," the younger Ferris told them, "you can no more manage it than I. Wellin is too old to fight her sickness. You have to let her go."

"Ferris is right."

The queen raised a weak hand as she spoke, her voice hardly more than a whisper. But the older Ferris had heard it all before and remembered exactly what was said. Brizen caught his wife's wrist before it fell back to the coverlet. The Ferris by the bed, sensing the queen wanted to talk to the king alone, started to rise.

"No," Wellin croaked, her voice as close to the end as the rest of her. "Please stay. Brizen, Meran, you will allow Ferris and me a moment alone, will you not? We shall not be long."

Husband and son bowed, then left with Trier. None of them noticed the invisible women in the corner.

"You've proved your point," whispered the older Ferris as the door closed. "I don't need to see any more."

"Shh. I want to know what she told you." Mims crept closer to the bed.

Just like her father, the older Ferris told herself. Too curious for her own good. Maybe the woman really was Hubley. Bothered that her daughter would stoop to spying, yet proud of her power all the same, Ferris said nothing more.

The younger Ferris sat on the bed and held the queen's wrinkled hand in her own smooth one. At least I stayed young and pretty, thought Ferris, knowing that was what her younger self was thinking at the same time. Then, just as her younger self had, she felt ashamed for thinking such a horrible thing for the second time as well.

"I am not sorry, you know," said the queen.

"Pardon?" said the younger Ferris.

"I said, I am not sorry." Wellin's voice grew firmer. "Brizen forgave me, as you know well enough, so I have never needed to forgive myself. We both wanted a child so much. I do thank you, however, and love you all the more for your reticence. A lesser woman would have whispered my secrets to the world."

The younger Ferris stiffened. For the first time in her life, the older recognized the gesture as one she had learned from Giserre. "I would never do such a thing."

As if the apparent difference between their ages were real, Wellin patted her companion's hand. "That is why I have always trusted you."

"We've been friends a long time, Wellin. Now is not the time to start saying things you might regret."

"I am not trying to be rude," said the queen crossly. "But I did want to tell you how unfair it has all been, how terribly one-sided. I should have been the one whose husband left her, not you."

The younger Ferris softened. Across the room, Mims squeezed her mother's hand. The older Ferris found she appreciated the queen's admission just as much the second time. And it helped to be comforted by her daughter, too.

"Don't say such things," said the Ferris on the bed. "We've both done our share of good and bad."

"Yes, but our happiness has been unfairly portioned, all the same. My husband had every reason to leave me, and did not. Yours had no reason at all."

"The difference is in them, not us."

"That is true." The sick woman coughed lightly. The younger

Ferris wiped her friend's mouth with the handkerchief she held in her lap for just that purpose. "Through no fault of my own," the queen went on, "I seem to have landed the better choice. Greedy though I was."

This time the younger Ferris didn't contradict the queen. The older knew why. Wellin's words had the same effect on her the second time, even when they were expected. She had been greedy herself. Thinking she could have it all, the man she had loved for so long and the power and knowledge he brought with him, she had paid no attention to the signs that he might have changed. Reiffen had turned out not to be what she thought, and their life together had ended.

"Life isn't fair."

The older Ferris heard the bitterness in her younger self's voice, though she knew she had tried hard to hide it. Had her disappointment and shame been so obvious all these years?

Wellin's loving laugh thickened to a heavy cough. The younger Ferris wiped the queen's mouth again.

"You used to have to tell Hubley that all the time," said Wellin when her fit had passed. "Not that she ever believed you. Meran was always much more agreeable, like his father. Speaking as a mother, I am very happy he did not turn out much like me."

"He looks just like you."

"Looks like, yes. Unlike his father, he has broken several dozen hearts already." There was no mistaking the pride in the queen's voice, or whom she meant by Merannon's father. "Unintentionally, of course, for on the inside he is the image of Brizen. Vain though I may be, I am much prouder of the way he takes after His Majesty. Not that I fail to appreciate his ability to enchant every woman he meets, mind you."

The younger Ferris made no reply. Her daughter squeezed the older's hand a second time.

"It is hard," the queen continued. "But I feel certain you will see your own dear child again. Reiffen cannot keep her forever.

He may not know that, but something will happen. Please, do not give up hope. I never did, and everything came out perfectly for me in the end."

"I hope you're right." Tears glistened in the younger Ferris's eyes.

Though she had kept from crying then only with great difficulty, the older Ferris found her current mood was much different. Everything had changed; Hubley had escaped from Castle Grangore. Now Reiffen was the one who was at his wits' end trying to recover Hubley, while Ferris stood with her full-grown and very powerful daughter at her side. More powerful than Wellin's son would ever be, even when he became king.

A thought struck her. If the mage beside her was Hubley, then that meant there was no need to be concerned about what might happen to the younger version of her daughter still wandering through Bryddlough. Avender really would protect her, otherwise this older Hubley wouldn't be standing here beside her.

Before she had time to think this new idea through, Hubley— or should she be called Hubley Mims?—pulled her mother back to the corner of the room. Ferris's younger self had gone to the door to let Brizen and the others back in.

"It's time to go," whispered Hubley Mims.

Quick as a Wizard, they were back at the cottage, though this time there was no cask by the door, and no Redburr. "I can do time or space easily and without preparation," Hubley Mims explained, "but not both. The only reason we traveled to Wellin's bedside so quickly was because I'd arranged the spell in advance."

"You knew Redburr and I were coming, didn't you." Ferris sat in the same place at the table she was going to occupy nearly two years in the future. "Just as you knew Redburr was going to follow me through the door."

"That's right." Pushing aside the ladder that led to the sleeping loft, her daughter began removing smudges and other magical items from the drawers behind it.

"Does that mean you already know what happens? To Hubley? To Reiffen and me?"

"Yes."

"Can you tell me?"

"No."

"Meaning you won't."

"Right again."

"Why not?"

"Believe me, Mother, there's nothing worse than knowing what's going to happen. Much worse than spying on your friends. You can get yourself in a lot of trouble if you know too much. Some day I'll tell you the story about how I tried to change things once and made everything much worse."

Ferris arranged herself more comfortably in the chair. "As long as I know everything's going to work out for you. When you're younger, that is."

Hubley Mims stopped what she was doing long enough to look at her mother. "So, you figured that out, have you?"

"Yes. The fact that you're standing there, more powerful than even Reiffen ever imagined, proves you're going to get through everything that's happening now."

Ferris's daughter pulled the last of what she needed from the cabinet and shut the drawers. "Don't think that makes it any easier, Mother. And we still have to worry about Father. But I'm glad you've accepted who I am."

"If you aren't who you say you are, Fornoch has given far too much away in revealing the Timespell. Which isn't to say that's not what he's doing anyway, knowing how mixed up the Wizard's purpose can be sometimes. And if it's your father who's done this, well, I can think of a lot more things he'd rather do with this sort of magic than try and trick me. He'd be back trying to stop the death of his father. Either way, it's a lot easier to just take your word."

"Thank you, Mother."

Though Ferris had accepted that Mims was her daughter, she still didn't feel any special love for the woman. The Hubley standing before her was someone she didn't know at all. The Hubley she missed remained far away, no closer to a hug and a kiss than when Ferris had set off to find her that morning.

She watched as the daughter who was probably older than she was prepared the Timespell, surprised at how similar it was to the magic of regular traveling. The same smudge pots on the table, the same restful concentration in the caster's face. But the memories that hurried through Ferris's mind as her daughter held her hand weren't the regular memories of a travel spell. Instead her awareness surged forward, day and night scrambling across the cottage in a rapid run of light and shadow. Like deer flickering through closely set trees, time darted across her mind.

"Well?" rumbled Redburr. "Are you going to do something? Or are you two going to just sit there all day holding hands?"

"We've already been and gone," answered Hubley Mims.

"And?" The Shaper turned his heavy head toward Ferris.

"She's Hubley. If Fornoch knows the Timespell, there's no reason he'd be giving it to us now. Not to mention she's a lot like her father."

"And you, Mother."

The bear took another lick at his empty bowl. "Well then. What do we do next?"

"Go back to Tower Dale," said Hubley Mims. "The younger version of me will show up soon enough."

"How long will we have to wait?" asked Ferris.

"Two days. After that, you'll get to face Fornoch at last."

22

Return to Valing

venderwoke the moment the wind stopped howling past his ears. Instead of the hard blumet mesh of the airship, he and Hubley were now lying on a soft bed. Night filled the window behind them; his lamp gleamed pale and thin around the room.

He recognized where they were at once. Hubley's spell had brought them back to her bedroom in Castle Grangore, the very spot they had been trying to escape in the first place. If Reiffen was home, Avender doubted they would get away a second time.

Thinking to wake the child, he rolled onto his side. Hubley slept beside him but, unlike Avender, she was below the covers. And the collar around her neck was the white of a clean night-gown, not the dirty dress she had been wearing on the airship. Or was it? Rubbing his eyes, he looked again. He could have sworn the collar was white before, but now it was dark brown. As he watched, it changed again, flickering back and forth between the two shades as quick as a blink. Small changes flashed across her face as well. A smudge on her cheek came and went with the same rhythm as the collar; her hair switched between tangled and combed.

It was almost as if there were two Hubleys sharing the same space, the one who had brought him here from the Abyss, and the other from . . . where?

Or when.

The night ended. Avender's lamp faded as full morning sprang up around him. The other Hubley disappeared. The one in the dirty dress took her place completely. Now she was lying on top of the quilts the same as he was, and the bed was made up as if no one had slept in it for days.

She opened her eyes. "Are we there?" she asked hopefully. Before Avender could answer, she went on. "I had the strangest dream. It was like I was in two places at once. Here, and here in my bedroom again, only it was the middle of the night. It was like I was remembering another of my old memories."

"I'm sure that's what it was," said Avender, not wanting her to ask anything more. Who knew where she'd take them if she realized she'd almost cast the Timespell. "Just another one of your dreams."

"Of course that's what it was," said a new voice. "What else could it be? She's been having strange dreams every night. Why, just yesterday—"

"Durk!" Hubley leapt up from the bed, dragging Avender with her. One-handed, she lifted the stone from his velvet pillow while Avender unwrapped the strap still holding them together.

"It's so good to see you!" she went on. "Avender's come back and rescued me! We've been to Malmoret, and the Stoneways, and fought sissit—"

"Rescued you?" asked the stone. "From what? Too much cake and presents?"

"Father's been holding me prisoner in Castle Grangore for years and years."

"Sssh." Avender put a finger to his lips. Removing Durk from Ferris's hands, he dropped the stone into his pack before their voluble friend could utter another word. "We have to get out of here," he whispered. "It would have been a lot better if you'd brought us to Valing. If your father's here, we'll never get away a second time. Can you do the invisibility spell?"

"Of course. That's the first thing I got Plum to teach me. How do you think we were able to steal so many cookies all the time?"

"Cast it then. At least that way we'll have some chance of getting out of here."

"That really won't be necessary."

For the second time, a strange voice intruded on Avender and Hubley's conversation. Looking up, they found Mindrell leaning against the doorway. Despite the bard's casual attitude, he regarded Avender warily. Given what had happened at their last meeting, Avender could understand why. Like Hubley, Mindrell didn't appear to have aged a day since that last meeting, either. Avender wondered if Reiffen had given him a Living Stone as payment for what he'd done. Or maybe he was using one of the other, messier, ways of keeping someone alive.

Pulling Hubley behind him, Avender reached for his sword. "You better let us pass."

Gracefully, the bard waved his arm to show they were free to go. Then he followed them into the next room. "Reiffen's not here. He disappeared into the cellars two days ago and I haven't seen him since."

"He'll be back," said Avender. "He has a charm that allows him to track Hubley wherever she goes."

"I know. I've been waiting for him to return with her. But you showed up instead. That was a pleasant surprise, especially the part about you having both your hands. I really did regret having to do that, you know. And the burying, too."

Avender was thinking it might be time to show Mindrell what being one-handed was like when Hubley tugged on his arm.

"We should take him with us," she urged. "That way Father can't make him tell we were here."

"He'll only help your father get us back if we do," Avender answered.

Mindrell shook his head. "No I won't. I told Giserre I'd protect her granddaughter, and that's what I've been doing. You think there's any other reason I'd have stayed here all this time? I've barely been outside these walls in thirty-one years."

Avender didn't like it, but he saw no alternative. Not unless he killed the harper in front of the child. Twice now Mindrell had nearly slain him. When the third time came, Avender was determined the chance would be his.

"All right, we'll take you with us. Hubley, can you cast invisibility on all three of us?"

The child concentrated, her forehead furrowed.

*"Hide us like it's darkest night.
Hide us so we're out of sight."*

"Someday, Hubley," said Mindrell as they disappeared, "I'll have to teach you to be a better poet."

With the child holding each man's hand, they hurried through the empty halls. Avender expected Reiffen to descend upon them at any minute. Invisibility could hardly be expected to stop so powerful a magician, especially in his own castle. If they got outside it might be a different matter. But why hadn't Reiffen returned? His charm had to have told him where Hubley was. The fact he hadn't shown up made Avender almost as uneasy as if he had.

By the time they reached the front gate there was still no sign of the magician. Opening the wicket, Mindrell led them outside. Avender thought about how Hubley had been with them the last time he and Mindrell had passed this way, though neither of them had known it at the time. Mindrell still didn't. She might have saved them all a lot of trouble, herself included, if she'd simply kept Avender from going inside. But that, as he was learning more and more every day, wasn't Mims's way. Still, no matter how much trouble she got him into, things had a habit of turning out all right. Flexing the fingers on his left hand, he decided to keep following her instructions.

"Our footprints in the road are going to give us away to the first person we meet," said Mindrell as they followed the dusty lane across the empty fields surrounding the castle and into the woods.

"I'm not worried about that." Avender looked up through the leafless trees at the clear blue sky. "At least while we're still invisible Reiffen won't be able to see us unless he's close to where we are."

"As long as he has that charm, we really can't hide."

Avender turned to where he thought Hubley was. "Do you know how your father tracks you?" he asked.

"No," the child answered.

The bard shook his head as well. "It's probably her Stone. I doubt Reiffen would have made it anything she could get rid of easily."

They walked on, their boots scuffing the road. Birds flew back and forth across the blue sky; a badger, who would never have been so bold had he been able to see the three travelers, shuffled across the road not two strides in front of them. Avender told the bard everything that had happened over the last two days.

At the Grangore Road they debated which way to go. Hubley was for continuing up the mountain to the Sun Road, but Avender and Mindrell disagreed. Grangore was closer, and the Granglough was there as well.

"We don't have to go all the way to Issinlough to find Dwarves," Avender pointed out. "And your father's magic doesn't work on Dwarves."

That convinced Hubley. The three of them in agreement, they started down the mountain toward the town that none of them had seen in a very long time.

Not until they were well into the farms outside did they meet anyone. They ignored a girl driving three sheep along the side of the road, but she didn't ignore them, and stared intently at the marks their feet left in the road as they passed. After that they started walking in the dry grass on the roadside.

"We'll never make it all the way into town like this," said Avender. "Sooner or later we're going to run into a dog."

"The spell never works with dogs," said Hubley.

"I know. You're father told me that a long time ago."

Making sure no one saw them reappear, Hubley removed her spell. A lazy hawk circled the sky high above, but, if Reiffen was the hawk, he didn't show it. The party made it the rest of the way to Grangore unmolested.

They found the town much larger than it had been thirty years before. Most of the streets and buildings they remembered had been torn down to make room for new ones. Granglough, however, hadn't been moved, and they found it after only a few wrong turns. A pair of sentries guarded the entrance jut as they had when Avender had first visited the place forty years before. Their black armor was the same, too, though Avender assumed the men inside had changed. Had they been standing guard outside Castle Grangore he wouldn't have been so sure of that at all.

"We've come to see Huri," he said when the guards asked why they wanted to go inside.

"A lot of people want to see Huri. That doesn't mean they get in."

Hubley subjected the two guards to her haughtiest stare. "I'm the magicians' daughter. In case you've forgotten, my father's been keeping me prisoner up at the castle, so it's very important I get to see my mother. Ferris, you know. If you don't let us in, I'm going to tell her to turn both of you into toads."

The guards exchanged glances but, when neither of them started hopping, they snickered behind their visors.

Hubley clenched her jaw, which reminded Avender of both her grandmothers at the same time. *"Rust,"* she said. The guards laughed some more.

Without another word, she marched right past them. Expecting the worst, Avender leapt after her. The guards tried to stop them but, stiff as statues, toppled to the ground instead.

"Very impressive." Mindrell stepped over them as the guards rocked awkwardly back and forth in feeble efforts to stand, their armor locked tight as rusted pipe.

Once inside, they had no trouble finding Huri. A boy escorted them to the Minabbenet, then ran off to fetch the Dwarf. Avender's lamp provided enough light to lead them down the steps into the large cave, but it wasn't enough to interfere with the glow of the gems arranged in patterns on the ceiling like the stars in the summer sky.

Huri recognized Mindrell and Hubley at once when he joined them, which was enough to persuade him to contact Issinlough on the Granglough mirror. But Avender had changed enough that the Dwarf only accepted who he was on the word of the other two humans.

The curious gathered as Huri went off to make his call, mostly humans but a few Dwarves as well. Though Mindrell had been seen from time to time by the women who had brought food to the castle, Reiffen had kept himself and Hubley locked up so long that most of Grangore wasn't sure they even existed. Hubley, who hadn't been around so many people in years, cowered by the table in the middle of the room as Avender and Mindrell held back the crowd.

A lane opened through the hall as a woman appeared at the top of the stairs.

"Mother!"

Hubley dashed across the room. Ferris met her in the middle, her daughter leaping into her arms. As if trying to make up for all they had missed in the last thirty years, they kissed a hundred hundred times. Desperately, Hubley clung to her mother's neck; Ferris wept with open joy.

Avender found himself sniffling too, and saw more than a few other eyes glistening in the crowd. Beside him, Mindrell cleared his throat several times.

Only after giving her darling another ten score kisses did Ferris greet anyone else, and that only because Hubley dragged her over to Avender by pulling on her dress.

"Aren't you even going to say hello, Mother?" said the child. "Avender's the one who rescued me."

The light bright against Ferris's face, Avender shaded his lamp with his hand, but the magician didn't recognize him at all.

"Avender? Is it really you? Have you come back, too?"

"It's me."

"You must have quite a story to tell." Ferris hugged her daughter once again. "Too bad we don't have time to hear it. I still have to get Hubley safely back to Valing. Are you coming with us?"

"Where else would I go?"

"We have to bring Mindrell, too," said Hubley, her arms still wrapped around her mother's waist. "He's on our side."

Ferris considered the matter. Avender saw that, like Mindrell, her eyes were the oldest part of her, with years and years of sadness bottled up behind them.

"All right," she said. "Mindrell's done what Giserre asked him to. He can come as well. Let Reiffen just try to get you away from me now."

She offered Avender and Mindrell her hands. The humans in the crowd shuffled back a few steps in the face of the magic they knew she was about to cast. With Hubley holding one hand and Avender and Mindrell the other, Ferris carried them home.

Giserre and Redburr were there to greet them when they arrived. Hubley hesitated for a moment, clutching her mother's skirt, unsure who this old woman with steel gray hair might be. Avender was also surprised. No one else he had met had changed at all, and to finally see someone who had was a shock. Giserre's beauty and bearing, however, were just the same. Recognizing her grandmother as soon as Ferris told her who she was, Hubley rushed to give her a hug. A quick embrace for the bear as well, and she was back at her mother's side.

In the meantime Avender let Durk out of his knapsack and set him in the middle of the nearest table.

"It's about time," huffed the stone. "And just as things were getting interesting, too. But, I tell you, I don't believe a word of it. Reiffen, holding his own child prisoner? Preposterous. Maybe in one of the more improbable melodramas you might get away with that sort of thing, but never in real life. Am I right? Excuse me, but is anyone listening? And what are you all going on about, anyway?"

When Durk, and everyone else, had quieted a bit, Giserre approached the bard. His dry amusement at all the sentiment being displayed around him vanished the moment the lady offered him her hand.

"I thank you for your service," she said simply. "Any gift that is in my power to grant is yours."

Bowing deeply, the bard brought Her Ladyship's fingers to his lips. "The opportunity to serve you, milady, is reward enough for me."

Avender grimaced. Unlike Giserre, he wasn't nearly as inclined to forgive Mindrell for what he'd done.

"And my son?" she asked as the bard let go her hand.

He shrugged. "I haven't seen him in two days."

"Have you?" The regal old woman turned to Avender.

"We've been running away from him, milady, not looking for him."

Giserre regarded Avender and Ferris with serene surprise. "Do neither of you find it odd that Reiffen has let Hubley get away so easily? Or that he is not paying us a visit at Tower Dale right now?"

"I do," said Avender. "I was thinking the same thing when we left the castle. But once we got safely away, I stopped worrying."

"Reiffen has made his own bed," said Ferris. "Let him lie in it."

"No, Mother." Hubley, who had gone back to Ferris's side the moment she left Giserre, looked up into her mother's face. "We have to find Father. What if something terrible's happened to him? What if the Wizard has him?"

Her mouth pinched, Ferris looked away. Giserre moved closer. Avender searched the magician's face closely for a sign of what it was she didn't want to say.

"If you know something, Ferris," said Giserre, "you must speak."

Ferris glanced at Avender as if for help, her eyes flickering between him and Hubley. "I'm not sure what I can say."

He understood her problem at once. "You met Mims, didn't you? I'm not sure how much you can say, either. But can you at least tell us what she told you about Reiffen?"

The bear lumbered forward. "That much ought to be safe."

"Who's Mims?" asked Durk.

"The magician who helped Avender rescue Hubley," said Ferris. "The one Redburr and I found when we tracked her to Grays Pond."

"She's very powerful," said the child. "And a little scary, too."

"Perhaps if Hubley left the room," suggested Giserre, "you could speak more freely."

"I'm not leaving." Hubley looked defiantly at her mother. "If you're going to rescue Father, I want to help. I'm remembering new magic all the time. Avender, tell them how we got past Huri's guards."

Kneeling, Ferris took her daughter firmly by the shoulders. "You've done enough already, dear. You need a bath, and dinner, and then maybe a long nap. But, whatever we decide, you're not coming with us. I love you far too much to let you take any more risks."

"Come, dear." Giserre reached for her granddaughter's hand. "Your mother is right. This is a discussion you cannot share. But

Ferris, if I ever learn you did not help Reiffen when you could, especially when he has not been himself for so long, I think I will be angrier with you than I have ever been with him."

"That's right, Mother," agreed Hubley. "Just because Father's been mean, he's still Father."

Their point made, grandmother and granddaughter marched out of the room.

Redburr was the first to speak after they were gone. "I'd be on your side, Ferris, only this may be the best chance to kill Fornoch we're ever going to get. Giserre's too old to come with us, but otherwise, if Reiffen is already with him, we'll be the same crew that killed Usseis."

"Oh?" said Mindrell. "I've volunteered, have I?"

Ferris gave the bard a scornful look. "None of us have, yet."

"What did Mims tell you?" asked Avender.

"That we would be seeing Fornoch again before this was all over."

"And Reiffen?"

The bear settled back on his haunches and licked his paws. "She said nothing about him. But we all know only one thing could keep Reiffen away from Hubley once she showed up in a place he could travel to."

"The Wizard."

"Yes," said Ferris. "The trouble is, she didn't tell us where he is, or I'd have taken every one of the magicians I've trained over the last thirty years and gone after him then and there. Instead I've scattered them all over the world trying to find him."

Avender raised his left hand. It was a moment before either of his friends noticed the thimble, and another before Ferris thought to ask the obvious question.

"Where does it go?"

"To Fornoch. At least that's what Mims told me. And if she told you we had to see the Wizard before this was over, I'd advise doing it. She knows what she's talking about. Hubley and I had a lot of trouble, but it all came out fine in the end. I take it she told you who she is."

"Yes."

"And where she's from," growled Redburr.

"Well she hasn't told me," said Durk.

Avender looked at the stone for a moment, then put him back in his pocket. "Durk's the last one we should tell any of this to. If he knows, everyone'll know."

Ferris agreed. "The last thing we need is every magician trying to figure out the Timespell for themselves. It's bad enough I had to tell them humans can make Living Stones."

"Timespell?" Mindrell's eyebrows rose. "And who is this Mims you keep talking about?"

Avender checked to see if Ferris agreed before he went on. She nodded. He supposed the bard had as good a right to know what was going on as anyone if he ended up coming with them. And, if he didn't, Avender would make sure he never told anyone anyway, now that Hubley was no longer in the room.

"She's Hubley," he explained. "An older Hubley, who knows how to travel through time."

"Travel through time?" Not inclined to disbelieve anything after thirty years of living with magic, Mindrell took a moment to think about what Avender had said. "Does that mean she already knows how this all turns out?"

"She gave us no guarantees, if that's what you're thinking," said Ferris. "Hubley may know what happens, but I don't."

"She's very careful," said Avender, "to say nothing about that sort of thing."

"Whatever we do," said Redburr, "we need to make up our minds. If Reiffen has been taken by Fornoch, the sooner we get to him, the better."

Avender remembered the feeling of cold, dry earth falling over his face. His wrist throbbed. He had no more urge to forgive Reiffen than he had to forgive Mindrell. Nor did he wish to rescue him from Wizards a second time. But Hubley expected it of him, both grown-up and child. And Giserre expected it, too.

"I'll go," he said.

"You agree with Redburr?" said Ferris. "You really want to do this?"

"If I can think we should rescue Reiffen after what he's done to me," said Avender, "I think you can, too."

"How dare you! He cut me off from my child for thirty years!"

"He cut me off from everyone for thirty years."

Like a shaggy boulder, the Shaper rolled between the quarreling friends. "Enough. This isn't about you two, it's about Hubley and Giserre. They're the ones we're doing this for. And would either of you really just leave Reiffen to the Wizard? Would you do that to anyone?"

Avender wanted to say yes, but he knew it wasn't true. There were worse things than being buried alive.

"Fine," said Ferris.

"Do we even know for certain Reiffen's with the Wizard?" asked Mindrell. "From what you've said earlier, I gather you're only guessing."

"Do you think we're wrong?" Ferris gave him her most patronizing stare. "After you've lived with him for thirty years?"

"If he isn't with Hubley," added Avender, "that's the only other place he could be."

"Are you with us?" Redburr asked the bard.

Mindrell glanced at the door that had closed behind Giserre. "If you insist. I never did want to live forever. But I'll need a sword. Preferably heartstone."

"Me, too," said Avender.

"There are several on the bottom shelf." Ferris pointed under the desk that ran along the workshop's northern wall.

When the men were armed, everyone grasped Avender by the hand. His fingers were already on the thimble when he remembered Durk.

"It wouldn't be fair," he said, removing the stone from his pocket and placing him on the table, "to make Durk come, too."

"Of course not," answered the stone. "But it's even more un-fair to keep putting me in your pocket every time you talk about something important. And where are you going, anyway?"

"To fight Fornoch."

"Really? Well, good luck to you. Quite right to leave me be—"

The stone's last words were lost as Avender twisted the thim-ble off his finger and whispered, "Return."

Grumbling, Hubley followed her grandmother down the stairs. At least there were new things to see out the win-dows: waterfalls, the shimmering blue lake, pigs rooting through the orchard. The views of Aloslomin and Ivismundra from Cas-tle Grangore, so spectacular to most people, had been boring her for some time. At least now she knew why.

"Bath or dinner?" asked Giserre.

Despite a sudden yawn, the gnawing in Hubley's stomach prevailed. "Dinner."

When they entered the kitchen, an enormous man, almost as large as the bear, stood up from the table. Soup dripped from his mustache.

"Hubley?" he asked. "Is it really you?"

"Yes." Hubley frowned severely. "Who are you?"

"Baron Backford," he said. "Willy."

Her lower lip trembled. For the first time she realized just how much things had changed. Everything she remembered was gone. Her grandmother might have become an old woman, but then Giserre had been an old woman from the start as far as Hubley was concerned. What had happened to Willy was much worse. Willy was her friend, and was supposed to be her own age. They should have grown up together, gone to dances and weddings and balls. But here he was, an old man with gray hair and more than a little bit of tummy bulging over the top of his breeches.

Burying her face in her grandmother's apron, she began to sob.

"I'm sorry." Baron Backford knocked over his chair as he backed hastily from the table. "I didn't mean any harm. I just thought, if you really had escaped, I might be able to say hello. All the magicians have gone, and I guess I should have gone, too."

Giserre waved Willy back into his chair. Sitting beside him, she pulled Hubley onto her lap and rocked the child back and forth, crooning a wordless song. A nod to the cook brought more bowls of soup and sliced bread with butter. Baron Backford fidgeted uncomfortably, no more sure what to do for Hubley now than he would have when he was twelve.

She stopped crying after a while. Feeling more like a child than she had since she was at least five, she rubbed her nose on the back of her hand.

"It's not your fault," she told the baron. "Everything's just so different." Pulling at the bridge of her nose, she fought off another surge of tears.

Giserre wiped her granddaughter's cheeks with a handkerchief. "And how is Lady Breeanna?" she asked, turning to the baron. "As hale as ever?"

"Mother is doing wonderfully," said Willy, glad of the chance to talk about something different. "She'll be thrilled to hear you asked about her. She's three-score seven next spring, you know."

"Does she still practice her archery?"

"Every day. How good of you to remember, milady."

"I remember, too," said Hubley. Plucking the handkerchief from her grandmother's hands, she blew her nose. "Especially that time she won the contest on your ninth birthday. That was the best ever, the way she showed all those stupid men she was just as good as they were."

The baron shook his head. "I haven't thought of that in years.

But I guess you wouldn't have thought so well of it if it had been your mother showing off like that. I was mortified."

"I'd love it if my mother won an archery contest. She just learned boring things when she was a girl, like ironing and how to bake pies."

Willy looked very serious, which made his mustache wag. "There's nothing wrong with knowing that sort of thing, too. Mother taught me how to cook and sew. You can't imagine how important that is when you're out on a campaign and don't have anyone around to do it for you."

"Doesn't your wife cook and sew?"

The baron looked down at his hands. Old as the hills though he might be, he was still Willy. "Wives don't go campaigning with you any more than mothers. Besides, I've never married."

"You've never been married? Willy, that's the silliest thing I ever heard!"

Willy pulled at his mustache. "Father didn't marry Mother till he was sixty-one. I'm only forty-three. I have plenty of time."

Hubley yawned. "I guess the girls are even sillier now than they used to be. You were the nicest boy I ever knew, and I'm sure you're the nicest man, too."

"That is enough catching up for now," said Giserre. Hubley's soup and bread lay untouched on the table. "Bath next, then bed. You two can talk more this evening, when everyone returns."

Hubley didn't miss the private look Giserre shared with the baron as her grandmother took her hand. She knew perfectly well how dangerous fighting a Wizard was. But, if no one else was going to talk about it, she would be strong and not talk about it, either.

"See you later, Willy," she said.

The baron knocked his chair over a second time as he stood and presented her with a military bow.

Her bath was waiting for her upstairs. Giserre added some soap flakes to make bubbles, then went off with Hubley's clothes.

Probably to be thrown out, she said, because they were too filthy to be cleaned.

Sighing, she lay back in the tub. Everything was going to be better now. Her mother and father would slay the Gray Wizard, just like they had the Black and the White before him. Then her father would stop being mean and they could all go back to Castle Grangore and everything would be the way it used to. Though it might be fun to visit Tower Dale from time to time. Giserre had said there was a wonderful pool for swimming at the bottom of the Small Fall, much better than Nolo's Glen. And maybe Hubley'd be able to come whenever she wanted, now she knew the traveling spell. No one would ever keep her locked up again.

Eyes closed, she lowered herself deeper into the tub until only her face showed above the steaming water. Thick vapor filled the room, which was the main reason she failed to notice the greasy cloud hovering just outside the open window. Black spots like bruises clung to it as the mist began to seep inside. Her nose twitched at the sour smell as the cloud settled gently around her and the tub, but by that time it was too late.

23

Inside the Manderstone

They stood at the edge of a weedy clearing. A goat munched on the bare branches of the trees on the other side, the rope around its neck tied off to the porch of a tumbledown cottage. Chickens pecked beside a tree stump with an axe embedded in the top.

Redburr licked his yellow teeth. "I guess even Wizards have to eat."

Twigs snapped as they left the woods, but the windows in the shuttered cottage remained closed. Perhaps the Wizard had already finished with Reiffen and gone elsewhere with the corpse. Avender shuddered at the thought of what Fornoch might do with such a prize: shape a nightstalker to haunt children, or a walking stench to travel the world as a lesson for those who thought to threaten Wizards.

They paused on the porch. The windows were shut, but the top half of the door stood open. Motioning for the others to stay back, Ferris peered carefully around the edge.

"Please come in."

The voice that spoke was soothing as cream. The last time Avender had heard it, the Gray Wizard had saved them all from the collapse of Reiffen's workshop after they killed Usseis. Why should Fornoch be any less helpful now?

"Whatever you do, don't listen to him," Ferris warned.

A spell at her lips, she pushed open the bottom half of the

door. Avender and Mindrell drew their heartstone swords and followed, Redburr behind them. They found Fornoch standing in the middle of the single room, his back bent slightly beneath the low thatching. Reiffen sat like a schoolboy on a stool with his back to his old friends, his eyes fixed on a tall mirror.

"We have been expecting you," said the Wizard. Only Mindrell returned his bow.

"Expecting us?" Arms outstretched, Ferris kept Redburr and the two men behind her. Their Inach swords would achieve nothing against the Wizard unless magic was first used to distract him. "How can you be expecting us? We only just found out how to get here."

"It was only a matter of time before you did. You are too good a woman to leave your husband to his fate, regardless of what has passed between you." Fornoch's voice was sympathetic, but his all-black eyes devoured everything that fell into them like bottomless pits.

Mindrell nodded toward Reiffen. "Looks like we're too late. Does he even know we're here?"

"I know." Reiffen's voice dragged reluctantly across the cottage. "We're all too late. I have tried everything I can, but the Wizard will not fight. All he wants to do is talk."

"That just makes it easier." Ferris made no attempt to hide her scorn. "Not fighting won't stop us. Avender, give me your sword."

Though it made him feel naked to face the Wizard without a weapon, Avender did as she asked. Ferris lifted the stone blade in both hands, the tip threatening to dip to the floor at any minute, and confronted the Wizard. He made no attempt to stop her. Scarcely believing it could be so easy to kill him after all these years, she aimed the heavy sword up at the Wizard's chest.

"For my husband," she said through clenched teeth.

She drove the sword forward with all her strength. Fornoch made no move. The weapon pierced him cleanly, far more easily than anyone had thought. So easily, in fact, that Ferris was thrown off balance. Like the blade, she passed right through her target, disappearing inside the Wizard for a moment before coming out behind his back.

"You see?" said Reiffen. "He will not fight."

Whirling, Ferris struck again. A sideways blow, with even more strength now that she was angry. The sword sliced completely through Fornoch's waist, flying out again on the other side, but the blade remained unblooded. The Gray Wizard regarded his attacker with an amused air that reminded Avender of Mindrell.

"It is no use," said Fornoch. "You cannot harm me. Fighting has never been my way. If you would like to discuss your anger, however, I would be happy to oblige."

"You aren't even here," accused Ferris. "This is all pretend. You're actually somewhere else—"

Terror gripped her face. "He's gone after Hubley! In Valing. Giserre and the apprentices will never stop him!"

"No, I'm here." Patiently, the Wizard tried to convince Ferris she was wrong. "I have never had more than a passing interest in your daughter. Though it will be interesting to see what the last few years have done to her."

Eyes blazing, Ferris raised her hands and spoke a word. A pillar of fire embraced the Gray Wizard, flaming to the ceiling. Straw crackled; the thatching above Fornoch's head began to smoke. But the Wizard remained unhurt, his smile as unaltered as his flesh. Ferris poured more strength into her conjuring: her shoulders shook, her face twisted. The thatching burst into flames. Avender wondered if she had gone as mad as Reiffen and intended to burn them all.

She hadn't. The fire around the Wizard vanished when she dropped her arms, though the roof remained ablaze. The Wizard's gray robes weren't even singed.

"If you will allow me."

Fornoch lifted his arm. Distant thunder rolled. Rain pattered on the cottage, building quickly to a downpour. The burning straw sizzled and went out.

Momentarily defeated, Ferris gave Avender back his weapon. But the furrows on her forehead told him she was still thinking furiously. It wasn't like Ferris to give up, ever, about anything.

Reiffen, on the other hand, already had. "You see?" he said. "It was the same for me. I tried to fight him when he came to me in Castle Grangore. Did you really think killing him would be that easy? He is not like his brothers."

"Is that not a good thing?" asked the Wizard.

"No. If you were like your brothers, I would have slain you years ago."

"Had I been like my brothers, you would never have had the chance."

Reiffen's sour mood deepened. "Believe me, I understand all too well that without you in the background, I would have accomplished nothing."

"I assure you, Reiffen," said the Wizard, "I did not interfere. You and your friends achieved everything on your own. You were magnificent."

"If we did, it was only because you allowed it. A word from you, and Ossdonc or Usseis would have bent me to their will."

"I did not wish that. I still do not."

"No. You prefer the way things have fallen out. Magic released on the world, and who knows what else with it."

"Was that not what you wished as well?"

Reiffen made no reply. Of course it was what he had wished, thought Avender. And what had Reiffen's wishing brought him? Power more than any human had ever dreamed of. Renown as great as any hero's. And yet, with all that, he had spent thirty-one years hiding his daughter from the world, and had stopped teaching what he knew to make sure he didn't have to kill any more of his pupils.

Raising his eyes to his wife and her companions, Reiffen pointed to the mirror. "Do you see what he offers me now? The mirror is a door. Beyond it lies a mander. A great mander, greater than any other creature Usseis ever made. Unborn it is, waiting for the touch of another mind. You've seen it already, the egg Nolo brought back from Ussene. I understand it has grown much larger since my last visit, and has been moved to the Bryddsmett. The mander lies coiled inside, ready to wake. With it I could roam the Stoneways at will, driving the sissit back into the darkest caves. Ascending the Sun Road, I could emerge on the surface of the world. No enemy could face me, no part of the world escape me. And I could come and go as I please. I could put the beast on and off like a cloak or a pair of shoes, as long as I had the mirror."

"Why would you want to be a mander?" asked Avender. "Isn't being a magician enough for you? Do you want to be a Hisser, too?"

"I have been a Hisser," said Reiffen. "But a mander is a creature I could never manage on my own."

"You'd be a Dwarf if you could manage it," said Ferris.

The Wizard shook his head. "Not even I can achieve that transformation. Bryddin are outside magic entirely."

"It's all a matter of traveling, isn't it?"

Fornoch looked at Ferris in surprise. Approval creased his face. "Reiffen chose most excellently when he made you his first apprentice, my lady. Better, perhaps, than I chose, myself. You have perceived what is not entirely obvious. But yes, the traveling spell is part of the magic. The mirror is the channel. I have wanted to teach Reiffen about mirrors for some time. What you and he have discovered so far is only the beginning."

"I don't think that is the only new use for the traveling spell you've shown us today," said Ferris thoughtfully. "Avender, please take my hand."

Again, Avender did as he was told. He knew by the look on

her face that Ferris had figured something out. His sword ready in his right hand, he approached the Wizard at her side. She reached for Fornoch's arm.

"It was a form of the traveling spell you used, wasn't it?" she said. "To escape my attack."

Before the Wizard could reply, the cottage whisked away. White clouds laced a clear blue sky above Avender's and Ferris's heads. Valing Lake gleamed between looming cliffs. Before Avender could wonder why Ferris had brought them back to Tower Dale, they had returned to the gloomy cottage.

"But that won't work for you now," continued Ferris, as if they hadn't gone anywhere at all. Avender wondered if anyone had even noticed they'd left.

The scene changed again. Not Tower Dale this time, but a meadow on the Shoulder that had been their favorite place to sled when they were children. By the time Avender recognized the spot, they were already gone.

"Kill him, Avender," Ferris said, her hand gripping the Wizard's sleeve.

Smoldering thatch reappeared. With all his strength, Avender thrust the heavy sword at the Wizard's chest.

He didn't strike slowly, but all the same Ferris must have taken them back and forth between Valing and the cottage more than a dozen times before his blow hit home. He recognized most of the places they went. The manor-house kitchen. The lower dock. Big Sheep Island. The Teapot. Southy. The Tear. The places he didn't recognize were those that must have meant more to Ferris than to him. Places her memory recalled more easily than his own. And in between them all, the cottage with its charred roof and muddy floor, the same scene again and again, only each time they returned, Avender's sword was that much closer to Fornoch's breast.

The air quivered with the throb of Valing Gorge. The sword pierced the Wizard's chest.

The world continued to dance as Ferris held fast to the Wizard's arm. The sword thrust deeper. Cottage to Grangore to cottage to New Palace to cottage to Minabbenet, the scenes flicked in and out of Avender's mind. He saw Dwarves and barons, farmers and thanes, but no one noticed him. He and Ferris were traveling too fast.

The Wizard stumbled backward. Avender let go the sword before he was pulled along. Ferris released his arm.

The world stopped moving. Black blood steamed on gray robes, dripping to the floor. Reiffen slipped off his stool as Fornoch clutched at the blade in his chest and toppled into the mirror.

He disappeared.

With an awful cry, Reiffen grabbed Mindrell's sword. Lifting the blade over his head in both hands, he charged the mirror. Even Avender knew that if Reiffen smashed the glass the Wizard would be trapped forever, wherever he had gone.

A large hand emerged from the center of Reiffen's reflection as he swung the sword, catching his wrists before he struck his blow. The Inach weapon rattled to the ground. Withdrawing into the mirror, the hand took Reiffen with it. The magician twisted, trying to escape, and threw his shoulder at the edge of the glass. The hand shook him like a feather, knocking his head heavily against the wooden frame before he disappeared beyond the pane.

The mirror rocked on its short, sturdy legs, but didn't fall. Black blood dribbled from the bottom of the glass.

Avender, and everyone else, hesitated before following their old friend, or trying to recover Mindrell's sword.

"What just happened?" asked Redburr.

Her magic spent, Ferris sank exhausted to the ground. "Fornoch was using a traveling spell to go back and forth from some other place. It's the opposite of what happens when a spinning wagon wheel goes really fast and you can't see the spokes.

Here it was the other places Fornoch was going that couldn't see him, which made it look like Fornoch was always here. Only he wasn't. So I started traveling back and forth with Avender until I matched the Wizard's pace. Once I felt his arm, I knew Avender could strike him."

"Clever lass." The bear's eyes glittered.

Carefully watching the mirror, the bard retrieved his sword. "Do you think he's dead?"

"Only one way to make sure." Avoiding the front of the glass, Redburr approached the side of the mirror.

"What about Reiffen?" asked Avender, knowing the bear's intent.

"Yes," said Ferris. "What about Reiffen."

Redburr shook his shaggy head. "You know Reiffen wouldn't think twice about smashing the mirror if it were us in there. Why should we?"

"I'm not Reiffen," said Avender.

The bard agreed with the bear. "Smashing the mirror is easiest."

"We need to rescue Reiffen first. We promised Hubley and Giserre."

"We have no idea what's on the other side of that glass," Mindrell argued. "Fornoch could be waiting in there with fifty sissit."

"I'll go in alone," said Avender. "If it's a trap, we'll find out soon enough. Then you can break the glass."

Ferris rose wearily. "I'll come, too."

"No you won't. You still have Hubley to take care of. If I see it's safe, then Redburr and the rhymer can come help, but not you. You're too worn out."

The last thing Avender wanted, however, was to get himself buried alive again, under glass or dirt. There had to be another way.

"Wait," he said as an idea came to him.

"What if the Wizard returns?"

"Stab him again."

He raced outside. The goat regarded him with velvet eyes as he raised his knife above its neck, then ambled away into the forest after Avender severed the rope. Untying the other end, he fastened the line securely around his waist and went back inside.

The Gray Wizard had not reappeared.

"Hold this." Avender tossed the free end of the rope to Redburr. "If I'm not back in a few minutes, pull me out."

Still squatting beside the mirror, the bear growled. But he picked the rope up with his teeth.

A last burst of caution made Avender hold his hand up to the mirror before he passed through. His fingertips disappeared, but they were still there when he drew them back. Mindrell's sword firmly in his grasp, he stepped through his reflection.

It was dark on the other side. Not the dark of lightlessness, but the dark of illumination obscured. Avender felt as if his eyes weren't seeing and not that there was nothing to see. Turning, he saw the mirror hanging in the blackness behind him like a door opening on empty sky.

Someone groaned. Reiffen, he hoped. With any luck, the Wizard was already dead.

"Reiffen?"

Heat and anger thickened around him. Hunger also, as bottomless as the Abyss. Hunger for rotting cattle and leverets by the shovelful, skinned and roasted. The pressure of it thrummed against his skull, like a beating heart that wasn't his own. Its pulse thumped steadily against his skin, quiet and dangerous as a resting snake.

"Reiffen? If you're here, you'd better answer. I can't stay long."

"Reiffen is here." The Wizard's voice poured over Avender from every direction.

"Where?"

"In front of you." Fornoch coughed, his throat thick with phlegm. Or blood.

Avender slid his right foot forward until his toe encountered something solid. Crouching, he touched what he had found with his hands. Cloth and hair. Carefully he patted along Reiffen's chest and shoulders. Nothing seemed wrong, until his fingers felt blood as thick as honey seeping beneath the ribs.

The pounding of the great heart quickened.

"Is he dead?"

"No."

"What did you do to him?"

"Not what I intended." The Wizard hacked again, longer and more wretchedly this time, as if his lungs were tearing. "I needed his Stone to save myself. You should be proud. A less skillful stroke, and I would not have had to avail myself of what your friend possessed."

"You can't blame me for this."

"Did I say that? I apologize. That was not my intent."

"Is he going to die?"

"Not if you leave him here. I will heal him when my strength returns. As it will soon." Another cough, lighter this time, as if to prove the truth of what the Wizard said.

"If I take him outside, Ferris can help him." The last thing Avender wanted was for Fornoch to be in charge of helping Reiffen.

"That is true. If you can take him outside. I lack the strength to stop you. And if I follow you, your friends would slay me in an instant."

Avender tugged at Reiffen, but the magician didn't budge. Dropping to his knees, Avender tried to lift him, but Reiffen was too heavy, as if his body was strapped to the floor. The great heart pulsed; unseen lungs swelled and tightened in time with Avender's own.

He searched the darkness once more for the Wizard. "You're doing this. Let him go."

"I would if I could." The Wizard coughed politely. "But it is not me. The mander senses the power Reiffen holds, and wants him for itself. Removing him will require more strength than you possess. A pity you did not bring Nolo. Though I doubt Nolo would have been able to pass the mirror."

Reiffen groaned. He stirred in Avender's hands.

"Avender, is that you?" Reiffen asked, his voice much weaker than the Wizard's.

"Yes. Can you get up?"

"No."

"You have to get out of here."

"I know." Reiffen's voice dropped to a whisper. "Fornoch is using me for a shield. As long as I'm in here with him, he thinks you won't smash the mirror."

"Actually," said the Wizard, the rasping in his voice almost completely gone, "I think just the opposite. Avender and his friends will find it much easier to smash the mirror than they believe. You have not been a particularly good friend to them over the last few years, Reiffen."

Reiffen's fingers closed tightly on Avender's arm. Avender tried once again to lift him off the ground.

"Don't leave me here, Avender. Please. I saved you once, remember?"

Yes, and all but killed him once, too. But Avender knew he couldn't resist Reiffen's plea, if only for Hubley's sake. He had rescued him from Fornoch once, and would try to rescue him again.

A tug on the rope around his middle warned Avender that his time inside the mirror was up. He reached for Reiffen's arm but, before he could get a solid grip, the bear had pulled him away. Spinning around, he tried to set his feet as he slid backward through the darkness, but there was no edge on this side of the mirror and he was pulled right through. Blinking at the sudden brightness, he tumbled out into the gloomy cottage. The pounding of the great heart disappeared.

"No!" he shouted. "I found Reiffen! You brought me back too soon!"

Ferris fell on her knees beside him. "Why didn't you bring him with you?"

"He's wounded. Fornoch took his Stone."

"What does Fornoch want with his Stone?" The last bit of color drained from Ferris's tired face.

"To try and save himself."

Redburr padded forward, blood glinting in his eye. His breath reeked of fish and beer. "Your cut almost killed the Wizard, eh, boy? Well, what are we waiting for? We still have another sword. Let's go finish him off."

Avender shook his head. "I don't think we'll find him. All I heard was his voice."

"You found Reiffen. Why not the Wizard, too?"

"Reiffen was lying at my feet, but I still might have missed him if Fornoch hadn't told me where he was. You can't see anything in there."

"If you were that close to him," asked Ferris, "why didn't you carry him out?"

"Something's holding him down. Fornoch, the mander, I don't know what."

Redburr snarled. "You saw the mander?"

"No, but I felt it. Almost like I was inside it. I could feel its heart beating, and its hunger."

Redburr turned back to the mirror. Avender noticed Mindrell already standing on one side of the glass. "There's only one thing left to do. Smash it."

"But Reiffen's still alive!"

The Shaper turned on him harshly. Flecks of white foam speckled his dark muzzle. Avender remembered the three or four times he had seen Redburr in a full-on rage. It wasn't a pretty sight, whether you were on the Shaper's side or not.

"You already talked me out of going back in there after the

Wizard," said the bear. "Do you want us to just wait out here till he gets better? Maybe he'll let Reiffen go, but then what? Another thirty years playing with us like a cat with mice?"

Avender remembered the pleading in Reiffen's voice, the fear he would be left behind. "What do you think?" he asked, looking at Ferris.

Her mouth set tight, Ferris took a long breath through her nose. The seeds of tears hovered at the edges of her eyes. "You've done everything Hubley and Giserre could ask. I lost him years ago."

That was enough for the bear. Rearing up on his hind legs, he took hold of one side of the mirror. Mindrell put his shoulder to the other.

"Fornoch said we'd do this," said Avender. "Which makes me think it's just what he wants us to do."

"Don't think," growled the Shaper. "That's what he wants us to do. Anything to buy him more time."

"Let me go in once more."

"No," said Ferris. "We have to do it now. The choice is mine."

Taking Avender's hand, she helped him off the floor. The Shaper and the bard each grabbed one side of the mirror and began to rock it back and forth. Even with the bear's great strength, it took several shoves before they got the heavy glass swinging. A final push and the enormous mirror toppled backward with a crash. A pair of great cracks stretched from top to bottom. Carefully Mindrell tapped the broken pane with the toe of his boot. When his foot didn't pass through, he picked up his heartstone sword and smashed the mirror completely, not stopping until the largest piece was smaller than his hand.

"That should do it," he said.

A spider dropped from the roof at the end of a single silken line. Ferris leaned on Avender's shoulder.

"I never even got a chance to talk to him," she said.

He put his arm around her. She bent her head to his chest.

Not since they had been children together had he held her so close. Smelling her hair, all their years together in Valing rushed back to him, the blue lake and the leaping nokken and the night raids stealing Enna Spinner's maple candy. And Ferris scolding him and Reiffen every time they didn't pay attention to her, or refused to take her with them, because she was a girl. Which hadn't been often, because ignoring Ferris had always been harder than ignoring a summer storm. Reiffen had ruled them both, the uncrowned prince demanding their fealty with his daring and his family's past. And now he was gone, like a barrel swallowed by the gorge.

Mindrell cleared his throat. "It might be a good idea to go to Issinlough."

Pushing away from Avender, Ferris turned on the bard in fury. "Can't you even give us time to grieve?"

"The rhymer's right, Ferris." Gently, Redburr nudged her with his massive head, the redness already washed from his eyes. "The mirror's smashed, but not the egg."

Weariness settled over Ferris like a fog. "Right. I forgot about that."

Avender remembered the angry hunger he'd felt inside the mirror. "The mander's in there, waiting to be born. And I don't think Reiffen's going to be the one in control when it comes out."

"I don't have the strength to travel to Issinlough right now." Ferris rubbed her forehead with the back of her hand. "I have to rest."

"There isn't time. Use your thimble to get us back to Tower Dale. One of the apprentices can take us on from there, but we have to get to Issinlough as fast as possible. We have to tell the Dwarves to break the egg." Avender shook his head grimly. "You wouldn't believe the power I felt in there."

"All right."

Rolling up her sleeves, Ferris held out her arms. The two

men laid their hands on her left wrist, while the bear set his paw on her right. Clasping her hands together, Ferris removed the thimble.

"Return," she said.

Hubley was waiting for them when they arrived.

24

The Mandrake

ubley didn't feel any older after her father's spell found her, but she did have to wrestle a bit with the thirty other versions of herself as they tried to order themselves in her mind. Each one thought it was her real tenth year and got very angry when the others tried to take over what it knew was its own proper place. Some wanted to be first, jostling for position right after her ninth birthday, while others fought to be last, trying to sneak in behind the current day. Hubley found it easiest to push the laggards away because she knew her memories were the most recent of any of them, but the earlier ones were harder to sort out. That was going to take some time.

Though her memories were unhappy and confused, Hubley herself was excited. Already she was seeing the snippets of magic her father had laid out for her over the years. None of them meant much on their own but, fitted together like puzzle pieces, they transformed into spells. Already she had discovered how to travel without falling asleep, and how to direct the spell to take her where she wanted. Who knew what else she would find wrapped up in the past, once she had the time to look for it.

Unfortunately, there were other things to do first. Her father had planted some very pressing memories in her mind in each of the last twenty years; apparently the whole idea of giving the last thirty years back to her was part of his plan to fight the Wizard. "You'll find the two halves of the firestorm spell in every other year," he had said in the most recent one, "and there's a decent disease in there I just developed. If you catch Fornoch off guard you might be able to kill him before he has a chance to do anything else."

So much for that idea. Her father hadn't anticipated her being stolen by someone she didn't want to kill. She'd have to mention that particular flaw in his plan to him after her mother and Avender brought him back from the Wizard.

Giserre returned with a nightgown, and Hubley allowed herself to be taken out of the bath and toweled dry. Even letting her grandmother tuck her into bed was easier than trying to explain what had happened. Giserre was no mage. But deciding to stay and watch Hubley sleep as well was a little much, so Hubley cast a quick spell that put her grandmother to sleep instead. After that she was free to move through the tower, as long as she stayed invisible. Secretly borrowing a dress from the same cook's daughter who had already lent her the nightgown, she found an apprentice with a thimble and compelled him to take her to the Tower's room of return. After a fight with Fornoch, her mother and father would most likely come back by thimble rather than ordinary spell.

Her suspicions were correct. "Where's Father?" she demanded when she saw he wasn't with them.

Ferris and Avender exchanged glances. The bear licked at a spot on the floor.

"We're hoping to meet your father in Issinlough," said Mindrell while everyone else was still deciding what to say.

"That's right," added Avender quickly. "We have to go right away. There's no time to even tell you what happened."

Hubley knew both men well enough to know they weren't telling her the whole truth. "You didn't rescue him?"

Her mother hugged her close. Hubley didn't think she'd ever

seen her so weak and tired. Her cheeks were hollow, her eyes shrunk deep behind her nose.

"It's too complicated to explain, sweetheart," she said. "I'll tell you everything when I come back."

"I'm going with you."

Her mother patted her absently on the head. "No you're not. It's too dangerous."

"I am too. You're too tired to do the spell. I'll have to do it."

"Hubley, I think you need to go back to bed. You're not making any sense. Avender told me you can only cast the traveling spell when you're asleep. And how'd you get down here, anyway?"

"I made Delmanour bring me. I'm not a child anymore, Mother. Father freed my memories. All of them. His spell only just reached me, but I remember everything now. He told me all about his plans, too."

Redburr padded forward. "Plans?"

"His plans to kill Fornoch if the Wizard ever captured me. That's what he was teaching me all these years. With what I know now, I could've escaped easily. Or I might even have slain the Wizard, if I caught him by surprise."

"But you weren't taken by Fornoch," said Ferris.

"Father didn't know that. He didn't know anything about Mims, so he cast the spell anyway just to be safe."

"This is all very interesting," interrupted Avender, "but we don't have time to talk about it now. What's important is to get to Issinlough. Hubley, can you really take us there?"

"Yes. Father taught me parts of the traveling spell several times. Now that I have all my memories again, I've already put the spell back together."

Ferris interrupted firmly. "Innich can take us. This is no time—"

Redburr cut her off. "Let the cub come. We're in a hurry, and it'll take time to find Innich. Hubley's obviously not what she was when we left, Ferris. And she'll be just as safe in Issinlough as here. Safer, even, with a couple hundred Dwarves around."

"If she's really got thirty-one years' worth of magic in her," Avender added, "she's probably better suited to this sort of thing than we ever were."

Ferris gave in wearily. Hubley held out her hands. The magic her father had given her brought with it not only knowledge and power, but confidence as well. She could take them wherever she wanted.

For now, that was Mother Norra's kitchen. Mother Norra was long gone, of course, which brought Hubley a twinge of sadness. Her Mims and Grandpa were probably gone as well, but she didn't have time for mourning anyone yet. Her father had a great deal to answer for once things were more settled.

"What's next?" she asked.

Avender nodded toward the window. Outside, a long airship slipped gracefully past the thick finger of the Halvanankh, the Bryddsmett at the end of its three blumet cables gleaming below. The manderstone, ten times larger than Hubley remembered, stood at the center of the bowl.

"Your father and Fornoch are trapped inside."

Her mother told her everything that had happened at the Wizard's cottage as they climbed to the top of the unneret, and how Fornoch had said he would heal her father. All that was left now was to see who would be in control of the mander after it hatched. Hubley could tell from her mother's sagging shoulders that she thought it was going to be Fornoch. The idea that her father was stuck inside some horrible beast was terrible, but still, he was her father. Why shouldn't he be the one who survived? He'd gotten away from the Wizard often enough before.

They sent the first humans they met off to find Dwvon and Uhle. "Tell them to meet us in the Bryddsmett," Redburr growled. "It's important."

At the top of the city they crossed a pair of shining bridges to the Halvanankh, then descended the long finger of stone. At the lowest windows they unfurled rope ladders and climbed down the last eight or nine fathoms to stand beside the manderstone.

Hubley's first impression had been right: the egg was enormous. The last time she had seen it, the stone had been shorter than she was. Now it loomed four or five fathoms above her head. Standing on its rounded end, it towered higher than the last blumet bench that circled the upper edge of the mett.

"At least it hasn't started to hatch," said Avender.

Following his lead, everyone put their ears to the stone. It was warm to the touch, and from within came a distant, hollow booming.

"Are Father and the Wizard fighting?" asked Hubley.

"I think it's the creature's heart," said Avender.

Fur rose on the back of the Shaper's neck and shoulders.

"Let's get it up on the edge of the mett." Leaning with one hand on the stone, Avender pointed back up the rows of silvery benches. "If we find out it's Fornoch, we push it over."

"And if it isn't?" asked Ferris.

"Push it over anyway," growled the bear.

"Why don't you go turn into a bat or something," said Ferris. "You're not helping at all. You know we'll make the right decision when the time comes."

Hubley thought about grabbing the Shaper and taking him far away. If her father had managed to survive being trapped with Fornoch inside the egg, he might last even longer if Redburr wasn't around when it hatched.

"Why don't you think Father can win?" she asked instead. "You said the Wizard was wounded."

"Yes," said Avender. "But so was your father. And the Wizard was healing faster."

Loss and longing brushed Ferris's face as she caressed the warm stone. "Even if he does win, sweetheart, what will he be like? Being trapped in a mander's body will hardly help."

"He'll still be Father."

"I have to say I'd rather find Reiffen in there instead of the Wizard," said Mindrell.

"We have to be ready, either way." Shading his eyes against the lamplight, Avender studied the ankh's windows for a sign that Dwvon or Uhle had arrived. "The Dwarves'll have to rig some sort of hoist from the ankh to lift it."

"I can do it," said Hubley. "The feather spell's one of my best."

Ferris examined the egg doubtfully. "It's awfully big. Can you manage the whole thing?"

Hubley didn't doubt she could. Many wonders were stored in her mind now. In time, she felt, she would make connections that even her father hadn't noticed. Already she had begun to see some peculiar aspects to the traveling spell that she didn't think had ever been explored. Like that dream she'd had just before waking up in Castle Grangore. She could even use some of them now.

> "Here and there,
> Now and then,
> Displace the weight
> To where and when."

The manderstone lightened easily, almost as if it wanted to fly.

"Nothing's changed," grumbled the Shaper.

"Not that you can see." Hubley poked the egg with a finger, but it was still too large to be easily moved, despite its weightlessness. "If we all try to lift it at once, we should be able to pick it up."

But the stone proved too smooth to grab. They found they could rock it back and forth by pushing on one side or another, but couldn't lift it off the ground without having it slip out of their hands. Redburr suggested knocking it over and rolling it up to the edge, but Avender stopped that idea by pointing out the egg might break in the fall. And getting it over the rows of benches still involved lifting.

"What you need is a sling."

Letting go the ladder he had descended, Nolo joined them. Dwvon and half a dozen other Bryddin followed. Hubley's heart lifted at the sight of her old friends. Before the Shaper and the humans could even figure out what they were doing, the Bryddin had fashioned one of the rope ladders into a double loop with handles that fit snugly around the base of the egg at just the right height for carrying, if you were a Dwarf.

Nolo looked to Ferris for further orders. "Where do you want it?"

"On the edge of the mett," Avender answered. "If you can just hold it there."

Without bothering to ask why, the Bryddin bent to the task. Somehow they all lifted at the same time without anyone counting down. A pair of smooth jerks, and they were carrying the stone over their heads as they ascended the benches. The egg swayed slightly. Even weightless, it remained awkward.

They got it to the top of the mett just in time. With a crack like the world splitting, a large, dark fissure creased the shell. Running from the top of the stone to a spot halfway down the side, the split was large enough to wedge a finger into. But the crack showed nothing of the creature inside.

Nolo looked down at the humans still standing at the bottom of the Mett. "What now?" he asked.

"Just hold it there," said Avender. "Keep it poised, so that if you let go it'll fall over the side."

"It won't fall unless you give it some weight."

Hubley understood Avender's idea at once. "I can get rid of the feather spell as soon as you tell me. All it takes is a word."

Another fracture split the egg's surface as the Dwarves shifted the stone closer to the edge. Jagged cracks webbed the shell between the two fissures. A third sharp report, and the top of the shell burst open, just like the smaller one Hubley had watched hatch in Uhle's workshop years ago. A long, black tongue snaked out to probe the night and lick the sides of the hole.

The next piece broke off the bottom. A crooked leg scrabbled for purchase on the blumet benches; the nearest Dwarf jumped back as claws raked the air.

Avender started up the mett. In the biggest explosion yet, a large piece of shell shot off the top of the egg. Bits of stone rained over Hubley and the others at the center of the dish. A foreleg slithered out the top of the egg, followed by an enormous snout. Smoke plumed above nostrils as large as Redburr's paws. A black eye blinked.

"Thank you for doing nothing hasty," said a voice as dark and sooty as the fumes leaking from its mouth. "It is always good to talk."

"Push it off!" roared Redburr. "It's Fornoch!"

"Not yet." Avender held back the Shaper's fury with his hand. "There's still time to find out what happened to Reiffen first."

He looked up at the mander. "Serpent, who are you?"

The cruel jaws smiled, revealing teeth as dark and shiny as its eyes. "Redburr seems to have answered that question already to his satisfaction."

"You admit you're the Gray Wizard?"

"Not any longer. The Gray Wizard is gone. The mandrake has taken his place."

"Is that what you call yourself? Mandrake?"

"I am a mandrake. The first of many, I hope. But you may continue calling me Fornoch if you wish."

"There! He admitted it!" Fur bristling, the Shaper stood upright on the first bench and roared. His fore claws raked the air. "No more questions!"

Avender signaled the Dwarves to ignore the bear. Addressing the mandrake once more, he asked, "What happened to Reiffen?"

"Oh, he is here as well. Would you like to speak to him?"

The mandrake smiled toothily. His voice changed. Wearier, and less confident, he said, "I'm here. Is that you, Hubley, standing in the middle of the mett? And Ferris? I'm so sorry. Nothing has come out the way I hoped."

Ferris bit her lip. Hubley restrained herself from running up to the egg. The mander sounded exactly like her father.

Redburr leapt impatiently onto the next bench, his claws scrabbling on the metal. "Just because you can talk like Reiffen proves nothing. The Gray Wizard could do that any time he wanted, and take Reiffen's shape, too."

"We'll ask him a question that only Reiffen would know." Avender turned back to the mandrake. "How old was I when I came to live with you and Giserre?"

The beast held his interrogator with a steady gaze. "You were six. It was three days after your mother died."

"And what did you do when Giserre told you the news?"

"I ordered you to bow. You refused, and Giserre said you were right to do so. 'Princes must earn fealty, not expect it,' she said."

"Everyone knows that's what happened," barked the bear.

"Ask him a harder question!" said the bard.

"I'll do it!" Hubley climbed up onto the first step. Her mother grabbed her from behind, though she had meant to go no farther. "Father and I had lots of time alone together, so there're lots of things only he and I know."

Even across the distance from the top to the bottom of the mett, Hubley found herself noticing nothing but the creature's dark, unblinking eye. Trying to keep her voice steady, because the mandrake was still terrifying even if part of her father was inside, she asked, "What did you give me for my birthday seven years ago? Not last year, or the year before, or thirty-one years ago, but seven years ago."

Her mother squeezed her hand. It was a very good question.

Hubley might not have known the answer herself had the memory not been fresh in her mind. If the mander was even close, she might think her father really was sharing the creature with the Wizard. And then what would they do? It was one thing to cast Fornoch into the Abyss, and quite another to do it to her father.

The beast's thin smile returned. Dark smoke shrouded the gray egg's shattered top.

"A doll?" the mandrake guessed.

"He's playing with us!"

Slipping wildly on the metal, the bear charged up the benches. Another loud explosion rocked the mett; a huge chunk of shell arced upward, blotting the city's lights. Ferris tried to pull Hubley one way, but her daughter wriggled free and went the other. The shell crashed between them. The floor of the mett shook; for a moment Hubley thought the dish would tear loose from its cables. But the Dwarf work held, and Hubley scrambled up after the bear as the shell toppled over behind her. Her eyes on Avender, she saw him give the signal to the Dwarves to push the egg into the Abyss.

"*Fall,*" she whispered.

The egg fell. Hubley caught a glimpse of the mander trying to pull itself free, and then it was gone, the Wizard and her father with it. A blur of red, and the bear had followed them over the edge before anyone could stop him.

"Redburr!" she cried.

"It's all right." Catching Hubley a second time from behind, Ferris wrapped her arms around her daughter. Hubley burrowed as deep as she could into her mother's dress.

"Hush, sweetheart." Her mother rocked her while murmuring in her ear. "Redburr will be fine. Remember the story about Avender and me running into the river in the *Nightfish*? We thought we lost him then, too, only he fooled us all by turning into a bat and flying free. He'll do it this time, too."

"But what about Father?"

Ferris squeezed her daughter tight. They both knew there was nothing she could say.

At the edge of the mett, Avender and the Bryddin watched the egg disappear. It didn't take long. The last of the Wizards was gone. When they could no longer see it, they returned across the benches to the center of the dish. Avender and Nolo lingered with Hubley and her mother, while Dwvon and the other Bryddin climbed back up the ladders to the Halvanankh. Mindrell stayed also, his hair gray with dust from the broken eggshell.

"Come on," said Avender. "I think we could all do with a hot meal and something to drink. I don't know about the rest of you, but I've had almost no sleep in the last few days."

"Neither has Hubley." Gently, Ferris guided her daughter toward the ladders. "You may have more memories than you should, but you're still a little girl. I say we go over to the Rupiniah till I'm rested enough to take us home."

Scaling the ladders, they pulled themselves back in through the windows at the bottom of the Halvanankh. Mindrell came last, huffing and puffing as he rolled onto the stone floor with a groan.

"What's wrong with you?" asked Ferris. "Except for pushing over the mirror, all you've done is stand around. The least you can do is wipe the eggshell out of your hair. You can't be that tired."

The bard brushed at his head, but nothing came off. Puzzled, he looked at his hand.

"There's nothing there," he said.

Ferris gave him a sharp look. "Didn't my husband give you a Living Stone?"

Mindrell shook his head, then rubbed his neck as if shaking it had made it sore. "My life was lengthened by other means, if that's what you're asking. Reiffen told me he wouldn't make another Stone."

Hubley racked her new memories, but none of them knew

anything about how to make Living Stones, or any other way of extending life. Their guesses, however, were not very nice.

Ferris grew concerned. "When was your last treatment?"

"A few months ago. I need them more often than Hubley needs hers. Is there a problem?"

"You're dying. Actually, first you're going to age rapidly until you look as old as you really are. How soon you die after that will depend entirely on what Reiffen put inside you."

Mindrell studied the age spots already freckling his hands. "I guess I should have expected it. Your husband never did think he'd paid me back properly for what I did to him."

"You paid your debt," said Ferris. "The rest of us have understood that for a long time."

His amusement undiminished, the bard quoted a bit of mocking rhyme.

"So the champion, his fate complete,
Fell down dead at his liege's feet."

Moving slowly to keep the bard from growing any more fatigued, they followed Nolo up the Halvanankh. Whatever satisfaction the party felt at the Wizard's defeat was lessened by the shock of Mindrell's sudden aging and the knowledge that Reiffen was gone forever. Hubley found her thoughts drifting as the realization grew in her that she would never see her father again. Though he had plainly been unbalanced by what Fornoch had done to him, most of what she remembered about him was happy. He had taught her a great deal, and had been kind and loving, and quick with praise. His lies she had only recently discovered, but she doubted they would ever come close to coloring what she thought of him, now he was gone. Not as long as she had thirty-one years' worth of tenth birthdays to celebrate instead.

She was still lost in her own thoughts when the bard stopped at the window she had just passed and pointed into the darkness.

"What's that? My eyes don't see as well as they did a few minutes ago, but it looks like a bird. Is it Redburr?"

The Dwarves, more accustomed to close work with metal and stone than distant peering, couldn't tell either. But Hubley found what the bard had spotted at once. A shadow blanketed the lights of the Rupiniah, moving toward the catwalks above. A long shadow, with wings and a tail.

Ferris leaned out the window beside her daughter. "It's not Redburr. Not unless he's decided to turn into a vulture."

"It's too big for a vulture," said Avender.

Hubley found the thing's head as it settled on the unneret. A wide snout with ridges where the eyes would be and a long neck above folded wings. A face she had just seen.

"It's Fornoch," she gasped.

"Fornoch?" said Nolo. "Manders can't fly."

"It is a mander," said Avender. "A mander with wings."

There was no mistaking the creature as it scuttled up the Rupiniah. Black as the Abyss, it climbed the unneret easily, its claws clutching balconies and windows. At a point where it could look down on the nearest catwalk, it paused and reopened its wings. The lights of the city shone dimly through the thin skin like stars through wisps of cloud.

"What's that on its belly?" asked Ferris.

"My sword," said Avender.

"Your sword?" asked Nolo.

"The one I stabbed Fornoch with when he was still a Wizard."

The beast coiled like a striking serpent. Hubley and the others tried to warn everyone on the catwalk, but their shouts were lost in the general clamor of the busy city.

The mandrake screamed. Not a human scream, but near enough to make the sound worse than if it had been. Then, more like a nokken in water than a lizard flying through the air, it launched itself at the catwalk.

Cries of alarm filled the darkness as the creature shot past the platform and looped its tail around the blumet grid. Humans and Dwarves scattered. The mandrake hung in the air, anchored by its momentum. Flexing its wings and tail, it pulled the catwalk downward until the bridge broke off from the Rupiniah under the strain. The mandrake uncoiled its tail; the walkway collapsed against the unneret on the other side. Any humans still holding on were shaken free. Long screams faded into the depths, reminding Hubley of the sissits' cries at the Backford Lamp. The Dwarves, however, didn't fall, and scattered like ants across the upside-down tower.

Folding its wings, the mandrake dropped toward the bottom of the city. With a clap like thunder, the creature caught itself just below the Bryddsmett by reopening them. Powerful beats sent it back up again, aimed this time at another catwalk between the Halvanankh and the inner ring of unnerets.

Avender turned to Ferris. "Can you do something? He'll destroy the city if he isn't stopped."

Hubley felt power thicken around them as her mother gathered the little strength she'd regained. Her own magic surged more strongly than she had ever felt before, coursing through her hands and chest and arms. She began to chant as thunderbolts raced out from Ferris's palms. The twin shafts of lightning struck the great lizard full on the back, knocking the beast away from its target. Shrieking in rage, the mandrake wheeled toward the Halvanakh on widespread wings.

> *"Candle, furnace, kiln, and byre,*
> *Help me set this beast afire."*

Balls of flame burst from Hubley's hands, growing hotter and brighter as they raced across the darkness. They splashed against the mandrake's hide, but were no more effective than her mother's lightning. The flying mander burst through the blazing clouds like a hound through a hedgerow, orange flame clinging to its black snout. Too late, Hubley remembered how Plum's fireball had failed as well.

"Out!" shouted Nolo. "Everyone away from the window!"

The humans scrambled up the stairs. Hubley felt a wave of heat sweep across her shoulders. The walls shook.

"Is that you, Ferris?" crowed the beast from outside. "I am coming for you next."

With Nolo pushing them from behind, the humans tumbled into the nearest cave. As he followed them inside they found the Dwarf singed black from head to foot, his hair and beard completely burned away.

"What in the world?" exclaimed Ferris.

Nolo shook his head in wonder. "The thing breathes fire."

"We have to kill it," said Avender more practically. "Anyone have any Inach?"

"Dwvon has some swords in the Rupiniah. In the room just above the Bryddis B'wee."

The ankh shuddered again. Stone crashed. Nolo led them up to the next chamber, where more windows opened out on the city. But no sooner had he stepped into the room than another stream of orange fire poured through. Though her mother shielded Hubley with her own body, Hubley still felt as if she had come much too close to a Dwarven furnace.

"Hubley," said Ferris when they had returned to the cave below. "It's time to go home."

"Home?" Hubley was appalled. "After all the times the Dwarves have helped us? How can we run away when it's finally our chance to help them?"

"You're just a child."

The Halvanankh shook as the mandrake pounded it again. Small rocks rattled down from fresh fissures in the ceiling.

"Your mother's right." Avender brushed dust from his shoulders. "You need to take her back to Valing to tell everyone what's happening. Let the more experienced mages help the Dwarves. And maybe they can bring some of Brizen's soldiers with them, too."

"I'm as good a mage as any of them." Just touching the surface of her memories, Hubley could tell her father had provided her with much more than fireballs. "Besides, someone has to go get the Inach swords you wanted. Mother's too tired, so that only leaves me."

"Sweetheart—"

"She's right, milady," said Mindrell. "None of the Bryddin will get past the creature without a good sword."

Avender disagreed. "I still say they should go home. Fornoch can't get to us as long as we stay away from the windows."

"He'll smash the whole city before any other magicians get here," said Hubley. "I'm the only choice."

Before anyone could stop her, she raised the image of the Bryddis B'wee in her mind. Ferris, still clinging to her daughter's arm, came with her.

Even knowing where they were going, mother and child both gasped when they arrived. The Abyss opened beneath their feet, the thick glass floor as clear as Dwarven art could make it. Through the windows, they saw the mandrake curled around the top of the Halvanankh, its long tail laced through a pair of openings at the point where the great ankh was attached to the bottom of the world. With the same strength the creature had shown earlier in breaking the blumet catwalk, it now strained to rip apart the stone. Its tail tightened; the rock between the openings exploded out across the night, sparkling as it fell.

The mandrake moved deeper in, and looped its tail around another of the pillars that kept the Halvanankh fastened to the bottom of the world.

"I don't believe it," said Ferris. "He's weakening the ankh. He's trying to make it fall."

Hubley saw what her mother meant at once. The Dwarves had mined so many passages out of the Halvanankh that it was hollow as a sponge. Already the mandrake had worked himself a third of the way into the pillar's top. Were it to remove much more, the ankh would surely fall.

The Bryddin had seen the same thing. Half a dozen had managed to channel one of the many streams that powered Issinlough's workshops and mills through a narrow hose. As Hubley and Ferris watched, they shot a powerful jet of water straight at the beast from the top of the nearest unneret.

Like a sputtering goose, the mandrake shook its wings and spat. The Dwarves aimed the hose directly at the creature's jaws. Steam hissed; a cloud formed just below the roof, but Fornoch's fire was drowned. He scrabbled for purchase on the wet rock as the Dwarves played the stream across his body, forcing him back around the ankh, where a second hose caught him from the other side.

Deciding he'd had enough, the mandrake dove off into the darkness. A great cheer rose from the people watching. Hubley's heart lifted at the thought they had found a way to defeat the creature so quickly.

Except they hadn't. Swooping on wide wings, the mandrake circled back. The Dwarves with the first hose tracked him as best they could, but eventually they lost him behind their unneret. The other hose was too far away to help. With one powerful wingbeat, the mandrake shot through the passage at the top of the upside-down tower and attacked his enemies from behind. The Dwarves popped out on the other side and scrambled away. Fornoch followed with a roar, the hose foaming between his jaws.

Wondering if the mandrake hated cold as much as he did water, Hubley squeezed her hands through the delicate stone lattice of the windows and cast what had just come together in her mind.

> *"Throw my cold across the night.*
> *Freeze the mander in its flight."*

Beyond her fingers the air bulged. Towers and catwalks bent as if seen through a growing bubble. When it reached the mandrake the bubble broke, encasing the creature in a crust of ice. The water spouting from the hose froze as well. For a moment it looked as if the mandrake was suspended over the Abyss at the end of a white stick. Then the stick broke with a sharp crack and the frozen creature fell.

A second cheer went up, louder than the first. The Bryddsmet swayed as the mandrake plummeted past. But almost immediately a burst of fire splashed the night below the city. The sound of ice shattering replaced the cheers; the smell of sulfur washed the air.

His wings unfrozen, the mandrake flapped back to the top of the Halvanankh. Ignoring the second hose, which couldn't reach him on this side, he went back to work with his tail.

"We have to warn Nolo," said Ferris. "There's no time to get the swords."

Hubley agreed, and took her mother's hand.

They found Mindrell alone in the room without windows, his head fallen to one side as if he were asleep, his hair as white as snow. When he didn't answer Ferris's question about where Avender and Nolo had gone, Hubley poked him in the shoulder to wake him.

He didn't move.

"Hubley," said her mother. "Get behind me."

Though she didn't want to, something in her mother's voice made Hubley obey. She had never seen a dead person before, and found herself as curious as she was repulsed. Her repulsion, however, grew as she watched her mother push back the bard's lolling head and look into his eyes. He was definitely dead.

All of a sudden it came to her that her father was gone as well. There would be no more spells, no more magic at birthday parties or two-headed kittens. It had taken the sight of Mindrell's corpse to do it, but now she understood. The mandrake was here, but her father wasn't coming back. Ever.

"Hubley." Her mother's sharp voice recalled her daughter to the world. "Now is not the time to lose control. You're the one who wanted to stay. Avender and I will need you to get back home. Do you hear me?"

Swallowing her tears, Hubley nodded. Her father would want her to be strong.

Avender came up the stairs as the ankh shuddered

"We have to get out of here," said Ferris. "Especially Nolo."

"He's already gone. What about the bard?"

Ferris shook her head. "Without the proper magic, he never had a chance. Once Reiffen went through the mirror, the spell lost its power."

Hubley was surprised at how little Avender seemed to care about Mindrell's death. Then what she had hoped never to re-member came back to her bright and hard, the night in her bed-room when Avender had lost his hand. She swallowed again, but this time it wasn't to hold back tears.

"Does Nolo think he can get past Fornoch without an Inach sword?" her mother asked.

"No," Avender answered. "He's gone the other way. He fig-ures it'll be easier to go back down to the Bryddsmett and climb the cables. The mandrake probably won't even see him."

"And if he does?"

"I asked the same thing. Nolo reminded me Dwarves don't fall."

"We need to make sure he gets away."

The ankh shook steadily with the force of the mandrake's attack as they descended the stairs. At the first window they stopped and searched for a sign of their friend. Rocks tumbled past, clanging off the mett like giant peas.

"There he is," said Avender. "On the cable."

Hubley looked where Avender was pointing but, before she could spot the Dwarf, she felt herself fall. The lights of Issinlough jerked up and away. Her knees bent as the ankh struck the Bryddsmett with a great crash, and then they were falling once more.

The window went dark. Wind whistled up the stairwell, growing so strong so fast that Hubley found it hard to breathe. And she had to cling to the sides of the window to keep from being blown away. Her mother and Avender were holding on as well.

"What happened?!" she shouted to make herself heard over the roaring wind.

"The Halvanankh has broken free!" Avender shouted in return.

"What about Nolo?! Is he still holding on?!"

As Hubley leaned out the window to see, Avender and Ferris grabbed her dress to make sure she wasn't swept away by the gale.

Looking up, she saw Issinlough shrinking rapidly overhead. Already its thousand lamps had merged to one. Still, there was enough light for the Bryddsmett to shimmer in the darkness below them like a moon. The bottom of the Halvanankh had punched through the center of the mett like a jester pulling his head through a hat, only upside down. The cable Nolo had been crossing rose like a long, narrow sapling in the darkness before her.

Dwarves don't fall, Hubley told herself.

"Can you see him?" Avender, his lamp screwed into place on his forehead, leaned out the window beside her.

"No." Her heart seemed ready to leap out of her mouth with the gale.

"There he is!"

Hubley followed Avender's pointing finger a second time. A small light shone about a third of the way up the blumet cable. It blinked out for a moment, then reappeared a little farther down.

Ferris pulled them back inside.

"Nolo's still there!" cried Hubley. "He's climbing down the cable! We have to help him!"

"It'll be a lot easier for him to get to us," said Ferris, "than for us to get to him."

Hubley saw her mother was right, especially when they started crawling back up the stairs in search of some place to get out of the ferocious wind. Having no weight made it hard to walk, and a lot easier to follow the gale up than fight it going down. If not for the horrible things that kept happening, the sensation of weightlessness would almost have been fun.

She found coming back to Mindrell's corpse was a lot worse than discovering it. But the windowless room was the best place for them to stay. Although the wind gusted through the entire chamber, it weakened as they moved away from the doorways. Hubley followed Avender and her mother to the side away from the bard.

They discussed how they might save Nolo, but had come up with nothing useful by the time he rejoined them.

Nolo had no ideas, either.

Considering his position, Hubley was surprised he wasn't more upset. Magic wouldn't work on him, and how else was he supposed to get back home? Was there an airship stashed somewhere in the ankh?

"Not that I know of." Nolo sighed. "Or anything to make one out of, either. I'll look for one, though, when I go through the place. We need to check for anyone else who might be trapped here before you go. No, Avender. Stay where you are. I can look alone. This wind'll blow you right off."

He didn't take long. The Halvanankh, which seemed so big

from the outside, wasn't so large within that Nolo couldn't search it quickly. His friends still hadn't thought of a way to help him escape by the time he came back with the news that they were the only ones left inside. All the other Dwarves had gotten away.

"No sense wasting valuable time trying to figure it out," he said after Ferris told him they had come up with nothing new. "There's a mandrake needs fighting up there."

Ferris hugged the Dwarf hard. Soot rubbed off on her cheek and dress. "Oh, Nolo. You can't really mean that."

"What's done is done, lass." The Dwarf patted her on the arm. "Cracked stone can't be mended."

Wiping her eyes, the magician loosed her hold. Small gray spots showed on the Dwarf's beardless cheek where her tears had smudged the soot. Hubley felt hot wetness on her own face before the wind swept it dry.

"There must be a way," said Ferris.

Nolo shrugged. "Ask Grimble. Maybe he can think of something. If I haven't already fallen too far for you to get back by the time he does."

"Can we get back?" asked Avender. "Will the traveling spell work on a place that's moving?"

"I don't know," said Ferris. "It's never been tried."

"At least I'm not broken. If you ever do figure out a way to bring me back, I'll be here." Nolo patted the tools hanging from his belt. "There's always stone to work. I figure I can do a lot to smarten this place up before I shut down."

Knowing her mother was doing the same, Hubley pushed her sadness away so she could memorize every detail of the cave. The weightlessness. The shadows from Avender's and Nolo's lamps. The smell of the soot still clinging to the Dwarf's leather clothing. The noisy rush of the air.

"Do you have any messages for anyone?" asked Ferris when they were done.

Nolo reached to tug at his beard, forgetting it had been burned away. "Buy a pint for Redburr for me at the Bull and Bass, will you?"

"That's all?"

"Aye. Unless you come back. Then you might bring a whole barrel with you. And you come too, lad." Affection twinkled in Nolo's eyes as he turned to Avender. "Though I can't really call you lad anymore, now you've got all that gray in your hair. I'd like to hear about where you've been these last few years. There's no time for it now, but the tale's a good one, I'm sure."

"I'll come."

"If there's any way to bring you back," said Ferris, "I'll find it."

"I'll be here."

Hubley wept as they embraced a last time. It was all so unfair. What was the use of magic, if you couldn't stop terrible things from happening to your family and your friends? Better off just grubbing in the dirt like everyone else if you couldn't change anything. Being back with her mother was more wonderful than Hubley had ever imagined, but, without her father too, it was going to be nearly as bad as it had been before.

"We need to decide where we're going," said Avender.

"That's simple," answered Ferris. "Back to Valing. We need to tell Brizen and the rest of the magicians what's happening."

"But what about the Dwarves?" Hubley rubbed her nose and sniffed. "We can't just leave them to fight Fornoch alone."

"We won't. Believe me, sweetheart, once I've got my strength back, we'll come back and get rid of Fornoch once and for all. But first I have to get my strength back. You'll have to be the one to take us to Tower Dale. Do you think you can do it?"

"Yes."

Ferris turned to Nolo one last time. "We'll be back, dear friend."

"Remember to bring the beer."

"We should take Mindrell with us," said Avender. "It's not what he deserves, but it's probably the right thing to do."

They crossed to the bard's side of the room. With tears leaking from her eyes, Hubley concentrated on her magic.

The Halvanankh disappeared.

25

Vonn Kurr

Giserre's face went white at the sight of the body slung over Avender's shoulder when they returned. Avender twisted to let her see it wasn't her son, but her alarm remained. The fact that Reiffen wasn't even with them frightened her even more than the thought that he was dead.

"We tried." Ferris's voice trailed away as she answered Giserre's unspoken question. "There was nothing we could do."

No matter how horribly Hubley felt her father's death, she knew her grandmother felt it more. Letting go her mother's and Avender's hands, she ran to Giserre and wrapped her arms around her waist. A moment later she felt her mother's arms around them as well.

How long they wept, Hubley didn't know. When they were done, her mother and grandmother took her upstairs to her bedroom and tucked her into bed. Shafts of moonlight from the room's single window thickened the sadness in their pale faces as they kissed her good night. Finally Hubley understood why Giserre had stayed with her father in Ussene. Reiffen had been all her grandmother had, and to part with him would have been worse than death for her.

As parting from Hubley for the last thirty years must have been worse than death for her mother.

She woke the next morning much later than she wanted. No

dreams had troubled her, and her sadness had sloughed away along with her fatigue. Rather than remembering her mother's and grandmother's sorrow, her first thought was that they couldn't possibly have waited this long to return to Issinlough, and must have left without her. If her mother thought she could get rid of her that easily, she was totally wrong. It wasn't as if she was an ordinary child. They would need every magician they could find if they were going to defeat the mandrake. Hubley knew her power was as strong as anyone's, except perhaps her mother's, and was confident no one would object, or be able to do anything about it, if she returned to Issinlough on her own.

Jumping out of bed, she discovered they'd even taken her clothes. As if leaving her in her nightgown was going to stop her. She was already collecting the travel spell in her mind to return to the wardrobe she'd found the day before, when someone knocked on the door.

"Come in," she said in her most irritated voice.

Avender poked his head into the room, her clothes in his arms. "Looking for these? Giserre took them last night to keep you from running away, so I stole them back this morning."

Hubley accepted Avender's peace offering and ducked behind the door to dress. "Have they all gone back to Issinlough?" she asked.

"No. Issinlough's already fallen. They went to Vonn Kurr."

"Issinlough's fallen? And Mother still thought she could just leave me here?"

"She wanted to, but I told her trying to leave you behind wasn't a good idea. You know too much magic now."

"Hmph. I'm glad somebody noticed. Why'd they go to Vonn Kurr?"

"The mandrake's on the Sun Road."

Hubley stopped with her boot half tied. "The Sun Road? Is he trying to get to the surface?"

"He was, but Huri took care of that when he and the rest of

the Granglough Bryddin destroyed Uhle's Gate. The beast can't get out any other way—none of the other roads are big enough for him. They did hope he'd try to dig his way through so they could knock the road down on top of him, but he turned around and headed back to the Abyss instead."

He told her the rest of what had happened over toast and eggs in the kitchen. Ferris had called a conference with Brizen and all the magicians, who met long into the night at Tower Dale. Lorennin, whom Hubley had last known as a girl not much older than she was, had made the dangerous trip back to Issinlough to see what the mandrake was doing. Her report, and the fact that Uhle had the presence of mind to bring his mirrors with him when he left the city, had kept Ferris and the others up to date on what was happening underground.

"The Dwarves think the mandrake can feel things in the stone the same way they do." Despite Hubley's impatient eye, Avender peppered his eggs briskly. "That's why he stopped going up the Sun Road even though he was still miles away when they broke the entrance."

Hubley sopped up her yolk with a piece of toast. "So, are they going to smash the roof at the bottom and trap him in between?"

"That was your mother's idea, until Uhle explained how the mandrake would probably be able to dig himself out if they caught him between two deadfalls. He thinks the creature can dig through loose rock, or at least bring down whatever he can get his tail around. But he can't break through walls or solid stone, especially if he can't move. So Dwvon came up with a better plan. They're going to try and bury him at the bottom of Vonn Kurr. Then they'll open up the drains on the Lower Lift and drown him. To top it off, you magicians will freeze everything. You gave them that idea when you cast the cold spell at the Halvanankh. Once he's unable to move, Findle and a few other Dwarves will tunnel through the ice and rock to slay him."

Delighted a spell she'd thought of had been included in the

plan, Hubley crammed the last wedge of toast into her mouth and wiped her chin. Once they got to Vonn Kurr, she'd show them she could do much more than cold spells now.

They couldn't leave right away, however, because Hubley had never been on the Sun Road. All her trips to Issinlough had always been taken magically, traveling with her parents. When a quick search of the tower turned up no one who could take them, they had no alternative but for Hubley to take them somewhere else instead.

Avender tugged at her hand as she was getting ready to cast. "Hold on a second. Where are you taking us?"

"To the Bryddis B'wee."

Avender shook his head. "It's not there anymore. You'll have to think of something else."

"Mother Norra's kitchen?"

"That's no good either. The mandrake smashed every unneret in the city. Do you remember anywhere close by?"

One of Hubley's favorite places in the Underground leapt into her mind. She hadn't gone there very often, as there was nothing to do but admire the view, but the memory of it was as complete as anything else she'd ever done in Issinlough.

"The Dinnach a Dwvon?" she asked.

Avender nodded. "That ought to do. I can't imagine Fornoch could have done too much damage to that. Not with all that water."

Closing her eyes again, she focused on the place where the eldest of the Dwarves had built his first forge. The image of the vast cavern loomed in her mind, the Issin flowing down the middle of its polished granite floor. At the open end, the stream fanned out into a wide sheet that poured into the Abyss as one of the Seven Veils, the lights of Issinlough gleaming in the darkness beyond like cobwebs strung with dew.

The smell of burning bit her nose, signaling that they had arrived. Opening her eyes, Hubley found she couldn't see the city at all. Thick smoke swirled past the edge of the cavern, long tendrils fingering the water and stone. In the light of Avender's lamp it looked as if they were staring at an immense spider whose crooked legs were holding its belly tight over the outlet of the cave.

Shuddering, Hubley stepped back. A gap appeared in the reek to reveal a small clutch of gleaming jewels, but even then it took Hubley a moment to recognize the once-grand view. Where unnerets had hung gracefully above the darkness, only stumps remained, clinging to the bottom of the world like broken teeth. Catwalks and bridges dangled like gaping jaws. Around them yellow flames flickered in the sockets of empty windows, their smoke pouring into the darkness black as blood. Even the Seven Veils, whose water had always shimmered with the glow of the city they surrounded, had disappeared. The mandrake had ruined it all.

Not wanting to look at the awful sight any more than she had to, Hubley turned away. Even though she'd been in the middle of the mandrake's attack, seeing what he'd done from the outside was a lot worse. The beast had ruined other lives besides her own. Dwarves had worked for hundreds of years to build their shining city, but Fornoch had destroyed it in a day. Not to mention all the humans who had lived here as well, some of whom Hubley had seen fall from the lamplit bridges to the dark below.

Taking her hand, Avender led her to the back of the cave. They climbed the stairs that led to the Upper Way, where they met a few human stragglers fleeing the city with whatever they could carry. Some looked questioningly at Hubley and Avender as they passed, not understanding why the two were going the wrong direction.

"How are they going to get home?" Hubley asked as the last of them vanished into the tunnel behind them. "The Sun Road's closed."

"There are other ways," Avender told her. "Mostly through the mines. The biggest problem will be food. But if we can take care of the mandrake, it won't be so bad. Huri and the others can reopen Uhle's Gate with a couple of days' digging. But first we have to kill the mandrake."

They saw no one else along the way. After a while Hubley felt a growing dampness in the air, the first sign they were approaching Vonn Kurr. Small passages led off on either side, to mushroom caves she guessed, where the Dwarves had set up small farms to capture the wet. Soon Hubley heard the rumble of the waterfall as well, shivering through the rocks and air.

They came out at the back of the deep near the bottom of the Lower Lift, across the cavern from where Uhle's Stair led on to what had once been Issinlough. The waterfall thundered before them, mist billowing past their faces and up into the dark. At its foot, the Brilliant Pool rolled like a twisting rainbow as the currents tugged at the hundreds of Dwarf lamps covering the bottom. Above the mist, the cliffs gleamed with lamplight of their own, a second Bryddin city carved from the stone walls. The roof was much too far away to see.

Hubley looked around her in awe. At least some of the beauty of the Underground remained. "It's a lot bigger than I remember."

"Looks like the Dwarves have been working hard since either of us were last here."

A Dwarf ran toward them from the Stair. "You folks must have made a wrong turn," he said. "The way out's the way you just came. We're expecting the mandrake back any time."

"We know," said Avender. "We've come to help. This is Hubley, the magicians' daughter."

The Dwarf peered at her. "You're the one who thought to try and freeze it, aren't you? When Ord and the others turned the hoses on it."

"Uh-huh."

"Good idea, that was. I hear the magicians are calling it Hubley's Cone of Cold." The Dwarf gave Hubley a quick nod and wink. "We'll be using your spell again, when the beast comes back."

A large bat fluttered out of the darkness. Hubley started as it came straight toward them, but Avender only braced himself as it settled heavily on his jacket.

"About time you two showed up," the bat squeaked.

"Redburr! You're alive!" Hubley might have given the Shaper a happy squeeze, only he was terribly ugly, especially his squashed-up nose. She could only imagine what he'd been eating.

"Of course I'm alive." Redburr snapped his wings smartly, then folded them across his chest like a baron thumbing his lapels. "When everyone else was running away, I kept track of the mandrake by clinging to his back. Your mother sent me down here to let her know when you arrived."

"Where is Ferris?" Looking up, Avender scanned the dark cliffs around them.

"Positioning the magicians. The beast has made better time coming down the Sun Road than we thought. He's less than fifteen minutes away."

"Will Dwvon have the trap ready in time?"

"Yes."

"If the mandrake can feel stone the way the Dwarves do," asked Hubley, "won't he know what Dwvon's doing?"

"Probably. Uhle and your mother think that's why he's in such a hurry. He doesn't want to get trapped in the Sun Road, you know. But he's not as cautious as he was when he was a Wizard, or he'd never have left the Abyss in the first place. He'd have been safe as long as he stayed there, where he can make the Dwarves fall and they can't do anything to him. Here in the Stoneways it's only a matter of time before they catch him."

"Good," said Avender. "Where do we go?"

"Follow me."

Releasing his grip on Avender's jacket, the fat bat wobbled away across the cavern. Water drops frosted Avender's and Hubley's hair as they followed the Shaper to the stair that led up into the deep on the other side. The tall, thin figure waiting to meet them turned out to be Trier, whom Hubley barely recognized as her parents' old apprentice. For one thing, she looked terribly old, as old as Avender, and for another she was wearing the sort of long, beautiful robe that baronesses wore more often than magicians. The last time Hubley had seen her, Trier had worn the same homespun clothes as everyone else. But, now that she was the king's magician, Hubley supposed things were different.

"Your mother sent me to make sure you had arrived." Stooping, the woman kissed Hubley sparingly on the cheek. "We are all so happy you have returned. We feel your loss terribly."

Trier had never been Hubley's favorite among her parents' apprentices, and the cold sympathy the woman expressed for her father didn't help. Redburr, hanging from a nearby carving in the stone, flapped his wings in irritation at the thought that Ferris had sent someone else to make sure he found her daughter.

"Is Plum here?" Hubley asked, remembering the apprentice who had been her favorite.

Trier hesitated before replying. "Plum? Unfortunately, no."

Hubley had learned to know what it meant when people didn't like answering questions about her old friends. "He died, didn't he."

The king's magician pursed her lips and nodded.

"How?"

"Helping your mother. A long time ago."

Hubley didn't want to ask any more. The more she learned about how much the world had changed since she'd last been a part of it, the more she wished she could go back to just being ten.

Leading them up the stair, Trier explained the details of

Uhle's and Ferris's plan. The magicians were already spread out among the lower apartments, waiting for the trap to be sprung.

"But won't the water run out the Uhliakh?" asked Avender, pointing toward the broad avenue that led to Issinlough. Or what had once been Issinlough.

"Eventually," Trier told him. "But that is not our worry. Dwvon will bring down enough stone to clog the exits thoroughly. We are expecting ten yards of rock, and another thirty of water. It will take some time for that much water to seep through. By then I am sure the Bryddin will have found a way to eliminate the mandrake entirely."

She left them in one of the apartments the Dwarves had carved from the side of Vonn Kurr's enormous shaft, explaining she and Ferris would be on the other side, to balance Hubley's strength. Redburr flew off as well, to see if there was anything he could do to help out Uhle and Dwvon at the head of the deep.

Hubley leaned against the pale moss that decorated the top of the balcony railing, and waited with Avender for her mother's signal. Ferris was supposed to flash a light when the Dwarves on the Sun Road told her the mandrake was nearing the top of the deep. That would give the less experienced magicians the extra time they needed to ready their spells. Even some of the more accomplished had prepared their magic beforehand, storing their power in small shells and other devices from which the magic could be quickly freed. But Hubley's father had taught her well. Her spells formed naturally, at the shaping of her mind and fingers. As far as she was concerned a simple cold spell, which amounted to no more than draining heat from one place to another, could be done without aids of any kind.

The waterfall roared; light rippled through the mist like bright snakes coiling.

A brighter light flashed at the corner of Hubley's eye.

"Here we go." Avender pushed aside a tall white fern that was blocking his view. "You ready?"

Hubley nodded. Now her gaze was fastened on her mother's and Trier's hiding place. The second flash would signal the trap had sprung. Dwvon had explained it would take a third of a minute for the stone to fall the length of Vonn Kurr, and that the magicians should wait for the water to rise before they cast the Cone of Cold. Hopefully the falling rock would catch the mandrake by surprise, knocking him out of the air. But if it didn't, the magicians were to make sure the beast didn't escape by casting whatever spells they could think of. Hubley wondered if she could slow the creature by freezing the waterfall's mist.

"What's that!"

Avender craned out over the balcony, his eyes on the Brilliant Pool. In his haste, he knocked some potted toadstools at his elbow rattling down into the gulf. Following his gaze, Hubley saw two people bathed in the pool's bright light in the middle of the floor. A man and a boy.

Not a boy, she realized, but Findle. And that was Merannon admiring the dance of the lights beside him. Even at this distance, Hubley recognized the golden lamp glowing at the prince's forehead as the one that had nearly rescued her at the bottom of Malmoret. Did they even know what was going on?

A terrible look came into Avender's face. "No!" he shouted. "Get out of there! Merannon! Findle! Get out!"

Hubley grabbed his arm. "They can't hear you, Avender. The waterfall's too loud."

"Then we have to go get them." Avender seized Hubley by the arms. Not even during their wild escape from Malmoret and the falling airship had he looked so desperate. "You can do it. You can use the traveling spell to go down and rescue them."

"But what about the signal? What if Mother gives it while we're down there?"

Avender's fingers tightened, pinching her painfully. "There's still enough time. Once we have them, we'll run for the Upper Way. I know we can make it. Hubley, in the name of your father and mother, please do this one thing for me. That's Wellin's son down there. The heir to the throne."

Hubley swallowed hard and wondered if she could do it. She'd had her full power barely more than a day; she still wasn't sure what she could and couldn't do. But if she didn't try to rescue them, an already horrible few days would become unimaginably worse.

Then the second signal came, and there was no more time to decide. Without thinking, she shifted. She didn't need to think: she'd been just where Findle and Merannon were standing only a few minutes before. The apartment disappeared, replaced by the mist and thunder of the pool. Grabbing hold of her friends, she thought of the place she had just left as something crashed to the ground beside her and nearly knocked her off her feet. The first of the tumbling stones. But Avender braced her with his shoulder and arm so she didn't lose her hold, not even when something smooth and hot coiled around her wrist.

An eyeblink, and they were back in the apartment. Her left hand was empty: in her haste she'd forgotten that the spell wouldn't work on Findle. Behind her an enormous roar filled the air, swelling up and around them like a blast of wind. Covering her head with her arms, she cowered on the floor. Whatever held her wrist didn't let go, but the din was so overwhelming she couldn't do anything but hide.

It seemed to last for hours. When it stopped, Hubley's ears still throbbed. Her skin tingled. Opening her eyes, she found herself staring into the mandrake's enormous black orb.

She started, but the thing around her wrist held her tight. The creature's tongue. Its other end disappeared between the beast's black teeth. One snap of those immense jaws and Hubley would be swallowed like a frog by a heron.

"What on earth?"

A cold breeze started at Hubley's back as Merannon scrambled away, fumbling for his sword. The mandrake's eye followed them, but the rest of the creature didn't move.

"It's stunned," said Avender. He seized Hubley's hand. "Quick. Take us somewhere else. Anywhere but the surface. Before it recovers. Before it breathes fire. You can do it, Hubley, I know you can."

Worn to her bones, Hubley closed her eyes. But the spell wouldn't come quickly. For the first time in her life she found her power wearing thin. Now she understood how her mother had been so exhausted after the fight with Fornoch. And here she was, about to fight him as well. The thought terrified her. Had she had more time to think, her fear might have overwhelmed her. But there was no time for thinking, and she knew at once that Avender was right. They had to get away. If the mandrake broke free, he might kill them all. Her mother and the other magicians didn't know that, thanks to her, the beast had escaped their careful trap. Only she could stop him now. If she could just regain a tiny bit of her strength before the mandrake regained his. The Dinnach a Dwvon was close, and she had just been there. She remembered the dark, and the smoke swirling across the broken unnerets. The smell of ruin in the cave.

The air warmed. The last of her strength dribbled away. The mandrake was huge, and traveling with it had taken every speck of power she had. But she'd done it, and brought them safely away. Opening her eyes, she saw Avender let go her hand and dash along the creature's side. Cruelly he wrenched the blade from the creature's belly. The mandrake trembled. Coming back to stand at Hubley's side, Avender raised the sword above his head.

Like a worm being swallowed by a bird, the beast's tongue slithered back into its mouth. The sword slashed down. Stone chips flew from the spot where the tongue had stretched a moment before. Smoke oozed from the mandrake's mouth and nostrils.

Avender raised the weapon for another blow.

The mandrake wheezed. Scales clanking, it tried and failed to move away.

The sword flashed. A great gash opened across the top of Fornoch's jaw. The beast quivered.

"It will take a while to slay me, you know," it croaked. "And I will be recovering the whole time."

Hubley screamed as Avender, refusing to listen to the beast, stabbed it in the eye. Black blood oozed, smoking on the sword and ground.

Fornoch's voice grew stronger. "Can you be sure you will slay me before I recover enough to slay you? One breath will do it. I have had the wind knocked out of me in my fall, but, be assured, once I catch my breath, I will kill you. I am not so weak as I once was. Talking no longer slakes my thirst at all."

Moving past the mandrake's dripping eye, Avender thrust the sword deep into the soft flesh beneath its shoulder. So deep, he had to brace his foot on the creature's flank to pull the blade out again. The mandrake shivered like a child who'd played too long in the snow, but didn't stop speaking. Hubley grew faint at the sight of so much gore.

"If Findle were here," the creature rasped, "he would tell you a mandrake's heart is buried deep inside its body. Far deeper, in me, than you can reach with your sword. To find it you will have to butcher me the way you would a cow."

Avender drove the blade into the creature's belly a second time. Blood hissed to the ground in small pools and flowed across the floor to the Issin. The river steamed.

"I will slay the child as well." The mandrake's smoky breath melted behind small balls of orange flame. "Mothers. Fathers. Children. I will slay them all. Though I shall hunt the Bryddin, first."

Shifting his feet, Avender swung the sword sideways. The creature's hide ripped open. Flesh as red as uncooked meat gaped between the edges of the wound. Blood spouted. Avender staggered back as it splashed his face and arm.

The mandrake coughed. This time the flame shot farther from its mouth, crisping the beast's own blood on the polished stone. Avender stumbled forward, readying another cut.

"No!" Hubley shouted as loudly as she could.

Avender's boots almost slipped in the mess at his feet as he turned and looked at her.

"He's going to kill us!" she said.

"No." Avender gestured with his sword. "I'm going to kill him."

To prove his point, he brought the stone blade down on the mandrake's foreleg. Fornoch groaned as the limb fell twitching to the ground. Righting itself, the severed leg skittered toward Hubley. Avender skewered it on the point of his sword, then flicked it back toward its body. Twisting awkwardly on his three remaining legs, Fornoch gulped the leg down before it could run away a second time.

Hubley sat weakly on the stone. Beside her, Avender's face and arm were black and scabbed where the creature's blood had seared away cloth and skin.

"I want to go home," she said.

"We can win, Hubley. This is no time to give up. He killed your father."

The mandrake's long snout swung toward them. Though the eye that faced them was blind, the creature seemed to know exactly where they were. Its nostrils flared.

"Look out!" cried Hubley.

Avender saw the danger the same as she. Pushing her down, he raised his sword. As if a shield that thin would ever help. With a roar even louder than the cave-in at the bottom of Vonn Kurr, the mandrake breathed.

Orange and yellow flame parted against the flat of the heartstone blade, but Avender's body was still swept up in the licking heat. Hubley didn't hear him scream, but she smelled his burning skin. His body turned black as his arm and toppled to the ground. Writhing in pain, he tried to crawl away.

She retched, even as her nose filled with the rot of roasted flesh.

The fire stopped. The mandrake set his wounded eye on Hubley. "Eventually," he said, "I will burn him until the Living Stone rolls from his belly like grit from a goose's gizzard. And then I will cook you."

"No you won't."

Looking up, Hubley found Mims standing over her friend like a goodwife at her hearth.

"You!" cried the beast, his anger and dismay both terrible. "Impossible. You were only a slave. How did you escape Ussene?"

"I was warned."

"But . . ." Smoke puffed from the cruel curve of the beast's great jaw. Hubley, who had thought Fornoch would burn Mims the way he'd burned Avender, wondered if something else was about to happen instead.

"Your appearance explains much," the beast continued in a calmer voice. "I should have known Reiffen was not strong enough to knock Ossdonc down when he was only fifteen."

"He did most of it himself."

"I suppose there have been other times you interfered as well. And yet you have waited until now to reveal yourself, when I can no longer take advantage of what you know." The creature waved its stump. "Not that it matters. I have accomplished all I set out to do. The Dwarves are ruined. Bryddlough is mine."

"No it isn't," said Mims. "Hubley, summon your magic."

The mandrake hissed. Avender moaned as a tendril of fire curled across his feet.

"I can't," Hubley answered weakly.

"You can," insisted the magician. "Look to your Stone."

As if it had heard Mims's command, Hubley's Living Stone

began to throb. Strength surged from her belly, flooding her body. Her breathing quickened; her lungs filled with air. Unbidden, the magic formed in her mind, almost as if Mims were casting the spell for her.

The beast opened its mouth to burn them; the spell burst from Hubley's hands. Mims launched her magic at the same time. The two spells mingled smoothly, as if they'd been cast by the same person. A cone of ice formed in the air in front of them, its tip pointed straight at the mandrake's throat. With a flick of their wrists, the magicians hurled it forward.

The beast gagged as the plug lodged deep in its throat. Its jaws gaped. Mims swept Hubley up in her apron and pulled them both to the ground. Before her face was covered, Hubley saw the mandrake's eyes widen in fury and fear, its cheeks puffed around the icy cork like a croaking frog.

Half an enormous thunderclap thumped hard on Hubley's ears, so brief she wasn't even sure she'd heard it. Then the world went strangely silent; Mims's apron bowed beneath a sudden wind. Solid chunks of something Hubley didn't even want to think about rained down on them like large, heavy hail. Her Stone's strength ebbed, and a wave of dizziness forced her to close her eyes. She shuddered, afraid that, even if they had blown up the mandrake, the beast was still going to bury them in the end.

The hail stopped.

Still weak, she opened her eyes as Mims swept the apron aside. Lumps of mandrake plopped to the ground. Though Hubley's ears throbbed as if they'd been boxed and she still couldn't hear a thing, her sense of smell was unaffected. The stink was awful. A fine red mist filled the cavern, settling slowly onto the chunks of charred gristle and bone that spotted the floor as far as the Abyss. She watched fearfully, half certain the lumps would start slithering together like greasy slugs the same way the mandrake's claw had scuttled away on its own after Avender sliced it off. But only one lump moved, the largest.

Her dizziness came back worse than ever when she realized it was Avender. The Wizard was gone, but so was so much else. Her father. Nolo. Maybe even Avender, too.

Tired to death, and wishing none of it had ever happened, she swooned.

26

Hubley's Tenth Birthday One Last Time

Y ou're sure we shouldn't move him?" asked
Ferris.

Hubley Mims's shadow flickered across her
younger self as she leaned over the bed. Loose
strands of hair cobwebbed the sleeping child's
face with pale gray lines.

"Avender'll be much better off here," she
answered. "You know as well as I do, the more
he sleeps, the quicker he'll heal."

"What about you?" Ferris nodded toward
the Hubley that actually felt like her daughter. "What we need to
do will be much easier in Tower Dale. And Giserre will want to
help, too. For someone who hates magic, she's become quite
good at this sort of thing."

"We have everything we need right here. You and I will do
fine."

Ferris made a disapproving face but didn't argue. The last few
days had shown her daughter to be the far more powerful magician. More powerful even than Reiffen.

Her mouth pursed at the thought of her dead husband, but
the feeling passed. That mourning had been over and done with
long ago.

"You know," she said, "there are still a lot of things you
haven't explained. I'd love to know how you got into Castle
Grangore to rescue Avender without Reiffen catching you."

Hubley Mims looked at her mother through the tops of her eyes. "I could have gotten into Castle Grangore any time I wanted, Mother. Father's alarms have never worked on me. But they would have told him if Avender had left, so I couldn't free him until after Father was gone. That's the beauty of the Timespell—you don't have to do things in order. If you went up to Castle Grangore right now, you'd find Avender was still buried. I won't be digging him up for a couple more days. After that, I still have to reattach his hand, and feed him up till he's back to full strength. It's going to be months before I can send him back to rescue me."

"Why do you have to reattach his hand? Doesn't he have a Living Stone?"

"Yes, but he'd already lost his hand before Father gave him the Stone."

Ferris nodded, a little closer to understanding her daughter's complicated plan. Living Stones only preserved what was already present. Just as she couldn't save Wellin with a Stone once the queen's sickness had begun, so also a Living Stone wouldn't re-grow a hand that had been cut off before the Stone was swallowed.

"How did you get his hand?"

"The Timespell, Mother. I was there the night it all happened. That's where I got that silver coin I showed you. The spell of return worked even after Mindrell cut it off. All I had to do was travel back to Valing and pick it up, along with the reliquary you'd put his finger in, then bring it forward to the same time I dug up the rest of him. I knew that once you discovered the reliquary was stolen, you'd think it was something Father had done."

"As I did." Ferris pushed a lock of the sleeping Hubley's hair back from her face. "Can you also explain how he got so old? Avender should be the same age he was when he swallowed the Stone."

"He was worse when I dug him up—he looked like he was ninety. But he's been getting younger ever since. I think what happened is that his body went through a lot of stress while he was buried, and the Stone only did what it had to, to keep him alive. Keeping him young was more than it could manage."

The explanation made sense. Ferris had never wanted to know much about Living Stones, to keep their temptation as far away as possible.

"I don't suppose you've thought about how you're going to explain this to everyone," she said. "How there just happens to be a magician running around who no one's ever seen before. Or do you want everyone to know about the Timespell?"

Hubley Mims shook her head. "No. That wouldn't be good at all. I'm going to make them think Fornoch trained me. I'll tell everyone how he started teaching me magic after the fall of Ussene, but that I turned on him just like Father once I learned everything I could. Sending me to steal Hubley was the last straw. How could I possibly do anything so horrible to Giserre's grandchild after all the kindness Giserre had shown me in Ussene? It was only natural I chose to set her granddaughter free instead."

"How will you ever get anyone to believe that?"

"I won't even try. Grandmother will do it for me. She's the only one who'll recognize me."

"And what about Hubley? What are you going to tell her?"

Hubley Mims looked down at the sleeping child. "As little as possible. She can know about the Timespell—she'll figure out soon enough that she almost cast it once. But she shouldn't know who I am."

When Hubley woke, the first thing she saw was a small spider spinning against the cottage wall. Its strands shone like silver, the ends disappearing into the shadowy nooks around them as if the sunlight were the only thing holding the delicate web in place.

This time, instead of being terrified, she only felt relief at finding herself in Mims's cottage.

"Feeling better?"

Relieved that her hearing had returned, Hubley was surprised when her mother sat down on the bed beside her instead of Mims. Her mother's thimble and wedding ring clicked together as she settled her hands in her lap. Mims loomed smiling behind her, her long gray braid uncoiled and draped across her shoulder.

"How did I get here?" Hubley asked.

Mouth pinched between joy and tears, her mother brushed back her daughter's hair. "Mims brought you. I came later, when we found you weren't where you were supposed to be in Vonn Kurr."

"Is Avender here, too?"

Mims pointed up at the loft. "He is, but I thought you'd prefer sleeping downstairs. The salves I'm using on him smell pretty bad." She waved a hand back and forth in front of her nose.

"Is he going to be all right?"

"Of course. He's got a Living Stone, doesn't he? You know that, you're a magician. I've given him something to help him sleep, but he's still in a lot of pain."

Her mother patted Hubley's hand. "Another few days of rest, and he'll be fine, sweetheart."

"And the mandrake?"

"Don't you remember?" Mims flipped her braid back over her shoulder. "We blew him to pieces."

Hubley remembered, but she'd had to make sure. All the same, she would have brought the Wizard back to life in an instant if it meant she could bring her father back too. Trading one parent for the other was not what she'd had in mind when she decided to trust Avender the last time she'd been in Mims's cottage.

"Did you find anything that looked like Father?" she asked.

Mims sadly shook her head.

"Not even his Stone?"

"We looked." Her mother took Hubley's hand in both her own. "A lot of the creature was flung into the Abyss by the explosion. We think your father's Stone must have gone that way, too."

Not wanting to think any more about how much she already missed her father, Hubley asked why the Wizard had done it. "Why'd he turn himself into a mander?"

"He didn't want to turn himself into a mander," Mims answered. "He wanted to do that to your father. But we were wrong when we thought this was about us. Fornoch wasn't really concerned with humans at all, but with the Dwarves. They're the ones whose sudden appearance ruined his plans back when your great-grandfather was king. Fornoch taught your father magic because he wanted humans to be strong enough to fight the Bryddin."

Hubley frowned. "Why would we want to do that? The Bryddin are our friends."

"Yes, but some humans steal lamps and other things from them just the same. It's human nature to be selfish. Angun's distrust of us isn't entirely wrong. What Fornoch hoped would happen was that he would get your father into the mander, and that the mander's nature would take over and your father would murder all the Dwarves. You'll understand how that could happen once you start casting transformation spells. Even when you turn yourself into something as inconsequential as a mouse, you tend to forget what it's like being human."

Hubley remembered the mandrake's greedy eye staring at her in Vonn Kurr, as if the creature had wanted nothing more than to devour every living thing in sight. Not a human's hunger. Or a Wizard's, either, she supposed.

"Fornoch wanted to make us just like him," said her mother. "Selfish and cruel, and not caring about anything in the world but ourselves. Your father died helping us stop him."

"I know." The idea that the wizard had wanted her father to kill Dwarves made her think again about what had happened at Vonn Kurr.

"What about Findle? Is he all right?"

"We don't know yet. Uhle and Dwvon are still digging. But I'm sure they'll find him."

Mims didn't look nearly as confident about what the Dwarves would find as her mother did.

Sitting up, Hubley looked around the rest of the room. Several pots simmered on the hearth, though the table didn't seem set for a meal. A white cloth covered the end nearest the fire, several gleaming tools laid out on top. Hubley recognized a few of them as the sort her mother used when she was doing the particularly messy bits of her doctoring.

"Are those for Avender?" she asked uncomfortably.

Her mother pursed her lips.

"They're for you," said Mims firmly. "With your permission, of course."

"Me? Aren't I all right?"

"Yes," soothed her mother. "But we still have to undo what your father's done. Unless you want to stay ten forever."

Hubley didn't have to think long about that. Despite all the magic she knew, everyone still treated her like a child. She'd never really be able to use her power properly until she grew up, and that wouldn't happen unless her mother removed her Stone.

The corners of her mouth tugged down. "Will it hurt?"

"Only a little," her mother answered. "If Giserre were here, she'd tell you the pain goes away after about a week. Though you'll still be sore for a while."

Hubley's empty stomach growled. "Can I have something to eat first?"

"No food," said Mims. "Your Living Stone's in your belly, remember? I don't want to have to hunt through half-digested pieces of egg and curdled milk when I'm trying to find it. And you're more likely to get sick if there's food in your stomach once we start poking around."

"You're always in such a rush, Hubley," said her mother. "We have other things to talk about, too."

"We do?" Hubley scooted back on the bed nervously. "Did something else happen in the Stoneways? Did someone else get hurt?"

"No." Taking her daughter's hand, Ferris rubbed it tenderly. "You know everything that happened. You saw it all, which is more than I can say. I didn't even know our trap had failed until I came here looking for you, and Mims told me what happened. It was a brave thing you did, getting Fornoch out of Vonn Kurr. Otherwise he might have slain us all."

"Avender told me to do it," said Hubley. "I'd never have thought of it on my own. I was too scared."

"That's not true." Using her apron to protect her hands, Mims removed one of the steaming pots from the fire and set it on the table beside the tools. "Don't underestimate yourself. Avender didn't tell you where to go, you did that. If you'd acted without thinking, you'd have brought Fornoch right to Castle Grangore. And if that had happened, we'd never have been able to stop him. No, you did the best thing possible. You and Avender both."

Looping her arm around Hubley's shoulders, her mother hugged her tight. "You were wonderful. Whatever else happens, you should never forget that. Merannon would have died if you hadn't been there. Though it's also true you should never have been anywhere near Vonn Kurr in the first place."

"Avender said it was all right."

"That's not what I meant. You were only there because of what your father did to you. You shouldn't have all that power any more than you should have stopped growing. You're only ten. For someone your age, you know far more magic than is good for you. If you really want to come home, you're going to have to give up the magic as well as the Stone."

"Give up magic!"

Hubley's mother pushed her gently back onto the pillows.

"Not all magic, dear," she said. "Just what your father taught you while I was gone."

"You know your mother's right," said Mims. "You do have all those memories, but they're not the same as having lived thirty-one years. They don't add up. They only sit there, side by side, like bacon in a pan. Except no one ever put the pan on the fire, so it's not done. You may have as much power as your mother and me, but you don't have any of the wisdom that should go with it."

"But won't it be enough if you just take the Stone out and let me grow up?"

"Eventually. But there's no guarantee you'll live that long. You know perfectly well you wouldn't have made it past today if I hadn't shown up. I won't always be able to do that, you know."

Hubley felt she should resent what Mims was saying, but she knew it was true. She hadn't been able to help Avender at all when he'd tried to kill the mandrake.

"So you're saying I can't keep my memories?"

"Yes." Unwrapping her arm from her daughter's shoulder, her mother looked Hubley in the eye. "That's exactly what we're saying. Your father should never have done this to you. It wasn't fair. Not then, and certainly not now. If you keep on this way, you're just going to get in trouble."

Mims shrugged. "Who knows? Things might even have worked out better at Vonn Kurr if you hadn't been there."

"Don't say that."

Her mother looked crossly at the older woman, but it was too late. Mims had voiced Hubley's greatest fear. Already Hubley was thinking about how Mims had looked so grim when she'd asked about Findle. If Findle was broken, it was because Hubley hadn't been able to save him. It might not be her fault the Dwarf had shown up at the bottom of the deep at just the wrong time, but that didn't make her feel any better. Maybe Mims and her mother were right. Maybe she really wasn't old enough to handle so much magic, or the responsibility that came with it.

"I know it feels like it was your fault," said Mims more kindly, "but it isn't. Someday it might be, however. Especially after I leave."

"You're leaving?" cried Hubley in dismay. "Where will you go?"

"I don't know yet, but I've been here long enough. I've been watching your parents, and you, for years."

Ferris's forehead wrinkled. "You have? Since when? I never saw you until three days ago."

"That's because I kept out of the way. And I didn't watch you nearly as much as I did Hubley and Reiffen. I wasn't as worried about you."

"I never saw you either," accused Hubley.

"Yes, you did. I brought vegetables to Castle Grangore now and then after your father shut you in. Not as often as I would have liked, or he and Mindrell would have gotten suspicious."

"That was you?" Hubley tried, but couldn't recall the goodwife's face. Her father had never let her meet the woman, though she'd often watched longingly from the top of the Magicians' Tower as the farmwife crossed the open meadow to the castle gate.

"Sometimes," said Mims. "But I've been here long enough. I only came to do what I had to. Someday you'll understand how difficult it is to stand by and watch horrible things happen to everyone you love. But you don't know that yet, which is one of the reasons you shouldn't have so much power. It takes a while, and a few mistakes, to know better than to try and interfere. You're far too young for such horrible lessons. When you need to learn them, I'll come back. But, as you grow older, the temptation to fix an imperfect world will be too great. Much better for you to let me take that temptation away entirely."

"So take it then." Hubley prepared herself for a good long sulk. "Take my memories. Father used to do it all the time."

"Hubley—" started her mother.

"I'm not your father, Hubley," said Mims. "I won't take them from you. You have to give them up yourself."

"And if I don't?"

Mims shrugged again, as if the matter was entirely out of her hands. Hubley tried to think of what she wanted more, to be a marvelous magician, or a child. What had happened in Dinnach a Dwvon and Vonn Kurr hadn't been nearly as exciting as she'd expected. Mostly it had just been terrifying. And what if Findle's fate really was her fault? What if someone else might have found a better way to rescue him if she hadn't interfered?

"How many memories are you going to take?" she asked.

"All but this last year. That's when things finally changed."

"Will I get them back?"

"You'll have them the whole time." From behind her back Mims produced a large pink shell.

"Is that mine? The one father gave me on my last birthday?"

"Yes. I brought it from the castle." Mims's iron thimble glinted as she returned the gift.

The shell felt cool in Hubley's hands, as if the warmth in the room had no effect on it. "It's my best present ever."

Mims nodded. "I know. That's one of the reasons I brought it. But it's not even close to being filled yet, so I thought we'd put your extra memories inside. That way you'll always have them nearby."

Hubley frowned. "But won't that mean I'll be able to get them back whenever I want?"

Mims shook her head. "I don't think so. Not until you figure out how to open it, which you're not going to be able to do for a long time. Correct me if I'm wrong, but you don't even know how to control the sounds yet, right?"

"No. Father said I had to figure it out myself."

"Exactly. Just like you're going to have to figure out how to get back your memories yourself, too."

"So, you're not taking me back to that cave with the mussels?"

"No." Mims's voice was calm and reassuring. "No mussels."

"All right." Hubley cradled the shell against her chest. "It's not like I'm really losing them."

"No, dear," said her mother. "You'll have them with you all the time."

Telling Hubley to lie back on the bed and close her eyes, Mims slid forward till she was sitting beside her. Ferris held her daughter's hand. Hubley felt the older woman kiss her once on the forehead, and place her fingertips gently on Hubley's temples. The rest of the room drifted away.

Her mind wandered while she waited for the spell to start. She remembered the mandrake rising out of the darkness on black wings to spit tongues of fire at Issinlough, his long tail flicking in rage. She remembered the thump of Avender landing on the airship beside her and the cries of the sissit as he threw them over the side. She remembered the look on her father's face, angry and impatient and hurt, before she ran away from him in the mussel cave.

The last time she'd ever seen him.

She almost leapt up then, almost refused to let the memories go. The years alone with her father were all she had left of him. Never again would they share another meal, another lesson, another spell. Never again would they share anything at all.

Only Mims's assurance that she would get it all back kept Hubley in her place. Eyes squeezed tight to hold back her tears, she tried to remember everything she could, to hold on as long as possible to every minute she'd ever spent with him.

Her birthdays flew away. And the gifts her father had made for her: books that flapped their leaves like butterflies and hovered in the air, snapdragons that nipped at cats like snakes, fish that swam through the earth like scaled worms. Riveted by her father's skill, she watched him as the long days faded. The autumn sun sank red behind Ivismundra's bronze shoulder; the night darkened. The hollows in Hubley's memory filled with quiet earth and settled back to stillness.

"We are here, Father."

Brizen let go his son's and Trier's hands. The magician bowed slightly.

"I believe the guests are assembled outside, Your Majesty," she said. "They have been lucky in getting especially fine weather for this time of year."

"Thank you, Trier. You must be eager to see old friends." Merannon waved his hand cheerfully toward the door. "I can help my father from here."

The king's magician raised an eyebrow in a look that managed to be both stern and questioning at the same time. Brizen winced. Ever since Wellin's passing, Trier had been assuming more and more the tone of his nursemaid rather than his adviser. Not that he could blame her.

"Very well," she said. "I have brought you to the room of return, which is situated on the first level of the cellar. Follow the corridor to the right and you will come to the stairs."

"We remember the way," Merannon replied.

Bowing again, Trier left. Brizen and his son followed at their own pace. Now that he was older, the king found the shock of traveling to be much more tiring than in the past. Sometimes he wondered if his heart was likely to stop on one of these trips. Had anyone but Ferris asked him to do this, he would have refused. As it was, he had arrived out of breath and with his heart hammering.

"You brought the gift, Father?"

Brizen nodded and patted his chest pocket. Ribbons hung from his uniform and braid from his shoulders. Neither he nor Merannon had met with Hubley since she saved the prince's life at the bottom of Vonn Kurr, so this was more than a social visit. Hubley was a hero now, as much as her father before her, and king and prince had come to pledge their thanks as well as their good wishes. So much he owed the child and her family. Still, no matter how much he had envied Reiffen's fame when he was younger, Brizen had long since decided that limiting one's opportunities for heroism was much the better path, at least judging from the way Reiffen's life had played out. He and Ferris had lost so much.

They paused to rest on the middle of the stair. "You know, there was a time when I thought Hubley would be my heir," said Brizen.

"It is a good thing Mother finally had me, then."

"A very good thing. She would have been very proud of you."

Merannon looked up, confused. Sometimes, when certain emotions played across his face, Merannon looked too much like his mother for Brizen to bear.

He missed her so much.

"How so, Father? I have done nothing. Had the magicians' daughter not saved me, I would be dead now. There is hardly anything to be proud of in that."

"No, but you did not hesitate. You and Findle went straight to the heart of the danger the moment you heard what had happened."

"We had no choice. Not after what everyone told us when we docked at Grimble's workshop. And Findle was quite confident he could handle the creature. All the same, I am glad Avender spotted us when he did."

"All Wayland and Banking are glad."

Arriving at the top of the stairs, they found themselves in the middle of a great commotion. The kitchen, as Brizen recalled. A woman he guessed was the cook was shouting, the scullions and potboys grinning at her behind their hands. Before Brizen could see what was happening, someone noticed him and announced, "The king!" Everyone stopped what they were doing and bowed. Brizen, long used to this sort of thing no matter how much he tried to stop it, waved his hands for them to rise.

A red-brown hill came forward. The Shaper. "There you are," he said. His red tongue hunted for bits of apple pie in the vicinity of his nose. "Ferris sent me to greet you."

"She most certainly did not!" The cook's livid face appeared behind Redburr's giant haunch. "I told Ferris I'd quit if you set foot in my kitchen ever again, and so help me that's just what I'm going to do!"

Untying the strings, the irate woman hurled her apron to the ground and stamped out. The bear ignored her. Instead he eyed the several undercooks she'd left behind.

"Who's in charge now?"

Fingers pointed at an unfortunate young man, who shook his head vigorously. Redburr bared his yellow teeth.

"All right, Barks. They need more cake and beer at the party. Especially beer."

"Y-yes, Redburr." The new cook pulled at the neck of his apron, as if he had thoughts of quitting too. "R-right away."

"Come on, then."

Wagging his shaggy head for the king and his son to follow, the Shaper headed outside. Brizen leaned carefully on Merannon's arm and did his best not to slip on the pie-covered floor.

"Is it true?" Merannon asked the Shaper when they were out in the sharp sunlight. "Has Hubley forgotten everything?"

"No. Only the parts she didn't need. Don't make the mistake of thinking she doesn't remember anything from the last few days. She knows she's a hero, and she's reveling in it."

Rounding the tower, the small party ambled down the stone path toward the lake. Even on a dull autumn day, Brizen told himself, Valing was the most beautiful place in the world. Solitary pines soared high above the ridgeline like slender giants. Sailboats cut the dark blue lake like the tips of gleaming knives.

"How is she feeling?" he asked.

The bear snuffled an acorn off the path. "About as good as can be expected, with that belly wound Ferris gave her taking out her Stone."

"And are the other rumors true, that you have all been aided by some mysterious magician whom no one has ever heard of before?"

The bear nodded his massive head. "That's what they tell me."

"Is she here?"

"Not yet. But she's supposed to come soon."

The path emerged into a meadow but, instead of following the trail to the edge of the cliff and down the steps to the dock below, Redburr led them toward the sunny northern edge. What Brizen's old eyes had first thought to be a cluster of sheep turned out to be the party. The iron chairs and tables usually set out in the tower garden had been shifted to the edge of the lake. Guests milled around them, plates of cake and glasses of beer in their hands, mostly local folk whom Brizen didn't recognize. And there were children, too, which surprised him. Except for Wilbrim, few children had ever attended Hubley's birthday parties.

As it had in the kitchen, the noise stopped at the sight of the prince and king. Everyone bowed, at which point Brizen spotted Baroness Backford waving her cane at him from a seat close beside Hubley's. Her son stood behind the child's chair like a courtier, holding her plate. Hubley waved also from the middle of a chair stuffed with pillows and blankets, her grandmother at her side. Though the child tried to stand as Brizen approached, Giserre gently pushed her down.

"Grandmother," she scolded as Brizen and Merannon joined them. "I'm not an invalid."

"You may stand." Ferris appeared with glasses for her royal guests. "But no curtsying. Those bandages Grandmother put on you this morning will tear."

Ferris offered Brizen her hand. He kissed it gallantly.

"Your Highness," she said. "Merannon. Welcome to Tower Dale."

"It is our honor to be here," Brizen answered. "As has happened so often before, we are in your debt."

Ferris dismissed his gratitude with a wave. "You know perfectly well, if we ever got down to counting, the ledger would be full on either side. Are you already forgetting how Merannon rescued Hubley first?"

The prince inclined his head, acknowledging the compliment. "Actually, milady, Findle and I failed. It was Avender who rescued your daughter at the Bavadar Lamp. Without his daring leap, the sissit would have kept their prize."

"Really, Merannon," Ferris laughed. "Sometimes you're too much like your father. Your mother, on the other hand, knew better than anyone the right time and place to toot her own horn."

"It is why we loved her," said Brizen.

"Really?" said Durk. The king noticed the stone had a prominent place among Hubley's pillows, a large pink seashell nearby. "I thought it was because she was so beautiful. I never saw her myself, of course, but everyone always said so. Queen Loellin's mother was quite the beauty in her day, too. Have I ever told you the story of how we met once? She wasn't married to King Grinnis yet—"

Hubley covered the stone with another cushion. Muffled protests sounded from underneath the embroidery and down.

"You're just in time for the games," she said, sliding carefully off her chair. "We're going to start with pin-the-leaf."

"Will you permit Merannon and me to present you with our gift first?" inquired the king.

Hubley's eyes lit up. "Another present?"

"Do not be greedy, Hubley," said Giserre.

The other guests clustered around, especially the children, all of them eager to see what a king's gift looked like. Hubley accepted the small box Brizen offered her with a swift thank-you, then tore off the wrapping with nimble fingers. Inside she found a fish-shaped brooch with chipped tourmalines for scales and small, topaz eyes.

"It was Wellin's," said the king. "She wore it when she was ten, I think."

Hubley held out the brooch so Brizen could pin it on her dress. The nearer guests oohed and aahed as the child showed it off.

Proudly wearing her latest present, Hubley led the party on to the games. Brizen was disappointed there was to be no magic; he had always loved the displays at Castle Grangore, rockets exploding and impossible animals cavorting around the garden. There had been something with talking cats, once, he recalled. But he understood why that particular tradition had been abandoned, at least this year. The magical displays had always been more Reiffen's gift than Ferris's.

It did not take much to cajole him into the game. Giserre tied the blindfold around his face, but only Hubley was bold enough to spin him. The other children looked on in awe. He shuffled unevenly on his feet, dizzy after a single turn. Taking pity on his age, Hubley led him to the large beech they were using as a target. Tears started behind the light cloth binding his eyes as he remembered playing this game with Merannon years ago. For all Wellin's faults, he had been fortunate to share her life.

"Not there, Your Majesty." Hubley laughed from close beside Brizen's hand. "You'll trip over the chair. This way."

Fingers fumbling along the bark, he fastened his leaf to the tree. The other guests clapped and cheered. Lifting his blindfold, he discovered he had pinned his token far around the side of the trunk from the robin's nest that marked the target. But others had placed their leaves farther away than his. For an honorary grandfather he had not done badly at all.

Hubley's turn was next. He bound the handkerchief securely around her face, peering with weak eyes to make sure the knot was tight. The children darted in to spin her around many more times than she had spun him but, even with no one helping, she pinned her leaf directly on the nest. Laughter followed, and good-natured teasing.

"Cheat!"

"She used magic!"

"His Majesty didn't tie the blindfold tight enough!"

Then Hubley tugged the handkerchief off her head and pulled on the edges to show it had been knotted securely, and her new friends accused her even more loudly of having used magic. And more cake was served and Ferris brought out a jug of cider, and the king, exhausted by the hue and cry, settled wearily into an iron chair beside Giserre, Merannon attentive at his side.

Now that he was close enough to get a good look at her, Brizen thought Giserre had aged since the last time he had seen her, her stern, dark beauty finally gone.

Hubley raced back to them, almost knocking the glass from Brizen's hand.

"Mims and Avender are here!" she cried.

The king looked where the child pointed as she dashed away one more time. A stout woman was approaching across the meadow, accompanied by a limping man.

"Here comes the real hero in all this," said Merannon. "I look forward greatly to hearing his tale."

"Yes, we all have a lot to thank him for." Brizen placed a fond hand on his son's arm.

As the two figures came closer, the king saw that the woman wasn't so old as he or Giserre, though she was old enough to have hair as gray as theirs. Looking more like a goodwife than a magician, she stumped her way forward. Hubley danced at her and Avender's hands.

Beside him, Giserre gasped.

"My goodness," she said. "It's Spit."